Wedding Bell Time

SOPHIE TOOVEY

eloquent elephant

Text Copyright © Sophie Toovey, 2023.
Cover illustration by 2V Studios

The right of Sophie Toovey to be identified as the author of this work has been asserted by her under the Copyright, Designs and Patents Act 1988.

ISBN 978-1-7393893-4-5

All rights reserved. No part of this publication may be reproduced, distributed, or transmitted in any form or by any means, including photocopying, recording, or other electronic or mechanical methods, without the prior written permission of the publisher, except in the case of brief quotations embodied in critical reviews and certain other noncommercial uses permitted by copyright law.

This is a work of fiction. Names, characters, places and dialogues are products of the author's imagination or are used fictitiously.

www.sophietoovey.com

To Andy, Megan and Joshua

1

Michael

'It makes sense for me to drive; I'm the one who knows where we're going.'

My girlfriend Jen jangles the keys of her dad's car and strides off towards the Ford Fiesta in the staff car park.

It makes sense for *me* to drive so that we arrive without injury or accident… But I don't say that out loud.

Instead, I sigh and follow Jen, and climb into the passenger seat. At least she's not driving a bus this time. *That* was a nail-biting experience.

Jen adjusts the mirror slightly, starts the engine, and the radio blares out an inane autotuned song. I buckle up my seatbelt.

As the car pulls out of the school gates, narrowly missing a bollard on the left side, Jen revs and flies over a speed bump, whilst humming along to the song.

'Michael,' she says, cutting out of her humming, 'you don't have to hold the dashboard.'

I didn't even realise I was doing it. Survival instinct, I guess.

'Sorry.'

Jen drives in the way she generally approaches life: without much forward planning. She relishes the twists and turns that seem to crop up unexpectedly, although she insists she's driven this way a hundred times before. She isn't fazed by the multiple hazards: cyclist, cat, traffic lights, busy junction.

'You should sit back and enjoy the ride,' she says, jerking the car around a tight corner. My stomach lurches.

I like to be in control. A smooth, well-planned drive, arriving early to the destination. As Jen points out when we park in front of a brightly-coloured Primary school building, we are only two minutes late. Because we zoomed over several mini-roundabouts and took liberties with the red light.

'It was amber,' Jen argues.

It was red.

The first thing that strikes me is how small the school is compared to ours. Primaries are generally smaller than secondaries, and at Whidlock County, the high school where Jen and I work, we have almost a thousand students. This school probably holds four hundred five-to-eleven-year-olds. I suppress a shudder.

'Jen, it's great to see you.' The receptionist smiles. It's the usual reaction to Jen. Her hair fizzes with dark curls, her eyes are like warm chocolate, and her skin is coffee-coloured silk. Today she's wearing a scarlet sweater and a black skirt that flares over her knees. I wish I could put my arm around her waist, but it wouldn't be professional.

'Hi Clare.' Jen knows everyone in this county. She grew up here, lived at home while she studied for her degree, and got her first teaching job in the school that she went to as a pupil. 'This is Michael.'

'Nice to meet you.' I nod.

As we sign in, I'm scanning every wall and trying to fight the rise of panic. It's all smiley faces, handprints, 'Working together, having fun' kind of motto. My worst nightmare.

'Sally's waiting for you, if you want to go on down,' the receptionist says.

Jen beckons me through the door with a giant tree painted over it. As I reach it, I see that each apple on the tree has a word like 'kindness' written on it.

Apparently, Jen has been running this Shakespeare project for a few years now. She goes into a local primary and helps them to put on a mini-Shakespeare play. We're both English teachers, and now that I'm Head of Department, I felt that I ought to see how this project worked. And I also agreed to come in a rash moment when Jen challenged me to get involved a few months ago.

I started at Whidlock in September, and in some ways it feels like a lifetime ago. Life before Jen, anyway. I met her on my first day, putting up a hideous cat poster in her bright orange classroom, and I had no idea what to make of her. The more time I spent with her, the more I wanted to get to know her. I've never been bored when I'm around Jen. That's good, because I'm a very boring person. I like my plain suits, my shirt-and-tie combos, and my black organiser. Neat, organised, but boring.

Somehow Jen agreed to be my girlfriend, and every day when we meet in the kitchen at work I half-expect her to break up with me.

It's November, and soon we will have been together for a month.

I've never had a girlfriend before. This is major.

Before I can reflect too much upon this milestone in my twenty-nine year-old life, Jen opens a classroom door and I am shocked at the sight of thirty ten-year-olds acting out a silent slow-mo sword fight with eerie synth music rippling through the air.

I almost grab Jen's arm. I'm not sure I can do this.

2

Jen

Michael looks as though he's going to bolt.

I give him what I hope is a firm but encouraging smile, and motion for him to step forward and lead the way to the front of the room. My friend Sally waves enthusiastically, as the two students in front of her try to execute one another with imaginary swords. The soundtrack is perfect, the strings building to a dramatic climax, and by this point many of the students are now lying on the floor, clutching injuries or dying a prolonged agonising death.

Sally stops the music and the students come back to life and face us.

'Fantastic work, everyone!' She claps her hands. 'Bradley, I really liked the way you reacted as Sam drove his sword into your side. Melody, try to slow down your movement as you fall to the ground. Maybe stretch out your hand, like you're trying to hold on to your last moments.'

She extends her arm with a desperate expression.

'Like that.'

I catch a glimpse of Michael's face. Still in shock.

'I'm so excited that Miss Baker and Mr Chase have joined us today!' Sally continues. 'I can't wait to show them what you've been working on.'

It's the battle at the end of *Julius Caesar*. At the front, Brutus, Cassius, Octavius and Antony take centre stage, with the rest of the class as soldiers behind them. They show us their whole performance from the beginning, an enthusiastic, if a little Samurai-inspired, rendition of the war. At the end, I clap and grin, and nudge Michael when he continues to stand there, open-mouthed.

'Break time,' Sally calls.

The class disperse, with one boy lingering behind.

'Do you want to see a trick?' he says to Michael.

Without waiting for an answer, he pulls out some cards and fans them in front of Michael, then flips one over to reveal an Ace, then makes it disappear again.

'That's fantastic!' I say, when it becomes apparent that Michael doesn't know how to respond.

'I'll just go and grab some drinks,' Sally says, leaving Michael and me alone in the classroom.

'Are you okay?' I ask, nudging him to break his trance.

'I don't know if I can do this,' he says.

'Of course you can,' I say. 'Just go with it! They're kids. They want to tell you things and show you stuff. It's cute. By the time they get to us, life has kicked that out of them.'

'I'm an English teacher.' Michael huffs. 'I don't do slow motion sword fights to synth music or card tricks.'

'Maybe you should.' I grin.

'It makes sense of why their literacy is so poor when they start Year 7,' Michael says gloomily, pointing to a board of 'key words'. 'Fiery is spelled wrong. All this 'two stars and a wish' feedback, and no one has highlighted any of the errors in these pieces of writing.'

'English isn't Sally's specialism,' I admit. 'But she does a great job of getting the kids excited about Shakespeare. She uses drama and music to engage their interest.'

Michael sighs.

'It's going to be a long day.'

Most teachers would enjoy the opportunity to be off timetable to visit a feeder primary school and help develop a play as a fun extra-curricular project. Michael, however, would prefer to teach the rules of direct speech to our Year 11 boys' group, who are challenging to say the least.

He perks up when we look at some of the famous speeches of the play with the group, and do more analytical activities on how to speak the lines, which words to emphasise. This is more familiar ground. But then it's time for a final run-through with the battle scene. By the time we are back in my car, ready to return, Michael leans back in the seat and closes his eyes. He doesn't even have the energy to hold the dashboard.

I smile to myself, enjoying a moment to stare at his clean-shaven face, his dark hair slightly ruffled and out of place over his pale forehead. My stomach gives a little skip. Michael doesn't know how attractive he is. I remember watching him teach for the first time, how magnetic he was at the front of the classroom.

He was definitely out of his comfort zone today.

At one point, I went to the bathroom and came back to discover him, back pressed against the wall, shrinking away from two students duelling. I snigger as I turn the key in the ignition, and the car comes to life. Maybe I should suggest an impromptu dinner date tonight, to help him recover from the trauma.

Then he opens his mouth and I quickly change my mind.

3

Michael

'What a waste of a day,' I groan, sinking my head back against the firm headrest, a headache blazing behind my left eye. 'I've got so much to do tonight.'

A few minutes pass before I register that Jen hasn't replied. I glance across at her, and her mouth is set in a firm line. She's looking straight ahead at the road.

'Is something wrong?'

Her eyebrow is slightly raised, and she doesn't reply. It's the silent treatment again.

'What have I done wrong?' I ask in resignation. There is no figuring out in this situation.

'You haven't *done* anything,' Jen snaps. 'In fact, I'd say you had a pretty easy ride today.'

I blink.

'Today was many things, but it was *not* easy.'

'So, a very difficult waste of time then?'

Oh.

'I didn't mean it like that,' I sigh, rubbing my temples. I wish that actually worked in improving headaches.

'So what did you mean, then?'

The silence rings in the air, along with the pulsing thud in my head.

'Okay, it wasn't life-transforming. We didn't achieve any top grades or win accolades from the Royal Shakespeare Company. But just because something doesn't churn out data, doesn't make it a waste of time,' Jen says angrily.

I really don't feel up for an argument right now.

'I'm sorry,' I say, as genuinely as I can. 'It's not my strength, working with younger kids.'

'In a few years' time, those children will be sitting in front of you, and you will be trying to help them understand *Romeo and Juliet*.' Jen violently strikes on the indicator and changes gear. 'Maybe they might remember putting on *Julius Caesar* in primary school, and think that Shakespeare might not be so bad after all.'

We swerve around a roundabout, gaining speed.

'The impact of this project may be hard to *quantify*,' she continues, as the car flings off the roundabout and into a side street. 'I believe it forms an important component of our transition work and builds a relationship with these pupils, which makes it easier for them when they move up to our school.'

'I'd rather they didn't remember me as the one who taught them to mime a battle with trippy music in the background.'

'They'll probably remember you as the uptight one who kept checking his watch and didn't want to be there.'

She seems to lose some of her rage at this point, sighing and thankfully taking her foot off the accelerator.

'It worries me, Michael,' she says, more carefully this time, 'that you're so obsessed with numbers and spreadsheets that you miss the bigger picture.'

Now it's my turn to raise my eyebrows.

'How is a bunch of primary kids acting out *Julius Caesar* in a way that is, at best, mediocre, the bigger picture?'

'That's exactly what I mean.' She pulls the car back through our school gates. 'You don't value it, because it's not a number.'

I don't know why she is so against numbers all of a sudden. Nice, predictable spreadsheets. You never have to argue with them.

The car rolls into a parking space and she switches off the engine. The noise suddenly cuts into silence. Neither of us move.

'I was going to ask if you wanted to have dinner tonight,' she says, looking down at her hands in her lap. 'But it sounds like you're busy.'

My stomach twists. Yes, on the one hand, I love the idea of seeing her. Any time with Jen sparkles with excitement, even if it's just cooking spaghetti. But it makes everything so… complicated.

'I thought we agreed that we should only see each other at weekends,' I remind her.

Well, it was my idea. She did agree to it – perhaps a little reluctantly.

'Since we went away at half term, I've barely had any time alone with you,' Jen says. 'We've had some dates, and they've been lovely, but I was moving out of my flat and back into Dad's, then we were celebrating my promotion with my family, and now this weekend, you said you wanted us to meet up with your friends.'

My 'lawyer friends', as Jen refers to them. She's still slightly baffled that I studied Law as well as English at uni.

'I can cancel that if you want,' I say, a little too hopefully. I'm slightly dreading introducing Jen to them, because I know they will love her. If I mess things up –which is looking very likely right now– then I'll never hear the end of it.

'I'm not suggesting that,' she says, shaking her head. 'You barely have a social life as it is. I just mean, if we could see each other in the week as well, then it gives us more time together.'

'We do see each other every day in school,' I point out.

'Yes, but it's not exactly quality time, is it?'

As if to prove the point, the bell rings in the distance, and students start streaming past the car, talking loudly and some of them waving and shouting, 'Hi Sir!'

'I've stayed at yours before,' she says, continuing her argument, 'so why can't I just stay over again and come with you to school in the morning?'

'You know David's funny about it.'

Our Headteacher, David Clark, has made it clear that he doesn't want us to be in a relationship. If he hadn't promoted us both recently, I think we would be in a tenuous position, but he's being sued at the moment and has got bigger fish to fry than to plug the draining bath tub that is my love life.

The fact is, when Jen stayed at my house, it was an emergency. We weren't really *together* then. And, well, things have changed since then. If she wants to stay over, I don't think she means the guest room.

When I mentioned my love life, you might think the phrasing ironic, because I've never had sex before. And I'm not sure I'm ready to tell Jen the reason why.

4
Jen

Not for the first time, I consider how much I dislike David Clark. Even setting aside the fact that he's had more promotions than I've had hot dinners, becoming an executive Head while still in his thirties (when most of us are trying to get an extra few quid for dinner duty), his manoeuvrings to promote Michael involved telling me to withdraw my application for the same role. Then he ignored me when I told him a pupil was threatening to turn up at my flat, and my laptop got stolen. So when Michael says I can't stay over his house because *David* doesn't like it, a lightning bolt of anger blazes through me.

'Great, well as long as David's happy, then I guess it doesn't matter that I never see you. I'm only your *girlfriend*.'

I know I sound petty, but the way that Michael always caves to that guy REALLY annoys me. Does he want to be with me, or not?

He shifts in the passenger seat awkwardly, and pulls at his tie to loosen it. I stifle the urge to rip it off him: I could either attack him with a passionate kiss so that he can't keep refusing to take me home with him, or use it to strangle him. It's 50-50 right now.

'I struggle to concentrate when you're around,' he says, mopping his brow. 'I need to keep on top of the paperwork, otherwise David's going to regret promoting me. I don't want to give him any excuse.'

'I'm busy too, you know,' I point out. I just got a whole-school responsibility for Additional Learning Needs. 'I resolved in half term that I was going to make more effort to have a better work-life balance.'

'That's good,' Michael agrees quickly. 'I just need you to trust me when I say it's for the best that we don't try and bring our relationship into the working week.'

So we're boyfriend-and-girlfriend on the weekend, but colleagues Monday to Friday. Michael doesn't seem to realise how lame that is.

It's getting to the end of autumn, and school is surrounded by trees with the last of their brightly-coloured leaves, and an increasing amount of bare branches. The sky seems permanently grey, and the air has a sharp edge of cold. People have started discussing Christmas shopping in the staffroom, and my best friend Steph suggests a Saturday meet-up.

'Sounds great,' I say, rinsing my mug in the staff kitchen. If I book social events into my calendar, then I will be forced to do something other than work the whole weekend.

My new role is exciting, and I don't officially start it until January, but it is definitely overwhelming with the amount of paperwork I need to read through. Natalie, the timetabler, is going to make changes to my timetable as well so I have fewer lessons to teach. At the moment, I'm muddling through – which is generally the story of my whole career.

Michael, on the other hand, has gone into overdrive with his new position as Head of Department. He doesn't officially take over from Geoff until January – but he's immediately thrown himself into it and Geoff's busy with senior team duties anyway. We're running mock exams next week and he's already created what feels like ten different spreadsheets for us to fill in.

'This one is for the item level data,' he says, showing us in a department meeting, 'then this one is for the pie chart, and finally this one creates a line graph.'

I catch Judy's eye and stifle a giggle. She's retiring soon and doesn't care much for Michael's techno-whizzy stuff.

'Finally, I have some other news,' Michael says, just as we are beginning to pack away our pens and diaries. 'Liz will be returning shortly.'

My immediate reaction is shock, for two reasons: one, Liz has been off sick since September, because she was Second in Department and the new Head scared her off so that Michael would get the promotion, and two, Michael has said nothing about this to me, even though he must have known about this for a while. It's another reminder of the professional/personal divide between us.

'That's good.' I recover, although I'm really thinking about how awkward it's going to be when Liz has to report to Michael. HR is not going to be his strong point.

'Get ready for some fireworks,' Judy mutters to me, while Michael is preoccupied at his computer.

'Hopefully it'll be fine,' I whisper. 'Geoff, Michael and I sorted the scheme of work over half term anyway. We can ease her back in gently.'

'I hope you don't get stuck in the middle.'

Judy gives me a meaningful look, then towards Michael. I swallow down a ripple of misgiving. Surely Michael would have the sense to tread carefully with Liz, rather than going in all guns blazing? But Michael doesn't seem to get the fact that not everyone works at the same break-neck pace as him. Case-in-point: the elaborate spreadsheet, when the students haven't even done the exam yet.

'Are we still on for these drinks tomorrow?' I ask Michael, once Judy has gone and we're alone in the classroom.

'Of course,' he says, methodically packing some books into a box and perfectly aligning them. 'Shall I pick you up at seven?'

I nod. 'What's the dress code?'

Michael shrugs.

'It's a bar. There's not a dress code.'

Jeans and a decent top then. Plus heels.

'I'm looking forward to it.'

I sidle closer to him and press my lips to his. He pulls back after just a split second, looking pointedly at the open door. Okay, so we got caught by the cleaner once. It's just a kiss. We're not plastered together like gross Year 9 students, in the middle of the corridor.

'Great,' he says, picking up the box.

I grab my bag and follow him out to the car park.

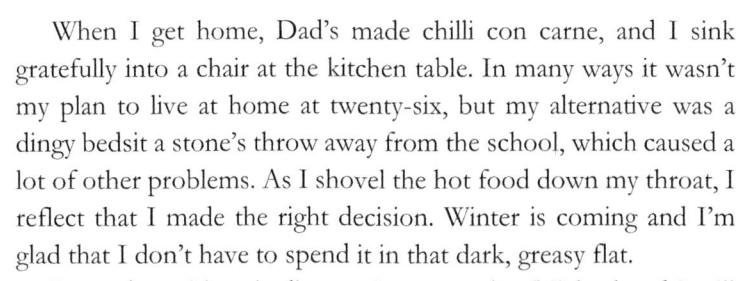

When I get home, Dad's made chilli con carne, and I sink gratefully into a chair at the kitchen table. In many ways it wasn't my plan to live at home at twenty-six, but my alternative was a dingy bedsit a stone's throw away from the school, which caused a lot of other problems. As I shovel the hot food down my throat, I reflect that I made the right decision. Winter is coming and I'm glad that I don't have to spend it in that dark, greasy flat.

I wonder, with a tingling excitement, what Michael and I will do for Christmas. What presents we'll choose for each other, what family traditions we might share together. I still haven't met his parents, so maybe this might be a good opportunity. With two weeks off school, there's plenty of time for visiting. Maybe I'll be able to stay in Michael's house again. Whenever I've been there, it's immaculately clean. I don't know why, but I feel at home with him. It's been so long since my last dating disaster, I'm hopeful that this relationship is going to last. Maybe, just maybe, this is it.

'How's Michael?' my sister Katie asks me, dryly, on the phone that night. She's at uni studying veterinary science, and she'll be finishing soon for the holidays. It will definitely be more crowded in the house when she's back. More reason to escape to Michael's.

'He's obsessed with spreadsheets,' I reply, 'but it's all good. I'm going to meet some of his friends tomorrow.'

'Are they rich?'

'Well, I think they're lawyers or solicitors or something.'

'You'll probably need a mortgage to buy a cocktail then.'

'I'm not going to drink much,' I assure her. 'I need to keep my wits about me.'

It turns out, it isn't the lawyers who are the problem.

5
Michael

As we enter the bar, I catch a glimpse of myself in the reflection of the shiny glass door. I'm an average guy, wearing a forgettable navy shirt and dark pair of jeans. Jen joked that she thought I didn't even own a pair. She looks fabulous, glittering with a jewelled necklace, brightly patterned top and eyes like diamonds. I know what my friends will be thinking: what's a girl like this doing with me? I often ask that question myself.

I can tell Jen is nervous, because she gives a high-pitched laugh at every barely-funny comment that's made. Kyle, Alex and Dan were my housemates at uni, and Dan's wife Louise is here too. She engages Jen in conversation, and I sip my drink, feeling the novelty of being out in a bar.

'Congratulations on the promotion,' Dan says, raising a glass to me.

'He'll be a Head next time we see him,' Kyle jokes.

I'm not sure if that means I don't see them very often, or that I'm forging a clear career path. Maybe it's both. I would like to lead a school one day, but it sounds arrogant to say it out loud. I turn to smile at Jen, but she's staring into space with a slight frown on her face.

'I hope you're not working too hard,' Dan comments.

'Yeah, with all those holidays you get,' Alex jibes. 'Half term the other week and Christmas soon.'

'What can I say?' I shrug. 'I can't compete with you, bringing Whidlock's criminals swiftly to justice.'

'Someone's got to do it,' Alex grins.

I get a drink and relax into the evening. It's unexpectedly enjoyable to be with friends; I'm beginning to think there may be something in Jen's whole work-life-balance mantra, although I didn't particularly appreciate her forcing me to listen to whale music with the lights dimmed when we went away. That feels a long time ago now. I look across and she's smiling and laughing with Louise.

'Jen seems great,' Dan comments to me quietly. He's a thoughtful guy, wise beyond his years.

'I'm glad you all approve,' I say, half tongue-in-cheek, half serious.

'I don't think you've ever introduced us to anyone before.'

I shake my head.

'Never been anyone worth it.'

'I know you take this stuff seriously,' Dan says. 'Why don't you bring her to our house for dinner, and then we can get to know her better?'

I haven't gone to Dan's for months, and my first impulse is to make an excuse not to go, in case it's awkward. But Jen seems happy talking to Louise and it feels nice to do things like this: to have friends and go for dinner. I know Jen would want to.

'That would be really great,' I say.

Everything is obviously going too perfectly, because then David Clark walks up to me, with a girl on his arm.

'Michael!' he shouts. 'Fancy seeing you here! I'd like you to meet my girlfriend, Adele.'

The girl looks in her early twenties, with hair dyed blond and her eyes caked in green and gold make-up. She raises her hand to wave hello, and her nails are like multi-coloured talons.

'Hi,' I say, aware that Jen is looking over now to see what's going on. 'Nice to meet you.'

'And you!' she says enthusiastically.

'Michael and Jen work in my school,' David says, indicating towards Jen. Adele looks over at Jen with a sudden flare of interest.

'Oh, are you two together?' she asks, obviously unaware that David has spent the best part of the last few months trying to stop us forming a romantic 'entanglement'.

She tugs on David's arm, hard enough to jolt his arm downwards and almost lose his smile. I never thought his smile looked fixed until Jen pointed it out. Now I can't see anything else.

'We must have dinner together,' she says.

Jen must be hearing this, because I can see her expression change from the corner of my eye. I'm worried she's going to outright refuse.

'How about we cook, at your place?' She turns to David, who is unable to contradict her suggestion. 'Next Saturday?'

David shrugs and gives a reluctant smile.

'I suppose so... Great idea.'

'I'll need to check with Jen,' I say hastily. It's the closest thing I've got to a get-out-clause.

'Jen!' David shouts over. She's always said he's obnoxious and I'm seeing more evidence of it every time he opens his mouth. 'Would you and Michael like to join us for dinner next Saturday?'

Jen looks speechless, and her eyes move to meet mine. I know what she's thinking: say no, Michael! But how can I? He's my boss, I've known him for years, and his new girlfriend is practically jumping up and down on the spot with excitement of playing hostess. Like she can read my thoughts, a shadow of disappointment crosses her expression.

'Sure,' she says, with all the enthusiasm of someone on death row.

She's going to kill me.

6
Jen

'Why didn't you just say no?' It's the question I keep asking Michael, all the way as he drives me home. 'You know I can't stand him! And who is this girlfriend anyway?'

'I have no idea,' he replies, and his mouth is set in a firm line. 'Look, it's just dinner. We'll go, we'll eat, then we'll go home. Simple.'

'Can't you just message him to say we've double booked?'

'That would be lying.' He frowns at me reproachfully. Michael's always good at taking the moral high ground.

'Okay, just say we don't want to come, then.'

If honesty's the way he wants to play this, then so be it.

'No,' he says firmly, then sighs. 'I don't pull out of things I've committed to. If I've said I'll go, then I'll go.'

Whilst part of me admires Michael's stoical reliability, I can't help but feel frustrated that he's tied us up into a situation I do not want to be in. Why has he always got to be so *principled* about everything? It's exhausting.

'Well, I don't know what I'm going to say to him,' I take a different tack. 'Thank you for overcoming your misogyny to promote me, David. Can you pass the butter?'

'Please don't,' Michael says, with no trace of irony.

'I don't get you.' I press my fingers to my temples. 'You know he's a jerk. He tried to split us up. He's being sued by someone from his last school! And yet, his girlfriend asks us to dinner, and you just say 'Yes. Three bags full. Would you like a bottle of wine?"

'You've got no reason to dislike Adele,' he points out. 'Neither of us even know her. She seemed keen to be friendly.'

'She probably wants David to pay off her student loan.'

'Jen!' Michael doesn't see the funny side when he's in this mood.

He pulls up outside my house, and takes a few breaths before speaking.

'Please,' he starts, 'you've got to be careful what you say. I know you have strong opinions, but this isn't the place… I mean, just go along with it, okay? Let's put the past behind us. He's still our boss.'

'Is that why, when your friends joked that you would be Head next, you said nothing? Because you actually want to be like David?'

I'm looking at him anxiously to contradict me, but instead he avoids my gaze, looking down at his hands.

'Is it a bad thing to have goals?' he says, not meeting my eyes.

'You just got a promotion,' I point out. 'Can't you just be satisfied with that?'

He twists his watch, and looks out at the deserted street.

'You know what your problem is?' I speak as the idea crystallises in my mind. 'You can't stay still. You have to do stuff, all the time, because you're scared of what happens when you stop.'

I recognise in him that same restlessness I had when my mum died. I didn't want to face the pain and the grief.

'What are you scared of, Michael?'

I speak the question into the heavy atmosphere of the car. The engine is running but the absence of speech makes a wall of silence between Michael and me. He turns to me, and I can see genuine confusion on his face.

'I don't know.'

I avoid discussing the Michael situation with Katie; the relationship feels too new to dissect it with her like a dead mouse. Plus, I'm keen to keep her opinion of Michael as positive as possible.

Maybe I just need to accept that dating a guy like Michael is going to be very different to my previous boyfriends. Not that I've had that many. My first love, Jamie, spent nearly every waking moment with me… But we were at school and we had nothing better to do than sit on cold benches eating chips together. Then there were a few different guys when I was at uni and when I started teaching, but nothing serious. This is my first 'real' relationship while being an adult and holding down a demanding job. I shouldn't be surprised that Michael and I don't really see each other outside school that much.

It's just that he's so busy, and even our dating life feels busy too. This weekend, we went to the drinks with his friends. The next day, he was doing marathon-training, and when I suggested meeting up, he called me and sounded exhausted.

'Sorry Jen,' he said. 'I think I'm going to get a few things done for school then have an early night.'

There's this rule about no-dates-on-school-nights. And next weekend, Michael's managed to book us a Saturday lunch at Dan and Louise's house, followed by 'supper' (whatever that means) at David Clark's house with the overly-enthusiastic Adele. Can't wait.

Part of me would feel excited about doing all of this if it meant going back to Michael's afterwards, cuddling up on the sofa, seeing where things go… But Michael seems content to drive me home and drop me off with a kiss each time. I don't want to invite myself over to his place. It just seems odd that he never wants to take things to the next level. I *know* he likes me, and I also know that I'm his first girlfriend… Maybe he wants to take things slowly. He's no ordinary guy.

I keep telling myself that this is a good thing.

7

Michael

I think Jen is beginning to suspect something.

When I dropped her home the other night, she lingered as I kissed her. Her face tilted up towards mine like a question, unasked. I don't know how to answer it. I'm hoping that with these social events booked in, it will give me time to figure out what I'm doing.

What am I doing?

With work, I have a long to-do list, but I feel confident in my ability to complete each task. I'm on safe ground. In this relationship, I'm hopping across landmine territory. Something might blow up at any moment.

I've never done this before.

I always looked at my friends with girlfriends and thought 'no thanks'. Sure, the beginning always seemed fun and attractive. But it never seemed long before there were flurries of text messages, agonised phone calls, slamming doors, stony silences and then the pain of heartbreak. If I'm honest, I congratulated myself that I avoided this messy process. I focused on my studies, and then my job, and without any distractions, I moved swiftly along my career path.

Some might find it hard to believe that I've reached the end of my twenties and I've never slept with anyone. The key thing is keeping your distance from any girl with relationship potential.

It all went out of the window when I met Jen.

When I started at Whidlock, I wasn't looking for a relationship. But Jen's so... magnetic. "Keeping my distance" turned into "walking into her classroom at every opportunity". I did display boards with her after school, ran a theatre trip, played 5-a-side football (okay, that didn't go too well as she ended up in A&E). I was spending more and more time with her without even realising what I was doing.

Even now, I could spend every day with her and it still wouldn't be enough. I love talking to her, finding more about how she thinks. She makes me laugh with her dry one-liners and expressions. She's beautiful, so beautiful.

I haven't watched many romantic films, but usually they end when the hero gets the girl. So my problem is: what next?

By some strange combination of fluke and dodging bullets, I've managed to get this far. Jen is my girlfriend. But I haven't worked out how to live my life with Jen as more than just a feature in school, or even at a weekend social. We've gone out for dinner, and a few dates, and now she's meeting my friends. I suppose I'll have to introduce her to my family at some point. Every aspect of Developing Your Relationship opens up a gnawing pit of anxiety in my stomach. The advantage of bringing home a girl when you're twenty is that no one takes it seriously. Now that I'm nearly thirty, my mother will probably start planning the wedding.

I haven't mentioned the W word, of course. Best not to run before I can walk.

I'm approaching this relationship much like my lessons. The key is having structure. Just as I never walk into a Year 10 group without a clear game-plan, I have no intention of just 'hanging out' with Jen. Like the unplanned lesson, it's sure to end in disaster.

The problem is, I sense that she's not happy about our clogged-up calendar. She's complained about not having any time alone together. If I'm not careful, she'll get fed up, and then my only relationship will be over before it's really had a chance to begin.

I need advice.

I scroll through the contacts on my phone to find the only person I trust to discuss this sort of thing. I press the call button.

'Hi Michael,' Dan says.

'Hi Dan. Are you still alright for us to come for lunch on Saturday?'

'Yes, we're looking forward to it. Any dietary requirements?'

I think for a moment. Is Jen a vegetarian? No, I've seen her eat bacon.

'I don't think so.'

I pause.

'I wanted to ask your advice.'

'Oh?' Dan gives a laugh. 'Not sure I've got any, but go ahead.'

'When you were going out with Louise, what kind of dates did you have? Or did you 'hang out', not doing anything special?'

'Uh…' I can hear confusion in his tone. 'Well, we did go on dates. Out for meals, to the cinema. But I suppose we spent a lot of time talking together too. Why do you ask?'

'It's just…' I sigh. 'I'm not sure I'm getting it right, you know. With Jen.'

'Have you asked her about how she would like to spend time with you?'

That sounds painfully direct.

'No, no not really.'

I'm glad he can't see me because I can feel my cheeks flush.

'You need to find out what her expectations are,' Dan says. 'And then you can figure out together how to plan your time.'

'Expectations,' I repeat. 'What kind of expectations?'

'Well, presumably she has had boyfriends before?'

A twist of jealousy gives me physical pain for a moment.

'Yes, she's told me that.'

'There may be things that she did with her previous boyfriends that she's expecting you to do.'

Jen hasn't told me much about said boyfriends. I haven't asked, either. I thought it was better that way. Now all I can think about is the foggy question mark in my head surrounding Jen's potential sexual history. So many complications.

'Dan,' I begin, 'do you remember me telling you about the Canadian chastity advocates?'

He laughs again.

'Yes, I do remember.'

'Well, it leaves me in a rather strange position.'

There are a few moments of silence.

'Did you sign up?' he asks. He sounds incredulous.

'Yes,' I reply. 'I thought it sounded... very sensible.'

It's really not as crazy as it sounds.

A bunch of Canadian students ran a lively presentation in an extended assembly about chastity. They explained that waiting to have sex until you were married was the best way to protect yourself from STIs and heartbreak. They had a vow they encouraged people to take, and they sold rings too. I grew up going to church so it chimed with what I'd already been taught. I signed up quite happily. After all, no girl was making herself available for me anyway.

I didn't realise that would still be true over a decade later.

'Thing is,' I continue, 'I've kept that vow... Possibly because I haven't met any woman who wanted to have sex with me. Well, maybe a few drunk women, but I didn't want to do it with any of them.' This is all coming out wrong. 'Anyway, my dad's a church warden and always said I should wait to get married first. Over time, I think it's become more important to me. Like the longer I've kept it, the more I don't feel right about breaking it now. Is that stupid? Irrational? OCD?'

Dan sighs.

'It's not stupid, Michael. Admittedly rare these days, but not stupid.'

I feel a small sense of consolation. Dan doesn't think I'm stupid.

'Louise and I… We're Christians, so we decided we wanted to wait until we were married. That's why I had to convince my parents to let us get married when we graduated!'

I remembered their wedding, and also vaguely that Dan had to work his legal powers of persuasion so that his parents didn't disinherit him.

'But it's likely that Jen is coming from a different place to you,' he continues. 'You need to be honest with her about how you feel, otherwise she's just going to feel confused.'

Yes, that sounds about right.

'So I need to talk to her, and tell her about the vow.'

'Yes.'

It sounds so simple, but I'd rather cover a whole day of P.E. lessons than have that conversation.

8

Jen

It's that stage of November when we get incessant rain. The kids in school move from class to class in a steaming, humid, soaking mass. I start reading *A Christmas Carol* with my mentor group, which always gets me into the festive spirit. Michael's boys' group have settled down a lot now that one of their ringleaders, Tyler, is behaving himself. Liz's return is postponed, so that's on hold for now. We run the mock exam and the marking fills every space in my week, but I've got the goal of clearing it before the weekend, so that I can enjoy the two dinner dates Michael's booked in.

Enjoy is perhaps the wrong word.

I mean, Dan and Louise seem absolutely lovely. I'm sure it will be so nice to have lunch with them. But David and Adele? I have no idea what we're going to talk about with them. The best part will be the free food. Whatever 'supper' involves. If it's just canapes, I'm going home.

With marking the mocks, putting the marks onto Michael's complicated spreadsheet, and then filling out another analysis sheet, the week passes fairly quickly. I sit at the kitchen table on Saturday morning, eating a croissant with Dad, and editing my fantasy story I've been working on for a while now. Since Michael went through it, I've been going through all of his suggested edits and comments, and it's given me inspiration to tweak the parts I wasn't sure about. 'Alice in Wonderland meets Game of Thrones' is my current tagline to describe it. Nothing refreshes you from the grim reality of Whidlock County like a fantasy world of assassins and sword fights.

'How's it all coming along then?' Dad asks, nodding at the laptop.

'Lots to work on,' I grimace.

I've definitely been very off-and-on with my writing, always struggling to fit it in around school. I've been using Katie's room as my writing zone, but this morning I brought the laptop down to have a change of scene. And eat croissants.

'Your mother was like that with her paintings,' he says. 'Always making alterations here and there.'

I still feel a sharp ache when I think about Mum. She died when I was in school, and Dad and I haven't really seen eye to eye in the past about her. She went to Jamaica after my grandparents died, to find her family, and then when she came back, we found out she was terminally ill. Dad is very forgiving, but even my good memories twinge with a bitter taste.

'It's hard to know when something's finished,' I say.

A comment Michael's made on the document makes my breath catch in my throat. It's the part where Alice, who has been chasing the shadowy form of her mother (instead of a White Rabbit), chooses to pursue her target rather than her mother when faced with a crossroads. *This feels wrong*, he's written. *Shouldn't she keep going?* No, I reason to myself. Alice needs to give up on chasing something that isn't substantial, and focus on her quest to assassinate the prince.

But the comment bothers me, in the kind of way when you feel intuitively that there's truth in something inconvenient. I close the laptop.

"I'm going to go for a walk to clear my head," I tell Dad.

My house is in a quiet suburb, next to a golf course, and I've got a favourite route that follows the path around the back of the houses, around the golf course perimeter, and through some woodland. It's muddy enough to need wellies, and I throw on a few layers under my thick winter coat. I always feel the tension ease once I get under the trees.

What if Alice did follow her mother? How would the story have to change? It feels like a Rubik's cube; once you move one thing, everything else has to shift too.

The heart of the story is what happens between Alice and the prince. The mother, like the White Rabbit, is a peripheral figure, so it wouldn't work for Alice to pursue her instead of him.

I have to admit, though, that Michael's instinct for story is very good. His sharp eyes spot anything out of place or inconsistent. He's actually a very good editor. Maybe we're both in the wrong job. I picture Michael and me, working from home (his home) and eating croissants in our kitchen before opening up our laptops.

Hmm. I think both of us would get bored pretty quickly without the interaction of school. Michael definitely thrives upon the high intensity. I love the social element; there's always someone to talk to.

On the ground a couple of metres away, a robin hops towards the side of the path. It reminds me of *The Secret Garden*, one of my favourite books when I was a child, where the robin points Mary towards the door, which leads her into the forgotten garden.

What if the mother (White Rabbit replacement) points Alice towards the prince, instead of a different direction? What if she goes through a door which leads into a maze? The cat-and-mouse possibilities are endless, along with building tension, perhaps an atmospheric fog...

By the time I get home, I've mapped out a new scene in my head, and bash it out on my laptop. It's changing the direction of the story, but I'm liking the feel of it. It's got an edge of raw energy which wasn't there before.

When Michael arrives, I'm just finishing up, and I call him up to Katie's room.

"I just wrote a new sequence," I tell him, springing up out of my swivel chair and meeting him in the doorway. "I can't wait for you to read it and see what you think."

I throw my arms around his neck and kiss him.

"Wow," he says, slightly taken aback.

His arms fold around me to hug me tightly against his chest, and when we kiss again, my stomach flips over.

His hand smooths across my back, then stops.

"I think I just found a hole in your hoodie," he says.

I pull back and survey my frayed appearance.

"I forgot I needed to change," I say. "Why don't you read it while I get ready?"

I check Michael's choice of outfit (smart jeans and a casual shirt, with a zip-up sweater), then leave him with my laptop while I go to my bedroom to find something suitable to wear.

Riffling through my wardrobe, I realise how ill-equipped I am for this kind of social occasion. Usually, Saturday lunch at a friend's house would mean going over Steph's for a bowl of pasta. Loungewear accepted. What do I wear for lunch with a couple I barely know? And also, given that we're heading to David's in the evening, what can I wear that will also be suitable for that?

It has to be something that I don't wear for work. That's most of my smart clothes out, then.

I decide to copy Michael's dress code. Smart jeans? Fine. I pull on some dark navy skinnies. Hmm, maybe they are a little faded at the knees. Oh well. Casual shirt? Too cold. I root through my packed clothes rail, impatiently pushing aside all of the cluttered hangers. Why do I have so many cardigans? Finally, I find a baby blue knitted jumper. I haven't even put any make-up on.

'Jen?' Michael says, outside the door. 'Can I come in?'

'Sure.'

He steps inside and smiles excitedly.

'I really like what you've done. It works so much better.'

'I'm so glad you agree,' I grin.

It's way more fun writing when someone else is reading it too.

'I think we should go now.' He checks his watch quickly.

I grab some earrings and a handbag and add a spritz of perfume on my way out of the door.

'You look great, by the way,' Michael says, kissing me at the top of the stairs.

I instantly sink into his arms, leaning against him like I've just exhaled every busy thought or anxiety, and enjoy that moment of my brain focusing on nothing but the soft warmth of his lips. His hands lightly rest on my waist, which probably is the only thing that stops me falling down the stairs. I'm so lightheaded, I don't think I could place my feet one in front of the other without keeling over.

'We really should go,' Michael says, but his eyes are holding mine and he doesn't move.

I move forwards and kiss him again.

'You owe me for booking us onto two dinner parties in one day,' I remind him. 'This is the least you can do to make up for it.'

'What else do you want?' he asks huskily.

I smile and smooth my hand across his collarbone, resting it over his heart.

'Lots of things.' I raise my eyebrow suggestively.

'We're going to be late,' he says, picking my hand up and leading the way down the stairs.

I call out a goodbye to Dad, feeling glad that he can't see me looking flustered. He'd be sure to read me like a 1970s Mills & Boon novel. I'm glad of the cool air when we open the front door.

Maybe there'll be time after the lunch to go to Michael's house and see what happens? I'm willing to follow Michael's lead so we're not late for Dan and Louise, but David and Adele... I'm sure they wouldn't mind if we were fashionably late. Heck, I don't really care if they do, given that I'm looking forward to their company like a cat in the vet's waiting room about to be neutered.

Now my similes are sex-obsessed.

I try to shake my railroading train of thought as I get into Michael's car. There are two identical gift bags on the back seat.

'I got some wine and chocolates,' he explains.

'Wow, you really think of everything.' I don't know why his organisation still surprises me.

I fidget in the passenger seat as he starts the engine. I can't stop staring at his hands, his strong arms, his broad shoulders... Looking at his profile, I love the angles of his face and his jawline. I bite my lip and imagine trailing kisses down his neck.

'Jen,' he says, and I watch his throat as he swallows. 'I wanted to tell you something, if that's okay.'

This is it. He's going to say he can't keep holding back; at first he thought he wanted to take things slowly, but now he's burning up with raging desire and wants to rip all my clothes off and ravish me in the back of the car.

'Yes?' I whisper.

'When I was younger, I took a vow of chastity.'

Okay, I wasn't expecting that. It's a metaphorical cold shower on my fantasies. I'm standing in a monsoon when I wanted an Indian summer.

'What?' My voice is an oddly high pitch.

'When I was younger, I took—'

Michael obviously thinks I didn't hear him the first time, rather than being utterly bewildered by the weirdest thing he's ever said to me.

'What, like a monk or something?' I interrupt.

'It wasn't primarily for religious reasons.'

Michael's doing his thing where he talks like a textbook. I stare as he changes gear and I can see him blushing.

'Are you going to explain this a little more clearly?' I prompt, when he doesn't elaborate any further.

'A Canadian organisation visited my school and ran an assembly. They were from a chastity movement, similar to True Love Waits, if you've heard of it?'

I shake my head.

'It's big in America,' he continues, speaking faster now. 'The idea is that you promise to wait until you're married before having sex.'

Sounds like something from the Bible belt that Miley Cyrus or Britney Spears might advocate before blatantly disregarding it in their next, mildly pornographic music video.

'Right,' I say. 'Why?'

'No contraception is 100% effective,' he says. Textbook tone is back again. 'Plus the risk of STI's. The safest way to have sex is with one partner who has only ever had you as their partner. I like the idea of waiting… for my wife.'

I process this silently, and I can feel his inquiring stare. I'm not going to lie, the fact that he said the word 'wife' is incredibly romantic and makes my stomach flip. The problem is that Michael and I are no longer alone in this car, but accompanied by the ghosts of my previous boyfriends. Am I going to have to explain how far I went with each of them, with facetious precision? Have I disqualified myself as a partner for Michael if I don't match his requirements of exclusivity?

'I went to Whidlock County, Michael,' I remind him. 'No Canadian chastity groups came to us.'

'Right.' He nods and focuses on the road. 'I realise it is a little... niche.'

I stare out of the window, at a house with a 'For Sale' sign and a lady with a dalmatian. How did I get from smooching on the stairs to this conversation?

'I mean it sounds very... noble,' I say, waving my hand dismissively. 'But Michael—lots of people *say* this stuff but they don't actually *follow* it. I remember in school, Miss Johnson told us that waiting for marriage was a Christian tradition, but not many people kept it now.'

'Dan and Louise did,' Michael says. 'Maybe you should ask them about it.'

'Yeah right!' I scoff. 'Hi, I've met you once, and Michael says you waited until you were married before you slept together. Is that true? Like I'm going to ask that!'

'I just wanted you to know that some people wait.'

'Are they religious?'

'They're Christians, yes.'

'But you told me that you didn't sign up for this for religious reasons.'

'Not primarily. But I was brought up in the Church as well.'

In the church? What does that mean? My mum's parents founded a Pentecostal church, but she ran off with a yoga instructor.

'Do you still go to church?' I ask, feeling on very uncertain ground. How is there so much about him I don't know?

'Not really,' he shrugs. 'Only when I'm home.'

He carries on driving, and I sit and fidget, forgetting about our imminent lunch and obsessing over why he's telling me this. This is forcing me to recalibrate our whole relationship... Maybe this is why he's been so weird about me going over to his house again.

'So you're telling me you're a virgin,' I say, struggling to process without verbalizing.

'Yes.'

'Right...'

He must know that I'm not. Is he going to judge me? I never had any religious beliefs to uphold. Unless you count not wanting to walk under ladders. Although that was largely because one time, I walked under some scaffolding and straight into a metal pole. I blame it on the rain, because my coat hood was up.

'Okay.' I try to focus on the issue in hand. 'I am surmising that you want to *keep* this vow of chastity?'

'Yes,' he says, trying to focus both on driving and on looking at me. 'If that's okay with you?'

Well, I don't know if I have much choice. I'm hardly going to coerce him. I've watched the 'consent is like a cup of tea' video too many times in awkward PSHE lessons for that.

'So we can't have sex.'

'Until we get married.'

I think I actually stop breathing. He said *until*.

'Jen, say something,' he frowns. 'What are you thinking?'

My mouth is opening and closing but no words are forming.

'Wow,' I finally manage to speak. 'I wasn't expecting this conversation.'

'I realise it's a lot to take in,' Michael says. 'This is Dan's house.'

He parks the car outside a red brick terrace. This Saturday lunch is going to be nothing like I anticipated.

9

Michael

I told Jen, and now she's freaking out.

Part of me thinks it's better to go on in to see Dan and Louise, in the hope that firstly, this provides a welcome distraction, or secondly, they can explain all this better than I can.

I mean, I think it's really romantic. Let's wait for each other. Let's make those promises till death do us part and then seal them physically. Nothing like all this 'swipe if you like', one-night stand culture.

But judging from Jen's reaction, she thinks this is Weird. Like I'm part of a cult. And I don't know how to tell her my viewpoint and beliefs without sounding like I'm judging her, because it doesn't look like she shares my convictions.

I hope this is not going to become a barrier between us.

We stand on Dan's doorstep, a hand span apart, and the reverberations of my confession create a volume of white noise around us.

Then Dan opens the door and we both give a middle-class, we're-fine, high-pitched 'Hi.'

It's been a while since I was last here, and I remember the distinctive red tiled Victorian floor, but what I'm noticing now is photos everywhere of Dan's wedding. We had not long graduated so we look fresh-faced and youthful in the pictures. I was an usher and we all had matching cravats. The ceremony was in a parish church and we spent hours wrapping ribbons around posts.

'Hi!' Louise walks out from the kitchen to meet us, holding a baby. 'Grace, this is Michael and Jen.'

Jen smiles and waves at Grace, who reacts with a sudden beaming smile. In that moment, my heart surges with love for her. I just know, with absolute certainty, that I want this to be it. I want to be with Jen forever. I want us to be living in a house together, with our wedding photos on the walls...

'What would you like to drink?' Dan asks.

I hand over the gift bag in a daze and ask for water. I'm vaguely aware of Jen nodding and chatting to Louise as we move into the kitchen and sit at the table. I take a glass of water from Dan and drink it mechanically, all the time wondering at this new revelation.

In the car, when I told Jen about my vow, I wasn't trying to use it as leverage for anything. I wasn't really thinking about exactly when I — or we – might get married. Since I graduated, I've focused on my career. I didn't have any girlfriends to distract me or raise any questions about my response to a Canadian chastity group. Now that I'm sitting in Dan's kitchen, and he's been married for years and has a baby, everything is suddenly in sharper focus.

I want to marry Jen.

'Michael?'

Jen's voice breaks into my trance.

'Louise just asked if you like Parmesan.'

I blink myself back into the conversation.

'Yes,' I reply. 'Thank you.'

Jen raises her eyebrows quizzically and then turns back to Louise. It's suddenly surreal, that I've been in and out of this kitchen before at various gatherings, but now I'm here with my girlfriend. The landscape of my life has altered and that night when

I took Jen out for our first date, I had no concept of what this would look —and feel— like. Everything feels better with her.

'How's things at school?' Dan asks me. For once, it's the last thing on my mind.

'Not very positive,' I admit. 'David told me the local authority want to merge Whidlock County with Prestfield, on Prestfield's site. Our buildings aren't fit for purpose.'

'What will happen to the staff?'

'Well, they will try to redeploy people, but there will be requests for early retirements, voluntary redundancies.'

I remember David intimating to me that if I continued to date Jen, he'd find a reason to get rid of her. But now she's been promoted, I don't think that's still something he's seriously considering. I hope not, given that he's invited us to dinner.

Dan grimaces.

'That sounds challenging.'

Even if we're both safe, Whidlock is going to turn pretty toxic when the news drops. I've been avoiding thinking about it.

'Pasta's ready!' Louise announces.

10

Jen

It doesn't feel as awkward as I thought it would, eating lunch at Dan and Louise's. The food is right up my street— tagliatelle with creamy sauce— and the baby, Grace, is grabbing pasta by the fistful and making a great mess in her highchair. Super cute. The house is lovely, but not super clean or fancy. By the time we have tea and cake in the lounge, I'm laughing at Dan's jokes and definitely not feeling like a clunky add-on into a well-established friendship group. In fact, this is actually something new, and something nice. Meeting Michael's friends and getting to know them is surprisingly enjoyable and being here, together, makes it all feel… grown up, somehow. It's so different to slouching around shopping malls with Jamie as a teenager, or student drinks with George.

'What's your role at the school?' Louise asks.

'I work with learning support to help students with additional needs, like dyslexia or autism,' I explain. 'I still teach English as well.'

'How do you find it, dating and working together?' She looks intrigued.

'Well, it's a bit mixed,' I admit, with a quick glance to make sure Michael's not listening. 'There's always a lot going on in the week, so we just meet up at the weekend.'

'Like you're seeing each other all the time, but you're not really spending much time together,' Louise suggests.

'Yes, that's exactly right,' I nod and take a sip of my tea. 'Michael once signed me up to drive a rugby team to a sports fixture so that we could 'spend some time together.''

Louise snorts with laughter.

'Bet he didn't do that again.'

I didn't see the funny side at the time, but now we're giggling about it, it's okay.

'I've never known him to have a girlfriend,' she says, once we've stopped laughing. 'And I've known him for years now. I don't think he's had much practice with dating.'

'You're right there,' I say, remembering his vow.

'It isn't a bad thing,' Louise says, 'but it must be harder to adjust to a relationship when you've been single for a long time.'

I sigh.

'When I was single, I just wanted someone to be there. Someone to walk with, watch a movie with, sit on the sofa with. The little things. But I don't know if Michael can switch off long enough to be 'unscheduled' and just… be.'

Louise gives a sympathetic smile, then gives Grace a toy to chew on.

'The start of a relationship is special, though,' she says. 'Dan and I have a lot of time to hang out on the sofa… and we probably end up dozing off if we put a film on! We don't get much opportunity to go out on dates like we used to do at the beginning.'

She's right, it's just the start, I remind myself. Plenty of time to reach all these milestones in my head. Even coming here today for lunch ticks off a stage on the relationship-barometer. I still haven't met Michael's parents yet. That's going to be a watershed moment.

'Thank you so much for a lovely meal.' I hug Louise as we get ready to leave. 'How about we cook for you next time? You can come to Michael's?'

Michael looks a bit dazed.

'That would be great,' Dan says enthusiastically, giving an exaggerated thumbs up to Michael.

'Great,' Michael repeats, but I don't think he even heard what I said.

'Are you okay?' I ask, once we're back in the car.

He looks at me, and his eyes burn with sudden intensity. He opens his mouth, but says nothing.

'Thank you for coming,' he says finally, turning back to start the engine.

'Where are we going now?' I ask. 'We've got a few hours before David's.'

'Fancy a walk?'

He drives a short distance and parks up by the river. The sky is its usual heavy grey but it's not raining. The air smells like fresh green leaves. I zip up my coat and Michael takes my hand, then leads me onto the path.

The river feels slightly sunken into the ground, with high banks on either side, the clay kind which creates a murky hue to the water. Whidlock is nicely hidden behind the trees and overgrown areas of the nature reserve. In summer there are wild flowers, but as it's November, there's only bracken.

We amble along, and even though it's not particularly scenic, it feels exactly the sort of ordinary moment that I was telling Louise we never shared. It's not a Saturday to write a postcard about, but compared to the endless, empty weekends filled with dreary work, this is blissful.

'I'm sorry if I dropped a bombshell earlier,' Michael says, looking apologetic.

Oh yes: the chastity vow.

'I'm glad you told me.'

It certainly explains a lot.

'Does it make you want to… find someone else?' He struggles to get the words out.

'No.' I'm slightly insulted he would even think that. 'I know this is all new for you. A lot of this is new for me, too. There's no need to rush anything.'

'How do you feel about meeting my parents?'

I guess 'no need to rush' isn't in Michael's vocabulary. Besides, he's met my dad and sister already. I can't help feeling a prickle of elation and fear. The fact that he wants me to meet them must mean he's serious, right? On the other hand, Michael took a long time for me to get to know. He's very intimidating. Will his parents be the same?

'That would be great.' I give a (slightly forced) grin.

'I was thinking we could stay at theirs next Saturday night, then go to church with them on Sunday morning.'

A few hours ago I didn't even know that this was part of Michael's life. I suppose I can sit through it as a sort of spectator. It's not my sort of thing and I don't want to be a hypocrite by pretending it is.

'Okay,' I nod, aware that he's staring at me to gauge my reaction. I give what I hope is an encouraging smile. 'I'm looking forward to finding out more about your family.'

The cynical voice in my head is reminding me that this is going to make it even more painful if our relationship fails.

11

Michael

I'm thinking if I can get Jen to come to my parents' church next weekend, I can measure how open she would be to getting married there.

I know church isn't her thing, but it's a beautiful, gothic building with stained glass windows, a real sense of history... It's the perfect venue. And I know it's in demand. Maybe I can get some contact details for the vicar and find out what the availability is like for the summer. July wedding, and six weeks off together for honeymoon. Jen's been talking about saving up to travel, so this is the perfect opportunity.

My phone buzzing in my pocket interrupts my train of thought. I release Jen's hand to retrieve it.

'It's David,' I read from the screen.

Jen raises her eyebrows. We're going to his house for dinner, so I'd better answer it.

'Hi,' I say, accepting the call.

'Hiya Michael, still okay for tonight?'

'Yes, we're looking forward to it.' It's not entirely truthful but I'm being polite. Jen rolls her eyes.

'Adele was wondering if Jen would mind helping her with some make-up she's been sent to try out.'

I lower the phone and hiss to Jen.

'David's asked if you can help Adele with some make-up.'

Jen makes a face and shakes her head.

'I'm not even wearing any,' she says.

'She's not wearing any make-up,' I tell David.

'That's perfect,' David says quickly. 'Adele will do everything. It's for her YouTube channel, would Jen be okay with that?'

I'm not really sure what he's asking, but I want to end this conversation.

'Yes, I'm sure it'll be fine,' I say. 'See you later.'

'What was that all about?' Jen asks, slipping her hand back into mine.

'Adele's got a YouTube channel.' I shrug, hoping this explains everything.

'That figures,' Jen comments. 'Don't know why she would need my help. I'm worried that I'm dressed too casually for tonight.'

'You look perfect as you are.' I bend down to kiss her.

By the time we've made a circuit, it's late afternoon. The sky was too cloudy to see much of a sunset, but the dimness of twilight has set in, and the chill is sharper. We head back to mine for a stopgap before we leave for David's.

'This has been a really good day,' Jen says reflectively, leaning against the counter as I make tea.

'You like Dan and Louise?'

It matters so much to me now, her approval. I get a surge of relief when she nods and smiles.

'They are so lovely. Grace is so cute!'

'Do you want children?'

It seems as good a time as any to ask this crucial question.

'Yes, definitely,' she says. 'Don't you?'

'Yes,' I reply, stirring milk into the cup. 'To be honest, it's not something I've thought much about up until now.'

'Too busy getting promoted?' she asks wryly.

'In some ways.' I hand her the steaming mug. 'When you're single for a long time, you try not to think about it, because it might never happen.'

'I didn't think guys worried too much about that.' She sips and stares at me over the cup. 'No biological clock ticking.'

'Yes, but you can't become a single male parent, unless you adopt, I suppose.'

This is not where I want this conversation to go.

'Is it something you've thought about?' I ask.

'Adoption?' She looks confused. 'Not really. I've always wanted to have children naturally.'

'And have you thought about that... much?' I'm vague because I'm treading on icy ground that might give way.

'It's not something I want right now,' she says. 'I've only just been promoted.'

What I really want to ask is: have you thought much about having children with *me*? But I chicken out and take a glug of tea instead. It's too hot and scalds my tongue.

We sit on the sofa, our mugs cooling on the coffee table, and my brain is leapfrogging from one major life goal to another. Until Jen moves closer and I feel the warmth of her breath against my cheek. My lips find hers and it's like the touchpaper is lit. We kiss and I can't think about anything anymore, only this sensation, this magnet pull that I've never felt with someone before. I cup her face because I don't know where my hands will end up if I don't. She pulls back, breathless and flushed, opening her eyes to stare at me, reflecting the raw desire in my own.

Only one coherent thought pops into my head: July is too far away.

12

Jen

I pull back from Michael, reeling from the heady dizziness of sudden passion. I have no idea how to navigate this ground. When I was a teenager with Jamie, we did whatever we had opportunity to do: a lot of snogging, basically. My uni boyfriends had clear expectations, which I went along with. I had no reason not to. My most recent (and by recent, I mean over a year ago) foray into online dating resulted in a few dates but I wasn't going to invite Ryan into my flat. I don't think he would ever have left again.

Now I'm here, with Michael, alone and in his house. But none of the usual rules seem to apply.

'I'm glad you're meeting my parents next weekend,' Michael says.

See what I mean? How did we get from smooching on the sofa to talking about his parents?

'Yes,' I say, sitting back and grabbing my tea, for want of anything else to do.

'Shall we see what's on?' Michael picks up the TV remote.

As long as it's not *Masterchef.*

The screen flickers and I see Kevin Costner. Michael goes to change the channel.

'Wait!' I cry. 'That's *Robin Hood: Prince of Thieves*!'

'You want this?' Michael looks slightly incredulous.

'Yeah, it's great.' I bat his arm down out of the trigger-happy position.

We watch until it's time to go to David's, and I'm seriously dreading this inopportune meal. I could quite happily practise my archery and shoot apples off David's head, strategically missing and hitting him instead. How exactly do you sustain conversation with someone who is smarmy, affected and insincere?

'Please try and be polite,' Michael warns me in the car before we go in.

'I can't promise anything,' I reply darkly.

David lives —unsurprisingly— in an elite suburb of the city. It's a small square of Victorian, red brick houses with distinctive period features. Two sporty, flashy cars are on the driveway— nothing if not anachronistic. Michael rings the doorbell, holding the gift bag, and I stand awkwardly, wondering how David is going to greet us. Will it be a hug like a long-lost cousin? Or a pretentious kiss on both cheeks, as if he's European?

It's neither. Adele opens the door, seizes my hand and literally drags me inside.

'Jen,' she says in an overly high-pitched tone, 'I'm so glad you've come! Thank you so much for agreeing to do this.'

She takes my coat, hangs it up, ushers me to take my shoes off, and I've only been inside thirty seconds.

'I'll take you straight to the studio, if that's alright,' she says, and it's not a question. 'David's in the kitchen,' she calls to Michael, pulling my sleeve in the opposite direction.

I've barely had time to take in my surroundings. So far, there's a lot of bright light, and white walls. Adele opens a door and guides me to a chair. As I sit, I notice the array of cosmetics on the table next to me. And a camera on a tripod, pointing straight at my face.

What exactly did Michael agree to earlier?

'That's a lot of make-up,' I say, allowing my alarm to colour my tone.

Adele is focused on her laptop, which is next to the camera, but I can't see the screen.

'They're a new start-up,' she says vaguely, 'aimed at people with darker skin tones. I thought you would be the perfect model.'

A stone-cold realisation begins to sink from my head down to my stomach.

'I haven't—' I stutter. 'I mean, I've never done any modelling…'

'Don't worry.' Adele waves a hand and then starts selecting compacts. 'You just need to sit back and relax.'

It's hard to do that when a YouTuber is trying to give you an unsolicited makeover. But this is my boss' girlfriend, and Michael told me to be polite.

'Sure,' I say through gritted teeth.

'I'm going to start with Compact 18, and this powder gives a great foundation.' Adele raises her voice slightly, not dissimilar to me when I'm teaching. She starts applying the powder to my cheeks with a generous dusting.

'I —er— don't usually wear much make-up,' I say tentatively, hoping she'll take the hint.

'This will look completely natural,' Adele assures me, before turning straight back to the table and selecting another product. 'I really like the design of this concealer stick, very neat to go in your handbag, and easy to blend in.'

She applies it to a sensitive spot just above my lip, her brow furrowed in concentration and I'm trying not to shrink backwards, which would be rude. She just is so close!

'Now for the eyes,' she says, brandishing an eyeliner pencil. 'This is the charcoal shade, and I'm going to go for bold definition.'

I absolutely loathe people touching my eyes in any way, so it's all I can do not to flinch. I close my eyelids and endeavour to keep my expression neutral, as Adele's pencil makes strong strokes right where my lashes meet.

'Now open them,' Adele instructs, 'and look up at the ceiling.'

She runs the pencil right underneath my eye, and I feel my eyes start to water.

'Wait!' she says, snatching a tissue and holding it at the corner of my eye. 'Now blink. That's right.'

By the time she's finished, my eyes are itchy and probably bloodshot. I definitely bear no resemblance to a model. There was a reason I chose teaching.

'This palette contains some great neutral tones.' She opens up a giant box of eyeshadows in about a hundred shades. It's like chocolates, but inedible. How disappointing. 'I'm going to use gold as an accent and a blend of the sandy shades as a base.'

'How long have you been doing this… sort of thing?' It's a lame question, but I feel like I should try and make conversation.

Adele looks insulted.

'A while now,' she says, swirling a brush into the eyeshadow until it's swollen up like a Christmas bauble. She applies it with a tad more force than necessary.

'It must be great to be able to try out new products,' I try again. If Michael were here, he would surely praise my civility.

'Mmm,' Adele says noncommittally. 'I'm especially impressed with the Bow Street brand. They offer high quality products at a high street price.'

My eyebrows knit involuntarily; she's sounding like a commercial now.

'Have you been seeing David for long?'

Her hand jerks and she mutters under her breath, before snatching another tissue and wiping my eyelid.

'Try not to speak while I finish this off, please.'

I don't know why she's turned cold on me, and I can't help bristling as she completes my totally-unwanted makeover. I mean, she could at least be more grateful that I agreed to do this.

'I expect he's a really busy man,' I say, aware that I'm deliberately ranging into a danger zone, but I can't resist it. 'Rescuing a failing school, hiring and firing people, fighting legal battles…'

Adele's face is inches from mine, and her eyes lock onto mine in a death stare.

'I think we're done here,' she says.

'Lovely, I'm starving,' I say.

She walks over to the laptop, clicks a button, then turns on me in an explosion of fury.

'What the hell? What do you think you were doing?'

'Sorry?' I blink my overly-golden eyelids at her.

'Saying all that personal stuff like that. Anyone could be watching.'

'Watching?' I narrow my eyes. 'What do you mean, watching?'

I look again at the camera on the tripod.

'Were you *filming* that?'

She facepalms, groaning.

'I was livestreaming on my YouTube channel!'

13

Michael

I'm in the middle of discussing the best method of roasting potatoes when Jen flings open the kitchen door. Her hair is bobbing with the movement and her eyes are painted like two gold hubcaps.

'Were you aware that Adele was putting make-up on me *live on YouTube?*'

Her hand rests on her hip and this is bad. Really bad.

'No,' I say immediately, looking at David, who gives a slightly smug smile.

'I did ask you over the phone. You agreed,' David says, turning back to the cooker to stir cream in a saucepan.

'I…' I try desperately to recall the conversation, while Jen glares at me with her most formidable animosity. I'd almost forgotten what it felt like. 'I didn't realise that you meant doing the make-up on YouTube.'

'Well, it looks fantastic.' David gestures towards Jen, putting on his charm. 'No harm done.'

Jen gives a sarcastic snort.

'Ha! I wouldn't be too sure about that.'

David looks at her, and his smile fades. She folds her arms and leans against the doorway.

'I mean, I'm sure she can delete it,' Jen shrugs.

'Delete what?' David's tone is menacing, but somewhat offset by his white apron and wooden spoon.

When Jen doesn't reply, he walks out to find Adele. As soon as he's gone, Jen turns her look of disdain to me.

'Jen, I'm so sorry,' I grovel, moving closer and taking her hand. 'I had no idea.'

'No wonder she was talking like an advert. I feel like an idiot!'

She gives a little noise, half-sob and half-laugh. I wrap my arms around her and squeeze. By the time she pulls away, she's laughing. It's all very unnerving.

'What were you saying to David?' I look down into her eyes, glowing like an Egyptian tomb.

'I said a few… personal things which he probably wouldn't want on YouTube,' she says, raising an eyebrow. 'Although I didn't realise I was on YouTube at the time.'

'What did you say?'

Before she can answer, David bursts back into the room.

'Why did you mention the case?'

His face is distorted with anger, and I've never seen him like this. He's usually a master of cool reactions.

I feel instant guilt because I'm the one who told Jen that David was being sued for unfair dismissal by a teacher at our previous school.

'I didn't say anything specific,' Jen spits back. 'Worried that your perfect image is going to be sullied? I would have thought you should be worried about how you're treating your staff right now.'

'I've given you a promotion,' David says. 'What more do you want?'

'An end to the glass ceiling and culture of misogyny that you have brought to Whidlock.'

Jen is truly impressive in these situations. She seems to be at her most eloquent when angry and under duress. Nevertheless, I'm standing in the kitchen feeling extremely awkward. I thought this sort of thing only happened in movies. We were supposed to be here for dinner and it's turned into a soap opera.

'You need to apologise to Adele,' David lashes back. 'She's worked so hard to build her following…'

'I don't bloody care about her following!' Jen's voice is getting louder. 'She didn't even ask my permission before she pressed the button.'

'I take full responsibility for this misunderstanding,' I interject, holding my hands up. 'I obviously did not grasp what David was asking on the phone earlier. Please, both of you, accept my apologies. Let's not spend our Saturday night arguing.'

'Well I'm certainly not going to spend it here.' Jen stomps towards the front door.

I give David an apologetic look.

'I'm sorry, David.'

I hurry after Jen, out to the car, and she climbs in and slams the door shut.

'I can't believe it.' She shakes her head, stunned with anger and disbelief.

'Jen—' I begin.

'Just drive!' she snaps.

I pull out and move through the neighbourhood, then spot a McDonalds and park outside.

'We need to talk about this.' I turn off the engine. But when I look at Jen, there are tears in her eyes. 'Come here.' I attempt to hug her across the gear stick.

'No,' she says, leaning forward and grabbing tissues out of her handbag. 'I need to get this stuff off my face.'

She pulls down the mirror and wipes away the shimmer, sniffing.

'I didn't know, Jen,' I say helplessly. 'I'm so sorry.'

'I know,' she says, with a sigh of resignation.

The silence is heavy.

'Are you mad at me?' I ask.

She doesn't answer for a few seconds.

'Do you remember when you said that it wasn't about you rescuing me, but me saving you?' she says.

I remember. We were sitting in my car, just like we are now, pulled over in a layby. Then we kissed…

'Well, sometimes I need rescuing too,' she says, and her voice catches.

'What do you mean?'

She seemed to be doing a pretty good job of kicking David's ass without my intervention.

'I mean that we would never have gone to David's in the first place if you had asked me before agreeing to it.'

'It was in the bar, it was busy, Adele put me on the spot…' I argue, then sigh. 'I thought it was a good opportunity to rebuild the relationship with David.'

'Rebuild?' Her voice is shrill. 'Well, I was always at Ground Zero with him anyway. You don't actually want to be *friends* with him, after all that's happened, do you?'

I look out of the window at the brightly lit restaurant with balloons at the entrance. I wish everything was as simple as getting a Happy Meal and a free balloon.

'I think that, given he's our boss, we both need to find a way to get along with him. Professionally.'

'That doesn't mean we need to spend Saturday night with him.'

'Okay, I'm sorry.' I can't help a pinch of anger creeping into my tone. 'I'm not like you. When I'm put on the spot, I don't have eloquent speeches. I just want to keep the peace.'

'Real peace doesn't overlook injustice.'

This woman is amazing. I'm breathless just looking at her eyes, shining with tears rather than cosmetics now, and I reach out to touch her cheek.

'I love you, Jen.'

She blinks at me, her mouth opening in shock.

'What?' she says.

I realise that a seismic event is occurring, and it's in the McDonalds' car park.

'I love you,' I repeat.

For an awful moment I think she's going to break up with me. Then her hands cup my face and she pulls me into a kiss. When she draws back, she's laughing and wiping a tear away.

'I love you too, Michael,' she says. 'Even though you drive me crazy.'

14
Jen

The email arrives at lunchtime on Wednesday.

At the Governors' meeting last night, a new HR policy was approved concerning staff interpersonal relationships. Dating relationships are strongly discouraged between staff members within the school, and may result in disciplinary action. This does not apply to married couples who both work at the school.

I shut my laptop lid and grab my bag to head into the staffroom, simmering with anger. So this is how he decides to punish me. David Clark, you—

'Have you read the email?' Michael appears in the doorway, his forehead furrowed.

'Oh yes,' I reply. 'HR: the perfect weapon.'

He steps towards me and takes my hands.

'Jen,' he says quietly, 'please don't go off and vent about this. I have a few ideas how to approach this and I need you to trust me.'

I meet his gaze, and his grey eyes are soothing. I sigh.

'Alright,' I concede. 'But can we take a walk or something, just to get out of here for a bit?'

'Sure.'

Wrapping up in our coats, we head out of the school gates and along the streets. The sky seems permanently cloudy, but there are some patches of sunlight breaking through. I take some deep breaths and instantly feel calmer. Breathing different air, getting into a different space, just has such a profound impact.

'So what's your plan?' I turn to Michael expectantly.

'Let me talk to David,' he says. 'And then we'll go from there.'

'What if he says he's not going to change the policy?' Which is exactly what I think he's going to say. 'Are you going to break up with me? Or are we going to have to meet in secret?'

I'm kind of joking but kind of not: this feels like the sort of thing Michael would do, in order to stay on David's good side and not rock the boat.

'Jen, I love you and I'm not going to break up with you,' Michael says firmly. I can't help smiling, but I note he hasn't ruled out the secrecy option. 'Let's not talk about it anymore, it'll just wind you up. How about we make plans for our trip this weekend to my parents?'

This trip is definitely making me nervous now. Michael wasn't an easy person to get to know. What are his parents going to be like? For an English teacher, Michael's not very good at describing them.

'My dad is… quite a direct person. You always know where you are with him. My mum is quiet, and she loves Jane Austen and the Brontës, so you should get on well.'

This is slightly reassuring, but it's hard to picture what his family dynamic is like. His younger sister's a similar age to Katie, my sister, and she's not at home anymore.

'Maybe we can all meet up together!' Katie says, as we talk on the phone later that evening.

'I haven't met her yet.' I roll my eyes. 'We're going to church on Sunday. I think they're quite religious.'

'Oh,' she says. 'Is Michael religious?'

'I don't really know,' I say. 'He doesn't seem to be, to me.'

Apart from the chastity thing, I add silently.

'I hope they're not judgy,' Katie says. 'Can you think of any religious people who aren't judgy?'

'I can, actually.' I smile. 'Michael's friends, Dan and Louise. We went to their house for dinner and it was actually really lovely. Unlike our non-dinner at David's.'

'How is Mr Clark?'

'He's introduced a new policy: no dating.'

'What?' Katie sounds shocked.

'I know.'

'So what are you going to do?'

'Well, Michael's going to talk to him…'

'I bet that's a fun conversation,' Katie says dryly.

'And Michael said he's not going to break up with me.' I'm grinning from ear to ear now at the memory. 'He said he loves me.'

'Wow, you guys have been together for, like, a month now? Must be getting serious, hey?'

'I don't think Michael can do anything else,' I say. 'He does everything 100%. No half-measures.'

'He is intense,' Katie agrees. 'But in a good way.'

If his parents are as intense as he is, I'm in for a long weekend.

I can't shake off my worries about the new policy, though. I post on a WhatsApp group with two of my friends from school, Deena and Clare, to get their opinions. They're lawyers, so hopefully they can shed some light on the legalities.

Me: Can they enforce this?

Deena: It feels a bit invasive to me. Surely lots of people meet at work and start dating?

Clare: It's also the sort of thing that they wouldn't need to act on unless something inappropriate happened on site or with students present.

Me: What if, for example, some students saw me and Michael when we were out somewhere together?

WEDDING BELL TIME

Deena: So what? It's a free country.

Clare: I also think the policy sounds old-fashioned with the marriage clause. What if a couple have been together for years and they don't want to get married?

Me: Maybe this is a classic example of David talking to the right people and getting this through.

Deena: Go to your union rep and ask them to challenge it.

Now that is a good idea. Plus my rep is Judy, and she has no fear when it comes to taking on the establishment. Especially as she's retiring soon.

Me: Hey Judy. I'm a bit concerned about the new HR policy of no dating, because of Michael. Can you query it from a union standpoint?

Judy: Already on it. Don't worry.

That gives me some relief, anyway.

I muddle through the rest of the week, marking books and fielding millions of emails. Michael's love for me still hasn't changed his mind on the whole midweek date amnesty, but I need to clear everything for the weekend, so maybe it's a good thing. When we finally reach Friday, he picks me up from my house and loads my suitcase into the car. I kiss Dad goodbye.

'I'll be back on Sunday.'

'Have fun,' he says.

Lessons pass and once the final bell rings, Michael comes to get me from my room. We walk out to the staff car park, and Joseph Vermont, a Maths teacher, gives us a Look.

'Have a good weekend,' Michael says chirpily.

I can't be bothered to be nice, so I just glare at him until he looks away.

Michael's car is beginning to look a lot less pristine than usual, and I congratulate myself on my influence. There are some hair bobbles in the side tray, sweet wrappers in the glove compartment, and a lipstick under the radio. I pick it up and pull down the mirror to apply it.

'Don't,' Michael says.

'Why not?' I ask, affronted.

He revs the engine and starts to roll the car forwards.

'Well, firstly, I'm about to drive off, so you could end up with it all over your face,' he says, looking both ways across the junction before pulling out onto the road. 'Secondly, you look better without it. You're beautiful.'

He turns down into a side street, and then swerves the car into a space next to some garages.

'And thirdly, because I want to do this.' He kisses me suddenly. 'Without getting your lipstick all over my face.'

'Very compelling reasons,' I manage to articulate, before pulling him down to kiss me again.

It's the moment we've been waiting for all week. When our lips touch, it's like breathing oxygen underwater. It's like the sudden, dizzying swoon of a pungent alcoholic drink. I lose my thoughts, my words, and everything except this completely consuming feeling and emotional pull. His hand touches my thigh, and I gasp. My whole body leans towards him, screaming to be touched. I slide my hand down his back and feel him shiver.

'M-m-Michael,' I mutter from the back of my throat. 'I want you.'

'I want you too,' he murmurs, moving his mouth away from mine and kissing my cheek instead. 'But I should focus on driving.'

'Your mind on other things?' I joke.

'There's probably some kid around filming us, putting it all on YouTube,' Michael grins. 'Just like in London, you're never more than six foot away from a rat. In Whidlock you're always in proximity of a school kid.'

I laugh, but I look nervously around, just in case.

15

Michael

I don't know what's come over me. I'm not the sort of person who snogs girls in cars.

As I restart the engine, I grip the steering wheel tightly. I've always prided myself on my discipline and self-control, on the fact that I've managed to keep my vow for so long. Now I'm starting to wonder if it was merely a lack of opportunity to break it.

Taking the road towards my parents' home, I'm in autopilot and my mind is all over the place. I'm acutely aware of Jen, and every time she moves I get a fresh hit of her perfume. I keep glancing sideways at her and it's hard to drag my eyes away from roving all over her body. I clench my jaw tightly and stare at the traffic with grim determination.

'I didn't think it would be this busy,' Jen says, leaning forwards to put the radio on.

Now I can smell her shampoo —apples?— and I nearly forget to take the right exit.

Once we leave the busiest roads, the sun is setting and giving a golden glow to the cold, barren fields. My parents live just over an hour's drive away, near the coast. It's not a place with sandy beaches, it's more cliffs and estuary, but the rugged beauty makes me feel at home. The ground is covered with heather and gorse.

'Like *Wuthering Heights* out here,' I smile at Jen, knowing it's her favourite novel.

'When was the last time you visited?' she asks.

Too long ago. With starting my new job, and then going away with Jen in half term, I haven't been here since the summer.

'August, probably,' I reply.

She looks at me with one eyebrow raised.

'So, are you going to tell me anything about your parents? I would like to be a little more prepared.'

I tighten my hands on the steering wheel, and feel my neck tense up.

'Their names are Ezra and Heather,' I begin.

'Ezra's an unusual name,' Jen comments.

'I suppose,' I shrug. 'My grandfather was very religious. He wanted all of our names to come from the Bible.'

Jen blinks. Another thing that she probably finds weird.

'Do they go to church every week?'

I give a dry laugh.

'Yes, sometimes more. My father's a warden.'

'What's that?'

'He helps with… different things,' I say vaguely. I don't really know.

'Is he still working too?' she asks.

'Yes, I can't see him giving up work anytime soon.'

I don't think I've ever seen my dad sit down in one place for longer than thirty minutes, except for the classical concerts he used to take me to. I picture the piano, and feel the ache of not playing for so long.

'He's very musical,' I tell Jen. 'He's an amazing pianist. He taught me.'

'You play piano?' She sits up straighter to look at me. 'You never said!'

'It's not something that I really think about when I'm at school.'

'What about your sister— does she play, too?'

'Rachel plays a bit, but her main instrument is the clarinet. She used to play in all these different orchestras—go on tour around Europe, that sort of thing.'

'Right,' Jen says slowly. 'You all sound scarily talented.'

'It's not a big deal,' I say. 'It was just... Music was always part of our lives.'

Jen sighs. I double take to check her expression.

'What's wrong?'

'It's nothing,' she says, putting her elbow against the window and gazing out at the scenery.

'No, it's not,' I push back. 'Tell me.'

She rolls her eyes, then looks back at me.

'For most of us, music being 'part of our lives' means listening to the radio on the weekend, not playing Mozart all over Europe.'

'We listened to the radio too.'

'What, Classic FM?' she jokes.

'Well... yes.'

I can't erase the music of my childhood and turn it into the Spice Girls just to make Jen feel better.

'What's that castle over there?'

She's looking across to some stone ruins on the cliff top.

'Bestward,' I answer. 'We can go there tomorrow, if you like.'

'Yes please.' She flashes me a bright smile. 'I bet the views are amazing up there.'

'The view is amazing wherever you are,' I say.

She rolls her eyes and laughs but looks pleased at the compliment.

We enter the town area and drive through the residential streets.

'Wow, it's swanky round here,' Jen comments.

I don't suppose I've ever stopped to notice, really. It's normal for me. But comparing it to Whidlock, the homes are more upmarket, the gardens are well tended, and everything feels greener and cleaner, somehow. When we pull up outside my parents' house, I'm aware of their large, detached property, the cars on the driveway… Jen looks slightly in awe. I unclick my seatbelt, ready to open the car door, but Jen's still staring at the house.

'What are your parents' names again?' she asks.

'Ezra and Heather.'

'Right.'

We get out of the car and I take her hand and squeeze it.

'Don't worry, I'm sure they'll love you.'

The front door opens and my parents move forward to welcome us. Dad is his usual wiry self, wearing his round glasses and a long-sleeved shirt, while Mum's hair is a silver-white colour, long over her shoulders. Dad gives me a tight hug and then shakes Jen's hand. Mum puts her arms around me and kisses my cheek, then grasps Jen's hand with a broad smile.

'Come in,' Mum beckons, 'I hope the traffic wasn't too bad.'

We sit in the lounge, Jen perching at the edge of the sofa. Mum makes some tea while Dad clears his throat and smiles politely at Jen, pushing his glasses up his nose.

'Have you been working at Whidlock County for long?' he asks. It's a mild-mannered question, but the subtext is clear: he thinks she's only recently qualified.

'Five years,' Jen nods in response.

'Jen's just been appointed as the Additional Learning Needs co-ordinator.' I give her an encouraging smile.

'Oh right,' Dad says. He clearly has no idea what that means.

'Do you live close to the school?' he asks next. I guess it's hard to switch lawyer-mode off.

I stifle a laugh. Jen used to live in a flat a stone's throw away from the school's entrance, but now she's back at her dad's, she's a little further.

'Fairly,' she says. 'I live with my dad, and it's only about ten minutes' drive.'

'I see,' Dad says, clearly thinking this through. 'So, have you always lived in that area, then?'

'Yes, I went to Whidlock myself as a student.'

Thankfully Mum walks in at this point, and smiles warmly.

'That's lovely,' she says. 'You must know it really well.'

She gives Jen a cup of tea... literally. It's a bone china cup with a saucer. It shakes and wobbles as Jen holds it. Why is my mother re-enacting a Jane Austen tea party? No one uses cups and saucers anymore.

Mum next enters with a tray with a full-blown tea set: teapot, sugar pot, milk jug. She deliberately avoids my stare. I've literally never seen her use this before.

'Would you like sugar?' she asks eagerly, holding the tray out to Jen.

'I'm fine, thank you.' Jen shakes her head.

Mum looks disappointed and slides the tray onto the coffee table. The room is awkwardly quiet as Jen drinks tea and chinks the cup back onto the saucer again. When Mum produces cups and saucers for all of us, the sound is echoed four-fold.

'Where did you study for your degree?' Dad asks Jen. I'm beginning to feel awkward at how many questions he's asking. It's like a socially acceptable form of interrogation. Jen told me the first time I met her, I fired about twenty questions at her in one go. Now I'm starting to see where I picked up the habit.

'Just the local university,' she says. I know this is a sore point because she had to look after her dad and sister, so I hurriedly switch topic.

'We visited a local primary recently, for a Shakespeare project that Jen runs.'

'That sounds like fun,' Mum says enthusiastically. 'Which play is it?'

'*Julius Caesar*,' Jen answers. She nods towards the wall of bookshelves. 'I can see you have quite a library here.'

'Buying books is my weakness,' Mum confesses.

'Are those first edition Penguins?' Jen asks.

'I just try to pick them up on special occasions,' Mum blushes. 'The last one I got was *Jane Eyre*, on Rachel's graduation.'

'I love the Brontës!' Jen's eyes light up.

'I was saying in the car how much the landscape looks like *Wuthering Heights* around here,' I say. 'I thought I could take Jen to Bestward tomorrow.'

'Oh, right,' Dad says, adjusting his glasses again. 'Around what time?'

Dad is a bit uptight about scheduling the whole weekend. And I know that's rich coming from me.

'Probably around eleven.' I wave a hand vaguely.

'No need to rush,' Mum says, with a look at Dad.

'We usually have lunch at one o'clock.' Dad's lips press together in a thin line.

'We'll be back by then,' I reassure him, inwardly annoyed at his tone. Dad always eats at the same time every day, on the dot, and I'm partly annoyed because I'm exactly the same.

There's me trying to convince Jen that we're just a Normal Family. Seeing the way that she is with her dad and Katie has shown me how different other families are. I get the impression they just came and went as they pleased when they were teenagers.

'I think dinner's nearly ready,' Mum says, breaking the tension.

Jen springs to her feet.

'May I use the bathroom, please?'

'Of course.' Mum ushers her into the hallway.

'How's work going?' Dad asks. 'Settling into your new role?'

'Yes, I think so.' I briefly remember the disastrous dinner at David's house, but Dad doesn't need to know about that.

'Are they okay with… you and Jen being together?'

I avoid his penetrating gaze.

'I'm not sure.'

Dad picks up on my unease straightaway.

'You've got to be careful, Michael,' he says. 'Keep David and the governors on side. You don't know what's going to happen to Whidlock.'

I have a pretty good idea, but it isn't pretty at all. Merging Whidlock with Prestfield will create a melting pot of kids from a challenging catchment area, a staff crisis with redundancies and 'redeployments', and huge workload with fewer people to shoulder it.

'I'm keeping our relationship separate from work,' I tell him.

'That's easy to say,' Dad scoffs. 'Somewhat more difficult in practice, though.'

'I hope you're telling Michael how glad we are that he's met someone,' Mum says, walking back into the room with a pointed look at Dad. 'Careers aren't everything, you know.'

'Of course,' Dad agrees quickly. But his expression says otherwise.

I think Dad's biggest disappointment in life was that I didn't become a lawyer. He would never admit that, but he's made so many barbed comments about the poor salary in teaching (it's really not that bad) and that it's not too late to change career path, it's obvious what he really thinks. Maybe he imagined becoming partners in the same firm together like some sort of father-son act.

My throat constricts, the mere thought of it stifling my breath.

One thing's for sure: I don't visit my parents to enjoy a relaxing weekend. Jen's presence makes it bearable, but I'm starting to wonder what I've brought her into. So far, she's been interrogated, given tea in an antique heirloom set from the nineteenth century, and I'm already on edge.

And it's only been half an hour.

16

Jen

I'm in the cleanest bathroom I've ever set foot in.

In fact, this whole place reminds me of a luxury hotel, not that I've had much experience of those. The towels are plush and dazzlingly white. Expensive hand wash and lotion are by the sink, with polished taps and a mirror so perfectly smudge-free, I'm actually wondering how Heather cleans it. Our toothpaste-flecked mirror never looks this clear.

I wash my hands, then push the dispenser for some lotion. A huge blob drops onto my palm, so then I have to rub it up my arms and over my neck to use it all up. I stare at my reflection. The area under my eyes is looking grey and shadowy. I just need to keep smiling so no one sees that.

Katie's texted to ask how it's going.

It's posh, I reply. I could add more about Ezra's obvious disappointment in me, but it stings too much to put into words. It's clear he thinks I'm completely lacking in ambition, a sort of 'homebody' nobody, the last kind of girl he wants involved with his son.

Heather seems lovely, though. Maybe if I just focus on winning her over, she can work on Ezra for me.

Walking down the stairs, there are framed pictures on the wall of Michael's graduation and his sister, Rachel's, too. I haven't met her yet. Michael says she works for an environmental charity. I really hope she isn't hard to get along with.

I've never had to navigate getting-your-boyfriend's-family-to-like-you before —none of my previous relationships were ever serious enough— but now that I'm here, it's like a fist is clenching and unclenching constantly in my stomach. It matters so much that they like me.

The dining room is decorated in expensive wallpaper, and a heavy mahogany table fills the room. As I take a seat, I gulp at the layers of tablecloths, runners, placemats, cloth napkins and multiple sets of cutlery. There are wine glasses and tumblers, a pitcher of water with ice cubes in it, side plates and bread rolls in a basket. Michael pours me a glass of water, while I wring my hands in my lap, afraid to touch anything.

'We will now say grace,' Ezra announces.

I bow my head hurriedly and he says a prayer. My hands feel sweaty, although it's nearly December and this house is several degrees colder to what I'm used to.

'Vegetable soup.' Heather places a bowl in front of me.

'Thank you.'

I think it's the round spoon I need —I wait for Michael to pick his up to be sure— then finally try to eat as daintily as I can.

I know I should be grateful for a three-course meal, but honestly, it's pure torture. It feels endless. When Heather's sat down with us, the conversation is much lighter, but she spends most of the time scuttling back and forth to the kitchen. I offer to help but she shakes her head. It leaves me to listen to Ezra's conversation with Michael, which seems to consist of Ezra relating information about people they know and strongly suggesting that Michael speak to all of them at church on Sunday.

'Christina Patterson recently qualified as a doctor,' he says. 'She'll be home at Christmas, so you can catch up with her then.'

Oh dear. Clearly Christina is a much more suitable girlfriend candidate than me.

'The Pattersons are organising our camp conference for next summer,' Ezra continues. 'It will be held in Somerset. I was hoping you would consider coming.'

Michael lays down his spoon and dabs his mouth with a napkin.

'Actually, Dad, I want to keep the summer free.' He looks at me. 'Jen's been wanting to go travelling for a while now.'

Does he mean, he wants to come with me? I look at him in surprise. Michael never said anything about this. The idea of lying on a sun scorched beach by a bright turquoise ocean is infinitely more appealing if he's going to be next to me.

'What are your plans?' Ezra asks me.

I take a sip of water and shrug.

'I... haven't really made any... yet.'

'I did wonder,' Michael says, 'whether you ever thought of going to Jamaica? Do you still have family out there?'

I'm truly floored by this conversation. My mum's family were Jamaican, but since my grandparents died, and she died, I lost touch with pretty much all of them. I felt so bitter about Mum that I didn't really care that much.

A sudden image of Alice, pursuing her shadowy mother, pops into my head. Maybe it's time to change my own narrative.

I certainly never considered going out there. But maybe I should. If Michael would be going with me, it changes everything.

'I'm not really in touch with them,' I admit. 'But it's a great idea. We should look into it.'

Ezra gives a slightly pained smile, then I notice the piano.

'Michael said that you're an amazing pianist,' I say, unashamedly changing the subject. I'm pretty desperate by this point to find a safe subject.

Ezra shoots his son a quick, appraising look.

'Did he? I hope he mentioned his own considerable achievements.'

He gestures towards the wall above the piano. There are framed certificates covering it.

'I'd love to hear you both play,' I say.

'Do you play an instrument?' Ezra asks.

Does the recorder count?

'No.' I smile and sip my wine. Michael covers my hand with his and squeezes.

Heather enters, carrying dinner plates in from the kitchen.

'Guinea fowl,' she announces.

17

Michael

Mum's gone more than slightly overboard tonight. It's clear that I've never brought a girlfriend home before. I'll have to tell Jen that we don't normally eat like this.

I wish Dad would lighten up a bit. The conversation feels like wading through treacle.

'Martin's going to Australia for Christmas to see his brother,' he says, referring to a friend at work. Given that none of us know Martin that well, it seems a fairly irrelevant piece of information.

'What do you normally do at Christmas?' Mum asks Jen.

'It's just me, my dad and my sister,' she replies. 'Quiet, really.'

'Perhaps you could come here to stay before Christmas,' Mum suggests, with a smile at me. 'We have a lovely candlelit carol service; it's really magical.'

'That would be wonderful,' Jen says.

That's when it hits me: it's the perfect proposal opportunity.

My mind whirs into action, creating a to-do list. Buy an engagement ring for a Christmas present… I'll have to order it as soon as possible to make sure it arrives in time…

'What if Rachel's friend comes to stay?' Dad asks.

'Oh, I'm sure they won't mind staying in Rachel's room.' Mum brushes off the issue.

I can't concentrate on anything for the rest of the meal. Once we've eaten lemon meringue and had coffee with mints, Jen repeats her request to hear us play piano, so I play some duets with Dad. It's just as well that I can play them on autopilot, because my mind is racing. I even manage not to rise to Dad's suggestions that I could have taken my music further (although how this fits with his lawyer ambitions for me, I don't know).

'What did you study at A Level?' Jen asks, as we walk up the stairs together.

'English, Music and Maths.'

She makes a face.

'You did English, History and... Drama?' I guess the last one.

She nods. I guess that explains the Shakespeare project. I wonder if anyone would notice if I sat in the audience with an eye mask on, with huge eyelashes printed onto it, and slept through the performance. Probably not.

Carrying the bags into the spare room, I check Jen has everything she needs. She seems a bit overwhelmed. I would be too, if I were in her shoes. She probably wants to call Katie, so I retreat to my old room, pacing back and forth until I feel calm enough to go to bed.

By 8 a.m. the next morning, I've chosen the ring and I just need to find out Jen's size.

I listen out for her to go into the bathroom, and then dash across the corridor and into her room. I look at the bedside table: yes, there's a ring on there. I use an app on my phone to scan it and identify the size, then tiptoe back to the door and slip out again. I'm just walking across the landing when Dad calls,

'Morning.'

Great, he must think I'm sneaking out of Jen's room because I stayed there last night.

'Just going to get dressed,' I call over my shoulder, escaping back into my room.

I finish the online order and feel a surge of relief.

After breakfast, I drive Jen to Bestward and it's a windy, overcast day. The car park is empty and we follow the worn path to the stony ruins. Jen immediately lays a hand on the rough exterior.

'You can feel the history!' she says, grinning widely.

I can't help but grin back.

On the edge of the cliff, we look down to the dark sea water, crashing against the rocks. The tide is in. Jen's curls blow around her face, and we stand holding hands, with the seagulls calling to each other overhead.

This is the perfect place. How will I do it? Should I read a poem? A sonnet might be good… 'The marriage of true minds'? Perhaps I could leave some sort of treasure hunt trail? Should it be daytime, or sunset?

Jen's kiss silences my manic thoughts. It's like we're at the edge of the world, and my stomach sparks and fizzes like a firework display. Not long. Not long now.

I drive back to my parents' house with the calm certainty that we'll be engaged by Christmas, married by Easter, and then everything will be fine. No more HR policy to worry about. No more vow to keep. No more questions from well-meaning friends or relatives of 'have you met someone?' It's the logical next step at my time of life, and I can't wait.

18
Jen

I love Michael, but I think I understand why he doesn't come home very often. It is full on.

Our visit to Bestward is like an oasis amidst a non-stop rotation of conversation and meals. And the meals! We've had every delicacy except caviar. I've eaten muffins, and crumble, and cake, and then been offered chocolate gateau. Steph will have to take me on a punishing run every day next week to make up for all this.

Michael seems in a very good mood, and I'm happy that I've had this opportunity to meet his family. I've had some nice chats to his mum, when she's finally let me into the kitchen to help make some tea. His dad is nothing if not valiant in his attempts to keep a conversation going at all costs. But the moment I'm dreading has finally arrived: Sunday morning church.

My grandparents used to run a church when they were alive, and we visited a few times. There was a strong contingent of Jamaican people there, and the singing was fantastic. The preacher would usually stop regularly to encourage the congregation to shout 'Amen' if he made a particularly salient point. They met in a small hall that was made from corrugated iron, probably just after the war.

So when we arrive at Michael's family's church, I feel completely out of my depth.

It is an ornate, medieval building, and we walk there because there's no car park. There are stained glass windows, and ancient tombstones amidst tufts of grass. At the door, there's someone in robes, who gives us several different books as we enter. There's the musty smell of stone, cobwebs and damp curtains. Michael squeezes my hand.

'Okay?' he asks.

I'm actually terrified, but I can't say that.

The organ is playing with the kind of funny, breathy notes of church music. We shuffle into a polished, dark wood pew. I'm surprised at how many people are in here. There's a fair number of white-haired participants, but also some families, and one lady at the back has a dog. Ezra and Heather smile and wave to people, and Michael methodically looks up the hymns and prayers and bookmarks the right pages.

I should have asked in more detail what this service was going to entail. My throat is constricting and I wish I'd brought a bottle of water.

'Do you like the ceiling?' Michael asks, pointing towards the arched roof. There are ornate gold painted leaves and carved flourishes into the cornices.

'Yes,' I whisper. I'm actually most impressed by the waves of heat coming through the vents in the floor. Medieval and modern at the same time.

The organ stops and a man, again in robes, walks to the front. He looks in his forties and actually (apart from the robes) pretty normal.

'Good morning,' he smiles. 'I'd like to give a special welcome to any visitors here with us today. You can follow the service on page seventy-four.'

As Michael holds open the book to me, I realise that he's following a written script. In the bold type, everyone joins in. It reminds me of school assemblies.

'Almighty God, our heavenly Father, we have sinned against you and against our neighbour in thought and word and deed, through negligence, through weakness, through our own deliberate fault. We are truly sorry and repent of all our sins.'

I falter a little, although Michael carries on and I can hear his voice above everyone else's. It seems a bit dreary, starting with sin and confession. I thought that was what Catholics did. To consider all the possible sins of actions, words and then things that I didn't do that I should have done, I would need way more time than the vicar allows in his short pause. When I'm saying that I'm sorry and repent, what exactly does that mean? Because if I'm honest, I don't even know the extent of my sins, so I probably will just do them again.

There are readings and I enjoy listening to these. Different people come up to the front to read, and one of them is a story I've heard before, about the short man called Zaccheus who climbed a tree to see Jesus. Then everyone stands up to sing and I stand there awkwardly while Michael's parents sing loud enough for all of us.

The vicar comes forward to speak.

'Today we're focusing on a story of total transformation,' he begins. 'Zaccheus was a cheat, deeply unpopular, and greedy. But when he met Jesus, he vowed to pay back four times what he owed, and give half his possessions to the poor. People didn't understand why Jesus chose him, out of everyone there. But Jesus says that he came for people just like Zaccheus. He came to seek and save the lost.'

He spends half an hour explaining the story. It's funny, usually I'm the teacher, the one explaining everything. I'm not used to sitting and listening. But everything he says is so clear. He really brings the story to life and helps us to understand the time, the culture, and what Jesus was doing. I thought it was a simple children's story, but he makes me see that it has much deeper layers.

'You may not have a lot in common with Zaccheus, at first glance,' he says, drawing to a close. 'You may be very good at paying your taxes, at never cheating anyone. But you can still be spiritually lost too. When Jesus said he came to save the lost, he didn't just mean a small section of people who were particularly bad. He meant everyone. Which of us can honestly say that we have always loved God and others perfectly? Sin isn't so much as what we do on the outside. It's who we are on the inside.'

Inexplicably, I think of my mother, and my eyes blur with sudden tears. I know that I've carried around a lot of anger towards her since she died. People always feel sorry for me, because I lost my mother at seventeen, but I don't feel the way they expect me to feel. It's not the longing sense of loss that wishes she were still alive. It's the burning desire for justice that was never satisfied. And I feel guilty about that, because I know I should forgive her and let it go. If I was truly going to confess my sins, I should start with that. But I know that I want to hold on to my bitterness. I'm lost, but I don't want to be found.

19

Michael

So far, so good. Jen appears to be enjoying the service, although the singing is a little reedy and it's definitely outside her comfort zone. Simon the vicar seems friendly and approachable, so I fold the notice sheet with his contact details and tuck it into my pocket. Hopefully I can ask him about the church's availability for weddings and maybe provisionally book a date.

It feels like everyone wants to come and talk to us at the end, so we're one of the last to leave. I overhear Mum talking with a friend.

'This is Michael's girlfriend. I think she might be The One!'

Hiding a smile, I turn to Jen and take her hand to lead her back outside. I'm glad that Mum is so enthusiastic. Dad, on the other hand, seems to have a false smile that more resembles a grimace permanently fixed on his face.

Back at the house, Mum disappears into the kitchen to prepare a Sunday roast to end all others. Turns out she put a joint in the oven at five in the morning and as soon as she opens the door, clouds of steam billow out and fill the kitchen, setting off the smoke alarm. Jen hurries in to help, and finally Mum can't refuse. That leaves me and Dad alone in the lounge.

'Are you and Jen... serious?' he asks, in the same tone I'd imagine him using if he was asking if I had been caught dealing drugs.

'I don't see the point in *not* being serious,' I reply. 'We're not kids at school. I'm nearly thirty.'

'That's what concerns me,' Dad says, with a sigh. 'You haven't known her for long and already you seem very attached.'

'Why is that a bad thing?' Annoyance creeps into my voice.

'I just think you shouldn't rush into anything,' he says. 'It takes time to really know someone.'

'Dad, I've never met anyone like her before. I've never had a girlfriend before. I wouldn't just choose someone random I barely knew. We've spent a lot of time together through work.'

After school theatre trips, 5-a-side football where I accidentally injured her... So many good memories.

'You've never had a girlfriend before. You don't have much experience with women. The fact is, Michael, you're a catch! You have a nice house and a good job with a steady income...'

'Dad, I don't think Jen is going out with me because of any of those things.'

'She's obviously not used to our kind of life.'

I raise my eyebrows.

'Dad, you're being a snob.'

'I'm not holding it against her, I just want to warn you that you may encounter difficulties later on...'

'Why? Look, as kind and lovely as Mum is, we didn't need a three-course meal the other night. She doesn't need to impress anyone. That's what I love about Jen's family, you can just be yourself and no one thinks any less of you.'

'What does her father do?'

'He's retired.' I've told him this before, I'm sure of it. It's one of the first questions Dad always asks about any of my friends.

'Sorry about the delay!' Mum appears in the doorway. 'Won't be long. I just realised I forgot to get an extra bottle of red, there's only the white.'

Dad makes a tutting noise.

'What's wrong with white wine?' I ask, flaring up again.

'You're supposed to have red with beef.'

'I know, I must have misread the list…' Mum says apologetically.

'I'll go and get some.' I jump up, needing to leave the house before I explode. 'I'll be ten minutes.'

'You don't have to,' Dad says sulkily.

I grab my coat and slam the door a little harder than necessary.

Every time I come home, I remember all of the frustrations that boiled inside me as a teenager. I was good at hiding my emotions, and staying unperturbed on the outside. Dad is just so petty sometimes. I don't understand why Mum just accepts it.

And what is he driving at with his 'words of advice' about Jen? Maybe it's the fact that he's a lawyer; he's more suspicious of everyone. The idea that Jen would be with me because of my house just seems a bit laughable to me. We're not living in an Austen novel. My two-bed semi isn't Pemberley.

It just bothers me that he doesn't seem to want me to 'be serious' with Jen. He spent most of my teen years lecturing me on the importance of steering clear of romantic entanglements, telling me I was too young, then telling me I needed to study, or later, focus on my career. He was thirty-five when I was born, so he must have been in his early thirties when he got married. Why can't he be happy that I've met someone, like Mum clearly is?

It annoys me the most because what's the alternative to being serious: sleeping around? Given Dad's church background, surely he doesn't want that?

I walk to the corner shop and buy their best bottle of red wine. As I queue up to pay, I notice that even the corner shops are different in this area, more upmarket. There are packets of mixed nuts and posh crisps around the till, rather than slushy machines and cheap packets of sweets. There's no denying that we're worlds away from Whidlock here. I trudge back to the house, seeing the pristine homes and expensive cars in the driveways. No wonder Jen's been feeling uncomfortable. I didn't think we were that different in our backgrounds, but now I'm starting to realise that maybe we are.

Does that matter? No, of course not. I can't let Dad's parent paranoia get to me. I love her, and that's all that matters.

20
Jen

I don't know why, but something happened between Michael and his father and now the atmosphere at dinner is thick with tension.

The cutlery squeaks on the porcelain plates, and Michael gives me an apologetic smile when I catch his eye.

'Anything coming up in school?' Heather asks.

'We have a Christmas shopping trip planned,' I reply.

'I think technically the trip is titled 'A Visit to Parliament',' Michael points out with a smile. 'Though I don't think the students signed up because they were excited to meet their MP.'

'You're going to London?' Heather sounds surprised. 'That could be stressful.'

'The theatre visit gave me confidence that we could pull it off,' Michael grins.

I remember sitting next to him in the theatre, before we got together. It was the first time I felt that spark with him. And I also hit him in the face by accident.

'It's not really our trip,' I remind him. 'It's a History Department one. We're just hijacking for the ride.'

'The major plus point is that we miss the Year 7 disco,' Michael adds.

This is true: two hours of standing around while kids awkwardly stand around too, obnoxious music blaring from the speakers with wildly inappropriate lyrics. I won't miss that.

Everyone falls quiet again and Heather looks anxiously at Ezra. It's a relief when we finally clear the plates and Michael seems keen to leave.

'So you'll come for the carols, won't you?' Heather asks me, pressing her hand warmly on my arm.

'I'd love to.'

She kisses Michael and he hugs his dad awkwardly, then we bundle into the car. The air is definitely colder now, and I rub my hands together while the engine starts. Heather waves enthusiastically, her eyes misty with tears. Ezra watches us pull away, and then lowers his eyes and puts his arm around his wife like someone just died. It makes my stomach shift uncomfortably.

I look across to Michael. His jaw is set and his eyes are far away, thinking. I lean back and wait for him to speak.

'So, what did you think?' he says finally.

'It was great to meet them.' I'm being truthful here. I feel I understand Michael better now that I've seen inside his home.

'But?' he prompts.

'It was quite… intense.'

'I know,' he sighs, running a hand through his hair. 'I don't even know why. We didn't have to go anywhere to do anything… It's so different with your Dad and Katie.'

I'm glad he said it, not me.

'I think they are really chilled out, whereas your parents…'

'Are not,' Michael finishes, raising his eyebrows.

'Your mum made a lot of effort.'

'We don't normally eat so many courses.'

'That's a relief!' I laugh, but it fades quickly.

In school, Michael and I are in this bubble of teachers and pupils, where the outside world seems so far away. It's not to say that we think the same way about everything, but in Whidlock, we're equals. There's no social pecking order... apart from David Clark's favourites. Meeting Michael's parents lifts the curtain on a whole different scene, one that I'm not part of, and one where I very much feel like I belong in a different act.

I'd always enjoyed times when Michael came over to my dad's, and we would have a take-away, or go to the pub for Sunday lunch. Now I'm starting to wonder if it all seems rather second-rate. Has he secretly been wishing we spent more money on a better bottle of wine? Or wincing at our cupboard of cheap supermarket snacks?

But the real issue, the one that neither of us are talking about, is the fact that his dad doesn't like me. That's the burning hot poker that's twisting inside me in a crush of embarrassment and stinging pain. And anger. Why am I not good enough?

'Thank you,' Michael reaches over and squeezes my hand. 'For being willing to come.'

I smile, and the car ploughs on into the waning hours of Sunday afternoon.

———

I feel exhausted by the time Michael drops me home, so I run a bath. About thirty seconds after I've sunk into the water, Katie rings.

'I'm in the bath,' I groan.

'You can still talk,' Katie says, undeterred. 'Come on, I want to hear all about it.'

'It's too much... I don't know where to start.'

'Describe the house.'

'Victorian, detached, high ceilings, four bedrooms.'

'They're loaded then,' she comments. 'What do they do again?'

'Lawyers,' I say.

'Figures,' she replies. 'Right, so what about them? What are they like?'

'His mum is lovely.' I start with the positive. 'She's very sweet, cooks an insane amount of food. We had so many courses for Sunday lunch today.'

'That sounds good!' Katie approves of food, so this is high on her priority list. She's probably hoping she can wangle an invitation over there sometime. 'What about his dad?'

'Ezra is… quite serious.' I'm searching for words.

'Right, so not too many jokes then.'

'Yeah, they don't really joke that much.' I try to remember how often we laughed over the weekend. It's hard to remember because I think it wasn't very much.

'Did you have to go to church?'

'I didn't *have* to go,' I remind her. 'I *wanted* to, because I wanted to join in with what they were doing.'

'Was it a snore fest?'

'Actually, no.' I think back to the vicar's warm personality. 'I quite enjoyed it. It's not much like the church Grampa and Gram used to run. It's more traditional.'

'I guess Michael's quite an old-fashioned guy, isn't he?'

The sort who takes a vow of chastity. Katie would have a field day if I told her.

'Yes, he is. That's not a bad thing!'

'No, just as long as his parents don't have an arranged marriage for him or some weird betrothal he hasn't told you about.'

'He's not an aristocrat, Katie. Or a medieval prince.'

But there is a sophisticated doctor in his church that his father would love for a daughter-in-law.

'The main thing is, did you like them? And did they like you?'

'I did like them,' I sigh. 'I think his mum likes me, but his dad… I'm not really the sort of girl he expects Michael to choose.'

'Why not?' Katie bristles. 'You're smart, funny, gorgeous… What else does he want?'

'I don't know,' I answer honestly. 'I really don't know.'

21

Michael

I knock at the same time as I barge my way into David's office on Monday morning. He looks up from his laptop, and raises an eyebrow at me.

'Michael?' he says, as though I have no right to be there. 'Can I help you with something?'

'The HR policy,' I say. 'You can't stop me from dating Jen.'

'The policy was voted in by the governors,' David says in a soft purr. 'They felt quite strongly that staff should be discouraged from romantic entanglements. Very unprofessional, you know.'

'I have never been unprofessional.'

'Yet,' he enunciates crisply. 'What happens when you break up?'

'We won't.'

'Oh, so you're getting serious, are you?' he mocks. 'Long-term singleton Michael gets a girlfriend, and within a few weeks he *just knows she's the one*. Sounds like you've been watching too many rom-coms.'

'It's none of your business.' I try to breathe to control my temper. Don't rise to the bait.

'Everything that happens in this school is my business,' he snaps. 'And you might try to compartmentalise your life, Michael, but with relationships, I can tell you now, it doesn't work. Things get messy.'

'I will give you no reason to be concerned.'

'Believe it or not, I'm trying to protect you, Michael.'

He stares at me, his composure gone. There's more depth of feeling here than I realised. We have known each other and worked together for years now. Part of me believes him, that in his own, twisted way, David is on my side. But I'm seeing more and more what cost is involved in playing David's game.

'You can't control me, David.'

The door opens and Joseph Vermont pokes his head into the room.

'Sorry, I was just wondering—' he begins.

'I'm just leaving.' I turn on my heel and open the door fully, letting Joseph in, and walking out past him.

I didn't expect anything different. This doesn't change the plan.

It's always the way, though, that a snag hits where you least expect it.

I'm late to the staff room at lunch because David forwarded me an email from Inspire to Achieve with a ridiculously long evaluation form to fill in, marked 'urgent'. I walk in to see Jen sat with Steph and Sean, the French teacher, laughing hysterically at some anecdote he's relating with exaggerated arm movements.

'His face was so red I thought he was going to spontaneously combust!' he says. 'And I said, I really think we should pull back. And he was like, "I've got to beat him," gulping air like a bullfrog. Just crossed the finish line a nanosecond ahead.'

Sean is one of those larger-than-life personalities you can hear down the other end of the corridor when they're teaching. He wears trendy shirt-and-tie combos, and deliberately doesn't shave in the morning so he sports a stubbly I-just-got-out-of-bed look. Funny how he manages to wax his hair into place, though.

'Hey.' Jen notices me and pats the seat next to her. 'Come and join us.'

For a moment I contemplate going back to my laptop.

'Sure.' I shrug and sit down.

It quickly becomes apparent that it's impossible to hold any sort of conversation around Sean. He's got to be the centre of attention all the time, constantly talking and bantering. And what I really don't get is how much Jen and Steph are lapping it all up. They keep laughing at his very unfunny jokes. At one point Steph says,

'Oh, Sean, you're such a scream.'

What does that even mean anyway?

'I was hoping to recruit some of you intelligent types for my pub quiz team,' he says. Oh, so that's the reason he suddenly appeared in the staff room. 'Farmer's Arms, every Wednesday. What do you say?'

'I'm in,' says Steph.

'What about you, Michael, you seem like the brainy sort,' Sean says, every word grating on my nerves.

'No thanks, I don't go out on school nights.'

It sounds heavier than in my head, but oh well.

'How about you, Jen?' Steph asks.

'It sounds like fun,' she says.

I nearly choke on my sandwich.

'Are you all right, Michael?' Jen pats my back.

'I'm… fine,' I cough, turning puce.

'You should get some water,' Sean says, unhelpfully.

In the kitchen, Jen comes over to me as I gulp down a glass of water.

'You are okay with me going to the quiz, right?' she asks.

'Of course,' I say. 'I was just… surprised really. I mean, it'll be quite late for a school night.'

'Well, I know that you don't want to hang out in the week, so I figured, this might be a good way for me to spend time with friends.'

She makes it sound like I don't want to see her in the week, when I'm just trying to keep work stuff separate. *Things get messy*, David said.

'It's fine,' I snap, and stomp back to my classroom.

22

Jen

The pub is on the edge of a suburb on the Prestfield side of Whidlock. It has a log fire, an artificial Christmas tree swamped with tinsel, and three quiz teams made up of locals, and then us.

'Team name?' the quizmaster asks us, looming over our table with a brown clipboard and a chewed pencil. He's basically saying 'who are you?'

Sean looks around at us and gestures for us to come up with something. Jason, from the Music dept, shrugs and sips his cider.

'Come on, Jen, you think of something.' Steph nudges me.

'Please Mrs Butler.' I say the first thing that comes into my head, an old poem about a teacher.

'Perfect.' Sean high-fives me.

The guy writes on the clipboard and gives us a picture quiz sheet. It looks like headshots of every person featured in *The Sun* this week.

'Ooh, give me the pen.' Steph grabs the sheet and starts scribbling.

With Steph's knowledge of soap opera stars, Jason's catalogue knowledge of pop music, and Sean's effervescent encouragement, we go through each round with a respectable score, though nowhere near the genius levels of the Smart Bananas team. At one point, I get a text from Michael.

Michael: How is the quiz?
Me: Great. You should come next time x

He doesn't message back though.

'How was your time meeting Michael's parents?' Steph asks, when the guys are at the bar.

'Good,' I say noncommittally. 'Bit posher than I expected.'

'I'm not surprised,' she snorts. 'He looks like the type to have a trust fund.'

I never really asked Michael about how he managed to afford his house, but I realise now his parents must have helped him out financially.

'They're lawyers.'

'Even better,' she jokes, but I don't laugh. 'What's the matter?'

'I think his dad would prefer him to be with someone else.'

'Really?' She sets down her drink. 'Why do you think that?'

'He just… wasn't very enthusiastic.'

'Are you the first girl that Michael's taken home?'

'Yes.'

'Well then, it must be a lot for them to get their heads around,' Steph reasons. 'It's always hard for parents to let go.'

'He's nearly thirty and he hasn't lived at home for years, though.'

'He's still their kid though,' Steph points out. 'Parents don't stop being parents.'

I think of Mum with a pang.

'Some do,' I remark.

'You know what I mean.'

'Next week we'll be doing a special Christmas quiz,' the guy with the microphone announces, to some half-hearted cheers in the background. 'Bonus points for teams wearing Christmas hats.'

'Love it,' Sean says. 'Come on, team.'

I'll have to drag out the bag of Christmas partywear down from the loft. Elf with oversized ears or classic Santa hat?

'Your phone just buzzed.' Steph pushes it across the table to me. 'Maybe it's Machine Man.'

I grab it to see who it is.

'It's not Michael,' I say. 'It's about the Parliament trip.'

I read the message quickly. I'm really looking forward to going to London with all the Christmas lights and I'll be gutted if it gets cancelled.

'We're one staff too short so we need someone to come with us,' I tell the others.

'When is it?' Sean asks.

'Friday.'

'Count me in, then.'

'Thanks Sean,' I say gratefully, and start texting the History department.

Michael's reaction the next day is less enthusiastic.

'You invited Sean?'

'The trip would have been cancelled otherwise!'

'I'm sure they would have no shortage of volunteers to go Christmas shopping in London,' he sniffs, riffling through papers on his desk, even though they are already organised by class, task and probably in alphabetical order.

'Sit next to me on the bus?' I ask, feeling like I'm back in Year 8.

'Of course,' he says. 'But no holding hands. The policy and everything.'

'I know,' I sigh. Michael hasn't said much else about the policy, although he reassured me that he would talk to David.

That evening, it's the Shakespeare show. I sit next to Michael and shoot him warning looks when he fidgets or (barely) suppresses a yawn. The synth sword fight scene of *Julius Caesar* is an epic success and I give Sally a hug at the end. When I find Michael again, he's on his phone and looks up guiltily.

'Trying to hide your secret life in MI6 from me?' I joke.

If I didn't spend so much time with Michael, I would seriously believe that he was actually an undercover agent, given how frighteningly efficient he is in everything.

He rolls his eyes and grins, and for a moment, his phone is flat in the palm of his hand, and I see Christina Patterson's name.

I don't want to sound jealous by asking him why he's texting her, so I ignore it, pick up my coat and prepare to go out into the freezing night. But I think about it before I go to sleep, and resolve that I'll try to ask Michael about it on the trip tomorrow.

23

Michael

There are so many reasons why I dislike school trips.

Number one: the volume of noise ratchets up to twice the usual level—which is already above my comfort zone. You're also more confined in a small space being packed onto a coach with around forty-eight students, far more than the average class, making the sound even more deafening.

Number two: staff are clumped together and want to chit-chat the whole time, adding to the noise level and with no consideration that some people may just want to sit without speaking and try to zone out from the general melee with meditation, headphones or ear plugs.

Number three: everything takes too long. Getting on the coach, getting off the coach. Travelling. Counting heads. Checking and double checking the first aid kit. I think of my endless to-do list and wish that I had the ability to get more things done without offending anyone or appearing to be a boring jerk.

It's a plus point that I'm next to Jen, and this was the carrot on the stick which tempted me to sign up, but I didn't factor in Sean, who sits behind us and addresses Jen in every other comment he makes in his overly-loud, performance voice.

'So I said "wait a minute! You can't argue with 'Lady Marmalade' because it was number one with 'Under the Bridge' as a double A single." He goes, "I thought it was a B side." I asked Siri and Siri says *All Saints released Lady Marmalade in 1998 as a double A single.*' Sean does an accurate impression of a computerised voice, and Jen giggles. I roll my eyes. '*Voulez-vous couchez avec moi?*'

Now he's singing. Badly. And entirely inappropriately. I might have to get the ear plugs.

Thankfully, once we get there, Sean is staffing a different group. We are meeting Whidlock's MP and walking around Parliament, which subdues the kids into some sort of stupefied reverence. As Jen would say, you can smell the history.

'Have you heard about the development plans for Whidlock County?' I take the opportunity to ask the MP as we walk ahead, down a corridor.

'Yes,' she replies warily. 'I think, with equality as the main focus, it should be a positive move.'

I have no idea how equality will be served by the proposal, but this isn't really the time or place to argue, so I merely raise an eyebrow in response.

At one point, I probably would have relished the idea of merging Whidlock, a failing school, with Prestfield, and totally restructuring the staffing and leadership, ready for a transformation. Now that I've taught in Whidlock, I've been surprised at how good the standard of teaching is, how responsive the pupils are to learning, and Jen's argument that most of the school's inadequacies stem from lack of funding is not lost on me. However, there are definitely *some* staff who are dead weight, *some* who seem to feel no sense of responsibility. I imagine Sean, larking around at this very moment. He seems to be in this for free trips and the holidays.

The same could be said for some of the MPs. We watch PM's questions and the level of jeering and shouting rivals the racket on the bus earlier. *Equality* burns on repeat in my ear, but the plush seats and the elaborate rituals of our country's system scream the opposite. Suddenly I feel weighed down. Can we really make a difference? Is this trip broadening our students' horizons, or merely confirming unhelpful stereotypes?

'You seem far away,' Jen whispers, looking concerned.

I sigh, then force a smile.

'Just tired, that's all.'

When our slot is over, we congregate outside the building and everyone's taking pictures. Sean snaps a selfie with Jen and shouts that he's uploading it to social media. I bite my tongue. The atmosphere is lighter because the 'official' business is done; now it's time for freedom. Marge Cook, the Head of History and a truly formidable woman, explains the rules.

'We will walk in our designated groups towards Piccadilly Circus. Your group leaders will choose a specific location as a meeting point. You must remain in groups of four. You must remain on foot and in the vicinity at all times. You must meet your group leader at the time they give you in order to walk back to the pick-up point for the bus. Make sure you have the emergency mobile number as well.'

Then we're walking into one of the busiest parts of London; the Christmas lights are dazzling, the air smells of cinnamon doughnuts, and the streets are full of shoppers and performers. It is so glamorous in a way that poor Whidlock could never be. Part of me misses the buzz of being in a city.

Jen's eyes are sparkling as she looks at all the window displays. We pass a jeweller and I catch sight of diamonds like the one I've ordered, and feel a flip of excitement. Part of me wants to draw Jen's attention to the rings, just to see her reaction, but I also don't want to ruin the surprise. Just before I do anything stupid, one of the pupils calls a question over to Jen, and she's focused on them as we pass the window by. Probably for the best.

We finally reach the outer edges of Regent Street and I address our small group of lanky sixth formers and girls with too much eye make-up.

'Miss Baker and I will be in this café.' I gesture behind me. 'You have our emergency number. Split into two groups of four and stay together at all times. You have one hour.'

'Have fun!' Jen adds, beaming, as they scatter into one of the world's biggest cities.

'I need a coffee,' I say.

24

Jen

It's magical, seeing all the beautiful Christmas lights, and sitting inside the coffee shop by the window with Michael. It would be perfect if it started snowing, like in the Hallmark movies, but it doesn't. Still, I stir my tea and bite into a chunk of shortbread and reflect that as far as school trips go, this one is in my top three. At least.

Michael seems distracted.

'Hideous prices,' he mutters, shrugging out of his coat. 'Almost makes me wish for that snack van of yours.'

'It isn't my personal snack van,' I laugh. He's such a snob. 'But once you taste their bacon baps, there's no going back.'

'I suppose I'm paying for the privilege of sitting and watching immensely wealthy people live their lives.' Michael gestures out of the window at shoppers with Jo Malone bags and expensive coats.

'Not everyone in London is rich,' I point out. 'Anyway, don't be in a bad mood. We didn't have to do anything for this trip.'

'True,' he acknowledges. 'All the same, I think I should be paid extra for sitting within a one metre radius of Sean on the coach.'

'Michael!' I mock-scold him. 'He's really not that bad. I don't know why you dislike him so much.'

Michael pulls out his phone and after a moment, holds up the screen. It's the school Instagram page. Sean's selfie of us is on there.

'Are you jealous?' I ask. Part of me feels pleased if he is, though part of me feels annoyed too. Does he expect to monopolise my friendship? I still haven't asked him why Christina is texting him.

'Mmm,' Michael murmurs, his attention back on his phone.

Not exactly the reply I was hoping for.

'This can't be right,' he says, his tone sounding serious.

'What?'

He holds up the phone again. It's a snapshot of two students from our group outside Piccadilly Tube station. The caption is 'Off to explore London @WhidlockCounty'.

'It must be a prank,' I say, gulping down tea. I don't want to believe that two students would be as stupid and as irresponsible as to hike across London on the Tube.

'What if it's not?'

We stare at each other.

'I'm ringing Marge,' he says, phone to his ear.

I twist a napkin tightly. Just when you think you have a moment of relief… Why didn't I choose a data-entry job, or work in a supermarket? The pay may be better for teachers, but this sick feeling of anxiety churns away years of my life.

'Right,' Michael says, his eyes meeting mine across the sugar-dusted surface, steam still rising from his unsipped coffee. 'I'll ring you back.'

He lowers the phone.

'We have to ring all the kids in our group to find out where they are.'

We split the list between us, and suddenly I feel like a cross between a police officer and a secret agent.

'Tom, it's Miss Baker. Where are you?'

'McDonalds.'

You take a bunch of teens to London and they end up in Maccy D's.

'Who's with you?'

'Theo.'

'Put him on the line please.'

Once I've confirmed that Theo is there—and judging from the background noise, it certainly sounds like a busy fast food restaurant—I continue my interrogation.

'You're supposed to be in a group of four. Where's Kye and Lucas?'

'I… don't know, Miss,' Tom stalls.

'Did they go off on the Tube? It's very important that you tell me the truth.'

'I don't know, I just wanted to get some food.'

'If you know where they are, you have to tell me.'

'They joked about taking the Tube, but I don't know if they actually did it or not.'

'Where would they have gone?'

'Kye said… it might be fun just to see how far they could get, in the time limit. They said they'd make sure they were back on time.'

'Oh, well that's all right then,' I snap impatiently, 'if Kye and Lucas tell the Tube drivers, I'm sure there will be no delays or mishaps or just the fact they are in the wrong part of London!'

People are beginning to stare at me.

'Let me know as soon as you hear anything,' I hiss.

I relay the conversation to Michael.

'I tried their phones but it goes straight to voicemail. They must be on the Underground,' he says glumly.

'What kind of stupid, sick idea is this?' I'm so cross that my hands are shaking.

'See how far you can get…'

'Sounds like a dare to me,' Michael comments. 'One of those TikTok challenges or something.'

He calls Marge and the verdict is that we should stay put until it's time for everyone to return. If the two boys don't appear, then we'll have to launch a new phase of action. The others all pop by to prove they are in the vicinity, so our hour is taken up with comings, goings, phone calls, and Michael stalking the boys on social media.

'No more posts,' he reports. 'Either they gave up, or they've got no signal.'

The time is up, and the students troop back to the meeting point. Michael and I nervously shift around, our eyes on the clock ahead. It's three o'clock and the lights are glowing against an increasingly grey sky. I shiver. I don't want to be stuck out here, in London, once it gets dark.

Michael is poised to ring Marge.

'I'll give them one more minute.'

Then Tom gives a shout and Kye and Lucas run, red-faced and breathless, to join the group. They look jubilant and high-five each other. I feel Michael bristle with disgust.

'Why didn't you answer your phones when we called you?' he barks, and they straighten up, looking more uneasy.

'Sorry, bad signal.' Kye shrugs. Bad idea. I can feel Michael stiffen with rage.

'Because you were on the Tube?'

'No,' Lucas denies it.

'What was the Insta post all about then?'

It's Michael the interrogator. He really should consider an alternative career working for Special Forces.

'We need to start walking to the coach,' I remind him. 'Let's get to the bottom of this once we're there.'

We herd the kids back towards the coach pick up point, meeting another group along the way. The wind is definitely colder and I feel suddenly exhausted. I think with longing of curling up with a cup of tea on the sofa...

The coach is parked at a bus stop, but there are traffic cones directly in front of it, and some workmen in high-viz jackets are scowling at the driver. There are two sets of doors to the coach, so the other group enter by the driver and we take the middle door. We usher the kids in, but keep Kye and Lucas outside. Michael begins.

'Now I want an honest answer from you about where you were.'

There is a sullen silence. Finally, Lucas says,

'We just went on the Tube.'

'Why?'

No one speaks.

'You *knew* you were supposed to remain in the shopping area. You were not meant to use any form of public transport. There is a risk assessment in place, and you breached about five different sections.'

Michael takes a breath, building momentum.

'Do you have any idea how irresponsible you have been? How much worry you have caused? Mrs Cook has made so much effort to organise this trip, and now we might never be allowed to run it again, because of you.'

The other group have all boarded the coach. A builder beckons me over.

'Look, do you think you could get this coach to move?' he says. 'We need to cordon off this area.'

'I'll speak to the driver,' I say hastily, and leave Michael to continue his listing of the boys' heinous actions.

I step up to the driver and relay the message. Looking down the bus, Sean gives me a wave. Marge is snivelling into a tissue at the front, being comforted by Miranda the Art teacher.

'Are you all right?' I ask her, dumping my bag onto the luggage rack.

'I'm going to have to report this incident,' she says. 'David will have a field day. He already wants to put me on capability because our department is too "old-fashioned".'

'The boys were stupid. It wasn't your fault. At least they're back safely and Michael is giving them the dressing down of their lives.'

'Why don't you ring Janet?' Miranda suggests. Janet Patchell is Deputy Head, and infinitely superior to David Clark.

'This is a bus stop. I've a legal right to be here,' the bus driver says, raising his voice, with the window down.

'I'd better get them inside,' I say, and run to the middle door, where they are still standing in the street.

'You are about to go to university, where you will be treated like adults. You need to grow out of this childish, irresponsible behaviour.'

I step out onto the street and lay a hand on Michael's arm.

'We need to go,' I say. 'Boys, get on the bus.'

They board the coach and I stay with Michael. I wish I could hug him, but David's rules hang over us. He looks tired and oddly defeated.

'They went to King's Cross,' he says.

A huge international travel station.

'Oh.'

'If the press find out...'

'They won't,' I say quickly. 'They didn't post on social media, did they?'

'No,' he says. 'But they'll brag about it and they probably took photos. David will go ballistic.'

He rubs his forehead, contemplating the prospect. Why did they have to be in our group? There was nothing we could have done to stop them.

On cue, Michael's phone rings. He stares at it and then holds it up to me. David Clark.

That man's instinct for trouble is uncanny.

'Hello?' Michael answers, before I can stop him.

The bus starts to reverse, beeping. Michael gives me a worried look. I wave my hand.

'He's just got to move away from the cones,' I explain.

Michael covers his free ear with a hand to block the noise, then turns away, taking a few steps down the street. I cross my arms over my body, feeling jittery with cold. Then I watch, like it's in slow motion, as the bus pulls away.

'Hey!' I shout, just as a pneumatic drill starts to churn up the pavement.

In my mind, London streets are full of nose-to-tail vehicles, inching forwards every second. This must be the one time a school trip coach has ever pulled out into the road and zoomed off, accelerating from 0 to 30 mph in less than five seconds.

I stare at the road in disbelief, but only the fumes remain.

I go to grab my phone from my bag, then I remember I left it on the bus.

I rush to Michael, gesticulating wildly. He lowers his phone.

'The bus!' I shout. 'We've got to ring Marge.'

'I'll ring you back,' he says quickly, swivelling round to face the empty space where the bus was meant to be. He scrolls through his dialled numbers to find Marge on the list.

'It's engaged,' he says in frustration, hanging up.

'Try Sean,' I suggest.

'I haven't got his number.' Michael looks insulted at the idea of it. 'Maybe I should ring David back and get him to find Sean's number for me.'

'Do you really want David to know?' I say incredulously. The guy hates me enough to fire me as it is. 'He'll probably spin this whole thing to prove how the fact that we're dating has made us unprofessional and negligent.'

'I'll keep trying Marge.'

Surely someone will have noticed by now… The kids, maybe? No, they're probably all sharing photos of Kye and Lucas at King's Cross.

I start shivering again. Michael puts his arm around me and rubs up and down my sleeve. I feel like crying but I haven't got the energy.

'Um…' Michael says, and it's so uncharacteristic that I stare at him. 'I'm running out of battery.'

25

Michael

I HATE trips. I am never doing this again.

Why didn't I pack a power bank? Better still, buy one of those vests with power banks sewn into them? I mocked them at the time, but I would buy ten of them now if I had the chance. I scan the street, desperately hoping for a dodgy vendor to appear.

'I just want to go home,' Jen's voice cracks.

I fold my arms around her and squeeze tightly. Stuff David.

'Don't worry,' I say reassuringly. 'I've got enough battery to ring David and tell him we'll get the train back. He can ring Marge to explain.'

David had seen the boys' photo post—of course—and was ringing me to fish for information because he couldn't get through to Marge. I brace myself as I press the green button, trying to ignore the red battery icon in the corner of the screen.

'Michael, what's going on?'

'The bus left. Sorry, I don't have much battery. Can you tell Marge we'll get the train home?'

'What about the ratio?'

'I'm not standing on the street while you try to get the bus back here. It's dark and freezing cold. Just ring Marge now please.'

I hang up.

'Wow,' Jen says. 'That was brutal.'

'We need to get out of here before they start digging up this pavement too.'

The builders are isolating an increasingly large area of the road, presumably because it's rush hour and they want to be annoying. I take Jen's hand and we set off towards the nearest Tube station. The initial horror of the bus leaving is now replaced with a surge of adrenalin, and I bounce along the bustling street feeling a buzz of excitement that I don't have to endure a two-hour coach ride with hyperactive students and Sean.

My phone starts ringing. Marge.

'Hi.'

'Michael, I'm so sorry—where are you? We can come back.'

'I'd rather not,' I cut her off. 'Listen, my phone's almost dead. We couldn't stay where you left us because of the roadworks. It's late and freezing and we just want to get the train home.'

'I think David really wants you to be on the bus,' Marge's voice is wobbling. She was already crying when we left her.

'It's too difficult to arrange a rendez-vous,' I repeat. 'I really need to conserve power on my phone. We're getting a train and I'm hanging up now.'

I pocket my phone and start walking towards the Tube entrance. Jen hesitates.

'Are we going to be in trouble?' she asks. 'Maybe we could find a way…'

'Do you want to go home, or not?' I sigh. I don't want to take it out on Jen. 'I don't know where we are well enough to find a safe pick up point. It's rush hour and we'll delay everyone. It was an unforeseen circumstance and I will tell David that we made the best decision we could, given the situation.'

'All right.' Jen still sounds unsure, but follows me into the station. She stops to point out a kiosk. 'They might have a power bank.'

WEDDING BELL TIME

I shift impatiently while she approaches the vendor.

'Hi, I wonder if you can help me…'

I have to marvel at Jen's people skills. Her voice is warm and honey-smooth, and the guy is instantly nodding, gesturing to me and fishing out a power bank from the packet.

'I will charge it for you now,' he says.

'Thank you so much,' Jen gushes.

The guy even plugs my phone into his own charger so I can take another call from David. I stand awkwardly, leaning low over the counter because the cable can't reach, as Jen chats happily with our new friend.

'Michael, we need to get you back on the bus.'

'Well I'd love to hear how you're planning on doing that, David, from Whidlock.'

'You just need to find a landmark or something…'

'Hmm, Big Ben?' I joke.

'This isn't funny, Michael. This trip is in breach of health and safety regulations.'

He sounds uncannily like me. Is this what I sound like? I hope not.

'The problem is, David, sometimes things happen in real life that you can't plan for. Or, you have to adapt the plan.'

The guy's a teacher, for crying out loud. If he hasn't learnt that yet, there's no hope.

'What's the name of the Tube station? Could I send them back there?'

'You're just going to delay everyone and really annoy the parents. They're always there waiting an hour before you arrive back as it is.'

I've struck the magic reason here, and he falls silent for a moment.

'If anything happens on the bus on the way back…'

'It won't,' I say, with completely false confidence, like I know what's going to happen in the next three minutes.

'We already have a huge screw-up on our hands with the boys' Tube journey.'

'That was teenagers being irresponsible. I don't know how we could have prevented it. We'll just have to give them consequences and ban them from future trips —get a strong message across.'

'I just wish we could have a day where something doesn't blow up in our faces,' David says. I do, actually, feel sorry for him in this moment. It's rubbish being the Head and everything comes back on you. The county, the parents, the stake-holders… everyone expects you to have super-human powers to prevent disaster or avert every crisis.

'You can't control the choices students make,' I say, sounding like a bad self-help guru. 'You can control how we respond and follow the processes. That's all they can ask for.'

My neck and back are straining and I'm getting funny looks from commuters.

'I need to go now,' I say. 'Just tell Marge to carry on and we'll see her tomorrow.'

'Look, this has 75%, see?' The vendor shows me the power bank.

'Great.' I straighten up and unplug my phone. 'I'll take it.'

26

Jen

Safe to say, I didn't expect to be sweating on a stuffed commuter train when I dressed this morning. I've gone from freezing outside to boiling in my woollen jumper.

'I couldn't do this every day,' I say to Michael, shaking my head at the poor people who lose hours of each day on these sardine-packed trains.

'Hmm.' Michael's messing with his phone and the power bank, texting Marge. 'Less kids to deal with, though.'

'Ah yes, your alternative career in law.' I feel sick just thinking about it. Would we ever have met if Michael had become a solicitor? Or some kind of high-powered barrister? Perfect for Christina Patterson… I squash that thought down where I can't see it anymore.

I look at Michael's profile, his jaw set as he swipes the phone screen, and his brow furrowed. His expression is intense. I used to find him unsettling, but now there's a familiarity which has brought understanding. Every now and then, I catch a glimpse of his other lives and possibilities. That scares me.

In Whidlock, we're both English teachers. All right, he's a HoD now and set for some senior role in the next few years, but generally speaking, we're equal. When I went to his parents' house, though… We weren't equal anymore. They clearly see Michael as exceptional—which he is, in so many ways. But I'm very unexceptional. It makes me feel like I have no right to claim him.

I've only recently been able to call him my boyfriend, and I just feel like an imposter. It doesn't help that in school, it's all got to be hushed up. I've got nothing to be ashamed of. So why do I feel, even now on this train full of strangers, that I should fold my arms and refrain from touching or embracing Michael in any way?

Maybe I should let him initiate contact.

I glance around the train carriage. Two ladies are opening Jo Malone bags, and I feel a stab of envy. Wouldn't it be amazing to have the money to buy luxury perfume?

'Now we should be able to catch a connection to Whidlock from Swindon,' Michael says, finally looking up. 'It'll take about an hour from here, and then that train will take thirty minutes… Do you want me to book a taxi from the station?'

His brain is whirring, calculating all the travel times and processing ten times faster than me.

'Uh… I'm not sure…'

The perfume ladies giggle, and a waft of 'Orange Blossom' fills the carriage. Michael coughs.

'What is that?'

'Jo Malone,' I say, then decide it's worth a hint. 'I'd love some perfume like that.'

But Michael keeps coughing. I don't think he heard what I said. He loosens his collar, then waves his hand at me.

'Michael, are you okay?'

'I'm allergic,' he croaks out, gasping for breath. His face is turning a deep shade of red and he stumbles out to the luggage area, pushing past peeved travellers who are standing in the gangway.

I rush to follow him, tripping over bags and narrowly avoiding a lady holding a coffee.

'Is there a window we can open?' I look around, but they don't seem to have those kinds of windows on trains anymore.

'Would you like some water?' A passenger holds out a bottle to Michael.

He shakes his head, still coughing violently, and gasping. He staggers into the toilet cubicle and starts running the tap and splashing his face and neck while everybody tries not to look.

'I think I should press the emergency button,' I say, my eyes lighting upon it.

Michael shakes his head violently and tries to say no, but can't speak.

'Michael, you're having an allergic reaction. I'm pressing the button.'

I push the red circle, and the light comes on, but nothing happens immediately.

'Do you have an EpiPen?' the helpful passenger asks. They must be trained in first aid or something.

'Michael, do you have an EpiPen?' I ask, practically shouting, although I have no idea what to do if he says yes. We've done training in school but It's Not The Same.

Slightly purple, he continues to shake his head. Or perhaps it's just convulsions.

'Here.' The lady with the coffee hands the drink to another passenger and produces an EpiPen from her bag. Who knew?

'Just stab it into his leg,' she says, looking at me expectantly.

Oh hell.

Trying to look as if I've done this before—which I have, in training, but It's Not The Same—and with my hand shaking, I press the pen into his thigh and he gives a loud cry. Maybe I did it too hard.

'What's occurring here?' A train staff person arrives and I'm not kidding, that's what they say.

'He's having an allergic reaction.' I think I'm actually crying now.

'If you just lower yourself to the floor.' It's the First Aid passenger, hauling Michael under his armpits.

'All passengers move into the next carriage, please,' the train guy shouts. 'Shall I call an ambulance?'

Michael's coughing begins to calm, and he manages to gasp, 'No!'

Is this part of being British, or something? You go blue in the face but you can't push the red button and you can't call an ambulance, because you don't want to make a scene?

'How far is the next stop?' I ask.

'Ten minutes,' the guard replies.

'I'm… fine,' Michael pants. He does sound better. The First Aider is checking his pulse.

'Just take deep breaths,' she says.

I think I need to take deep breaths.

'It's okay, the adrenalin will take effect immediately,' Coffee Lady tells me.

'Th-thank you so much,' I stutter. 'I had no idea he was allergic…'

I still have no idea what Michael is allergic to. Perfume?

'… had an allergic reaction…' The guard is speaking on a phone.

'I'm fine,' Michael repeats, slightly louder this time. He still looks red-faced but he seems to be breathing properly.

'The paramedics will board the train at the next stop,' the guard tells me. 'They'll check him over and then see what to do next.'

I nod, cupping my face in my hands and feeling tears on my cheeks. I may not be in Michael's league, or anywhere close, but if I lost him, I would never get over it.

I'm in deep enough that I don't care now if his parents wish I was Christina Patterson with letters after my name and a fast-track to a six-figure salary. He's mine, and I'm claiming him before anyone else can get a look in.

27

Michael

This is definitely one of the worst days of my life.

Time seems to have slowed down to a painful rate. How long have I been awkwardly strewn over the filthy train carriage floor, just outside the open door of the toilet? It's probably just been five minutes, but it feels like an hour in one of the seven circles of the Inferno. Even if my face wasn't burning from a reaction to the perfume, my complete sense of humiliation would be enough.

Maybe this is some sort of divine punishment because I didn't go back on the coach.

I try to tell Jen I'm fine and she doesn't need to be crying and wringing her hands, but lying on a train by the exit door negates the 'fine-ness' of the situation somewhat. In the end, I just give up and submit to the inevitability of it all.

When the train pulls into the next station, the doors open and I catch a glimpse of a National Rail SWAT team on the platform. Two paramedics in high-viz jackets jump on and start assessing me, while presumably all the other train doors are rammed full of passengers trying to get on or off with one door out of action because That Man Had a Reaction to Perfume.

Well, it's an allergy to limonene (an oil found in citrus peel) actually, as I tell Jen. I rarely get close enough for much of a reaction but that Jo Malone stuff is pungent. No wonder it costs five gold bars for a bottle.

'The swelling has reduced,' the paramedic says, cold fingers prodding my neck. 'Are you struggling to breathe?'

'I'm fine.'

I really should think of a different response.

'We should probably take him in for monitoring,' the other paramedic says.

What, and be stranded in A&E to be sent home at midnight once the last train has gone?

'That's not necessary,' I say in my best assertive tone, although being on the floor lessens the impact. Not enough projection.

'We can transfer him to First Class,' one of the train workers says.

'Yes,' I nod enthusiastically. 'That sounds much more necessary.'

'We'll provide you with another EpiPen just in case. You should go to your doctor tomorrow to get checked over,' the paramedic advises.

'Can I get up now?'

I fold down the annoying tiny corridor seat and lever myself to a standing position. I pat the smooth grey plastic of the wall, trying to find something to grip onto. There's nothing, so my palm stays flattened against the surface.

Jen takes my arm and we follow the train worker to the First Class area. Someone immediately offers us refreshments and as the train judders into movement again, I reflect with some satisfaction that this whole escapade resulted in a seat upgrade and a free panini.

Jen is still jittery and keeps looking around in hypervigilance mode in case anyone else took out a mortgage to buy luxury perfume with citrus oil.

'Why didn't you tell me you had allergies?' she says, like I'm some kid who forgot to bring their medical form on the trip.

'I only have one,' I argue.

'I could have unpeeled an orange right in front of you at any time and set you off.'

'I've never seen you eat an orange.'

'That's not the point.' Jen frowns. She looks cute when she does this, though I know better than to tell her in this moment. 'We should really raise awareness of this. Put a poster in the staff room.'

I splutter on the mouthful of coffee I just drank.

'What—a poster, with my mugshot and 'NO CITRUS'?'

'You could have died.'

She's really not in the mood for joking.

'You saved my life.' I decide to put a positive spin on it. 'How can I ever repay you?'

'Number one, get your own EpiPen so I don't have to borrow one from a stranger,' she says, her voice rising, and I know a crusade is beginning. 'Number two, tell me your allergies. Number three, stop being British when you need help.'

'Okay!' I hold my hands up. 'I will try to deny my cultural roots in moments of life-or-death crisis.'

To my horror, Jen starts crying again. Then does that thing where she tries to explain why she's crying, but she's crying too much to make any sense, so I just make soothing noises and pretend I understand.

'[unintelligible noise]... hard day… [unintelligible noise]... so scared…'

'It's all okay now,' I say, patting her shoulder.

I look around and pass her a napkin in lieu of a tissue. She blows her nose then sniffs, wiping her face.

'I don't know what I'd do if I lost you,' she says with sudden, quiet calmness.

I grasp her hands and my heart bursts with the excitement of this intense emotion being reciprocated. That I found someone to love, who actually loves me back, seems outlandishly impossible.

I think about the ring, and I can't help grinning.

'I want you to talk to David again,' Jen says, her tone still serious. 'I don't want to have to pretend that this doesn't exist, or that it's only part-time on the weekend.'

'I know,' I squeeze her hand. 'Don't worry. I told you, I've got it all under control.'

Two weeks until Christmas, and counting.

28

Jen

'Do you and Christina message much?'

I finally ask the question I've been thinking about since nine o'clock this morning.

'Not much.' Michael shifts away slightly, reaching for his panini. He's avoiding eye contact.

'I didn't realise you were friends.'

There's no way of saying this without sounding petty, I know.

'We grew up in the same village,' he says, waving a hand.

It bugs me because to me 'growing up in a village' means everybody wearing each other's hand-me-downs and having a Christmas party with someone's grandad as Santa in the community centre, whereas to him it means 'being a chorister and taking your first communion together' and Joules wellies with gilets.

'I think your parents may have signed a contract to betroth you.'

'It's never been like that between us.' He shakes his head.

'Did she ever want to go out with you?'

'No,' he scoffs.

'Did you ever ask her out?'

'No.'

He looks at me as though I've suggested flying to the moon and back.

'Then how do you know she never wanted to go out with you? She might have said yes.'

'No one wanted to go out with me.'

'So how come you asked me, then? Was it obvious I liked you?'

He considers, sipping coffee.

'I think it got to the point where I couldn't *not* ask you. I was desperate enough that I couldn't go on without asking you.'

I smile at the memory of that insanely tense and turbulent season. What is this season we're in now? 'Going steady?' Why does my language for relationships come from 1980s movies?

'You've changed my life, Jen,' he says. 'I'll never be the same again.'

He kisses me before I can properly process this, and then holds up his phone.

'Should I book a taxi?'

It feels like midnight by the time the train pulls into our station, but it's only 8 p.m. Michael gets a pizza from the take-away by the taxi rank. Amongst people arriving for a night out, decked in heels and (thankfully) cheap perfume, we finally bundle into a taxi which takes us to his place.

At this point I'm feeling exhausted, intoxicated by the idea of finally being alone and not on The Trip To End All Trips. I find a bottle of wine and pour two generous glasses, as we settle on the sofa to eat. It's Friday night again, and now the horrors of the trip are a distant memory. Some rubbishy TV show is on, but I don't want to change anything in this moment. I could be happy with this. I don't want anything else.

Except when I kiss Michael, and then I do want Something Else. Very badly.

As soon as our lips meet, I feel the desire unfurl and bind us closer and closer like a rope being stretched taut. My hands grip his shoulders, tighter and tighter, and there's no time to take breath, it's too vital to drink him in…

I might be succeeding in getting him to forget his vow. He's responding, and I know it can't be just me who feels this magnetic force pulling us together. I slide my hand under his shirt to feel his skin, warm and smooth. It's irresistible.

But then I remember: precautions. Neither of us is prepared for… that. What does it matter? Imagine if I got pregnant with Michael's baby… The thought is not the panic-filled warning it always has been before. Maybe this proves that this time is different. Maybe I'm finally ready for a grown-up relationship. Of course, his dad wouldn't like it, but in the end…

Just as my hand grasps at a fistful of shirt, preparing to pull it off, Michael's phone rings. He grabs it off the coffee table and I see the caller ID: Christina.

'Sorry, I've just got to take this,' he says, and untangles himself from me, leaving me on the sofa and hurrying away to the kitchen.

Disappointment extinguishes my 'becoming a parent' daydream. Worse still, distrust niggles at my certainty that Michael is The One. Has he really been honest about Christina? Why does he need to leave the room to take her call? Why is he even considering answering the phone right now, when he could be with me?

My head feels giddy with the wine and I wish I had my phone. I'm so cut off without it and I just hope my stuff is all okay, that Marge remembered to take everything off the bus for me. I hope she is all right too, and that David isn't going to come down on her like a ton of bricks for what happened with the boys on the Tube.

'Sorry about that.' Michael returns, looking sheepish, but offers no further explanation. He just sinks down onto the sofa next to me.

'Why was she ringing you?'

'Just organising an ... event... at Christmas.'

'Oh?' First I've heard of it. 'Is this to do with the church?'

'Yes.'

'Will I be going too?'

'Yes.'

'Are you hiding something from me?' I scan his face. He meets my gaze and takes my hand.

'Trust me,' he says.

It's not a 'no'. I withdraw my hand.

'Funny how, before I met your parents, you never mentioned church to me. Once.'

'It didn't really come up,' he replies.

'I don't get it,' I shake my head. 'Like, either it's important to you, or it isn't. My grandparents lived and breathed their church. They must have been there practically every day of the week.'

'I may not be devout like them, but it doesn't mean it's not important to me.'

'So important that you never talk about it?'

'Why are you angry about this? It doesn't affect you.'

'Your *sacred vow* affects me.'

'I don't expect you to understand it, but I do ask you to respect it.'

'I would, if you were more consistent in practising your religion. The only thing you seem to follow is your schedule.'

'A minute ago you were about to rip my shirt to shreds, and now you're just tearing my faith apart instead. What's the matter?' Michael snaps.

'Do you have any idea how hard it is to be with you sometimes?' I'm cross, and I don't care what I'm saying because it's true. 'You look down on someone like Sean, because you think that he's 'inappropriate' and plays fast and loose with the rules, and yet as soon as that bus pulled away, you were frog-marching me to the Tube station, ignoring what everyone said about finding a way to get picked up.'

'Well, I'm sorry for trying to take care that you weren't shivering on the pavement all night!' Michael raises his voice to match mine.

'It was more that you didn't want to hang around waiting for someone else to make a decision,' I point out. 'Just like on the train, you preferred choking to pulling the emergency cord and getting an ambulance. You're so stubborn sometimes; it's ridiculous.'

'Anything else you want to say?' He gestures to the air. 'Any other glaring faults that you need to make me aware of, because I'm such a terrible specimen of human being? Because that's what I am: human.'

'Then stop acting like a robot.' My voice drops to its normal level. 'Can I stay tonight?'

He looks at me and he knows what I'm asking.

'Jen,' he says. 'I love you, and that's why I want us to wait. Please. Don't make it harder than it already is.'

'You're the one making this difficult!' I raise my voice. 'I'm sorry but *no one* makes a vow as a teenager and feels they have to keep it as an adult!'

'I do.'

The irony of his response isn't lost on him either.

'Jen, one of the most important lessons my parents taught me was to always keep my word. They never lied to me, and if they said they were going to do something, they did it. I have massive respect for that. That's the kind of person I want to be. You may not care about chastity vows, or keeping a dinner appointment, but

I'm sure that you'd want me to keep my wedding vows... if we got married.'

He adds the last phrase hastily, then clears his throat.

This situation is so odd, I feel completely disorientated. Michael keeps mentioning marriage, fairly casually, when most guys seem to run a mile from it. Surely this is a good thing? But the stupid vow, and the way he always has to keep his word, threaten to tie us up for the rest of our lives. Honesty is good, right? But then it makes every time he kisses me feel dishonest, like he's making a promise he can't keep. I don't think Michael understands that in his black-and-white world.

'Sometimes we make a promise with the best of intentions, but we can't follow through,' I point out. 'We can't punish ourselves forever. Sometimes you have to let things go. Circumstances change.'

He looks at me for a moment, then takes a deep breath.

'I know you don't like talking about it...'

My heart skips a beat. He's going to talk about Mum.

'But when your mum left, your dad could have—'

'That's irrelevant to this discussion,' I snap.

'I don't think it is,' he says gently. 'Your dad could have said "she's broken her vows to me" and moved on. But he was faithful and looked after her when she came back.'

'What good did that do?' I feel the emotion bubbling in my throat. 'She never realised what she'd done! Dad just... overlooked it because he didn't know how else to deal with it! Do you know the damage that caused? How hard it was?'

He wraps his arms around me, and I sob. I still feel so angry, but I need him right now.

'Look, I'm not saying she was right, and I don't want to sound glib because I wasn't there,' he says. 'I just want you to know that

I want to be faithful. I want to keep my promises. And I hope you can see that as a good thing.'

'I don't understand,' I whisper, shaking my head, tears still streaming down my cheeks.

'Trust me,' Michael repeats.

I don't really have much choice.

Interlude

Alice pressed herself against the cold stone of the castle wall. The moon was bright enough to cast a shadow, and in the thick darkness of the recess ahead, she thought she saw movement. Alice exhaled through her mouth, grasping her staff. She had come too far to give up now.

She inched along the gravel, still pressed against the wall, sidestepping noiselessly. As she grew closer, she thought she heard the sound of someone breathing.

She reached the end of the wall, before it curved around, and stood poised for a moment. An owl shrieked and she swung herself around the corner, raising her weapon. It instantly clashed with something metallic. Sword?

It was almost comically silent, the next furious minutes where they blocked one another, lunging with sharp hisses. By lowering the staff and jabbing, she finally had the satisfaction of hearing a grunt. It was a man.

He was good at fencing, but he obviously wasn't used to combat. She pivoted and swiped his legs with the staff, easily dodging his attempt at jabbing her, and aimed a kick at his groin while his balance was off. He groaned properly then. She used the staff to strike him across the midriff, then across his back. He was kneeling by now.

"Stop!" he cried out, panting for breath. "Do you know who I am?"

She looked down at him in amusement. Her eyes had adjusted more and she could make out the outline of a figure staggering to his feet. He was thin—

not the bulky guard type. When he stretched out his hand, his skin seemed pale in the grey shadow.

"I am the prince," he said, straightening up.

"So what?" she replied, and went to beat him again. He blocked her, but then she jabbed him in the chest with the end of her staff.

He stumbled back, coughing, and she then swiped upwards, catching his neck under his chin. He fell to the ground, clutching his throat.

She didn't have time for this.

"I need you to get me inside the castle," she said, ignoring his gasps.

Document comments:
Michael Chase: Is this violence necessary?
Jen Baker: Yes.

29

Michael

Christmas can't come soon enough this year.

After the London trip fiasco, Jen is definitely off with me. She suspects something is going on—which it is, although not the way she thinks it is—and she seems particularly vehement about my supposed hypocrisy.

I mean, nobody's perfect.

You'd think that things would wind down at the end of term, but David's roped me into different meetings with agencies who are supposed to be helping Whidlock improve. I'm one of the first to arrive in the morning, and the sun is just rising, ribbons of red cloud spanning the horizon. There's frost on the ground and I take a moment to stare at the sky. The radiant glow gives a halo to our grimy, dilapidated school. It's a rare moment of transcendence. Perhaps I am doing something good here, making a difference. It's a sign of divine approval.

'Grab me a coffee, will you?' David calls to me as I walk past his office.

I roll my eyes and push the door a little more forcefully than necessary.

When I walk back through the empty staff room, a cold draught blows through a gap where the window won't close properly. This building. David's office is warm—too warm, in fact—and he leans back in his executive chair as he barks out the paperwork he needs for the meeting.

'Data analysis for Year 11? Intervention plans? Provision for students in target groups?'

'I shared it all with you last night.' I open my laptop, feeling like it was just five minutes ago I was staring at the screen, as if I hadn't slept. School bears an alarming similarity to Groundhog Day at times.

'They were at Prestfield yesterday,' David tells me, sipping his coffee.

It's strange: in moments like this, it's as if the dinner/YouTube incident never happened. David's good at compartmentalising. I know it's all filed away, ready to be produced at an opportune moment for blackmail or emotional manipulation. Right now he's cool and collected, making small talk to hide his nerves at this meeting. I wonder where Vermont is, and why David can't get the Senior team to do this due diligence.

I hear the sound of voices in the corridor as more staff arrive, and try to pick out Jen. I imagine her making her usual mug of tea, in the *Wuthering Heights* mug I bought her. *Whatever our souls are made of, his and mine are the same.*

'Don't you think?' I realise David is staring at me.

'Sorry, what did you say?'

'Never mind,' he snaps impatiently. 'You seem away with the fairies. Where is Vermont?'

On cue, the door bursts open, and Joseph enters with a flustered expression. I've hardly ever seen him discomposed. He sits next to me and fumbles around with his briefcase.

'You're late,' David says, unnecessarily.

'Sorry.' Joseph avoids eye contact. He doesn't give any reasons or excuses, which I can tell annoys David, but then the phone rings.

'Yes… Yes I'll meet them.' He replaces the receiver. 'They're waiting in reception.'

There are two emissaries from the local authority, both dressed in black suits. I can tell it's going to be one of Those meetings. David turns on his usual charm, but within two minutes of them sitting down, the questions begin.

'What is your forecast for exam results this summer?'

'What action are you taking to help pupils in your target group?'

'How do you know these figures are accurate?'

There doesn't seem to be a good-cop, bad-cop routine; they're both bad cop.

Vermont and I struggle through our sets of data for Maths and English, and I help to bail David out of answering a couple of awkward questions about students with additional learning needs (Jen has filled me in on all of that, as it's part of her new role). When it's finally over, I retrieve my respectable Fair Isle patterned sweater and pull it over my shirt. It's Christmas jumper day.

The corridors are now full of hyper kids wearing elf hats, jumpers with flashing lights, along with shorts, ripped jeans, and other inappropriate items for a school day in December. One kid is dressed in a Captain America costume. I catch sight of Jen, wearing a giant snowflake fluffy jumper and a headband with snowball pom poms. She loves all this. Her classroom has coloured lights and a mini Christmas tree.

'Nice jumper,' she comments with an ironic smile.

I shrug.

There's a commotion as two boys kick a football down the corridor. I catch it swiftly and take it with me to my classroom, ignoring the cries of protest. A tiny girl is waiting for me, and she immediately starts twittering about homework being lost and the dog eating it.

'Okay.' I hold a hand up to stop her mid-flow. 'I will speak to you in the lesson.'

My Year 9 class is waiting, a fizzing excitement amplifying the volume of their usual noise.

'Sir, are we doing something fun today?' one of the boys asks hopefully.

'English is always fun,' I reply dryly, shoving the football under my desk.

It's going to be a long day.

At lunch, I find Jen in the staffroom, taping a large notice to the wall. My face is on it, surrounded by a border of oranges, with the text:

CITRUS ALLERGY
Please do not eat citrus fruit in public areas when Michael is present.

'What are you doing?' I stare at the picture of myself.

'Making sure that you don't have another anaphylactic shock.'

'I give it half an hour before that poster is defaced.'

'As long as the message is clear, I don't care.'

The snowball pom poms wiggle as Jen shakes her head at me. The note of annoyance is permanently in her voice.

'Did you bring your EpiPen in?' she asks.

I hold open my jacket, to show that it's in my inside pocket in case of future emergencies.

'I'm looking forward to taking you to the carol service,' I say in a softer tone, hoping she will respond.

'Will Christina be joining us?'

She's really got a bee in her bonnet about this.

'She'll be there,' I hedge.

'It will be great for you two to catch up,' Jen says bitterly.

'You're the person I want to spend time with.'

I wish I could pull her tightly in, squeezing the grey fluff of her jumper and stroking her back comfortingly, but I just stand there.

'We've got the special Christmas quiz this week,' she says. 'Why don't you join us?'

I'd rather squirt lemon juice in my eye than sit with Sean at a pub quiz, but I'm starting to worry that Jen's hatred of me is returning in full force, which may have negative ramifications for my planned Christmas proposal.

'All right,' I agree. 'But no elf hats.'

30

Jen

When Quiz Night finally arrives, I'm wearing my hat with oversized elf ears and a red elf dress, which would be rather raunchy if I wasn't wearing it over a pair of jeans. My Christmas bauble earrings flash with surprising vigour considering the batteries in them are a few years old. The plan is for Michael to come over for some food before we leave, but he doesn't turn up until past six.

'Sorry,' he says wearily. 'David asked me to help with some data he's got to submit by tomorrow.'

'Why can't he ask Geoff, or someone else who's actually on the Senior team?' I ask. 'I hope he's not making you do all the work and then taking the credit for it.'

My dad's made cauliflower cheese, and I dish Michael up a bowlful, batting away memories of his mother's cordon bleu. He eats ravenously.

'This is really good,' he says.

I pour him a glass of water and silently celebrate this victory for humble normality.

'I haven't had time to change.' He looks down at his suit.

'Why don't you borrow one of my dad's Christmas jumpers?' I suggest.

'Sure.' He looks pained at the thought.

I run upstairs and root around in the wardrobe. There's a tame option, similar to the one Michael wore to school, and then a more outlandish Rudolph option with a light-up nose. Bingo. I hand it to Michael, along with a Santa hat.

'But—' he begins to protest.

'You said no elf hats. You said nothing about Santa hats. Plus we get extra points if you wear it.'

He pulls the jumper over his shirt and tries the hat on in front of the mirror.

'I look ridiculous.'

'A bit of humiliation never hurt anyone.'

Michael insists on driving, even though he's never been to this pub before, and I could have taken my dad's car. He seems to carry an atmosphere of stress, perhaps left over from school, but simple things like changing lane or a roundabout seem to be ramping up his sense of annoyance.

'Unbelievable. They really should signpost that exit more clearly.'

I press the heating controls to make the car warmer, and he flicks it off with a huff.

'It's boiling in here.'

I begin to wonder if this was a good idea.

I've always known that Michael is an uptight kind of person. He doesn't relax or chill out very easily. I guess my hope is that I help him to smile a bit more and find a life outside of school. But now I'm worried that I'm adding an unidentified package to the fun-loving, well established quiz team, and it might just be a bomb about to explode.

After reversing into a tight space, checking his mirrors a million times and complaining loudly about the car park dimensions, Michael slams the car door with more force than necessary. I walk round to his side and take both his hands in mine.

'Michael,' I speak firmly, 'we are going here to have fun. You need to calm down. Take some deep breaths, or something.'

'I'm fine,' he says.

See, men do that too: saying they're fine when they're patently not.

I readjust the pom-pom on the end of his Santa hat, and trace my finger down the side of his face.

'I love you.'

'Really?' He breathes out. 'I thought you were still mad at me.'

'I'm not,' I say, although it's true I have been annoyed at him since the trip. 'Let's just put things behind us and enjoy tonight, yeah?'

'Hey, Jen!' Sean appears in the pub doorway, beckoning frantically. 'It's about to start!'

I hurry to follow him inside, Michael a few paces behind me. The pub is hot and packed with loads more people than last week. Everyone has turned out in force, with a colourful variety of hats too. Michael and I have to squish onto a narrow chair, awkwardly placed at the corner of a table, and barely have time to perch before the round begins.

'Who is generally recognised as writing the poem 'Twas the Night Before Christmas'?'

Sean shrugs and looks at me. Michael gestures for the pen and writes down neatly *Clement Moore*. I give a thumbs up.

The questions rattle on, but the atmosphere is louder and rowdier than before. In the first break, Sean heads to the bar and returns with a tray of shots.

'What is this, happy hour?' I laugh.

'Aren't you driving?' Michael asks suspiciously.

'Nah, we're sharing a taxi back,' Sean says, giving everyone a shot.

Michael pushes his back onto the tray.

'What is it?' I ask. I'm not really the drinking type.

'It's a snowball,' Sean says. 'You'll love it: brandy, peppermint schnapps and cacao.'

Michael sniffs disapprovingly.

'Come on, Jen,' Steph prods me. 'Live a little.'

'Alright.'

'Three, two, one…' Sean counts down.

Jason seems unperturbed, but Steph and I make faces at each other as our throats burn.

'Whoever gets the next question wrong has to drink the spare,' Sean challenges.

'What if it's Michael?' Steph says, giggling.

'I'm sure we'll think of something,' Sean says, with a glint in his eye.

'What is the name of the last ghost to visit Scrooge in *A Christmas Carol*?'

'Christmas Future,' Sean says.

'It's actually the Ghost of Christmas Yet to Come,' Michael corrects him.

'Same difference.'

'You won't get the point,' Michael says in frustration.

'I think it's time for another round.'

Sean starts to get up, but Jason says,

'I'll get this one.'

'What is the best-selling Christmas song ever?'

"White Christmas',' Sean says immediately.

'I think it's Mariah Carey,' Michael says, then looks to me. 'What do you think?'

'I really don't know,' I shrug. 'Steph?'

'I feel like I hear Mariah Carey a lot more on the radio and in shops than the other one,' Steph says.

'Yes, but 'White Christmas' has been around way longer, so it's made more total sales.'

'That makes sense,' Steph concedes. 'Okay, put it down.'

When the answers are revealed, it is 'White Christmas', and Sean jubilantly shouts,

'Yes! I knew it! You're having a forfeit now.'

Michael scowls and turns to his phone, while Sean heads off to the bar again.

'Here we go,' Steph mutters to me, knocking back the rest of her gin and tonic.

I'm sipping lemonade, having realised that juice is a bad idea with Michael's allergy, although it's unlikely to cause a reaction unless it makes contact with his skin. He holds his phone up to me triumphantly.

'Look, I *was* right,' he says. ''All I Want for Christmas' is the Christmas single with the most digital downloads.'

'I don't think Sean's going to care.' I wish he would let it go. Can't he just be wrong for once? The overly competitive vibe from Michael and Sean snapping at each other's heels has made tonight way more stressful than it should have been. It's also uncomfortably hot and crowded and the open fire is making it more sweltering. There's a line of sweat on my forehead under my elf hat.

'Time for your forfeit!'

Sean is back, holding a glass with a milky liquid. Michael wrinkles his nose.

'What is it?'

'Eggnog. Non-alcoholic,' Sean adds, setting it down with a flourish.

'I found evidence that I was actually right.'

'Drink it! Drink it!' Sean chants, slapping his hand against the table.

Michael looks to me for a way out.

'It's not going to kill you,' I say, feeling irritable.

Something shifts in Michael's eyes and he grabs the glass and downs it. Too late, something clicks with what I just said.

'Your allergy!' I shout, springing to my feet as he places the empty glass down on the table. 'Sean, is there citrus in it?'

'What?' Sean looks confused. 'It's milk, egg...'

I catch sight of the blackboard with 'Christmas drinks' listed on it and, in slow motion, see the words 'orange zest'. I look at Michael, who is wiping his mouth with disgust.

'Where's your EpiPen?' I yell.

He goes to search his jacket pocket, then remembers he's wearing my dad's Christmas jumper. He shakes his head.

'It must be in the car.'

'Quickly!'

I grab his arm and drag him out into the car park. He's still holding a hand over his mouth. He fumbles in his pocket, hands me the keys, then turns and vomits.

Terrified, I unlock the car and throw open the back door, finding his jacket and turning it over, nearly tearing it with trying to access the pocket. When my fingers close over the EpiPen, I draw it out and rip the cap off with too much force, so it skitters over the concrete. Holding it in my fist, and grateful for the video tutorials I watched obsessively after the London incident, I push it into his thigh and hold it for ten seconds, while he coughs and splutters.

'Please, God...' I find myself praying, paralysed with fear.

'Is he all right?'

Sean, Steph and Jason come running out.

'I'll call an ambulance,' Jason says, pulling out his phone.

'I'll go and see if anyone can help.' Steph rushes back into the pub.

'I'm so sorry,' Sean moans. 'I didn't know…'
'Michael, say something,' I cry.
He pulls the Santa hat off his head and tosses it to one side.
'Never again,' he answers.

31

Michael

This must be the new worst day of my life.

I think I preferred it when Sean was just a general annoying idiot. Now he's fawning all around me, trying to make me amends, when if I felt better I'd punch him in the face. He throws his arms around Jen, supposedly to comfort her, as I empty the contents of my stomach in the freezing cold car park.

Steph emerges from the pub with a blue roll of paper towels.

'Here you are.' She hands a wadge over to me.

It feels like no time at all before a paramedic's car pulls up, and I'm being assessed… for the second time in a week.

'Your blood pressure is normal and there's no anaphylaxis,' she tells me. 'But you probably will continue to vomit through the night. You need to drink plenty of water to avoid dehydration.'

'On it.' Steph goes back inside the pub.

'If it was less busy, I'd suggest you come in for monitoring, but the reality is, A&E is packed, and you'll probably be stuck in a waiting room. Have you got somewhere to stay close by?'

I shake my head, closing my eyes.

'I'm half an hour away.' I hear Jen's voice. 'I've been drinking so I can't drive… We can't take him in a taxi if he's vomiting…'

'The pub will have a room,' Sean pipes up. 'Look, you can stay with him. I'll sort it.'

'Thank you,' Jen says gratefully, to the guy who nearly killed me.

So I find myself in a double room with Jen, running back and forth to the bathroom, sleeping in a feverish blur, with her trying to give me water every two minutes. I suppose I should feel grateful, but the thought stuck on repeat in my head is, *I have to be better for tomorrow.* I've planned too much for everything to fall apart now. If I can just get through this biological blip, everything can go according to schedule.

At 4 a.m., when it's still pitch dark like midnight, my stomach is well and truly empty and my throat is raw. I finally close my eyes and rest. Whatever battle my body's been fighting is over for now.

The next time I wake, I can hear Jen talking.

'Absolutely not.' Her voice is raised. 'I'm not leaving him.'

My eyes open, focusing on the radio clock on the bedside table. 7:30 a.m. The deadline for phoning in sick.

'Thank you,' she snaps, then adds sarcastically, 'Merry Christmas.'

'Jen,' I croak, but it sounds more like an incoherent grunt.

'Michael?' She rushes over and feels my forehead. 'Drink this.'

She hands me a glass of water. She's still wearing an elf dress, but at some point she lost the jeans.

'You look hot,' I say without really thinking, after taking a few gulps.

She laughs.

'So do you.'

I look at her apologetically.

'I'm sorry. You probably didn't get any sleep.'

'I've had better nights,' she says lightly. 'I'm beginning to think that we can't do anything normal. Ever. Something catastrophic will always happen.'

'Thanks for getting the EpiPen. I didn't twig at all that there might be anything in the drink.'

'No, you were too busy being a jerk.'

Ouch.

'I'm sorry,' I repeat.

She sighs and buries her face in her hands.

'You were unbearably competitive,' she says. 'You judged me for drinking a few shots. Then you put yourself in danger because you're too arrogant to tell people about your allergy and take precautions.'

She's obviously been thinking up this speech all night, while I've been vomiting into the toilet.

'Did I remember this wrong or did you tell me to drink it because it wouldn't kill me?'

'I'm sorry, those were careless words, and as soon as I said them I realised…' she says. 'Please don't blame Sean. It wasn't his fault.'

'The guy is a total tosser and you're actually defending him!' I argue hoarsely, the impact somewhat lessened by my voice giving out on several syllables.

Stop it, Michael, I tell myself. This is meant to be the most romantic day of her life, and you've kicked it off by arguing.

'Why don't you try and get some sleep?' she says, yawning. 'We don't have to get up yet.'

'Sure,' I say, turning away from her.

She settles down beside me, and once her breathing is steady, my eyes ping open.

I've got too much to recalibrate to sleep.

We're not going to school today… what will we do about clothes? Maybe this could work to our advantage by allowing us to leave earlier than originally planned. But we are in the wrong location with none of the resources we need. And instead of feeling like I can take on the world, I'm exhausted and possibly dehydrated too. I grab the glass of water and glug back some more.

I need a shower.

Fifteen minutes later, I quietly close the door on Jen, still sleeping, and go to find the landlord. He's talking to a cleaner in the lobby area, and eyes me suspiciously.

'Feeling better?' he asks.

'Yes,' I reply brusquely. 'I need a few things… Do you have a Wi-Fi code? And do you offer breakfast?'

32

Jen

When I open my eyes, daylight is streaming past the feeble, lopsided curtains. I turn to check Michael, and discover I'm alone in the bed.

'Michael?' I ask, listening for movement.

He clears his throat. I look across the room and he's fully dressed, and pouring tea into a mug.

'Would you like breakfast in bed?'

I squint at him. My head feels like it's been bulldozed by a train, and I'm not the one who was throwing up all night.

'I thought I was supposed to be looking after you.' I take the mug of tea he holds out, sipping it gratefully.

'I'm fine,' he replies.

I stare at him over my mug. From a distance, he would look like normal Michael. Up close, he's pale and strained.

'You need to ring your doctor,' I say.

He gives a sigh of irritation.

'You need to get checked over.'

'I did last time, and it was pointless.' He rolls his eyes.

'You need another EpiPen.'

'I know.'

He hands me a plate of toast.

'Signal's rubbish in here. I'll go downstairs.'

He leaves, the door clicking shut behind him. I swig more tea, looking around for a clock. 8:30 a.m. The surgery phone line will be jammed and they probably won't have any appointments left. I close my eyes and lean back, throbbing pain behind my eyes. I just want to keep Michael safe, but it feels like what was an innocuous allergy could now create regular life-threatening situations.

In any other circumstance, we would be a romantic couple, enjoying a weekend break. But as I pull on my jeans, my stomach churns with the empty nausea of a bad night's sleep in a strange place, like a New Year's party when I was seventeen.

The grimy mirror does nothing for my skin. Nor does last night's eyeliner.

At least I won't have to deal with David Clark today.

When Michael returns, I've finished my tea and gathered my belongings.

'All sorted?' I ask.

He nods.

'Let's go.'

Michael drops me home, and I shuffle up to the front door, feeling vaguely concerned about him driving as he pulls away. He's had barely any sleep and an allergic reaction. But he's got that steely expression and I know it's useless to argue. I'm too tired, anyway.

I greet Dad and then trudge upstairs, aching for the comfort of my own bed. Not for the first time, I reflect with gratitude that I no longer live in a filthy flat above a chip shop. Coming home has its benefits.

When I next wake up, it's lunchtime. I check my phone and Michael's texted: Pick you up at two. I'd better get a move on.

Imitating a badly acted zombie in a B movie, I stagger around, throwing random clothes into a holdall. Christmas jumper, spare jeans, sparkly top… I throw in my make-up bag and a book, then head to the bathroom.

'Fancy a bacon sandwich?' Dad calls up the stairs.

I love Dad.

When Michael arrives, I've showered and eaten and I'm a little more presentable… but I still look ragged. He looks his usual energetic self, perhaps a little more than usual. He strides around, grabbing my bags and whisking me off like we've got a plane to catch.

'What's the hurry?' I ask, kissing Dad goodbye and running to catch up.

'Just want to beat the traffic.'

On the passenger seat, there's a wool blanket.

'Just in case you get cold,' Michael says, starting the engine.

I fold it over my knees. Thoughtful, but it's not actually that cold. Plus, he's got the heating blasting too. He turns the radio on, and impatiently skips through every station, swerving the car a little.

'How are you feeling?' I venture, once he's settled on a station playing Christmas songs.

'Fine,' he says, then gives me a quick glance with a smile. 'Much better.'

'What did the doctor say?'

He doesn't reply.

'Michael?'

He changes gear, and I see his jaw twitch.

'You didn't go, did you?'

'I had other things—'

'Like what?'

I stare at him in disbelief. It's the last day of term and we weren't even in school, for crying out loud.

'I have another EpiPen, and I'll get it sorted while I'm at my parents.'

I remind myself that he's an adult; he can make his own choices. I breathe in deeply.

The scenery starts to change as we approach the coast, and a creeping sense of dread invades my peaceful contemplation. All the emotions and memories of meeting his parents come back, and now with the added pressure of Christmas, and all the unique ways families celebrate, and being a stranger. Michael's fingertips drum the steering wheel and I guess this excess of adrenalin stems from his nerves too.

He exits the main road and the car climbs a hill.

'Thought we'd take a slight detour,' he says.

I recognise the ruins of Bestward come into view. I turn to Michael in surprise. Michael doesn't do detours. He has an odd, fixed look in his eye. That's when I realise that something is about to happen.

33

Michael

Considering I could have died yesterday, things are going surprisingly well. I can't with any accuracy say how much sleep I managed last night, which might account for why my eyes keep closing for a second too long, and why I feel a gravitational pull to the ground, as if my body craves a horizontal posture.

But what's important is that I don't miss a moment of this life-changing event.

A low mist covers the fields, and gives an ethereal quality to Bestward. The sky is already turning a dusky grey, the sun pale and low on the horizon. It's the winter solstice and sunset is imminent. The place is deserted, and crows are cawing overhead. I would have preferred nightingales, but there you go. Nature doesn't abide by man's demands.

Jen looks stricken for a moment, and I can't wholly be sure whether the emotion of her expression is positive or negative. Does she find this a bit creepy because I sprung it on her without warning? Maybe I should have given her a note at this point to start it all off... Too late now.

'Shall we get some air?' My voice sounds higher than normal and slightly strained. I clear my throat as I open the car door and move round to help her out.

Jen gives me a look of suspicion—that's easy enough to decipher—as she accepts my hand and steps out of the car.

We fasten our coats up as the chill wind blasts our faces. It's not like that in the movies. There's no gentle wind machine to lightly ruffle Jen's hair; she looks like she's going through a vortex at high speed. I pull her towards the ruins, hoping that everything is in place and no one has disturbed it…

We step through an old, bare doorway, arched with stone, and Jen breathes in sharply. The inside of this rather sheltered area is covered with fairy lights like a magical grotto. Jen looks at me.

'What is this?'

'Perhaps you should go and read the message.'

I point to where a vintage teacup is placed, upside down, on a saucer, on one of the steps. Jen steps forward to lift it, and pulls out a piece of paper.

'"Whatever our souls are made of, his and mine are the same",' she reads, eyes meeting mine with immediate recognition. '*Wuthering Heights.*'

'I thought I'd start you off easy,' I shrug, trying to conceal how much I'm enjoying this. 'That's your first clue.'

'Is there something hidden here?' Jen smiles for the first time. '*Wuthering Heights*… is it something up high?'

She starts to look around, and I feel dizzy with happiness. No, actually perhaps I just feel dizzy. I place a hand on the stone wall to steady myself. Jen is bounding over to a raised section where she climbs up and reaches a window ledge.

'Aha!' she cries out, retrieving a jar. She opens the lid, pulls out another slip, and reads. '"O no, it is an ever-fixed mark that looks on tempests and is never shaken".'

'You know where that's from?'

'It's a sonnet, but I don't remember which one.'

'That doesn't matter anyway,' I grin.

'"An ever-fixed mark that looks on tempests"... Maybe the flag?'

She darts away, and I take the opportunity to briefly lower my head between my knees, just to get the circulation going. Then I stride around the wall to catch up with her. Well, stagger.

Jen is looking up and down the flagpole, and finds a tube of pencils hidden at the foot of it. She twists the lid and finds the paper folded inside it, giving me a smile of delight before reading it.

'"If I loved you less, I might be able to talk about it more. But you know what I am. You hear nothing but truth from me." That's Mr Knightley,' she says promptly.

She looks puzzled, and then starts walking around, looking for another clue. Suddenly I hear a bark, and a giant greyhound comes bounding towards me. I panic and move to the side, but I miss my footing and fall in slow motion, inelegantly sprawled on the wet grass while the dog salivates over my head. Right on cue, the music starts.

'Roger!' a woman scolds the dog, but with the inevitable isn't-he-cute undertone to her voice. 'Come here!'

The dog scampers away and I manage to stand by getting on all fours and then pulling myself up on a rock. In the meantime, Pachelbel's "Canon" is blasting around the ruins.

'Michael?' Jen reappears, just as I brush myself down and scowl at the dog and its owner.

'Don't know where that music is coming from,' the dog lady says, mystified.

'It's a Bluetooth speaker,' I say in annoyance, willing her with my eyes to Go Away.

'Ah, technology,' the woman says, with a shrug. 'I like these fairy lights, there must be something going on...'

'Yes, yes there is,' I say pointedly.

'It's a sort of treasure hunt,' Jen tells her.

I want to face palm.

'Ooh, that sounds like fun!'

'I'm stuck on this one,' Jen continues. '"You hear nothing but truth from me".'

'Well, I saw a big mirror as I came in from that direction,' the woman says, pointing.

'Brilliant!'

I watch in despair as Jen heads over there, accompanied by the woman and the dog too. What a way to ruin a moment. I surge with hot, venomous anger. I haven't bust a gut here to set all this up only to be thwarted by some dog walker with her stupid animal. I set off after them, calling to the woman.

'Er, perhaps you could take the dog and—' Here I resort to gesturing, a shooing sort of motion.

'Ohhhhh,' the woman inexplicably raises her voice. 'I see. I'd better leave you to it then.'

She clips a lead around Roger's neck, then gives me an over-exaggerated wink.

'I hope she says yes.'

As she finally walks off, Jen stops dead in her tracks and swivels round to face me, the mirror forgotten.

'Says yes?' she repeats. 'Michael… you're not… you're not going to *propose*, are you?'

I shift awkwardly, cursing every dog owner in England for stealing my proverbial thunder. The violins are playing majestically on my speaker and the sky is turning pink.

'Aren't you going to check the mirror?' I point towards it, seeing myself in the reflection. I look vampiric, I'm so pale.

Jen walks slowly up to the ornate frame, which is leaning against a wall. She tips it forward and untapes the folded paper on the back. She opens it out, frowns, then steps back to hold it out, facing the mirror, in order to read it in the reflection.

'"You are too generous to trifle with me".' Her voice is low, like a murmur.

Incidentally, mirror writing is hard to pull off. I had to try that one several times.

'Jen,' I say, ready for my big moment.

I kneel down before her—perhaps a little too enthusiastically, because I lose my balance a bit, but I put my hand down to steady myself, then fumble in my coat pocket for the small box. Her hand flies to her mouth. Perhaps she will cry with happiness when she sees the diamond. I open the box, hoping that from her angle, it's sparkling and lustrous.

'I love you. Will you marry me?'

My head pounds with adrenalin, and it feels like time stands still. The wind whips through the battlements and I involuntarily shiver, my hand still holding out the ring.

I think I expected her to say something by now.

'Michael,' she says finally, 'I didn't expect this…'

No, I thoroughly disguised every aspect of this perfectly executed plan, I silently congratulate myself.

'That ring looks amazing.'

'It's exactly your size. Would you like to try it on?'

'Well…'

I lift the delicate band from the velvet cushion and slip it onto the right finger. I've imagined this so many times. It does look perfect on her; I knew it would. But she still hasn't given me an answer.

'Will you marry me?' I repeat hopefully.

She doesn't speak, but she nods her head. That's enough for me.

34
Jen

I won't lie and say I've never imagined this moment, as I gawp at the prettiest diamond ring I've ever seen, but it feels like an out-of-body experience, or a dream. It doesn't feel real. I wouldn't be surprised if Michael produces a black hat and a whole flock of doves flies out.

I touch the diamond with the tip of my index finger. How did he know the right size? When did he order this?

'I love you,' Michael says, cupping my face and kissing me. 'Come and see the sunset.'

He pulls me out of the ruin and the sky is dappled pink and gold. Suddenly the dreariness of the day has melted away into a spectacular finish. A flock of birds, moving like the tail of a fish, sweep past us. Michael grasps my shoulder, his eyes gleaming with adrenalin and sunglow. I wonder if he's had any sleep.

'Perfect,' he sighs.

Slow to ignite, a spark of excitement fizzes my dull mind. I am going to marry Michael Chase. No more 'only meet up on the weekend' or stupid teenage pledges to separate us. Our lives are going to join together.

'We should go and break the news to my parents.'

Break the news. It'll be like taking a jack hammer to their cabinet of glassware. I gulp.

'Just need to collect up the lights and things.' Michael hurries back into the ruin and starts gathering up the fairy lights and other items. 'If you just take these…'

I hold out my arms for a bundle of lights and then head to the car, still in a daze.

'I should just text Christina too,' Michael says, tapping his phone manically. 'She helped to set all this up.'

Oh, so that was why he had been in touch with her. I blush, remembering my jealousy.

In the car, Michael winds down all the windows.

'Just a bit of fresh air to keep me awake.'

I frown and shiver into my coat.

'Do you want me to drive?'

'It's only down the road.'

Thankfully we arrive unscathed, but I'm conscious that we're bearing a giant bombshell. I can't even think about ringing Dad or Katie yet—not when I haven't even got my own head around this. Besides, perhaps Michael's dad will disinherit him or something. I brace myself as we approach the front door, decorated with a luxurious wreath. Heather opens it, with a huge smile, beckoning us inside and then hugging us each in turn.

'So good to see you.' She gives me an extra squeeze, and I swallow my sense of guilt.

'Merry Christmas.' Ezra enters the hallway, hugs Michael, then offers me his hand to shake. I put my left hand behind my back to hide the ring.

'Merry Christmas!' Michael chirps back, like Michael Caine as a reformed Ebenezer Scrooge. I half expect muppets to appear and start singing from the living room. 'I just gave Jen her Christmas present—take a look!'

He grabs my left hand and holds it out, the diamond sparkling like a star with its own gravitational pull. Heather gasps and then squeals, throwing her arms around me, obscuring my view of Ezra.

'Well, congratulations.' I hear his voice, quiet and understated. 'I'll go and get a bottle of champagne.'

Soon we're in the lounge, perched on the spotless cream sofas, holding champagne flutes.

'Cheers.' Michael takes a mouthful, then puts it on the side. 'I've just got to go upstairs a minute.'

I sip my drink nervously, while Ezra avoids looking at me, and Heather smiles shyly.

'So, when do you think the wedding will be?' she asks politely.

'We haven't really discussed it yet,' I croak, swigging more champagne.

'You could speak to the vicar tonight,' Ezra says.

Or I could just enjoy the carol service.

'Will there be many people there, at the service?' I ask, trying to steer the conversation.

'Probably around a hundred,' Ezra replies. He's coolly polite, but without Heather's warmth.

'I'm just doing a light supper before we go,' Heather says. 'Ezra, could you help me in the kitchen?'

She gives him a meaningful stare. He sighs, puts his glass down, and follows her. I down the rest of my drink and then sit back, my thoughts a hot mess. Ezra thinks I'm a gold-digger. What's my dad going to say? And Katie? Should I ring them now or wait till I get home? What about all the questions people are going to ask, like when's the wedding, where is it going to be? I feel overwhelmed just considering all of the possibilities.

I remember that Michael still hasn't returned. I tiptoe past the kitchen, where I can hear plates clattering and Heather and Ezra probably having an emergency pow-wow, and creep up the stairs.

I stand in the doorway of Michael's room, pushing the door open, and see him fast asleep on his bed.

Great.

I slip back downstairs and reclaim my position, perched on the sofa. The clock ticks and the sound echoes around the silent room. It's now twilight and the gloom seeps through the windows, framed with luxurious curtains. My eyes flit over the pictures and furniture; there's a Christmas tree this time, in the corner. It looks slightly Victorian with red bows and golden bells on it. It shouldn't surprise me: if I've learned anything about Michael's parents, it's that they like Tradition.

I check my phone and I'm just about to text Katie when the doorbell rings. I listen as footsteps tread the length of the hallway, the door creaks open, and there's the sound of greeting.

'Welcome home, darling. It's so good to see you.'

It must be Michael's sister, Rachel. I raise my eyes to the ceiling, sending 'wake up' signals. Please don't make me do this alone, Michael.

'Now, come on through, and you can meet Jen.'

I hastily rise to my feet in preparation, as a petite girl with a pixie haircut, the same dark shade as Michael's, steps into the room. She flashes me a smile and her eyes sparkle.

'Hi!' she says, reaching out and gripping my hand. 'It's so nice to meet you.'

She speaks in a confident, slightly-louder-than-normal way, but with warmth and enthusiasm.

'And you.' I smile back.

'Where's Michael?' She looks around for him.

'He's… fallen asleep.' I look apologetically at Heather, who is standing behind Rachel. Ezra's right next to her.

'Is he all right?' Heather asks with concern.

'He didn't get much sleep last night,' I say, before I realise how that sounds. 'I mean... I'm not sure if he told you... He had a reaction.'

I can feel my cheeks on fire and Rachel looks from me to her parents, before flopping down onto the sofa.

'Was it serious?' Ezra asks.

'A paramedic came. We gave him an EpiPen shot but A&E was full, so we stayed at the pub and he was sick.'

'Maybe we should cancel our plans,' Heather says to Ezra, laying a hand on his arm.

'Has he seen a doctor?' Ezra questions me.

'I wasn't with him for most of the day... but I don't think he has.'

Mainly because he was setting up clues and a diamond ring at the ruins of a castle.

An alarm beeps from the kitchen, and Heather hurries off, looking distressed.

'Why didn't you go to A&E this morning?'

'Dad, why don't you ask Michael?' Rachel intervenes before I can reply. 'I mean, if he's asleep, let him sleep for a bit.'

'Well, we were going to eat now.' He sounds annoyed.

'Just save him a plate for later.'

It's when we're sitting around the table, and I pick up my fork, that Rachel notices my ring. I'm not sure which was preferable: the deadly silence, or her loud exclamation,

'Is that an engagement ring?'

35

Michael

Generally I find power naps highly effective in giving the body a short dose of comatisation and then re-energising upon awakening. But when I open my eyes, it's with the sudden shock of realising I've been asleep, and the disorientation of having no idea what time it is.

I twist my watch and read that it's fifteen minutes before the carol service is about to begin.

I jump off the bed and leap onto the landing, bracing myself on the bannister while my bleary eyes adjust to see Jen and my family standing by the door, wearing coats and ready to leave.

'Wait for me.'

'Michael, are you all right?' Mum rushes towards me.

'Fine.' I run my hand over my face and attempt to walk down the stairs normally.

'We heard about what happened,' Dad says. 'Do you need to see a doctor?'

'No,' I reply curtly, then notice Rachel and give her a hug. 'Good to see you, Rach.'

'You look terrible,' she says, with an apologetic grin. 'Why don't you just go back to bed?'

'No, I don't want to miss it.' I shrug into my coat and pull my shoes on. I take Jen's hand while her eyes search my face, assessing me.

'Well, we need to leave now or we're going to be late.'

I can tell by Dad's tone that he's annoyed.

'Congratulations, by the way.' Rach gives me a nudge.

Dad stomps off out of the front door.

The cold night air helps to sharpen my alertness again. I inhale deeply and look up at the distant tapestry of stars overhead. The excitement of being engaged to Jen courses through me like electricity. I squeeze her hand as the village Christmas tree just outside the church comes into view. All these familiar rituals take on new meaning now that I can share them with her.

We join the funnel of people shuffling through the church doors, and Jen gives me a grin of delight as she sees the glow of hundreds of candles. Not all of them are real; there's plenty of LEDs and fairy lights too, but the effect is still magical. Dad mutters about being so far towards the back, but we can still hear the sound of the choir amplified in the stone arches of the roof above.

They begin with 'Silent Night'. It sounds unearthly, as their voices rise in a beautiful crescendo, and it seems spoiled when the whole congregation join in. In the hush at the end, it feels like a rare, treasured moment of peace. Every day I rush from one minute to the next, the hours measured by the school bell, and this kind of stillness seems impossible. Here, the quiet feels deep enough to actually penetrate my soul.

I've heard these readings and carols many times before, but somehow, tonight feels different. Perhaps it's the adrenalin from proposing to Jen; perhaps it's thinking of us getting married in this very building. Tears well in my eyes and I feel overwhelmed with the sheer beauty of life. I never thought I would find someone like

Jen, let alone that she would feel the same way. I have been undeservedly blessed.

36

Jen

Michael squeezes my hand and I shift against the hard pew. I've never experienced anything like this before. The choir are all in white robes, singing soaring harmonies like something on Classic FM, and everyone in the congregation is dressed in smart woollen coats, pashmina scarves or polished shoes. It's like going back in time to the 1950s or something. I mean, it's beautiful, and a bit eerie too. I don't know many of these carols well enough to sing along, so I strain my eyes at the tiny words and allow Ezra's booming voice to compensate for my own. He wants us to talk to the vicar about booking the wedding. What would I look like, walking down the aisle in this place? Out of place, that's what.

I know I'm not a religious person, but Michael isn't either, not really. So are we going to go through the motions of a churchy service with archaic vows? It makes me squirm, but even more: the thought of saying that to his parents.

Sorry, Ezra, but I'm not really religious...

That's not going to go down well.

My thoughts are rollercoastering round so fast I barely notice the readings and songs. Finally, a hush settles, and the vicar stands to give an address.

'I'd like to ask you all to take a moment to consider this question: what are your ambitions for your life?'

He gets my attention. I need to sort out my writing, and actually get something published. I suppose I've always wanted my own family, and getting engaged is a step towards that. I glance at Michael's profile. He probably wants to be like David Clark: running several schools by the time he's forty. It niggles me: the feeling of not being good enough for him.

'Mary was engaged. She was planning her wedding—as, I believe, some young couples among us are also doing.'

Surely he can't mean us? I look at Michael in surprise. His lip curls in a sly smile.

'She was willing to lay aside her ambitions, and to threaten her own hopes and dreams, in order to obey what God was calling her to do,' the vicar continues. 'It was not an easy path before her: the shame of being pregnant, the doubts of Joseph, and isolation from the community. But Mary's faith meant that she was willing to take a path of suffering, trusting that God would continue to do great things for her.'

It must be nice to have faith, really. It must make the darkness a bit brighter. Without expecting to, I'm thinking about Mum again. The darkness of cancer, of grief. Of refusing to forgive her.

'I'm sure everyone here can think of some suffering they had to go through, or perhaps are enduring right now. Perhaps this Christmas is painful. Remember that God is not far away, somewhere up there. Christmas is all about God coming down to this earth, as a helpless baby. This gave Mary hope. This gives us hope, too.'

His words juxtapose with the bleakness of my thoughts, and my eyes burn with the sting of there being no hope: Mum is gone. The finality of her death chokes me every time I think of it. There will be no recovery, no reconciliation.

'God may not take your suffering away,' the vicar says, and I refocus on his face. It's a crowded building, but it feels like he's talking directly to me. 'But God's solution for suffering was ultimately seen thirty-three years after Jesus was born in Bethlehem. In His suffering of dying, and then rising to life, Jesus broke the power of sin and death for you and for me. Anyone who believes in Him shall not die, but have eternal life. You see, just like for Mary, our hope comes from faith, not from our circumstances. Mary's circumstances would not have given her much hope. Perhaps yours don't, either. Faith sees things that are unseen, things that are eternal. May God give you eyes to see this Christmas.'

I'm still stunned into a stupor when everyone stands to sing the last carol, so I rise hurriedly and brush my hair out of my face. My hand touches something wet and I realise I'm crying. I sniff and search my pockets for a tissue. Nothing. I wipe my face as best I can, and my fingers shake as I turn the page of the hymn book. 'O Come All Ye Faithful'. It's a good job I can't sing because I would be such a hypocrite. I'm the opposite of faithful. If the suffering I've been through was a test, I failed. I didn't believe. I didn't trust. I didn't have hope.

O come let us adore Him…

God, is it too late for me?

All I can hear is the swell of the singing. Then someone gently prods my shoulder. I look to my right, and Rachel holds out a packet of tissues to me. I take them gratefully and try to clean myself up before the last song ends.

One advantage of being near the back is that we're primely located for a swift exit. Once the final blessing has been pronounced, Ezra stands and we shuffle along the pew and into the aisle, just a few steps away from the arch over the entrance. I hadn't counted on the vicar being there waiting to shake our hands.

'See you at midnight mass,' he says to Ezra and Heather, then shakes Michael's hand warmly. 'It's lovely to be able to congratulate you in person. Did you get my message about the course starting on January 5th?'

'Yes, we'll be there,' Michael says, with a sideways glance at me. We?

'Congratulations, Jen.' The vicar turns to me with a smile. 'I look forward to getting to know you better.'

I give a smile that probably doesn't hide my confusion at all, and then hiss to Michael as we move forwards,

'What does he mean?'

'Er, I meant to talk to you before the service but...' He looks ahead to where his parents are standing, joined by Rachel.

'Yes?' I press.

'I signed us up for a marriage preparation course.' He gives a sheepish grin.

'What?' I raise my voice without thinking, then continue in a hiss when I see his parents looking over. 'We only got engaged a few hours ago!'

'Good job you said yes, then.'

I stare at him until he shifts awkwardly.

'Michael,' I say carefully. 'There's something else you're not telling me.'

He takes a deep breath.

'I wanted to check whether they had availability for Easter, and that's when Steve told me about the course...'

'Availability?'

'Well, some people book these things two years in advance, so...'

'Wait, are you telling me you've booked the *wedding*?' I can't stop the shrillness of my voice now.

His face turns slightly red.

'It's just pencilled in...'

'With a permanent marker.'

I take a step away from him and shake off his arm.

'So come on then, Michael, what's the date for *our* big day? When were you planning to tell me: the week before?'

'Why don't we go back to the house and talk about it?' he says, looking around pointedly.

'Sure, I'll get my diary out and see if I'm free for one of the most important days of my *life*.'

'Michael!' Christina calls from the church entrance.

He gives me an apologetic look, and then walks over to her, completely ignoring my warning stare.

'Everything okay?' Rachel holds back from joining her parents, who have started walking home.

I stride forwards and she falls into step beside me.

'I can't believe he booked the church without even asking me—without even *proposing* to me first!'

She winces.

'Michael is… frighteningly efficient.'

'He's faster than a bolt of lightning, and I can't keep up.' I let out a sob involuntarily, wiping my eyes again. She must think I'm an emotional freak. 'I haven't even told my family we're engaged yet.'

'He's obviously so nuts about you that he wants everything sorted as soon as possible.' Rachel smiles. 'Look, I can talk to him, if you want.'

I sniff and nod.

'Sure.'

37

Michael

I'm very grateful to Christina for all her help, but right now I'm conscious of Jen stalking off and I really need to catch up with her.

'It was all amazing,' I say, my eyes following Jen. 'Thank you so much.'

'It was a pleasure,' Christina says warmly. 'You'll have to both come round for a coffee and we can catch up properly.'

I mutter something incoherent (best not to make any more rash social engagements without Jen), make my escape and dart towards Jen, but Rachel stops in front of me and grabs my arm.

'Give her a minute,' she says. 'I need to talk to you.'

'I've upset her,' I say, unnecessarily.

'Yes, but do you even understand why?' Rachel sounds exasperated.

'She didn't want me to book the church.'

'That's not the point, is it?'

I look at Rachel blankly.

'There's not many people like you,' she says. 'You get an idea and within half an hour, you've drawn the plans, hired a team and laid a foundation.'

'What's wrong with that? At least I get things done.'

'But your marriage isn't something to just *get done*,' Rachel points out. 'It isn't another item on your to-do list. If you treat it like that, Jen is going to give you that ring back and call it all off.'

'Did she say that?'

'No.' Rachel shakes her head. 'But you need to stop acting like a psycho.'

'Okay,' I say automatically, even though I have no idea what she means.

She lets go of my arm so I'm free to run and catch up with Jen, who is walking ahead.

'Jen,' I begin, 'I'm sorry.'

'For what?' she snaps, tightening her scarf and tugging on it forcefully.

'I was so excited I rushed ahead and I didn't think—'

'No, you didn't. Do you realise I'm going to call my sister and say, by the way, I'm engaged, and the wedding's in three months?'

'One hundred and twelve days actually,' I automatically correct her. 'More like three months and three weeks, to be exact.'

'Most people spend at least a year planning their wedding, often more.' She gestures wildly. 'Everyone's going to think we're crazy.'

'Since when have you cared what everyone else thinks?' I point out. I mean, she has a cat poster on her classroom wall. 'Besides, the reason that everyone takes so long to plan weddings is because the venues are all booked up. Which is why I reserved the church.'

'And what's this marriage course thing?' She ignores my argument completely.

'They encourage anyone who wants to get married in the church to attend it,' I explain. 'It's to help with communication—'

Jen snorts.

'Well one of us certainly needs some help with that.'

'So you're happy to do it, then?' I've got her with that one.

'Sure.' She sighs and raises her eyebrows. 'I just hope I'll have time for it with all the other things I've now got one hundred and twelve days to organise.'

'I'll do whatever you want me to do,' I promise.

'That's great Michael, and I appreciate it, but you're not going to buy my wedding dress. Or sort out bridesmaids. Or contact my family. And I want to know *exactly* what you're doing from this moment on. Absolutely no secrets. Do you understand me?'

'Yes.' I nod, wishing I didn't feel like some scolded Year 11 pupil.

'Now, when we get back, we're going to sit down *together* and work out what *we* both want. And we're not going to tell anyone anything until we've got that straight.'

'Right. Okay.'

Trying not to act 'like a psycho', I lead Jen back to the house, and she doesn't pull her hand away this time when I take it.

Back inside, Mum is preparing mulled wine and Rach is sprawled on the sofa on her phone.

'Do you want a drink?' Dad asks, appearing in the hallway as we remove our coats.

'Er…' I hesitate, looking at Jen. Her eyes glower a reminder: *you promised*. 'No thanks, we just need to… sort a few things out.'

Dad's face sets in disapproval, but he's going to have to get used to me having other priorities. *I'm* going to have to get used to having other priorities.

We go up to my bedroom, the only place we can really get any privacy in this house. Seeing the hastily left, unmade bed reminds me of how little sleep I've had. So tempting. I hand Jen my planner then collapse onto the mattress.

'Back page,' I direct, my voice muffled in the pillow.

She opens it up and sucks in her breath sharply.

'Potential venues for reception, photographers, florists, car hire, music… What were you going to do if I saw this before you proposed?'

'You never look in my planner.'

'Lucky for you,' she sniffs. 'This is completely overwhelming.'

She shuts the book and goes quiet for a moment. When I open my eyes to peer over, she's sat on my swivel chair with her head in her hands.

'Jen, don't be upset.' I reach out towards her.

'I just need to get my head around all this,' she says, lowering her hands.

I can just about reach far enough to brush her arm with my fingertips.

'Look, as long as we get married, I don't care about everything else. We can do whatever you want.'

She gives me a small smile.

'You might regret that.'

'Okay, no cat posters,' I add, closing my eyes again.

38

Jen

I'm sitting in Michael's room while he's dead to the world, in a comatose slumber. I run my hands over the smooth cover of the planner. What kind of wedding do I want? Is it okay to plan a wedding in three months? It feels like there are so many questions that I can't answer.

I think back to the church, the stone arches and the stained-glass windows. I imagine myself walking down the aisle in a long, white dress.

What's the alternative? Shuffling into Whidlock registry office, on the main street where all the buses wheeze and fumigate the atmosphere?

Or my dad's local parish church, where I barely know who the vicar is? It wouldn't seem right to slight Michael's family's church, when they have such strong links there, for a church I've never set foot inside before.

It seems that Michael's church is the best option. But three months' notice? What's the alternative? We could wait until Whitsun. But then, there's only one week off school, whereas at Easter, there's two. Or the summer holiday. Wedding peak season. I bet every venue would have been booked up for two years' in advance for those premium dates. Next Christmas? Do I really want to get married when it's freezing cold? Plus, that's a whole year away. Whilst the three-month option seems scarily close, part of me feels disappointed at the thought of postponing.

As much as Michael's vow is a pain, the idea of finally being together… living under the same roof, sharing a bed… Isn't that what I've been longing for? Surely his keenness for all this shows that he wants that too? Why would I put that off, just because I didn't choose the date myself?

What about this long list of things to book? More importantly, who's going to pay for all this? From staffroom conversations, I know that people spend thousands on their big day. Michael's family may be well off, but Dad can't afford it, nor can I.

I need to speak to Katie.

I bite my lip and tap the desk impatiently while the phone rings.

'Hey Jen.'

The sound of her voice makes me exhale in relief.

'Hey,' I breathe.

'Are you okay?' she asks, instantly alert.

'I just… I have some news.' I look at the ceiling and wait for a second, gathering my courage. 'Michael proposed.'

'What? Ahhh!' she screeches. 'Did you say yes?'

'Yes of course, you muppet,' I blurt, half laughing, but feeling tears in my eyes again.

'What happened? Tell me everything. Wait—can I be a bridesmaid?'

'Yes, please,' I say. 'Look, I'm going to need a lot of help. Like you might have to take the photos and make the cake too.'

She laughs.

'I'm serious, Katie, I don't know how I'm going to pay for all this stuff…'

'You only just got engaged, you can save up,' she replies airily.

'Well, that's the other thing I need to tell you… Michael's booked the church.'

'He's *what?*'

'Three months. I've got three months to plan a wedding. What am I going to do?'

Katie responds with her favourite stream of swear words.

'That's not helpful,' I comment.

'Can't you just change the date?'

'The summer's going to be all booked up. I don't really want to wait until next Christmas. Plus it's too cold.'

'Have you spoken to Dad yet?'

'No.' I massage my forehead. 'I can't ask him for a ten grand showpiece wedding. I need to work out how to do this in a way that won't bankrupt us for the next ten years.'

'What about Michael? Isn't he loaded?'

'His family are well off, but traditionally the bride's family pay for the wedding.'

Katie utters some expletives to give her opinion on this historic tradition.

'Again, not helpful,' I repeat.

'Okay.' She regroups. 'What are the options then? Get a bank loan? Remortgage Dad's house? Or just… go budget?'

'I don't want anything fancy.' I think of those gossip magazine wedding photo shoots and shudder. 'Just the people who matter most to be there. And a dress.'

'Right then,' Katie says. 'We'll go sale shopping after Christmas.'

My stomach flips. Me, buying a wedding dress?

'Dad's here by the way. Do you want to speak to him?'

'Yes. Yes, all right.'

I switch the phone to my other ear, bracing myself.

'Hello?'

'Hi Dad,' I say, in a forced cheery tone. 'Just wanted to tell you the news… Michael and I just got engaged.'

'Congratulations,' he replies calmly. He doesn't sound surprised. 'I hope it all went off okay, then?'

'You, you knew about this?' I look at Michael, but he's still out cold.

'Oh yes, Michael came round to ask my permission a while ago. I think it was while you were out at one of those quiz nights.'

My jaw literally drops.

'Oh,' I clear my throat. 'I didn't realise you knew.'

'Well, I didn't want to spoil the surprise. I'm sure everything was executed with perfect brilliance. Michael never seems to do anything by halves.'

'Yes, that's certainly true.'

'Anyway, you go off and celebrate. We'll have a good catch up when you get back.'

I hang up and stare blankly at Michael's old bedroom wall. I hold the engagement ring and twist it absent-mindedly. This is it, then. It's really happening. I'm engaged.

39

Michael

The sound of my phone ringing wakes me up. It stings to open my eyes, and the residue of a headache throbs as I reach out to grab my phone. Instead my palm hits a solid but warm obstacle.

There's someone in my bed.

I push myself up, the ringing still insistent, and grope around the sleeping form of Jen to find my phone, knocking over a glass of water and a pointless, ill-placed pot of pens.

She's not supposed to be sleeping in here, and my dad is going to Freak Out.

I finally grab the phone and see the familiar sight of David Clark's name on the screen.

'Hello?' I say, my voice clogged up with grogginess.

'Michael?' David usually sounds urgent, but this sounds more like panic. 'I've been trying to get hold of someone, and you're the first person who picked up. We have a situation.'

'What's the matter?' I ask, straining round to catch a glimpse of a clock. 7:30 a.m.

'The contractors arrived on site at seven this morning. They needed to replace some cabling in the Science block. One of them noticed a computer cable coming down from the ceiling. They think there's asbestos contamination.'

'Didn't we have a survey done recently?'

'We were given information by the local authority just to continue to contain the asbestos on site. Most schools in this area are under the same asbestos management plan.'

'Did you ring the council?'

'Yes, they're sending someone to consult with the contractor and getting in a specialist. But you know what this means.'

'What?'

'They were going to open a consultation on merging Whidlock with Prestfield. Now they'll probably fast-track the proposal and move us onto Prestfield's site.'

'How soon?' My head was throbbing anyway before trying to make any kind of calculation.

'I don't know.' David has never sounded so defeated.

'Look,' I say, sounding much surer than I feel, 'once they've checked the site, they will probably find it's just one area that needs to be blocked off. The rest of the site will function as normal. We'll just need some Portakabins to relocate the Science rooms.'

'Yes, Portakabins.' David starts to perk up. 'Okay, I've got to go. I'll keep you updated.'

I place my phone back down onto the desk and look at Jen, still sleeping. Blissfully unaware of the chaos that's about to erupt in our school. I rub my forehead and sigh, then peek under the blind to check the colour of the sky. Dark, with a patch of light breaking through in the distance. Perfect for a run.

I fumble around pulling on my gear, then I slip out of the back door and head for the coast path. All of the fuggy ill-feeling seems to dissipate into the clear, cold atmosphere, and I'm thankful for the restorative power of sleep. I feel like I could scale a mountain again. Without thinking, I'm heading for Bestward, drawn like a magnet to the place that's become the epicentre of my hopes and dreams in the last few weeks.

However messed up things are at Whidlock, I've got better things to think about. On reflection, I'm amazed that the proposal went as well as it did, considering I was catatonic for most of it. I make a note to send Christina some flowers to thank her for helping. I feel bad about how I had to dash off last night when things were going sour with Jen.

Now we're really engaged, we have a wedding to plan, and a whole future to map out. As I consider, I'm not even sure how much Whidlock is going to be part of that future. I never took the job with a view of it being a place to stay long-term. I never expected to meet Jen. How much is she tied to the school she used to attend as a student? How is she going to cope with the consultation process of merging it with Prestfield, which clearly is going to be a paperwork exercise? I know that Whidlock means a lot to her, but at the end of the day, a school needs to run efficiently. These old buildings are a nightmare. The central heating system is thirty years old and manual operation only. That means you can't put a timer switch on; the caretaker has to switch it on in the morning and turn it off at the end of the day. The asbestos doesn't surprise me. The health and safety of that school is a disaster zone. But Jen takes everything to heart, and I can see her passionately standing up against the Council's plans.

Both of us get too sucked into school as it is. We've got other priorities now. I wish I'd told David about our engagement, but there wasn't really time. That conversation will have to wait.

There are more immediate conversations I need to consider: with my parents.

I wince as I remember Dad's expression when I told them yesterday. And then I wince again as I realise I left Jen alone with them, drinking champagne, while I accidentally fell asleep upstairs. I wonder what they said.

There will be no avoiding a conversation today. I still haven't really asked Jen about what she wants, so I need to make sure we're on the same page before we face the barrage of well-meant curiosity and keenness from my mum, and barbed comments from my dad.

What if she says she doesn't want to get married in the church? She wants somewhere else, and we'll have to change the date, and start all over again?

I vaguely recall handing her my notebook last night. Yet again, I abandoned her to sleep. I hope she doesn't hate me already.

I check my watch and pound my feet a little faster; I want to be back by the time she wakes up, so she doesn't have to face breakfast alone with my family. What was Rach's advice? *Don't act like a psycho*. Right. Roger that.

40

Jen

The smell of Michael's aftershave wakes me up. It's that minty, woody aroma and as my eyes open, the blur shifts into focus on Michael's contoured torso, a towel round his waist.

'Wow,' I say, making him jump. 'That's a good view to wake up to.'

'Shhh,' he says, making more noise than I did. 'You're not supposed to be in here.'

He tries pulling on a pair of boxers with the towel still wrapped around him, nearly falling over in the process. I snigger.

'Surely now we're engaged…' I point out.

'We've come this far,' Michael says, whipping a polo shirt over his head. 'It's not long to wait.'

Something shifts in his eyes and he sits down on the bed next to me.

'That is, if you're happy to go ahead? Because we really don't have to keep the booking, if you'd rather choose something different. I'm sorry if I made you feel like you had no choice in your own wedding day.'

I smile. Having a good night's sleep, and next to Michael (even though it was contraband), has put me in an amenable state of mind.

'I thought about it, and I realised that if we don't go with your date, we'll be looking at delaying till maybe next Christmas.' I reach for his hand. 'I don't want to wait that long.'

He squeezes my hand and smiles with evident relief.

'Me neither.'

He leans in to kiss me, even though I must smell terrible, but I can't resist the opportunity to inhale him. It's like when I unwittingly sniffed a petrol cap as a kid and was nearly knocked out by the fumes.

'But Michael,' I say, once I have the power of speech again, 'I need you to understand that this can't be a high-class event. I don't want tuxes, and swans, and ice sculptures, and there's no way my family can afford that anyway.'

'Why do you think I would want that?' He raises an eyebrow.

I indicate with my hand, meaning to emphasise the house, but I end up pointing to his (very ordinary) desk chair.

'What I'm trying to say…' I clear my throat. '…is that your parents have a lot of money, and my dad…'

'This is our wedding,' he says. 'It shouldn't be down to either of our parents to foot the bill.'

'There's a lot of traditions that go with weddings…'

'We don't have to follow them.'

'Seriously? Says the guy who booked a church and took a True Love Waits vow?'

Michael's hypocrisy leaves me breathless sometimes.

'Okay, I mean the silly let's-spend-money-we-don't-have traditions.'

'So you're okay with keeping things simple?' I emphasise, as if I'm talking to a Year 7 pupil who doesn't know how to underline the date.

'Of course,' Michael affirms. 'Simple.'

He waits a beat before adding,

'So I'll cancel the twenty-piece band then?'

'What?'

'Just joking!'

He leaps up before I can whack his (annoyingly muscled) shoulder.

'Do you want to get dressed for breakfast? I saw my mum making cinnamon rolls.'

One of the best things about staying here is definitely the food. I can smell the delicious aroma as we walk down the stairs, and it helps to ease the awkward clenching feeling in my stomach about facing the family as an officially engaged couple.

Ezra and Heather are sitting at the dining table, and Heather greets us enthusiastically, while Ezra says 'good morning' with a frown, which somewhat lessens the effect. Heather passes us a basket of cinnamon rolls which are the size of my head, and then starts pouring coffee. Rachel isn't there, so I feel less bad for sleeping in.

'How are you feeling?' Ezra asks his son.

'Much better, thanks,' Michael says, tearing into his roll. 'Thanks so much for this, Mum.'

'My pleasure.' Heather smiles. 'Jen, do you take sugar?'

'No thanks.'

I clutch the coffee cup gratefully. I think I'm going to need something stronger than tea for this conversation.

'We were hoping to be able to talk to you a bit more last night,' Ezra begins, unable to resist the dig, 'but anyway… could you perhaps tell us a bit more about your plans for…' He clears his throat here, struggling to pronounce the words. '…getting married?'

'Well…' Michael chews and swallows. 'I booked the church for April 12th.'

It's the first time he's told me the actual date, and my stomach flips with excitement but also raw fear at how real and close that sounds. Heather must be thinking the same thing, because she gasps, and Ezra starts spluttering and choking on his coffee.

'Do you mean, *this* April? As in, this year?' he says incredulously.

Oh great. This is a foretaste of what everyone's reaction is going to be like.

'Yes,' Michael says in a 'why not?' kind of way.

'How exciting,' Heather exhales.

'What's the rush?' Ezra pushes.

Michael's jaw sets.

'I've found the woman I want to spend the rest of my life with,' he says, and a warmth spreads through my cheeks.

Ezra can't really say anything to that.

'Don't these things take a lot of time to prepare?' he says, with less certainty this time, looking to Heather for back-up.

'Well, it's a long time since we got married.' She gives a nervous laugh.

'Jen and I want to keep it simple,' Michael says, placing his hand over mine. 'We don't want a fuss.'

I catch Heather's eye and the flicker of disappointment in it.

'But we need your help,' I say quickly, to Heather in particular. 'We want you to be involved.'

Michael looks at me in surprise. I know I said I didn't want it to be a high-class event, but I don't want to cold-shoulder Heather when she's made so much effort to welcome me. If her cooking is anything to go by, she will be an amazing asset.

She smiles warmly.

'Whatever I can do, I would be happy to help.'

'Cinnamon rolls!' Rachel enters, with an old sweater and pyjama bottoms on. 'Thanks Mum!'

She plonks down into a chair and looks up.

'I haven't interrupted a wedding planning meeting, have I?'

'No,' Michael says decisively, pouring her some coffee.

'Phew,' she says, taking a swig. 'All that boring stuff about matching shades... *Magenta* not *red*, Martello... Just don't choose yellow and it will all be fine.'

'Well, I've already chosen a pineapple theme,' I announce. 'So there will be yellow.'

Rachel's jaw drops open and I see Michael gulp.

'Oh,' she says. 'Well, I'm sure that'll be great.'

'I'm just joking.' I grin. It was so worth it for that moment.

Rachel guffaws in relief.

'I can't believe you just did that to me.'

I laugh with her, and Michael grins and shakes his head.

'Michael, I approve of your choice,' she says, raising her coffee mug in a mock toast. 'Welcome to the family, Jen.'

Two out of three ain't bad.

41

Michael

After breakfast, Jen grabs my planner and we sit together on the edge of the bed.

'The first thing we need to do is draw up a guest list,' she says. 'Because once we've got an idea about numbers, we can find a venue for the reception.'

'Right.' I start drawing up columns. 'Your family, my family, friends.'

'My dad, Katie, and Steph,' Jen says. 'Deena and Clare.'

I jot their names down then look up expectantly.

'That's it,' she says.

'Don't you have any extended family?'

'Yes, but they're in Jamaica.'

'You don't think they might want to come?'

'I doubt it.'

'What about your dad's side of the family?'

'I have an uncle Max, but he's a recluse.'

'We should probably invite him, even if he decides not to come.' I write his name down. 'What about uni friends?'

'I was living at home, remember? I didn't have housemates. I had a couple of friends, but no one I kept in touch with. It was just too hard with everything going on at home.'

I reach for her hand and squeeze it. She's had such a tough time with her mum dying, and having to look after her sister.

'You write down your side now.'

I start with my parents, Rachel, then my aunts and uncles, cousins, Grandma, Dan, Louise, Alex and Kyle. Already this list is looking very unbalanced.

'What about David?' I ask, knowing what Jen's reaction will be.

'No way.'

I feel bad, but I can probably fob him off with 'close family only' or something along those lines.

'It's about twenty-five people.' I total it up so far. 'What do you think?'

'That's great.' Jen nods. 'It's small, manageable, keep the costs low. Now let's look at the venues.'

Using my laptop, we view all the hotels and country clubs in the area, but every single one of them is booked already.

'Let's take a tea break,' Jen groans.

I bring the notebook down with us, thinking I can scribble a few extra ideas while the kettle boils. Mum hears us coming and immediately starts arranging biscuits on a plate.

'How are you getting on?' she asks.

'We drew up a guest list,' I tell her. 'But all the venues are booked.'

'Can I see?'

I hand her the notebook. She scans through the names, her brow furrowed.

'It's quite a small list.' She looks at me questioningly. 'It might be good to go over it together some time.'

'Well there's no point adding more names when we can't find a venue to accommodate us as it is.'

'Have you spoken to Christina?' Mum asks, and Jen looks up from stirring the tea. 'Just because her parents were doing that barn conversion to rent it out for parties and weddings.'

'Were they?' I look at Jen. She's probably not going to leap at the idea, but it might be our only hope if everywhere else is fully booked. Plus it means I can properly introduce her to Christina, and make it clear that there is nothing going on between us. 'Maybe I should give her a call.'

Jen mashes the tea bag out of the cup and then discards it in the bin.

'Sure,' she says noncommittally.

I'll take that as a yes.

Growing up, we went to the Pattersons' on a regular basis: Sunday lunches, Christmas parties, birthday celebrations. Their old rectory house, set back from the road with a long driveway, has always been a place of familiarity. I can see from sideways-glancing at Jen's face that she's adding up the signs of privilege, from the cast stone pillars with pier caps when we drove in, to the large detached property with enough windows to signify five or six bedrooms. Jen is, it has to be said, a bit of an inverse snob. We stayed in the Cotswolds once and she caricatured everyone as wearing gilets and expensive wellies… which may have been true… But here, I just want her to let go of her hang-ups. This is a family I've known all my life. And as a potential wedding venue (even though I've never considered it as such), it may actually be perfect.

There are fairy lights wrapped around the trees at the front of the house, reminding me of Christina's decorating talent for my

Bestward proposal. Christina herself strides out of the front door to greet us, grinning broadly and waving as we clamber out of the car.

'Michael!' She crushes me in a hug, then surprises Jen by giving her the same treatment. 'Jen! I didn't get a chance to chat to you at the carols and I want to hear ALL about it!'

'I have to give Christina credit for making everything possible,' I tell Jen. 'Thank you so much for all your amazing work. I'm sorry I didn't get a chance to say it properly before now.'

'Well, it's always nuts at Christmas,' Christina says warmly, not showing any hard feelings. 'Come on in!'

We step through the door onto the weathered parquet floor. Rufus, an aged Collie, ambles up to me.

'He's still alive, then?' I comment.

'Don't listen to him, Rufus.' Christina ruffles his fur lovingly. She leads us through into the kitchen, where her mother, Juliet, is making what looks like five hundred mince pies.

'Hello!' she cries enthusiastically. 'How *lovely* to see you both. So sorry I'm tied up with this but I should be done in no time.'

'Wow, that's a lot of mince pies,' Jen comments, looking overawed at the neat duplicated rows across the worksurfaces.

'Mum started a catering club a few months ago,' Christina explains, putting the kettle on. 'Your mum's been going.'

Ah. That would explain the sudden penchant for gourmet.

'She's very talented. She's always been an excellent cook,' Juliet says, spooning mincemeat into pastry cases.

'Then Mum thought that maybe the club could turn into a business, given that the quality was so high.'

'Well, people need caterers, and I thought, why not? We're all retired, we've got time, and we enjoy it,' Juliet added. 'Nothing too full on, just a few parties now and then.'

'Is Mum doing this too, then?' I ask. I feel guilty that I had no idea.

'She seems keen,' Juliet nods. 'Of course, I don't need everyone to help with every order. I can see who's available and we work it out between us.'

Since taking early retirement, I definitely think Mum has been left with a lot of unexpended energy. I make a note to ask her more about this later.

'And it also ties in nicely with the barn,' Christina says, offering us chairs at the solid oak table and opening up a laptop.

She clicks a few pages, then swivels it round to show us a crisp, modern website with an artistic impression of a barn conversion as the centre image.

'Haven't come up with a name yet,' Juliet calls over. 'So if you have any flashes of inspiration, let us know.'

'It looks great,' I say, examining Jen's expression. Her face seems neutral at least, albeit not abounding in positivity.

'So, is it on site here?' Jen asks.

'Yes, I can show you in a bit,' Christina explains. 'It's around the back of the house. We thought we'd convert it to a venue so people can hire it for events. Then potentially, with Mum's catering, we could offer that as part of the service, but more bespoke than a hotel.'

Jen's eyes are wide as saucers, and I get it: it's the kind of ambitious project that few families would have the drive, resources or opportunity to even contemplate. But this could be the exact solution we need for a reception venue and catering, and in the grounds of the home of a close family friend. I just hope she can see the obvious perks of this arrangement, rather than just her mistrust of Christina and, generally, upper-middle-class people.

'Have you thought about what kind of food you want?' Christina asks Jen.

'Well, I hate canapes,' Jen begins, and I wince inwardly. 'I think wedding food needs to be substantial... without being pretentious.'

'Sure.' Christina seems unfazed by Jen's judgy tone. 'Have a look at this sample menu.'

She hands over a card with three course meal options: soup, chicken with mushroom sauce, and cheesecake.

'This looks good,' Jen says, a bit begrudgingly.

'Would you like to see the barn?'

Jen looks at me and I can see her conflict of not wanting to choose this option battling with a sense of inevitability.

'Yes,' she replies.

42

Jen

It's clear that Michael really wants me to like this.

Two days ago, if someone had suggested that I would be viewing Christina Patterson's barn as a potential wedding venue, I would have screamed with laughter. To be honest, the thought of viewing *any* potential wedding venue would have this effect. Now I've been thrown into this parallel universe where you need to know the difference between bruschetta, grissini and crostini, and arrange a seating plan with enough diplomacy that World War 3 won't break out before the Best Man's speech.

I'm drifting down the river, carried by the rapids, and all I can do is to go with it.

I mean, yes: it's a fantastic house. The barn is large and spacious, but as Christina talks about heaters and fairy lights, I can see that it could be a really special venue. Completely private with no other parties in the function room next door, as it would be with a hotel, or just other guests ambling around and stumbling into your group photo session. I also love the way that it would be (and I hate myself for using this word) *bespoke*; Christina makes it clear that we can dictate the menu, layout and setup, and how her mother loves trying new things and would be happy to accommodate us.

It does bother me that essentially we would be their guinea pigs, because they've never done a wedding before.

'So, what do you think?' Michael puts an arm around my waist.

'I'll give you guys some space.' Christina backs towards the door. 'Come back to the house when you're ready.'

Once she's gone, Michael draws me closer.

'Admit it, you like it more than you expected.'

I can't help but smile.

'It does seem pretty ideal really. Apart from the fact that they've never done this before.'

'But they'll work so hard to make sure they get it right for us,' he argues. 'Plus, with most places booked, we don't have a lot of choice right now.'

'I know,' I sigh. 'I'm sure they will do an amazing job. It feels like everything they touch is golden.'

'You're not jealous of Christina, are you?' Michael leans down to scrutinise my expression.

'What, of her flawless appearance, her impressive qualifications, or the fact that she's Grade 8 harp and a tennis champion?' I joke.

'You just need to get to know her,' Michael says. 'She's not one of those Instagram hashtag perfect life people.'

'Like David's girlfriend, you mean?'

'Exactly. Just because someone has a bit of money doesn't make their life perfect.'

'But it does allow them to make a huge amount more money because they can afford to convert barns in their back garden.'

Michael sighs in defeat.

'Is this going to be a yes or a no?'

I look up at the beams overhead, and the rustic posts, imagining them wrapped with ribbons and fairy lights. I picture tables with all our family and friends, candlelight, and soft music. I try to put myself in a white dress at the centre of it all, although this is hard to muster. The truth is, I have no reason to say no.

'Let's do this.' I seal it with a kiss.

We arrive back at Michael's parents' house on a sugar high. Firstly, Christina and her mother were over the moon when we said we'd love to hold the reception there. Secondly, Juliet insisted on us taste-testing not only her mince pies, but also her shortbread and mini pastries with white chocolate and raspberry filling (heavenly). But as we shut the door with a bang and stumble over each other to kick off our shoes and find Ezra and Heather to tell them the great news, Rachel comes out of the living room scowling and stomps upstairs.

When we step into the lounge, it feels like a courtroom.

Ezra and Heather sit on the sofa together, and Heather jumps up, flushing as she turns over a notebook in her hands.

'How did it go?' she asks.

'Great. We decided to go for it,' Michael answers, with a guarded expression and less enthusiasm than he showed five minutes earlier.

'That's lovely,' Heather says nervously, then looks awkwardly at Ezra.

He makes a gesturing motion with his hands to urge her to continue.

'Well,' Heather licks her lips. 'We thought we'd write down a few more names to… suggest… for the guest list.'

My eyes widen as I turn to Michael, who takes my hand in a mark of solidarity. He reaches out for the notebook and she hands it over. He scans it silently, while I peek to see a page of scrawling Mr and Mrs couples and families with double-barrelled names.

'We'll discuss it,' Michael says, in a tone not dissimilar to David Clark responding to a member of staff's request for a pay rise. 'But this would completely change the budget we've agreed with the Pattersons.'

'We realise that,' Heather says hurriedly, 'so we thought we would offer to pay for these guests to attend. So it doesn't affect your budget.'

Great, so now there will be ten Chases for every one of my guests.

'That's very kind of you,' Michael replies coolly. 'But it's not just about the budget. We don't want a big wedding. We'll review the names together but we need to be happy with the people attending.'

'Why would you possibly be unhappy with our oldest and dearest friends, who you've known your entire life, attending your wedding?' Ezra says incredulously. 'I could never face them again if I had to tell them you were getting married but they weren't invited.'

'You can blame it on me and restricted numbers,' Michael says, keeping his tone calm.

'The computer says no.' Ezra makes sarcastic air quotes then shakes his head in disgust.

'It's not about you, Dad,' Michael retorts sharply.

Ouch.

'I was just trying to be involved.' Ezra stands, and faces the door like he's about to leave the room. 'I notice your invitation to your mother to help didn't include me.'

I look down, because it was me who said it, not Michael.

'You don't look like you want to be involved,' Michael accuses.

Heather looks about to cry. Can I just leave, or will that look bad?

'This came out of nowhere.' Ezra gestures towards me.

So I'm *this* now?

'Funny, I didn't think the groom had to ask his own father for permission before proposing.' Michael's face is starting to turn pink.

'Why don't I make some coffee?' Heather says, her voice wobbling.

I use this as my excuse to leave too, heading up the stairs and leaving Michael to have it out with his dad alone. That's not a conversation I want to be part of.

As I get to the top of the stairs, I hear a sob coming from Rachel's room. I hesitate. Should I knock and see if she's alright? But she barely knows me. As I hover, I hear her talking. She must be on the phone.

'It's no good, I can't tell them,' I hear her say. 'I know. I know. Can we talk later? I love you.'

I probably shouldn't have heard that, and afraid that she might throw open the door and catch me eavesdropping, I tiptoe back to Michael's room and sink onto the bed. My sugar high has turned into a crash.

43

Michael

'Why can't you be happy for me?' I ask Dad.

He runs his hand through his hair, the same way I do. I can hear the clock on the mantelpiece ticking, and the same photo frames that have been there for ten years stare back at me. He sighs before speaking.

'I just feel this is all happening so fast. I don't want you to rush into something you might later regret.'

'You don't even know Jen yet. I've never met anyone like her before.'

Dad says nothing, but his scepticism is clear. A rush of anger surges through me.

'Sometimes it feels like nothing is good enough for you.'

'I never said that,' he snaps.

'You don't have to say it,' I respond. 'It's in your expression, your attitude.'

'I can't pretend to be happy about something if I'm not. You want me to lie?'

This is why you don't try to argue with lawyers. I take a deep breath.

'I want you to be polite, and content to reserve your judgement until you know Jen better.'

'By that point you'll already be married,' he says dryly. Classic Dad.

'Well it's your choice whether you want to be involved or not,' I tell him. 'But to *help*, not to *control*. You don't get to make decisions about our wedding.'

'So you don't care what your mother and I feel anymore? We supported you through university, we helped you buy your house, and we're offering to help pay for the wedding. And all you can say is that I'm trying to control you?'

'Why else are you brandishing a guest list with twenty extra people I haven't seen for years?' My volume has increased to match his, and I realise that everyone in the house can hear us. I consciously lower my tone. 'Dad, I don't want to argue with you.'

'It's not about arguing,' he retorts, with no sense of irony. 'People come into my offices every day to file for divorce. They all started out thinking they were making the right decision.'

It's a miracle that Mum isn't one of them. Biting my tongue, I walk away.

The contrast when we arrive later at Jen's house could not be starker.

We've barely got out of the car when Katie mobs us, hurtling at Jen like a cannonball, screaming.

'Aaaahhhhh! You're engaged!!'

She grabs me next for a crushing hug and pulls us inside, where Jen's dad is waiting to greet us too.

'Look at the *ring*! Isn't it gorgeous?' Katie holds Jen's hand under his nose.

'Let me take my coat off,' Jen laughs.

'Anyone want some fizz?' her dad offers.

We settle in front of the TV, squidging up on the well-worn but comfortable sofas. Things are much simpler here. There's no expectations, no hard stares, or raised eyebrows. I feel my shoulders relax; I didn't realise how hunched and tense I've been on the whole drive over.

Why does Dad still have the power to raise my blood pressure through the roof? I just want to get married. I'm emotionally spent, physically exhausted, but thinking about him makes all the anger churn up inside me again.

'You look tired,' Jen says, placing her wine glass on the coffee table. 'Are you driving back tonight?'

'I think I'll go to my place and get a good night's sleep,' I tell her.

'Make sure you text your mum,' she reminds me.

The guilt is instant: I know Mum will be disappointed that I'm not back there later. She always says I'm never there as it is.

But I can't face Dad again tonight.

In the end, David provides me with the excuse I need, messaging me to ask if I can call into the school site tomorrow. Even the chaos of unexpected asbestos is more attractive than spending time with my parents.

School emergency. Will be over as soon as I can leave, I text. Then I sigh with relief as I turn out the light.

I've seen David in a number of heated situations, his girlfriend's failed livestream being the most recent, but this time he seems really out of his depth.

The sky is clear and the ground is icy as I step out of my car the next morning. Expecting the car park to be fairly empty at 8 a.m during a school holiday, instead it looks like a number of Senior Team are here, along with some vans and heavy-duty vehicles.

It isn't hard to find David: he's wearing a builder's yellow hard hat, and he's shouting at Geoff.

'I need solutions!' I hear, as I approach. 'We have eight classrooms out of action, and we can't let the fact that it's three days before Christmas stop us from sorting this out. Sure, we'd all rather be somewhere else than here right now, drinking mulled wine and wrapping presents. The sooner we can crack this, the sooner we can all go home.'

He checks his phone, muttering expletives, and Geoff looks unimpressed. Janet Patchell stands, shivering in a heavy winter coat, but clutching a clipboard.

'Michael.' David greets me with relief. There is a hint of vulnerability behind his guarded expression. I can't help it: I do feel sorry for him.

'Hey,' I say, meeting eyes with the others. 'Do you want me to go inside and make some coffee?'

'That would be great,' David says, looking down at his phone again.

'Geoff, could you give me a hand?' I ask. I figure getting him out of there is probably the best way to diffuse the tension.

He walks with me into the main building, along the corridor to David's office.

'This must be stressful,' I say, redundantly, but it gets a grim smile from Geoff.

'Maybe I should get signed off with anxiety,' he jokes, then looks as if he regrets it instantly. 'Don't tell David I said that, will you?'

I shake my head, preparing the coffee machine.

'I'm not going to drop you in it,' I reassure him. 'I know what David's like.'

'Is he always like this?' Geoff asks.

'Wanting the impossible? Yes.'

I hand Geoff the first coffee; he deserves it.

'If you and Janet stand your ground, you'll be okay. He'll have to back down. But he'll try and make out that she suggested something different behind your back. Just, don't believe him.'

Geoff gives a short laugh.

'I thought you were his friend.'

I hold up the next cup of coffee.

'I'm making coffee to try to make him human. That says it all.'

'Sometimes I wonder if this job is worth it.'

Geoff sips his coffee, and looks at me thoughtfully. Here's this guy, on Senior Team just like I'd like to be one day, but he's questioning it.

'You're always going to get bad days,' I say, more to convince myself. 'This, too, shall pass.'

Geoff sighs and shakes his head.

'I think it's only just beginning.'

44

Jen

I barely see Michael over Christmas, but Deena and Clare are both staying with their families, so we finally have our long-awaited get-together. It involves a lot of shrieking, examining my diamond ring, wine and junk food.

'Tell me again about the castle!' Clare says.

'It was very romantic,' I recall. 'There were lights and a lady with a dog…'

'He planted a dog there?' Deena cuts in.

'No, they just happened to be there.'

'And he left you clues…' Clare is practically telling the story herself.

'It was like a treasure hunt trail, leading to where the ring was.' I grin as I remember it, although at the time I think I was too shocked to react properly. 'There was music and everything!'

'It all sounds great,' Deena says, holding up her hand as if she's trying to calm a horse. 'But last time we met up, you didn't even know this guy. I still feel we need a little more information.'

'I mean, it would be nice to meet him,' Clare adds.

'Maybe we should do engagement drinks or something,' I think out loud.

'Well, it will have to be quick otherwise it'll be after the wedding,' Deena quips. 'I mean, what about your hen do? We'll have to fix a date now.'

'Yes!' Clare starts scrolling through her calendar. 'We'll have a chat with Katie… Is she your chief bridesmaid?'

'Um…' I hesitate. 'Yes. I really want you two to be bridesmaids too - '

Their screams interrupt me and they crush me in a group hug, which I then try to pull back from to continue,

'But guys, this wedding, it has to be SUPER budget, okay? I don't have the money to just keep adding zeros onto things all the time. I'm already stressed about buying a dress for myself, let alone for you too.'

'Jen, relax.' Deena cuts her hand through the air. 'We'll sort it. Just as long as he's not a psycho.'

'He's not,' I say, perhaps too hurriedly.

'And didn't he ghost you one time?' Deena raises an eyebrow.

'No, because he saw me in work every day and tried to talk to me.'

'But you were kind of 'on hold' for a bit?' she pushes.

'He was worried that I was going to lose my job,' I explain. 'He was trying to protect me.'

'You mentioned the new HR policy of no dating,' Deena continues. 'So is this shotgun wedding basically his way of getting round the policy?'

I open my mouth to deny it, then realise that it probably is.

'A shotgun wedding is usually because the bride is pregnant,' Clare corrects her, then they both look at me with wide eyes.

'No!' I say emphatically. 'I am not pregnant!'

Though I'm not going to tell them that it's actually impossible, given our relationship virginity.

'No offence,' Deena says, in a way that is clearly going to cause offence, 'but I don't think a HR policy is a good reason to get hitched.'

'He loves me!' I protest, and look at Clare for back-up.

'The elaborate proposal suggests it's more than just meeting HR regulations,' Clare points out. 'I mean, you said your union were contesting the policy anyway, so it may well be overturned. Plus you could just say you were engaged and that would be enough to keep them at bay. You certainly wouldn't have to seal the deal so swiftly, and he must know that.'

'Yes, exactly,' I say, relieved.

'But maybe he wouldn't have popped the question so soon if the policy hadn't come up.' Deena is unwilling to drop her point.

'He did tell me he was dealing with it,' I remember, thinking out loud. 'I didn't realise he meant that he was planning to propose.'

I guess I had hoped it meant him sitting down in David's office, giving him an ultimatum: *The policy goes or I go*. Or something to that effect.

'Deena's probably right that the policy was a catalyst,' Clare muses, 'but let's face it: we aren't students anymore. We're over twenty-five. He's older than you, isn't he?'

'Yeah, he's nearly thirty.'

'Most of us want to settle down by then,' Clare argues. 'We don't want to be messing around on dating apps and being ghosted by guys who don't want to commit. So this guy comes along who's willing to commit to Jen, and you're trying to scare her off? Both of your sisters were married with kids before they were our age.'

'That's Nigerian culture though.' Deena waves her hand dismissively. 'Most of our friends won't marry until their thirties.'

'Yeah, because the guys won't commit until they're sure they have no other options,' Clare jokes.

'Jen,' Deena says, drawing my full attention. 'Are you 100% sure that you know him well enough to marry him? That this is the right decision for you?'

'Look, I won't say I know him perfectly,' I admit. 'Meeting his family made me realise there's a lot about him that I don't know. But I love him, and I want to stay with him. So that's why I said yes. What else was I supposed to say?'

'How about, can we review this again in six months?' Deena suggests, as if it's a dentist appointment.

'You can't really say that when there's a guy down on one knee, classical music blasting over an ancient castle, and a lady spying on you with a dog,' I observe dryly.

'You could say that now, though, if you're not happy.'

'I am, though!' I hold up my wine glass to toast my own success. 'Honestly, I wasn't expecting it… But once I'd had a chance to think about it, I realised that I was really excited. He did say that we could postpone it until Christmas, but neither of us wanted to wait that long.'

'Is there a reason why you don't just move in together?' Clare asked.

'He's religious,' I say, avoiding Deena's gaze, because this is her area of expertise.

'Whoa!' Deena says. 'You never mentioned this before.'

'I only knew when we visited his parents, and we all went to church.'

'What kind of church?' Deena asks. She probably has an encyclopaedic knowledge of denominations.

'An old-fashioned one, with stained-glass windows.'

'Anglican?' she asks. 'He's posh, then.'

'He's not,' I say automatically, though she's right.

'I bet it's all midnight mass, incense and vicars in white robes.' Deena nods sagely.

'Is he quite devout?' Clare asks, surprised.

'Um…' I hesitate again. How do I explain the fact that I had no idea he had any religious beliefs, given he had never mentioned them, yet he had taken a vow of chastity which he was determined to keep? 'It's complicated.'

'How?' Deena asks bluntly.

'I don't think he goes to church much, but I still think he's serious about what he believes.'

'That's like saying he likes swimming but never gets in the water,' Deena remarks.

'You can be a Christian without going to church, can't you?' says Clare.

'What's the point in that?' Deena shrugs.

'I suppose it's personal,' Clare says. 'I know you like church, but it's different for everyone.'

'They're my *family*,' Deena stresses. 'I get support from them that I wouldn't find anywhere else.'

'That's cultural, though,' Clare says. 'They're all Nigerian or Nigerian British.'

'Not all of them,' Deena responds.

I've been to Deena's church before, the one in London. I had stayed overnight on the Saturday and then she dragged me with her the next day. I realised why when I was still there six hours later. If she'd left me in her flat, I would have reported her as a missing person.

'Anyway,' Clare continues, signifying that the conversation needs to move on, 'if Michael wants to get married, and Jen wants to say yes, she has every right to do so, and we should just be happy for her.'

'When are we going to meet him?' Deena demands. 'Can't he come over here now?'

'That would be weird,' I point out. 'Why don't we go for drinks tomorrow?'

'I can't,' Deena says immediately. 'My family are having a big gathering. But you could all come?'

'Are you sure?' I ask. I always loved going to Deena's when I was a teenager. Her mum's cooking is amazing and she would help me with my hair after Mum left.

'The more the merrier,' she grins.

45

Michael

It would be nice if Jen had some friends that didn't terrify me, but she doesn't.

As we're ushered inside Deena's parents' house, I'm making my public debut as Jen's fiancé, and I've never met anyone here before. Even the hallway is rammed with people. I awkwardly follow in Jen's wake as Deena leads her to the lounge. I wore a shirt but I feel majorly underdressed. Deena looks like she's walked straight off a catwalk, with striking gold eye make-up and a fascinator that makes her taller than me.

'This is Clare,' she says to me, presenting the only other white person in the room. I shake her hand. 'We've heard a lot about you.'

It sounds vaguely threatening, so I give a half-cough, half-laugh—to be interpreted as the listener chooses. Clare smiles at me at least.

'Your proposal was very romantic,' she says.

'Thanks,' I say, and instantly regret saying something so stupid. Couldn't I just come across well for once in my life?

'Let me get you some drinks,' Deena says.

She raises a hand to let someone pass, and I notice her nails are about two inches long and elaborately decorated.

'You should try some of the food.' Clare points towards the buffet.

'It looks amazing,' I say, seeing a range of dishes with rice and chicken on the table.

'I should check about the citrus,' Jen says, laying a hand on my arm to stop me going to help myself.

She wanders off, leaving me with Clare.

'You have an allergy, right?' Clare asks, then looks down at her plate. 'I hope nothing I've got will set it off.'

'I'm sure it'll be fine.' I wave my hand.

It's exceptionally bad luck that my worst reactions have occurred when Jen has been there. I'm beginning to think she won't let me eat anywhere in public again.

'Don't worry about Deena, by the way,' Clare says, enigmatically.

'Should I be worried?' I raise an eyebrow.

Clare shrugs.

'She wants to grill you a bit.'

It's funny, I can cope with a crowd of Year 11 boys, a job interview panel, and a site with asbestos, but the idea of Deena's interrogation is truly terrifying.

'What about?' I try to stop myself stuttering to sound confident. Nonchalant.

Clare looks at me for a moment. Something about her reminds me of my sister, maybe something about the way she stares at me with a mixture of warmth and defiance.

'When you started going out with Jen, you went away together. Then you went off the radar for a bit.'

'I didn't want to give the Head any ammunition against her,' I explain, feeling my cheeks go red. 'But it wasn't the best idea.'

I wonder exactly how much Jen has told her friends, and what she said about me back then. She must have been really angry with me.

'Now there's this HR policy about no dating,' Clare continues, 'and it feels like your proposal is a bit of a knee-jerk reaction to it.'

Ouch. Where does she work, the divorce courts?

'I knew I wanted to be with Jen,' I say, trying not to get defensive. 'And I thought, what's the point in waiting around?'

'You can have the rice but you should avoid the chicken,' Jen says, returning.

'Is this Michael?' A woman I presume is Deena's mother joins us. 'I'm so glad you came!'

Before I can hold out my hand, I'm crushed into a hug and hold my breath in case there's more citrus perfume here.

'Thank you.' I pull back, subtly gulping in air.

She's wearing traditional Nigerian clothing with a head tie and puts her arm around Jen.

'I like him,' she says, with a broad smile. 'His face is nice.'

Before I can get too arrogant, she adds, in a stern tone to me,

'You treat her like royalty. She is like a daughter to me.'

I gulp and nod.

'So you met my mum.' Deena hands me a beer, grinning.

I take a long drink.

As the evening progresses, Deena drags Jen into the dancing hub of the room, and Clare kindly stays with me. We chat about music, and she used to play in a jazz band, but doesn't have the time for it anymore. I ask her about her job. I feel like she would get on well with Dan and Louise, and make a note to introduce them at the wedding. I'm taking Jen to theirs for New Year, and then the wedding will be that much closer psychologically.

'So how do your parents feel about the wedding?' Clare asks.

Her tone of voice suggests that Jen has said something to her.

'My mum seems okay with it.' I shrug. 'My dad is more… fixed.'
'Will he come round?'
'I don't know.' My tone hardens. 'I don't need his permission.'
Clare gives a laugh.
'We always try to move in the opposite direction to our parents, but we always end up back where we started,' she comments.
'Does Jen ever talk about her mum with you?' I ask.
'Not really,' Clare shakes her head.
'I just feel like… looking around here at Deena's family… It would be a shame if there was no one at the wedding from her mum's side of the family.'
'I know she has an aunt,' Clare tells me. 'She should definitely get in touch with her. But Michael… family is messy.'
'You don't have to tell me that,' I reply.

46
Jen

All in all, I think Michael made a good impression. Clare and Deena seemed to have a 'good cop, bad cop' routine, but I rescued him from the worst of the latter, swooping in with fresh drinks when I heard Deena ask how much his house was worth. The best part was when they started talking about law. Suddenly, they were all on common (nerdy) ground, and I was left sipping a mocktail while Deena talked about her latest crisis at work.

Which is why I feel like it's deja-vu, now we're at Dan and Louise's New Year party, and I'm again listening to lawyers talk shop. This is obviously penance for all the times I've subjected non-teachers to state-of-education rants.

'I was very glad not to be on duty tonight,' Kyle laughs. 'But I got called down to the Police station last night at two in the morning. The guy was Polish and didn't speak much English, so I rang my mum and she translated for me.'

'Your mum speaks Polish?' I ask.

'Yes, she grew up there,' Kyle explains. 'She's lived here for thirty years now.'

'Do you ever go and visit?' I can't help the question, which forms like a stab in my gut as I think about Jamaica.

'I haven't been for a few years,' he says. 'When I was a kid, we'd go over every few years and see my grandparents. Mum goes back more often now that we're not at home anymore.'

'She must miss her family.' A lump forms in my throat.

'Well, I experienced my first Nigerian party at Jen's friend's house,' Michael says, diverting the conversation.

'Wow, what was it like?' Louise asks.

'What was the food like?' Dan interjects.

'It was very good.' Michael smiles. 'And Jen has two lawyer friends, who were there, and they both interrogated me.'

'You obviously have very good taste in friends,' Alex jokes to me.

'Sorry, I think you'll find the catering somewhat more basic here tonight!' Louise's phone starts beeping and she swipes across it. 'The pizza's done.'

'I'll come and help.'

I follow her out to the kitchen and she gives me a pepperoni pizza to slice up.

'This looks so good!' I say, hoping she doesn't genuinely feel guilty.

'I was just glad that Grace went down okay,' Louise says. 'She hasn't been sleeping very well recently.'

'That must be tough.'

I gingerly drop the hot slices onto a plate and try to arrange them more attractively.

'So, did Michael's proposal take you by surprise?' Louise asks, with an eager grin.

'Uh... yes,' I decide to be honest. 'I had no idea.'

'Oh wow. That must have been a shock.'

'Especially as he was throwing up the night before because he had a drink which triggered his allergy,' I tell her, shaking my head at how mad those few days were.

'Oh no,' Louise frowns in concern. 'It's citrus, right? I always have to check that no one puts out juice by mistake, or something. Was he okay?'

'You know Michael, he was pulling off his elaborate proposal less than twenty-four hours later,' I smile dryly. 'We were on our way to his parents, and he proposed at this castle, and got his friend to help him set it all up.'

I give her the gist of Michael's perfectly executed treasure hunt. I'm warming to the fact that I have such a cool proposal story to share.

'I bet his parents were over the moon!' Louise says.

If only.

'His mum was really sweet,' I say carefully, 'but I think his dad didn't expect it. I think he thinks it's too soon.'

'Dan and I had a lot of conversations like that with our parents,' Louise says, with immediate understanding. 'We'd been together for two years, but we were only just out of uni.'

'Did they come round?' I ask.

'Yes, and they're great with Grace too,' she says. 'But it can take time.'

'We don't have much time before the big day though.'

I explain that we booked a date in April, and she nearly drops the platter.

'That's soon!' she says, her eyebrows shooting up. 'But then again, long engagements seem a bit pointless to me.'

'How long were you engaged?' I ask.

'About a year,' she answers. 'Like I said, we were quite young. If we were in your position, we wouldn't see the point in waiting that long now. I've had friends at church meet someone, get engaged, and married within a year.'

'Did it all work out for them?'

WEDDING BELL TIME

It sounds like I'm asking if they made it without splitting up. Maybe I am.

'Yeah,' she smiles. 'My friend Mel is pregnant now. It wasn't a big, fancy wedding. They had the church service, then they hired a village hall, and it was really simple.'

I breathe out, feeling relieved and hopeful. Maybe we weren't as insane as everyone thought. And by everyone, I mainly meant Ezra.

'That's what I want,' I say, taking my platter and following her back to the lounge. 'The problem is what other people expect.'

We add the platters to the table with other buffet food, and everyone crowds around to fill up a plate. It's definitely not a loud-music-and-dancing New Year's party, but we play a quiz board game and it feels relaxed, not like I've got to impress anyone. Michael seems to have calmed down away from the school site and David Clark. I've avoided asking him about the asbestos problem because I'm hoping he's been distracted by all these social occasions.

'A toast,' Dan says, raising his wine glass, when it draws near to midnight, 'to Michael and Jen. Congratulations on your engagement!'

Our glasses chink together and Michael kisses my cheek. My knot of anxiety has unravelled and I finally feel a streak of pure happiness. This is going to be a good year.

47

Michael

This is going to be the year I get married.

That's the thought looping round my brain on repeat as we pull party poppers, swipe annoying stringy stuff out of our hair, and hear fireworks going off (we go to the window but we can never see them). It's mad to think that this time last year, I didn't even know Jen. Now here she is, laughing with my friends, this unexpected gift of sunshine in my life. I pull her in for a kiss and taste the wine on her lips. Just four months to go and counting.

'You're not wasting any time, then,' Dan jokes when I tell him the wedding date. 'Good for you.'

It's such a welcome reaction after my dad's.

'I was going to ask… will you be my Best Man?'

'Seriously? Yes, mate!' Dan claps me on the back. 'I'd be honoured.'

'I might need your advice on a few things,' I say, enigmatically.

'I don't think I'm very qualified,' Dan laughs.

'You know. About *that*.' I make exaggerated eyebrow movements and hope he gets what I mean. 'And, in my sister's words, how not to be a psycho.'

I tell him about booking the church and Jen's reaction to the marriage prep course.

'You might want to work on your communication skills,' Dan suggests, with a smile. 'We did marriage prep. It was really helpful. I'm sure you'll find it good too.'

'Are you actually going to get the wine, or are you just using it as an excuse to gossip in here?' Louise interrupts, taking a bottle of Prosecco out of Dan's hands.

'What's the best thing we learned in marriage prep?' Dan asks.

'Just listen all the time to each other, then repeat back what you think the other person has said,' she says promptly. 'We pretty much spent our entire first year of marriage saying "What I think you're saying is…"'

'I thought the introvert-extrovert stuff was the most useful,' Dan says. 'You know, doing personality tests and figuring out how you both function. It helps you understand why things that work for you don't necessarily work for the other person.'

I wince. It sounds like this marriage preparation is going to be very in-depth.

'And all the stuff about your parents,' Louise says as a parting shot, before going into the other room.

'What about your parents?' I ask Dan.

'Oh, you know.' He sips his beer. 'They always ask questions like, "how did your parents communicate" because you generally imitate what you've grown up with.'

'That means I'm doomed then.' I roll my eyes.

'What's wrong with your parents?' Dan asks, in genuine confusion. 'They're great!'

'You should have seen my dad's face when I told them we were engaged.'

I can't get the look of shock and disappointment out of my head.

'Was he not on board with it?' Dan looks sympathetic.

I look across at the stack of discarded pizza boxes and sigh.

'He just has all these expectations for me, and I'm never going to meet them.'

'Has he told you that?'

'He may as well have.' I shrug.

'It might just be that he needs some time to get used to the idea.'

'I just felt bad for Jen.' I haven't said this to anyone, and now that I've verbalised it, it feels more tangibly real. 'I wanted it to be the best day of her life, and then the first thing we did was walk into my parents' house and have my dad scowling at us the entire evening.'

'Does he not like her?' Dan widens his eyes in surprise.

'I don't think it's anything to do with her.' I shake my head. 'I think it's more to do with me. What he thought I would have achieved by now. He thinks being in a serious relationship will hold me back.'

'What do you think?' Dan asks, surveying me.

'He's wrong,' I say simply.

Something passes across Dan's face, and his jaw twitches.

'Look, Michael,' he says, shifting his weight against the worktop, 'I'm not saying that he's right, but I do think you need to consider how marriage will change your life. It's a big commitment, twenty-four-seven. You can't just carry on working all hours of the day and night. Jen will need you. You will need her. You need to make each other a priority.'

'I know,' I answer automatically, although I'm not sure I do.

'Just remember, you can't put a relationship on pause while you want to go and work all out on something, then just press play when it suits you.'

'I realise that.' Although I can't help thinking it would be very useful if I could.

There's the sound of crying from the baby upstairs.

'Looks like Grace is teething again,' he says apologetically, before running off to see to her.

I drive Jen home, and say to her before she leaves the car,

'Have you ever done a personality test?'

'Which one?' she asks.

I blink. How many are there anyway?

'We'll have to spend a fun date night doing some together,' she says, her eyes sparkling as she shuts the passenger door.

Can't wait for that one.

Interlude

Alice pushed the wooden, panelled door holding her breath, hoping it wouldn't creak as it opened. A draught of mead-scented air filled with noisy songs caught her in the face. Behind her, she heard the prince inhale and held up her hand, pre-empting him. She was fed up already with his smart "advice".

She ran, on tiptoe, down the corridor, while the banquet continued and the volume increased. Hopefully they would all be too busy with their food to notice a stranger, if they bothered to look through the doorway out of the hall.

Suddenly the prince clamped his arm around her and scooped her into a walk-in storage cupboard. They stood, face to face, her eyes questioning him as he raised a finger to his lips.

"Don't see why we have to go out to check," a voice carried from the corridor.

It sounded not far from their door. Then there were the sound of heavy footsteps, thankfully passing by and fading into the distance. She let out her breath.

"Just as well I saw them," the prince whispered smugly.

She tried not to think about how close they were standing to each other in the enclosed space.

"What do you want, prince: a medal?"

"My name is Edward," he said, holding her gaze. A challenge.

She wanted to look away, but she couldn't. Her mouth felt dry.

"Looks like I just saved your neck," he murmured, and she shivered as though he had placed his finger on her throat.

"When I found you outside the castle," Alice said, her voice barely louder than a whisper, "were you waiting for me?"

"Alice," he said tenderly, "I've been waiting for you my whole life."

Document comments:

Michael Chase: I feel like I should copyright the things I say to you.

Jen Baker: I'll mention you in the acknowledgements.

48

Jen

It's the January sales, and Katie and I are going shopping. Deena and Clare are tagging along too, and I'm sure every shop in the street can hear us coming, our collective volume is so loud.

Bridal boutiques are the sort of place you always long to go into, but never have a legitimate reason. The dazzling creations of white tulle and lace in the window look like some Snow Queen extravaganza, given the season, and fortunately it's fairly quiet when we arrive.

'Good morning,' the assistant says, rather coldly. 'How can I help?'

'My sister needs a wedding dress,' Katie announces.

'Perhaps I should just have a look around,' I say, with visions of Katie forcing me to try every dress in the shop.

'Do you have any idea what style you'd like?' the assistant asks, in a tone that doesn't expect much from me.

'No, not really.'

Clare and Katie start cooing over various dresses, surging forward to examine them. Deena gives me a sideways glance.

'Every single picture in here is of a white girl,' she comments.

She's right. However diverse this country becomes, there are still so many reminders of how we're in the minority.

'I can wear a white dress though, can't I?' I ask, not entirely rhetorically.

'You can wear whatever you want,' Deena laughs. 'But it sounds like Mummy and Daddy Chase want the English country club style. Maybe that's what you should say to the *helpful* assistant.'

She rolls her eyes, and I hastily steer her further away from the woman's earshot. I touch the fabric of the first dress in front of me and turn the price ticket over.

'£2700!' I suck my breath in sharply. 'I had been saving for a deposit and it seems wrong to spend so much of it on something I'll only wear once.'

'Weddings are just silly money,' Deena pronounces. 'If you went into a cake shop and ordered a cake, it'd be, like £50. You say it's for a wedding, they're going to charge you £500.'

'Maybe I should just learn some new skills. Like flower arranging.'

'Don't think you're going to master dressmaking in time though,' Deena points out.

'Anything you like?' Katie walks over to join us, Clare following.

'I don't want to spend too much,' I tell them.

'What is your budget?' The sales assistant calls across the shop floor, inserting herself into the conversation.

'This is too much.' I indicate to the price label that nearly gave me a heart attack. 'I want something more reasonable.'

'These are couture gowns, you know,' she reminds me.

'Do you have anything on sale?' Deena asks.

She wrinkles her nose.

'We'll probably have a sale in February as stock comes in for the spring and summer.'

'Cutting it a bit fine,' Clare comments.

'When is your wedding?' the assistant asks.

'April,' I reply.

'Oh!' she says in surprise, then recollects herself. 'Well, I'm afraid most of these gowns need alterations to fit perfectly. Even if you chose one that was in stock today, you would struggle to have it prepared in time.'

'Let's find somewhere else,' Deena says. 'Thank you very much for your help.'

Once we're outside, the others look at me with sympathy.

'Don't worry,' Katie rallies. 'We'll find something.'

'She was unnecessarily rude,' Clare comments.

'It's cos we didn't have designer handbags and all that.' Deena pretends to walk in an exaggerated swagger across the pavement.

'So we know you don't want *couture*,' Clare says. 'What's the alternative?'

'H&M?' Deena shrugs.

She isn't far wrong. We troop into many high street stores, searching at the back for a wedding dress section. The problem is, it's January sales time, and the shops are rammed full of sale rails with little black dresses and glitzy jumpers. There are piles of clothes on the floor, and everything is in a total mess.

'What has been going ON in here?' Katie steps over a mass of hangers, with tangled up tops.

'Sorry.' A harangued assistant, dressed in black leggings and a black T shirt that says SALE in red letters, stumbles over to pick them up. 'We've been open since 6 a.m.'

'Man, some people need to get a life,' Deena says.

'I don't think we're going to find anything in here,' I say with a hopeless shrug. 'Why don't we get some lunch?'

We push our way through the crowds to a department store and manage, by some miracle, to grab a table.

'Selfie time!' Katie announces, holding out her phone while we cram our heads together and pout.

Deena and I go up to the counter together, leaving Katie and Clare to giggle over filters.

'It's not the end of the world if you don't find something today,' Deena says, taking in my glum expression.

'I know,' I sigh. 'I just wanted to get it sorted. As soon as term starts, everything will get busy again.'

'I know what it's like to have a stressful job,' Deena begins, 'but you can't do that whole 'disappearing' thing when you've got a wedding to plan.'

'What 'disappearing' thing do you mean?' I ask.

'You only have to look at our group chat.' She holds up her phone pointedly. 'July, August, you're posting away with all of us. September comes round and you are Off The Radar. You told us about Michael... because you hated the guy... Then you told us you were going on a date... Then suddenly you're engaged.'

'Sorry.' I avoid Deena's stare to scour the fridge for sandwiches. 'It was all a bit of a blur.'

'I know it's special, meeting someone new, and you get all caught up in it,' Deena continues. 'I understand that. I'm just worried that you've bitten off more than you can chew. Your big day is coming in four months and it won't do any good to put your phone on silent when you get stressed out.'

'I don't ignore my phone,' I counter, reaching for a tuna mayo baguette. 'I just don't always have the energy to reply to messages. I still read and keep up with what's going on.'

'That's lurking.' Deena raises a pencilled eyebrow. 'Just... let us help you, okay? We're all in this with you.'

'I'm not in trouble.' I roll my eyes.

'In approximately eight weeks, you will be.'

She's probably right. Once we've got through the checkout and returned to the table, Katie proudly shows me a new WhatsApp group she's created: WEDDING.

'What do you think?' she says. 'I've put us all on there, seeing as we're bridesmaids.'

'Don't get too excited.' I slide into my chair. 'At this rate, you'll be digging out your old prom dresses.'

'That's actually not a bad idea,' Katie says, grabbing her baguette from the tray.

'Except that we'll all be wearing totally different colours,' Deena says dryly. 'What is your colour scheme, anyway?'

I stir my tea in the teapot and set down the spoon.

'Not sure.'

'Please not pink,' Clare says.

I make a face.

'Blue could work with all our skin tones,' Deena says.

'Cross that bridge when we come to it.' I try to shut down the conversation.

'So, what did you think of the groom then?' Katie asks with a mischievous glint in her eye.

Here we go.

'I like him,' Deena says. This is what she's said repeatedly, which makes me think that really, she doesn't like him. Something about the lady doth repeat herself too much.

'And?' Katie asks expectantly.

This is the other thing: the way Deena says it, it's like there is a BUT coming. She takes a bite of her sandwich and shrugs.

'I mean, I still haven't spent much time with him yet,' she hedges.

'I had a good chat with him,' Clare chips in. 'I think he's a solid guy.'

'Solid?' Deena echoes with a shriek. 'What, you mean he's made of bricks or something?'

'He seems reliable,' Clare says.

'Well that's very romantic.' Katie rolls her eyes.

'I also thought his proposal was very lavish,' Clare continues. 'The fact that he went through with it, even though he was really ill… It seems sweet to me.'

'And it's a gorgeous ring,' Deena says, pulling my hand to examine it again. 'I can't believe he got exactly the right size for you.'

Once we've built our strength back up, we make our way through the maze of the store's third floor. It's quieter up here, away from the 50% off sale rails on the ground floor.

'Ooh, let me just look at this.' Deena stops and grabs a hanger, holding up a gold silk, floor length dress.

'That would look amazing on you,' Katie says.

'Would it annoy you if I tried it on?' She looks at me.

'Go ahead,' I gesture, and wander around to browse.

There's a tiny weddings section in the corner, with a few cute kids' bridesmaids' dresses, and then a few bridal gowns. A woman with the department store uniform (black shirt and silk scarf—my kind of style) is unhooking a stunning white bodice covered in diamanté jewels from a mannequin. She catches my eye.

'Sorry, don't mind me,' she says. 'I've just got to change over the display now that Christmas is over.'

'That's so beautiful.' I step nearer.

'It is,' she agrees. 'The skirt piece is a bit unusual but it really works. Let me show you.'

And just like that, she produces a satin, sweeping skirt with a long train, holding it up underneath the bodice. It's a rich, honey gold.

'Can I try it on?' The words are out of my mouth like a reflex action.

'Sure.' She looks surprised. 'Let me take it to the changing rooms for you.'

Carefully carrying the two-piece ensemble, she leads the way to the changing area, where Deena is posing in front of the mirror with the gold silk dress on.

'Jen!' Deena says. 'What have you got there?'

'Just found something,' I say, trying not to get too excited.

The assistant leads me into a larger sized cubicle, and then helps me into the dress. I hope she ignores my sweaty armpits and my discarded, washed-out bra. She fastens up the back of the bodice and it feels like just the right amount of tightness to fit without suffocating me.

'Okay.' She draws back the curtain and I step out towards the mirror.

I can't believe it. I look *incredible*. I stare at the image of a sophisticated bride… It's me!

'You look AMAZING,' Deena says.

'Whaaaaat is this?' Katie crashes into the changing room, and stops dead when she sees me.

I smile nervously at her.

'Do you like it?'

She blinks for a moment, and I realise she's blinking back tears.

'You look just like Mum,' she says.

Silence rings in the air as Clare catches up and peers at me over Katie's shoulder.

'It's *perfect*!' Katie cries, and flings her arms around me.

'I'm going to find us more dresses,' Clare says.

I hug my sister, and I allow my eyes to well up.

'I wish she could have been here,' I whisper so only Katie can hear.

'I know.' She squeezes me tighter. I hope she doesn't damage this thing.

'Group hug!' Deena throws her arms around both of us.

'Take this, Katie.' Clare has managed to find the gold silk in both hers and my sister's size.

Five minutes later, we are all shimmering in front of the mirror.

'Time for another selfie!' Katie whips out her phone again.

'I'll take it,' the assistant offers.

'This has to be top secret though,' she says, although her current volume means that the whole shop floor knows about it.

'How much is this, anyway?' Deena asks me, stroking the satin skirt.

'I don't actually know,' I say. 'How about we get changed and then have a pow-wow?'

We reconvene, back in our jeans, and the assistant places the dresses carefully onto the counter.

'Original price for this was £400,' she says. 'But because it was on display, I can cut the price to £200.'

'I'll take it,' I say, to squeals from the bridesmaids. 'Calm down, everyone. I want your honest opinion on the gold for you.'

'Love it,' Deena says. 'It was my idea, technically.'

'I will need to take up the straps a bit,' Clare says. 'But I think it will be fine.'

'I love the colour,' Katie says. 'Let's do it.'

WEDDING WHATSAPP CHAT
Katie: We got dresses!
Deena: I take credit for the whole thing.
Clare: I think the cafe was my suggestion.
Katie: Shall I add Michael to this group?
Jen: You'd better stop posting selfies then.
Katie: There will always be selfies. Just no wedding dresses.

49

Michael

The first day of the Spring term never felt so brutal.

To begin with, 'Spring' is a misnomer: it's January, and the frost gives the (usually grey) yard a diamond sheen. Secondly, we have the asbestos area cordoned off, and we've made a poor, barely doable schedule of lessons which are going to take place at Prestfield. The county has provided us with a coach and driver to ferry classes back and forth. What could possibly go wrong?

Plus, today is the day when Liz comes back.

I don't know her that well; I think she was only in for the first few weeks of term in September, but I didn't get a great first impression. Jen was too loyal to criticise her but clearly, she's not used to doing much work. As soon as David asked for basic paperwork, she freaked out. She's the Second in Department, so I need to figure out how we can work together. In a way that doesn't mean that I do all the work.

I meet Jen in the staff kitchen for our usual morning beverage.

'If your sister sends any more GIFs, I'm going to leave the group,' I tell her. This WhatsApp group is driving me nuts and I've only been in it for twenty-four hours. Leave it a while and there's three hundred new messages. Then it turns out it's just Katie, posting memes again.

'We just need to channel her,' Jen says, retrieving her mug and teabag from a filing cabinet.

'Why don't you ask her to find us somewhere to stay for a few days after the wedding?' I suggest, refilling my coffee machine. 'We'll do our proper honeymoon in the summer, but it would be nice to get away.'

'Okay.' Jen fills her mug from the urn, avoiding my gaze.

'What's wrong?' I ask. I wonder if I'll ever lose this constant paranoia that she's going to break up with me.

'We should probably talk… about a few things… to do with that.'

She gives me a meaningful stare.

'Sure,' I gulp.

I think I'd actually prefer the personality test.

'For a start, maybe I'd better go to the clinic,' she says, obviously thinking I will know what this means.

'What clinic?' I ask, when it becomes apparent that she's not going to tell me.

She sighs.

'The sexual health clinic, Michael.'

I jump and look around the room nervously.

'You can't talk about that here,' I hiss. 'It's unprofessional!'

'Just as long as we talk about it at some point.' She picks up her mug and heads for the door.

I can't leave the conversation on this cliff-hanger. I grab my coffee and follow in her wake.

'Why do you need The Clinic?'

I'm saying it like it's some secret location in a spy movie.

'It might be good to check a few things… and maybe get prepared. For the honeymoon.'

I have visions of Jen sitting in the waiting room and a Year 10 student walking in.

'Can't we just order some stuff online?' I suggest, still speaking in a low tone.

'By *stuff*, do you mean condoms?' she asks.

I nearly spill my coffee over my shirt. I think she's trying to give me a heart attack.

'Can you not say these words on site?' I say through gritted teeth.

'We could use a code word,' Jen says sarcastically. 'How about 'apples'?'

We finally reach the safety of her classroom and I shut the door decisively behind me.

'Yes, I am happy to order *apples*. You don't need to go through a humiliating experience.'

'I just thought it might be a good idea. It's been a while since I…'

My coffee tastes particularly bitter.

'How many… partners… have you had?' I choke the word out.

Jen glances at her (usually incorrect) clock.

'Do you really want to have this conversation at 8 a.m.?'

My stomach drops.

'It's that bad, is it?'

'Well, not everyone takes a vow of chastity.'

I don't understand why she keeps saying that like it's something bad.

'Is it double figures?'

'Not now, Michael.'

'It is, then!' My voice rises unintentionally.

'No, it isn't,' she snaps. 'I don't want to have this conversation now. It's unprofessional.'

She's so sharp, throwing my own words back so that they catch me round the neck like a boomerang.

'Are you going to meet Liz when she comes in?' she asks, changing the subject.

'Well, I was going to say hello to her at break time.'

'I think you should come to the staff room and be ready to welcome her.'

'All right,' I sigh. Sometimes Jen's treat-everyone-as-valuable mantra becomes exhausting.

But by the time I've sorted out some papers, spoken to David and sent some students out of the stairwell, I enter the staffroom again and Liz is already surrounded by well-wishers. Judy and Jen are on either side of her, and she's chatting with staff who have crowded round to welcome her back.

Liz has the kind of heavily made up face that is uncomfortable to look at. Her overly mascara-d eyelashes, the cakey texture of her foundation, and her yellowed teeth make for a slightly ghoulish effect, a sort of twenty-first century Miss Havisham. Her nails are elaborately painted and decorated with a pattern not dissimilar to birthday wrap. She's dressed in a too-tight, low cut dress and her perfume could knock out a football team. But I notice the way her hands shake when I greet her. Perhaps the elaborate get-up is some sort of shield.

'Hello, Liz,' I say. 'Welcome back.'

'Thanks,' she says, with none of the animation she was just exhibiting in her conversation with the others.

I'm clearly already the bad guy. Well, someone's got to make the hard decisions.

'I've looked at my modified timetable,' she says. 'I'm not sure about the Year 11 group. I think it might be a bit stressful for me right now.'

And within sixty seconds of talking to Liz, she has wound me up. We've had a nightmare covering her class for three months while she's been off, and most of my lessons get disrupted with me having to go into their room and sort them out because they have a different cover teacher who has no clue what they've already done.

'They are your most important group, which is why I've prioritised their lessons,' I say. 'They are very keen to have you back.'

'I can share my resources with you,' Jen says. 'We're all covering the same thing anyway.'

'Thanks, Jen,' Liz says, smiling at her.

I guess I'll just go, then.

'Congratulations!'

Steph barrels past me and ferociously hugs Jen.

'Everyone, look! Jen and Michael are engaged!' She addresses the staff room, brandishing Jen's engagement ring like the cover of *Hello!* magazine.

People start abandoning their coffee to come over and see for themselves.

'I obviously missed a lot, then,' Liz remarks.

'Isn't there a HR policy on no dating?' Joseph points out.

'My union has torn that policy to shreds,' Judy says, with finality. 'They won't have a leg to stand on.'

'When's the big day?' Sean asks, eying the ring. Read it and weep, brother.

'April 12th,' I say, perhaps with unnecessary relish.

'What, next year?' he asks.

'This year,' Jen corrects him, smiling at me.

'That must be a lot to organise,' Liz says, looking at Jen.

'Don't worry, Michael will be doing most of it,' she says. It's a joke but it's probably true.

I don't mind, though. As I watch Jen shepherd her Year 7 class towards the bus, all I can think is that April can't come soon enough.

50

Jen

By the time it's Friday, it feels like the longest week ever. Something about coming back after the holidays, combined with my new responsibilities as Additional Learning Needs co-ordinator, and bussing Year 7 to Prestfield for a class. At least I don't have the stress of driving the vehicle.

As much as I dislike Michael's 'no fraternizing on weeknights' rule (along with some of his other life choices), I wouldn't really have had time to see him anyway before now. When I climb into his car at the end of the school day, it feels like there are a bank of half-finished conversations between us... including the one about the clinic.

'I don't know what the marriage preparation course will include,' I begin nervously, 'but I think we should continue that conversation we started earlier this week.'

Michael glances at me, then changes gear and he speeds up onto the dual carriageway.

'All right,' he says, then looks straight ahead at the road, his jaw clenched.

'Do you have any religious views on contraception?' I ask.

He frowns, and shakes his head.

'No, why would I?'

Honestly, his changing views could give me whiplash.

'Right. I just… wanted to check.'

'I'm not a Catholic, Jennifer,' he drawls, but it's the wrong joke at the wrong time and I don't feel like laughing.

'What's wrong?' he asks, when he notices my face.

'I don't appreciate you making me feel stupid.'

'What?'

'Just because I don't understand the robes and the prayers and the… weird stuff.' I struggle to complete my own tripartite construction. Rookie error. 'I'm sorry I don't understand the difference between Catholic and… whatever you are.'

'Church of England,' he reminds me.

'Right,' I say, not without sarcasm. 'Because of course, you go to church every Sunday.'

'I never said that.'

'So what are we going to say to this vicar tonight, then?' I question him. 'Because if I know you, you're going to go in there and pretend to be super-religious, because you always want to be super at everything.'

'Where's all this come from?' He raises an eyebrow. 'I never said I was going to pretend anything. I just want to get married in my church, and all the couples have to attend the course.'

'It's your parents' church,' I correct. 'Not yours.'

'I grew up going there every week,' he counters.

'So now that you're nearly thirty, that's still relevant?' I return. 'The truth, Michael, is that you don't *go* to church, so you never found another one when you went to uni or started working or bought a house.'

'I thought you said you didn't like it when religious people were judgy.'

I must be getting to him, because he's deflecting big time.

'I'm just worried that your parents have very specific ideas about what they want, and I'm not good enough for them.'

He reaches over and squeezes my hand.

'I don't know how you can think that.'

I look out of the window. We've passed the city and we're driving alongside fields now, with the sun lower in the sky.

'Wait a minute.' It suddenly hits me. 'When are you thirty?'

'In a few months,' he says vaguely.

'Michael?'

He looks at me, and sighs.

'April.'

'What date?' I ask, my teeth clenching together.

'It doesn't matter,' he says.

I wait for five seconds before saying,

'I hope it's not—'

At the same time, Michael says,

'The thirteenth.'

I bury my face in my hands and moan.

'I used to worry about my mental state,' I say as I emerge again. 'But you…'

'What's wrong?'

He indicates and the car runs onto the slip road.

'You wanted to get married before you were thirty. Admit it.'

'Well, I thought it would be nice…'

'Nice?' I repeat in disgust. It is, after all, the English teacher's most hated word. 'Oh, sure. It's really nice to feel that you're part of someone's bucket list.'

'I thought those were for people who were dying.'

'There's also a few choice words that rhyme with bucket, but I'm being restrained.'

'I wanted to pick a Saturday that was in the Easter holidays, so that's why I chose April 12th.'

'Deena was just starting to trust you, and now if I tell her this…'

'Well she's an idiot if she thinks I'm marrying you for any other reason than that I love you. Besides, legally, she knows that I have more to lose.'

I was just drinking from my water bottle and practically spit it out.

'Excuse me?'

'I own a house. When we get married, it will become half yours. I'm the one who stands to lose half my assets. How can I be conning you?'

'Don't paint me as the poor orphan who gets transformed from their lowly background to marry the prince,' I scoff. 'I'm not Eliza Doolittle. And I may not own a house, but I have my deposit saved, which I've chosen to use on the wedding as a sacrifice.'

'I've told you, you should let my parents help…'

'I don't want that!' I cry, forcing him to lean back. 'I want things to be simple, and I don't want to be in anyone's debt.'

We fall silent for a few moments; the only sound is the car engine and the whoosh of passing traffic.

'I don't want to go to our first marriage preparation session arguing,' I say, in a calmer tone this time.

'Okay,' Michael replies, with an edge of frustration.

When we park up near the church, I feel my stomach lurch with anxiety. I have nothing to be afraid of. I don't need to impress anyone.

The church has an annexe that's brightly lit, and when we enter, Steve greets us with a wide grin. He's wearing jeans with a shirt, so he looks more normal. It's modern in here, with carpet, and chairs set out in a semi-circle. There is a table with a teapot and two boxes of pizza.

'Glad you made it,' Steve says warmly. 'Grab some refreshments.'

There are two other couples: one already sitting in the semi-circle, and the other are at the buffet table.

'Hi,' I say, sounding like a kid on the first day of school.

They introduce themselves as Violet and James. Violet's dressed in a blouse and skirt, with a pin that says 'Branch manager'. I'm guessing she works for a bank. She looks in her mid-thirties. James looks older, but it's always hard to tell with guys. His face is weathered and he's wearing a T shirt as though he doesn't feel the cold.

Michael, still looking annoyed, takes his plate and sits on the chair furthest away from the seated couple. I smile at them as I take a seat next to him.

'I'm Jen,' I say.

They both look around my dad's age.

'Matilda.' The woman, with a stylish silvery-grey bob, holds out her hand. 'Most people call me Mattie.'

As I take her hand, I notice she has some serious rings with jewels the size of rocks. Cut-glass accent too. She must be loaded.

'Benedict.' The man next to her nods his head.

They have cups of tea, but no pizza. Maybe they're going to have supper later.

I need to stop judging people. It's not their fault they're rich.

Once Violet and James have sat down as well, Steve takes a seat in the middle.

'Welcome to you all,' he says. 'Why don't we each introduce ourselves and maybe explain when you got engaged and when you're getting married?'

Violet is first.

'Hi everyone, I'm Violet, and this is James.' She speaks crisply, with confidence. 'We got engaged on holiday last year, and we're getting married this summer.'

Benedict is next after James, but he looks to Mattie to speak.

'We're a little more senior,' she jokes. 'We actually got married twenty years ago. It was a second marriage for both of us. We went through a bit of a rough spot, and now we want to renew our vows.'

Respect to them. I feel bad for judging them now.

Oh no, it's our turn. I'm next in the row, but Michael signed us up for this thing, so I stay quiet to force him to speak up.

'Hello,' Michael says, rather formally. 'I'm Michael and this is Jennifer.'

Why is he calling me that?

'We got engaged at Christmas, and we're getting married in April.'

I can feel Violet eyeing me immediately.

'Wow,' she says.

'That's so romantic,' Mattie sighs.

'I hope we don't have to compete to see who can pull off the most romantic gesture,' Michael says. 'The proposal nearly killed me.'

Mattie laughs, but I don't think he's joking.

51

Michael

'If your life together was a show or film right now, which one would it be?'

As Steve gives us a few minutes to confer together as couples, I note that I'm experiencing what my students face every time a teacher sets them a task: an eagerness to prove myself and come up with the best response, but an overwhelming apathy that can't be bothered to expend energy on it.

'How about *Jaws*?' Jen jokes.

She could at least try to take this seriously.

'*Countdown*?' I suggest. Jen pulls a face.

'*Ten Things I Hate About You*? It's based on Shakespeare so that's appropriate.'

'Next thing you're going to say is *You've Got Mail*.'

'I thought we were done being rivals anyway.'

'I guess no one's going to go for *Titanic*.' I look at the other couples, trying to listen in. I can overhear *Father of the Bride* and *Meet the Parents*.

'Not many movies are about engaged couples,' Jen points out. 'I can only think of *My Best Friend's Wedding* but that doesn't bode well.'

'Time's up!' Steve says.

My stomach curls up in panic.

'Jen, would you like to start us off?' he asks her.

She blinks and her face is frozen for a moment in a polite smile.

'*Beauty and the Beast*,' she announces.

Mattie screeches with laughter.

'Would you like to explain why?' Steve asks, with a wry smile.

'We work together,' Jen begins, 'and a lot of people find Michael quite… scary.'

Seriously? That's the best she can come up with?

'So you're the one who truly understands him,' Steve continues this creative interpretation. 'Good!'

It's nice to know that Jen feels she has to be a human shield between me and the rest of the staff. Case in point: Liz.

The evening rolls on. Steve talks about communication and sets a timer where we take turns to tell each other our thoughts without any interruption. Listening to Jen's stream of consciousness is like hopping on lily pads across not just one, but several ponds. And they're made of lava.

'I need to sort out cake for the writing club,' she says, 'and I missed a phone call from a parent today, which I need to chase up. We're going to your parents tonight and I'm not sure if they really like me.'

'Wait,' I say.

'No interruptions,' Steve calls.

I'm supposed to only use nonverbal techniques to convey empathy and encouragement. There's no universally recognised signal for 'don't worry, I'm sure they do, just don't take it personally because my dad is awkward with everyone.'

It makes me realise, though, how many thoughts are rushing through Jen's mind, and why she wants to have time together to talk. A few days without a proper conversation and I would have missed the equivalent of the *Harry Potter* series in sheer volume of thought.

I need to be a better listener.

'I'd like you to practise this during the week and we'll feedback at the next session,' Steve says.

Great: we've got homework.

At the end of the session I usher Jen towards the door, thinking about how hopefully Mum has cooked up another feast for us. She waves goodbye to the other couples.

'There's some really nice people here,' she says.

'Hmm,' I reply.

'I thought that task was really interesting. It's so hard not to speak.'

'Especially with the amount of thoughts running through your mind,' I comment.

We walk around the corner through the cold breeze to find my car, frost beginning to tinge the windscreen.

'Do you really think that my parents don't like you?' I ask, just before we open the car doors.

'Well,' Jen stalls, 'I get the feeling they weren't very on board with our engagement.'

We climb into the car, which is just as cold as outside. I start the engine.

'Do you need them to be on board with it?'

'I don't want to go against them.'

'They have nothing against you.'

'They wish I was more like Christina.'

'That's ridiculous,' I say. Surely my parents wouldn't attempt some medieval betrothal... would they? 'They just need time to adjust to the idea,' I continue. 'They struggle with change.'

Just thinking about going home, my stomach is clenching and I'm bracing myself for whatever my dad will say next. Will he grill me about the marriage preparation course so that I realise that I'm not prepared for marriage? Or will he just give a thin-lipped smile and let his deathly silence speak volumes?

I park outside their house.

'Jen.' I rest my hand on her knee before she can open the door. 'I know I don't say this enough, but you're the best thing that's ever happened to me.'

She kisses me, and the knot of pressure eases. It's a reminder that we're doing this together, and having her by my side makes the tough things seem manageable. Like staying over at my parents'.

'I take it I'll be in the guest room again,' Jen says, keeping her face close to mine.

'Not for much longer,' I remind her, squeezing her knee. 'We've done one session of marriage prep. Two more sessions to go.'

Jen gives a dry laugh, and unclicks her seatbelt.

'Michael, I know this course is just another tick-box exercise for you,' she says, 'but I really enjoyed this evening. Steve went through important points about communication, and I think we need to start putting it into practice.'

'We're English teachers.' I shrug. 'Surely we're great at communication.'

She gives me a Look with a raised eyebrow.

'Okay,' I admit, 'the listening task was good, and I know I should listen to you more often.'

'And maybe be prepared that when we're married, you can't just compartmentalise me into your 'weekend' box, because I'll be there every day. We will need to communicate *every day*.'

On the one hand, the image of Jen in my house, with me every day, is wonderful and everything I've ever dreamed of. On the other hand, potential hours of listening and important conversations stretch out into infinity. The mere thought is exhausting.

'I want to be the best husband for you,' I tell her. 'Whatever you need.'

'Just remember this isn't something you can get an A grade for,' she reminds me. 'It isn't a competition. It's just us, you and me, being together.'

I nod, but I'm instantly thinking: what if *just us* isn't good enough for her? What if I can't make her happy? What if she meets some other guy who's funnier, better looking, and can talk about astrophysics without seeming nerdy?

'I love you,' she says, in a softer tone.

For how long? is my gut reaction. I shake it off. That attitude is not helpful.

'I love you too,' I reply.

52

Jen

I can tell Michael's on edge by the way he's constantly drumming his fingers against his thigh. But so far, so good: we're at the dinner table with a delicious supper of some kind of savoury cheese tart, with walnuts and pears (no idea how Heather manages to pull this stuff off), a thick glass of wine, and even Ezra has laughed at our anecdotes from the marriage preparation course.

'How many sessions are there?' Heather asks, hopefully.

She clearly loves the fact that we'll be travelling here and staying over.

'Just two more,' Michael says.

Evidently, he can't wait to get the whole thing over and done with. Sometimes I worry that's what the whole of life will be like with Michael: always on to the next thing. Wedding before thirtieth birthday: check. Two point four children before fortieth... I haven't even asked him how many kids he wants yet.

'Oh.' Heather tries, unsuccessfully, to hide her disappointment. 'And what are your plans for tomorrow?'

'I thought we could leave after breakfast,' Michael says.

This seems a little harsh, treating them as a glorified B&B. I clear my throat to catch his attention.

'We don't need to leave straight away, do we?' I ask.

Michael looks surprised. He obviously thought I'd want to shoot off as much as he does.

'Well… no…' He hesitates, probably trying to think of an excuse or reason why he needs to get back.

'There's a special service tomorrow for the Epiphany,' Ezra says, then looks directly at me. 'If you enjoyed the carol service, you might like to come.'

An invitation! Clearly church is the way to Ezra's heart, and where I once would have kicked up a fuss about going to my grandparents' lengthy services, the idea of going back there doesn't repel me. There was something still and profound about the whole place.

'Yes please,' I agree before Michael can say no.

Later, when I'm lying in bed, I reflect with satisfaction on the day. Marriage prep was unexpectedly helpful and Ezra seems to be thawing towards me. It's a new year full of new possibilities.

But another thought stabs me like a knife in my heart: this year it will be the tenth anniversary of my mother's death.

The memories of that awful season of my life are enough to bring tears to my eyes, and as much as I try to focus on the positives (wouldn't she be happy now that I'm engaged?), the negatives stand out with the sharpness of black marker on a whiteboard. I'm getting married, and she's not going to be there to see it.

Even though I should think happy thoughts about my amazing dress, my glamorous bridesmaids, the venues and the menus, that one cold fact is enough to plunge them all into the silence of screaming underwater; nothing gets through.

It's enough to lace my dreams with a bitter aftertaste, and it's probably why I snap at Michael the next morning. He knocks at my door and sits on the bed while I rub oil into my scalp to help moisturise my hair.

'We don't have to stay all day today,' he says.

'Why not?' I ask.

'I just… didn't think we were going to stay. I didn't plan for it,' he says, betraying some agitation.

'What do you have to get back for?' I ask. 'If you want to go running, you can do it here. No one's stopping you.'

'It's not that.'

I catch his glum expression in the mirror, and turn to face him.

'You find it hard being here,' I state. 'I get it. But what are you going to do when you find it hard being with me? Work late every night to avoid me?'

'You know I would never—'

'Actually, I don't,' I say. 'I know how difficult parents can be. But I think you need to show more appreciation for the fact you have *both* parents, and they're willing to spend time with you.'

'You only just moved back in with your dad, and now you're telling me how to fix my relationship with my parents?' He runs a hand through his hair.

That stings.

'I made mistakes,' I say. 'I admit it. I've been able to put things right again. You can't do that until you're honest with them about how you feel.'

'They don't *want* honesty,' he says. 'They want me to be just how I've always been: the perfect son. It's just never good enough.'

'I think you're looking at it all wrong.' I turn back to the mirror.

'Cinnamon rolls!' Heather calls from downstairs.

After breakfast, we head out from the house to walk along the coast path that follows the cliff tops. It's a grey, cloudy morning and the wind is bracing, but hearing the crash of the waves and watching the white foam froth over the rocks makes me feel alive. So often at this time of year, it feels like I'm half asleep, like a sort of hibernation. Michael and Ezra soon outpace Heather and me; we're at the more leisurely end of the spectrum.

'It must be lovely to see the sea through the year,' I comment.

'Yes,' Heather smiles. 'It's so quiet in the winter. We have it all to ourselves virtually.'

'Did Michael and Rachel do much swimming, growing up here?' I ask.

'Yes, they loved it in summer.' She smiles at the memories. 'Seems a long time ago now.'

'We'll have to come so he can show me,' I say, 'before we go away. Maybe we could come for a weekend in June?'

'You're always welcome.' Heather beams.

I can't wait to start booking things onto our new joint calendar, which currently only exists in my head.

'I lost my mum when I was a teenager, too,' Heather says, unexpectedly.

'Oh,' I say. I don't think Michael ever mentioned it.

'I know what it's like, whenever you go through a milestone and she isn't there to see it.'

My eyes fill with tears, and the wind continues to whip my hair into a frenzy.

'Do let me know, if I can help with anything,' she says, laying a hand on my arm.

I manage a teary smile.

'Thank you, Heather.'

Ahead of us, Michael and Ezra are still keeping a good pace, when a horde of seagulls swoop down and bark noisily. Ezra twists round, loses his balance, and topples over. He catches onto Michael's coat, and pulls Michael down with him. As we hurry to catch up with them, they stand, their trousers covered in mud.

'Oh no!' Heather gasps.

I can't help laughing. Heather begins to giggle too, and Michael's expression of annoyance gradually melts into a reluctant grin. Ezra says,

'Sorry, son,' and then starts laughing too.

When I see Michael and his dad smiling side by side, the resemblance between them is uncanny.

53

Michael

There seem to be an endless amount of church services at Christmas, and the Epiphany service feels like a re-run of the carol service in some ways, though less well attended. Jen seems to actually enjoy it.

'I like the peace and stillness,' she says in the car, when we're finally on our way home.

Home. I keep thinking that it's going to be Jen's home as well soon. I already helped her move out of her flat and back into her dad's, and there was a lot of rubbish in boxes then. I shall have to resign myself to her stuff taking over. It's a small price to pay for having her with me 'till death do us part'. Steve mentioned the wedding vows at the end of the marriage prep session, so we'll need to have a conversation about those too. I look across at Jen as she leans back in the seat comfortably. All in good time.

'Do you want to come in for a bit?' she asks, when I pull up outside her dad's.

'I've got a ton of stuff to do for school.' I shake my head.

'Okay,' she says, and gives me a lingering kiss.

Not long now.

Trying to ignore the flatness of being alone in the house, I open up my emails and find a new one from David. When I told him I was training for a marathon, he started thinking about possible PR for the school. I had already entered and paid, but he said that it would be a great opportunity to raise funds. Now he's asking me to go to Bradley Cook's house tomorrow for a photo.

I don't know Bradley well, but everyone talks about him regularly in the staff room. He was diagnosed with leukaemia last year, and the PTA were joining his parents to fundraise for him. Perhaps David is thinking we can split any fundraising between Bradley and the school.

When I turn up, I'm grateful for David's ability to handle difficult situations. Bradley looks pale, but he's cracking jokes and seems genuinely happy to see us. His parents are visibly exhausted, but shower us with gratitude when we haven't even done anything yet.

Feeling humbled, I smile next to Bradley while David takes a photo, and consider how puny running a marathon seems compared with the battle this family is facing. If I can raise money as well, so be it.

'Fancy a drink?' David says hopefully, as we make our way outside.

'I've been at my parents.' I shake my head. 'Got a lot to catch up on.'

'And planning for the big day too?' he says with a jaunty smile.

'Well… a bit.'

I suppose marriage preparation courses count.

'How do you think the bus system is going?' he asks.

'Teething problems,' I comment, picturing the kids going wild instead of forming an orderly line on the yard. 'Given the circumstances, I think it's okay.'

'Yes.' He nods eagerly in agreement.

The reality is, it's not much fun on Monday morning. The temperature is about five degrees. There's black ice on the corner of the yard, and I have a headache already.

'No thank you.' I glare at a Year 7 who is edging towards the ice.

The classrooms we're using at Prestfield are pretty basic, but at least it's somewhere that isn't going to poison us. I suppose one bonus is that my lesson is twenty minutes shorter than usual. It feels like we barely cover anything before we have to jump back on the bus.

'Michael.' David grabs me in the corridor. 'Take a look at this.'

He shows me, on his phone screen, a poster with the photo he took yesterday of me and Bradley.

'Looks great, doesn't it?'

'Yeah,' I mutter, distracted by my Year 11 boys kicking a football in the corridor. 'Put that ball away!'

It's only the next morning when I come in and see my face plastered on every wall that it hits me.

SPONSOR MR CHASE, RUNNING 26 MILES FOR BRADLEY. 12TH APRIL

The marathon is on the same day as my wedding.

54

Jen

'12th April,' I remind Steph, sinking into a chair next to her in the staff room with my mug of tea.

'What's the rush?' she asks. 'Is Michael afraid you're going to turn into a pumpkin or something?'

'You know Michael.' I swig my drink. 'Everything has to be done as swiftly and efficiently as possible. He hates waiting for anything.'

'He's clearly a lot more romantic than I gave him credit for.' She grins. 'Robot guy's gone rogue.'

'I found numbers for every possible wedding supplier in his diary,' I confess. 'He booked us onto a marriage preparation course before he even proposed.'

Steph hoots with laughter.

'What does the course involve? Is it any good?'

'I did enjoy the first session, actually.' I fill her in on the key details. 'It made me realise that even though we see each other all the time in school, we're not always having proper conversations where we actually share something meaningful.'

'Ever since we came back, it's like Christmas never happened.' Steph gestures at staff walking busily across the room. 'The pace of this place is crazy. How's the new role?'

I groan and put my mug down.

'I've been booked onto training, and all these meetings, and with the shuttle bus I won't know whether I'm coming or going.'

'I'm sure it will get easier once you've got your head around it,' Steph reassures me.

'Maybe,' I say, doubtfully. 'This asbestos thing isn't helping. We have a support staff shortage and who's going to want to work here?'

'Didn't you say they were getting some Portakabins?'

I shrug.

'Michael said they were looking into it, but I don't know if anything came through.'

'Speaking of Michael, I see he's keeping himself busy.' She nods to a poster on the wall.

It's a cute photo of Michael with Bradley. There's a sticker on it saying 'SPONSOR ME'.

'He's been training for a while now,' I tell her. 'He won't have any problems running it.'

'Hello quizzers.' Sean bounds up and sits next to me. 'Can you make it this week?'

I pull a face.

'Not sure.'

'Oh, come on.' Steph nudges me. 'What are you going to do, write your seating plan?'

'Do you mean for my class or for my wedding?'

'Does it matter?' she says, and we both laugh.

'Our performance in the literature round will be sadly lacking without you,' Sean adds plaintively.

'I'll do my best.' I pacify them, but all I can see in my head is an overwhelming to-do list.

'Is Michael okay?' Sean asks. 'I feel terrible about what happened at Christmas.'

'You weren't to know,' I say, and an irrational flash of anger at Michael fizzes through me. 'He should check everything first.'

'It must be hard, though,' Steph says. 'I mean, anyone could eat an orange in the staff room at lunchtime.'

'Hence why I made that poster.' I point to the citrus allergy awareness one that I put up, noticing that someone has drawn an elaborate Edwardian moustache onto Michael's face. Teachers are worse than kids sometimes. Maybe the immaturity rubs off on us.

'Does anyone really *notice* what's on the walls, though?' Steph says incredulously. 'I bet if you asked someone what posters were up in the staffroom when they were on the yard, they wouldn't be able to name one.'

'Not even the union board?' Judy interjects, waving an Equalities poster which she then pins up.

'I notice,' I call over.

Steph looks less convinced.

'I had an email,' Judy says in a lower tone, moving closer to speak to me. 'The Chair of governors accepted the points I raised about the HR policy. She's asked to meet with me to discuss it, without David.'

She looks at me with a glint in her eye.

'Maybe I should bring up a few other things too.'

'Ask her where the Portakabins are,' Steph says. 'I'm tired of bus journeys.'

'Hear, hear,' Sean chips in.

'Perhaps you could spend your Christmas holiday ringing suppliers and see if you're any more successful,' Michael says acidly. I didn't even notice him come in.

Sean and Steph look down awkwardly and the atmosphere becomes icy.

'We know it's a difficult situation,' Judy says diplomatically. 'I just saw the posters—can I sponsor you for the marathon?'

Michael's expression changes. I wouldn't say he looks happier, though—his eyes widen slightly, as if in shock, then his brow furrows. He runs a hand through his hair, which he always does when he's stressed.

'Uh, yeah, I'll be sending out a link in a bit,' he says, his tone still snappy.

He storms off towards his classroom, and I feel everyone's eyes on me in a kind of 'What was that all about?' way.

'I think, er—' I clear my throat. 'He's got a lot on at the moment.'

He's certainly firing out enough emails to fill my inbox to maximum capacity (again). Amidst emails saying I've reached my storage limit, there are department memos, an agenda for our meeting, several different emails with huge attachments, and by break there's a new one he's sent to all staff with a link to a donation page for the marathon. I bookmark it—I use the red flag for anything important and then categorise it later when I get the chance (there are a lot of flagged emails clogging up my inbox)—then shut my laptop in frustration. Why is my fiancé determined to live at this inhuman level of intensity? I'm beginning to worry that he'll have a heart attack.

I look at my diary. I suppose I'm in no position to lecture him, when I'm cramming in meetings in an over-full schedule. I had an email from a parent asking if there was any support available for their child. I look the child's name up on the system: Kane Lewis. He's listed as having moderate learning difficulties and poor literacy. Who is his English teacher? Liz.

I go back to the email. *Struggling with spelling... Lacks confidence... Quiet in class...* He would have had a supply teacher while Liz was off, so that probably hasn't helped. I head for the staffroom to see if Liz is around. Luckily, she's chatting to Judy.

'Hiya.' I approach them both. 'Liz, do you have a minute to discuss Kane Lewis?'

'Sure,' Liz says. 'He's struggling, isn't he?'

'Yes.' I'm glad she's aware of this already. 'His dad emailed me about his spelling.'

'Basically, he doesn't know a lot of the sound patterns,' Liz explains. 'I bought some flashcards to use with my son, so I thought I could bring them in and see which ones he doesn't know, and then give him a pack to take home for his parents to work through with him.'

'That sounds great.' I try to hide my surprise. I had assumed that Liz was pretty switched off; she had been behind on the schemes of work in September, and then she was signed off for a few months. Maybe I misjudged the situation.

'I'll bring the resources to the meeting,' she says. 'There may be other students who would benefit from them.'

Our meeting is in Michael's room after school. He's not actually there when I arrive, and I wonder whether he's been roped into bus duty. Judy volunteers to make tea, and Liz supplies some chocolate biscuits. Geoff comes in, and it feels like the old, easy dynamic between the four of us from last year.

'I'm getting a puppy,' Judy announces.

She shows us photos of an adorable-looking King Charles spaniel.

'My sister got one last year,' Liz says. 'I think he's only just sleeping through the night.'

'Sounds like a baby,' Geoff comments.

'Well, I figured we need a new adventure.' Judy grins. 'Plus Lydia will come over more often because she'll want to play with him.'

I remember Judy showing me photos of Lydia's graduation, but that was two years ago.

'Where is she based now?' I ask.

'Sheffield,' Judy says. 'She's working in speech therapy.'

'Dylan's been going for weekly sessions with a speech therapist,' Liz says. 'I think he finds signing easier.'

'Does your son use sign language?' I ask. I've been reading about the need to train up support staff in this.

'Yes, he's very good at it.' Liz smiles and pulls up a picture on her phone to show me. 'I've been taking an evening class to learn it too. He has Down syndrome so his speech is a little trickier.'

Dylan is wearing a cowboy hat and striking a pose in the picture.

'He looks cute,' I say.

I'm feeling guilty that I never asked Liz much about her kids. Now I'm realising that her experience would be an amazing help when I'm so out of my depth with all of these different learning needs I'm supposed to be dealing with.

Michael bursts through the door, out of breath and flustered.

'Sorry everyone.'

He moves over to his laptop and starts setting it up, typing the keys aggressively.

'There's a tea there for you,' Judy says.

'Thank you.' He picks it up gratefully. 'I've just been talking to David. The Portakabins are arriving at the end of the week.'

'Which company is it?' Geoff asks.

'Well,' Michael begins, 'it's actually a parent's company. Do you know Jack Casey? He's best friends with Bradley. He told his mum about the marathon and the fundraising, and she rang up to say that her company is looking for a local charity to support this year, and they would like to make a large donation.'

'How large?' I ask.

'Ten grand,' Michael says. There's a collective gasp. 'Anyway, David asked her more about the business, and she mentioned

Portakabins, and then he said we urgently needed some... It all worked out perfectly.'

David Clark definitely seems to be a magnet for good things to just fall into his lap.

'Okay, so I sent you all the agenda for today's meeting.' Michael reverts back to business-mode. 'Item one: raising achievement.'

I think I need another chocolate biscuit.

55

Michael

This day is really not going well.

After running around the school slapping big red stickers over the date on every marathon poster (nearly meeting my training distance in the process), I manage to grab David after school.

'There's a problem,' I say, and explain about the clash of dates.

That's when he tells me about the ten-grand donation.

'You can't pull out now,' David says. 'Why don't you shift the wedding by a week?'

'I already got in trouble with Jen about the date,' I say. 'And now we've told everyone.'

'What time is the ceremony?'

'Two o'clock.'

'The marathon starts at nine,' he says. 'What's your expected time?'

'Three and a half hours?' I say.

'There you go then.' David smiles. 'What's the problem?'

'I can't tell Jen it's on the same day,' I say flatly. 'She will kill me.'

'Does she even need to know?' David shrugs. 'Look Michael, I'll be your wing man. I'll drive you there, bring your suit, pick you up and everything. I will promise that you won't miss your wedding.'

I feel like the stress is imploding in my skull.

I rush to our department meeting, late, when there's already way too many items on the agenda to cover in the time. I manage to plough through, talking fast and scrolling through slides on the screen at breakneck speed.

'Any other business?' I finally exhale at the end, ready to collapse.

'I'd just like to share these resources for students with poor literacy,' Liz says.

I've just finally taken a bite of a chocolate biscuit and I try not to choke in surprise.

'Jen and I have been talking about Kane Lewis, but we could send this pack home for other students too.'

She briefly explains it, and this could be really good… although I feel cross that there's so many things Liz could be doing to help as Second in Department.

'Thank you,' I snap. 'I'll send out the minutes tomorrow.'

I just want this day to be over now. I'm fed up with feeling like I'm dodging bullets, and the black folder with a pile of Shakespeare essays is weighing on me like a HGV.

Geoff, Judy and Liz gather their things and leave in a subdued mood. As I shove my laptop in my bag with unnecessary force, Jen stands at my desk and lays a hand on my arm.

'Do you want to grab a coffee before you go home?' Her tone is laced with concern.

Part of me would love it; part of me hates the thought of sitting there while Jen tries her best to communicate with me, and I (hypocritically) try to hide the fact that I'm going to run twenty-six miles before our wedding ceremony.

'I'm sorry, I can't,' I sigh. 'I'm going to go for a run and clear my head.'

'Okay.' Jen removes her hand.

I want to take her in my arms but knowing my luck, David Clark would walk in. Right now it's enough to stop him plastering my face over the whole town on these marathon posters.

'Have a good run,' she says, turning to leave. 'You can call me later if you want to chat.'

I miserably watch her walk to the door, almost forgetting to say, 'I love you.'

She looks back over her shoulder and smiles. Then she's gone.

56

Jen

Clare: How was marriage prep?

Me: Nice people. Good pointers on communication.

Deena: Did you tell Michael he has to ask you first before he signs you up for something next time lol?

Me: :/ He's acting a bit weird lately.

Clare: How do you mean?

Me: I don't know… Maybe he's just busy.

Clare: He's probably under pressure with the asbestos crisis, from what you've said.

Me: Yeah, I think so.

Deena: What happened with the HR policy of no dating?

Me: My union rep contested it. She's meeting with the chair of governors. Looks hopeful that it will be thrown out.

Deena: Maybe Michael's getting cold feet?

I laugh out loud at how ludicrous this suggestion is. Michael, who hares through life at a million miles an hour, get cold feet about something that was *his* idea in the first place?

Me: Michael doesn't change his mind about things.

It gives me some relief; even if Michael is a little short-tempered and preoccupied with work, I know he is looking forward to April 12th as much as I am. It's some consolation that the week passes quickly and the next marriage preparation session suddenly arrives. We haven't really had much time to practise the communication exercise, so we take it in turns on the journey to share about the week.

'I'll go first,' I offer. 'I've been working with Liz this week, and it's actually been really helpful and enjoyable. I didn't really appreciate her situation and her experience before.'

Michael raises an eyebrow but says nothing.

'I know she hasn't been very reliable at meeting deadlines in the past,' I continue, 'but I think she's come back wanting to do her job well, and we should encourage her when she makes the effort to bring something to the table.'

Michael's gaze is fixed upon the road, his eyes narrowing a little. He doesn't verbalise his disagreement, but it hangs heavily in the air between us. In the end, I break the silence.

'Michael?' I ask in irritation. 'Can you at least acknowledge that you were a little curt with Liz at the meeting?'

'I thought we were meant to be communicating about what's important to us, not criticising each other.'

'This is important to me.'

'You see the best in people,' Michael says, as if it's a bad thing, 'but at some point the narrative that everyone-has-a-contribution breaks down. Namely, when someone doesn't do their job properly. Things are going to get really awkward if you try to tell me how to manage someone else in my department.'

'I'm not trying to tell you how to manage—'

'Well it sounds like you want me to give her a medal for showing up and actually having an idea to offer.'

'You need to listen to yourself sometimes, Michael.' I cover my face with my hands and press my fingertips to my forehead for a moment. 'I know you can be kind, generous and funny. But times like this, you just sound like David Clark. There's a reason why he has no friends.'

'I've told you before, I don't agree with all of his decisions. I don't like him and I know he treated you badly. But I do acknowledge that he's a leader, and that he's out there on his own. He's shouldering a lot, and he has to make unpopular choices because it's what he believes is best for the school. It's easier to judge him when you're watching him from a distance. I've seen him up close these last few weeks; I've seen him struggle through an absolute minefield of health and safety issues where many would just quit. He's still there. He may not have friends, but that shows he's willing to make sacrifices to keep Whidlock open.'

Michael takes a breath and checks over his shoulder before joining the motorway. I try to compose the swirl of guilt and anger which muddles my thoughts. I've had an unshakeable conviction that David Clark is a charmer, someone more obsessed with image than substance, since he taught me ten years ago when I was a student. He hasn't done much to counter this image since arriving in September as our new executive Head. He clearly over-relies on Michael because they came together from his previous school, and he's closer to Michael in age than to the rest of Senior Team, who have children at university. Have I judged him wrongfully? If I misjudged Liz, there's certainly a possibility that I'm guilty of doing the same with David. But David told me to withdraw my application for the Head of Department role, which Michael got anyway, and has done everything in his power to split me and Michael up. I'm only surprised he hasn't discovered (or invented) some other HR policy which specifies that no staff members can be married, in order to prevent us. I imagine the vicar, asking the legal question 'If anyone knows of any reason why these two cannot be joined in holy matrimony, declare it now', and David Clark bursting through the church doors, wearing his usual suit, brandishing papers as evidence for his objection.

'I get so busy sometimes I forget to be nice,' Michael sighs. 'I'm not saying that as an excuse, trying to make out that it's okay to be a horrible boss. I don't want to be like that. I've just... been under a lot of pressure.'

'Is there anything I can help with?' I reach over and take his hand. He squeezes it.

'Once the Portakabins are set up, no more bussing around, and things will settle down,' he says with finality. 'I will set up a time to see Liz next week and I'll apologise for not being more positive.'

In some ways it's a satisfying response, but in another sense, it's a classic example of Michael always having the right answer for everything, smoothing over the cracks so that the illusion of perfection is maintained. It doesn't feel like anything I've said has really touched him deep down. That's not a kind of response you can force.

There's a lively atmosphere at the marriage prep class, and an increasing level of banter now that we're getting to know one another better. Steve gives us a warm-up task of sitting back-to-back, building something with some blocks, and then instructing the other person to build the same structure. Mattie's hooting with laughter so much she can barely hear Benedict's frenetic instructions, and Violet seems more distracted with Michael's strategy of giving me co-ordinates as if we're playing Battleships. When I say distracted, I mean laughing in disbelief while she tries to instruct James at the same time.

'Red block to C4,' Michael barks.

I roll my eyes.

'Michael, I have no idea what you mean.'

'Just imagine the table is a grid in 5cm blocks. Horizontal axis is labelled in letters, the vertical with numbers. Then you'll be fine.'

I place the red block in a random place on the table.

'Blue block to H4.'

I put the blue block parallel to the red one.

'Now the yellow block needs to be on C4 too,' Michael says. 'I should have worked out a system to indicate depth.'

'On top of the red block?' I ask, catching Violet's eye as she fails to suppress another laugh.

'Yes,' Michael replies.

'Well why don't you just say that, then?' I place the yellow block down with slight force.

By the time Steve calls us back together, I have made an odd pile of three blocks in a rough sort of triangle. Mattie's made a huge tower which wobbles precariously before falling down with a crash, and Violet's made a sort of bridge.

'A fitting metaphor for our topic this evening,' Steve says. 'When you get married, you are each coming from separate families to create a new family. You both have to help the other to navigate through the unique landscape that is your family. For some of you, your families may look quite similar from the outside. But every family has its quirks, values and behaviours that are acceptable or unacceptable. Your family has shaped who you are. Together, you two will create a bridge, and your marriage will be stronger than if you try to build a new structure with no support on either side.'

Steve gives us some questions to work through together. I scan them and my stomach queases. If my childhood is a landscape, it's pretty rocky and I don't like going there. Now that I've met Michael's parents, I wonder if Michael's childhood looks like an idyllic beach but is actually full of quicksand.

'How would you describe your childhood?' I read out, looking at Michael.

He reflexively runs his hand through his hair.

'Good,' he says blandly. 'Nothing out of the ordinary. We went to the sea in the summer, enjoyed Christmas all together.'

It seems facetious to say 'yes, but your dad is impossible to please.' If he can't articulate it, then he won't accept it if I say it.

'What about you?' he asks. 'Before your mum left?'

That feels like a very foreign landscape.

'I remember food.' I smile, hearing again the cheerful noise of the radio and the clatter of pans in the kitchen. 'Mum cooked Jamaican style: chicken, rice and peas. Dad cooked the classics: shepherd's pie, macaroni cheese. We always ate together.'

'How did your parents relate to one another?' Michael reads the next question.

I give a dry laugh.

'My mum was fiercely independent. She had opinions about everything. My dad just let her get on with it, really. He idolised her.'

'Maybe we're more similar to them than you think.' Michael squeezes my hand with a grin.

There's so much about my parents' dynamic that I just can't adequately express to him: the nuances of a white British guy with a second-generation Jamaican woman whose parents lived in the UK for most of their adult lives, but created their own community so that they continued their cultural traditions. Visiting my grandparents, going to their church, had the odd sensation of being somewhere different. I loved them, but I found them hard to understand, especially as we didn't see them very often. I can hardly expect Michael to 'get' something I don't fully grasp myself.

'If I went out with my dad, people didn't think he was my father, or that we were related, because we look so different,' I explain. 'After Mum left, Deena's mum had to help me with my hair, because my dad had no idea. If we have children with hair like mine, you might go through the same thing.'

'That doesn't change anything,' Michael says, smoothing the back of my hand with his thumb.

'Okay,' I swallow. 'Sorry, I've gone off topic. How about you answer the question now?'

'About my parents?' he asks, and shifts in his seat. 'Well, maybe it's the opposite. My dad has the opinions and my mum goes along with him.'

And gets steamrollered in the process. The problem is, Michael doesn't seem to see much wrong with this pattern.

'Do you think that's a good thing?' I ask pointedly.

'I'm sure Mum tells him her views when they're discussing something on their own,' Michael answers. 'But when I was growing up, she would never say anything to contradict him in front of us. That's good for kids, isn't it, a united front?'

'Not if they never see healthy ways of dealing with conflict,' I frown. 'It gives the impression that any disagreements have to be swept under the carpet. Plus, I've only met your parents twice, and both times I've seen your mum get upset because of your dad. If you grew up with that, then maybe it wasn't such a united front as you think.'

'Time's up,' Steve calls. 'Now, you may have heard phrases like 'you end up turning into your parents'. I don't think that's necessarily true. But what I'd now like you to discuss together is how your ways of relating to each other could mirror your parents' relationship in some ways. Where that is positive, that's great. But where it's a negative pattern, this is a good opportunity to identify it and talk about how you could change.'

I look at Michael, who checks his phone. He's probably counting down the minutes till the session finishes.

'Michael?'

He looks up guiltily, and slips the phone back into his pocket.

'When I tried to talk to you in the car about Liz, you got defensive and shut me down.' I take a deep breath. 'I need to be able to express my opinions when they are different to yours without being afraid that you're going to take it as personally offensive.'

'I don't mind hearing your opinions,' he replies, 'but I won't be like your dad and just say 'yes dear' to everything you say. You can't try to control me by heavily suggesting things, and then taking offence when I don't follow your advice.'

He's an expert debater. Sometimes I worry that our arguments will go on forever.

'I don't want to end up like my mum,' I sigh. 'But I don't want you to end up like your dad, either.'

57

Michael

By the time we get to my parents' house, I have the unsatisfied feeling of arguing over something that doesn't really matter, because I've hidden the subject that we really need to discuss. I don't feel right about hiding the marathon clash from Jen, but there's no good time to bring it up. What will I do if she says, in one of her final pronouncements, that there's no way I should do it and if I don't cancel it, the wedding's off? That's exactly the sort of thing she'd say.

'How is the running going?' Dad asks me.

'I'm on track,' I reply. Ironic really—it's the only thing I'm doing well.

After dinner, Jen's in the kitchen with Mum. Dad beckons me into the lounge. He hands me a manila envelope.

'It's a draft pre-nuptial agreement,' he says.

I cast a worried look over my shoulder to check Jen is out of earshot.

'Dad,' I hiss, 'this is really insulting. Do you honestly think we're going to get divorced?'

'I just wouldn't want to see you lose your house, if anything happened. Remember we gave you the deposit.'

'I'm grateful,' I say through gritted teeth, 'but you can't hold it over me, Dad.'

'Just take it and read it over when you get a chance.'

'Michael, do you want tea or coffee?' Jen calls.

'Coffee please.'

I stomp into the hallway and put the envelope in my bag. Having both parents as lawyers, I think my whole family has trust issues. *I don't want you to end up like your dad*, Jen said. Seeing the world as he sees it, I envision the scenario: Jen yelling at me that I've ruined her life, and packing a bag, and leaving forever. Divorce papers through the post. Putting my house on the market. The whole thing gives me physical pain in my stomach. A pre-nup isn't going to salve that wound; it would be like trying to stick a plaster over a haemorrhage. I just need to not screw this up.

Maybe I should approach Jen about changing the date. After all, it's a lot of stress on her to plan a wedding at such short notice.

I sit with my parents and drink coffee while Jen calls Katie, and amidst my non-committal responses to mindless small talk, I try to formulate a few choice phrases to broach the subject. *I've been thinking about the stress you've been under. I didn't really consider what planning a wedding in four months would be like.*

'Guess what?' Jen bursts in, her face shining, holding out her phone. 'Katie's booked us two nights at a luxury hotel for our 'minimoon', as she calls it. AND she's designed the invites. Look!'

My heart sinks as I see the scripted writing of the fatal date: **12th April** in bold black font. Why did I have to choose this date? Why did I rush everything?

'Do you like it?' Jen asks.

I've barely registered the gold feather and dark green leaf design.

'It's great,' I say mechanically.

'If we order them now, we'll be able to send them out by next weekend,' she grins.

'They look very elegant,' Mum says approvingly.

Dad catches my eye with a reproachful look, then picks up the newspaper.

We leave shortly after breakfast the next day, as we've finally arranged to cook for Dan and Louise as we'd promised. Jen's mood seems to have received an injection of fresh positivity and energy from the hotel and the invites, and she chatters away on the drive about finding her mum's recipe for chicken.

'I was thinking about what Steve said,' she continues. 'I don't need to be afraid that I'm going to make the same mistakes as Mum did. I can still celebrate the happy times, otherwise it feels like I'm dragging around a ball and chain whenever I think about her. It's ten years since she died next month. I want to mark it somehow.'

I've been wanting Jen to open up more about her mum, and find healthy ways of grieving, since I heard about her death, but I'm so preoccupied with my own sword of Damocles that I have limited enthusiasm.

'That's great,' I reply, flatly.

'Is everything okay?' she asks, examining my expression.

I do my best poker face. Then I attempt a smile.

'Everything's fine.'

'Can you pull over?' She points to an upcoming layby.

I indicate and move the car off the main road. It rolls to a halt.

'I'm enjoying the marriage prep course, and seeing your parents, but I want to *connect* with you,' she says. 'You've been really stressed at work. Do you want to talk about it?'

'Work is… not that bad,' I answer truthfully.

'Is it David?' she presses. 'Is he overloading you?'

I shake my head.

'He's been all right.'

'Is it… me?' she asks, searching my face. 'Have I done something?'

Guilt twists in my stomach.

'No,' I say, touching her cheek.

I can hear the soft noise of her breath. I lean forward, savouring the moment where our faces are so close but still a hair's breadth apart. She smells honey-sweet. Our mouths meet, and I can't think about anything else.

'I was beginning to worry you didn't like me anymore,' she says, breathlessly.

I answer her first with another kiss.

'I don't deserve you,' I tell her.

By the time we've stopped off at the supermarket, then arrived at my house, we can't wait to shut the door and be alone together. I never saw my hallway as a particularly romantic place, until Jen grabs me, causing me to drop the shopping bags in surprise.

'Kiss me,' she demands, and I'm not going to argue.

'I should probably put the chicken in the fridge,' I suggest, after a few minutes of what Brontë might call a 'passionate embrace'.

'I'm going to marinade it,' Jen murmurs against my ear, and it's unbelievably sexy though I have no idea why.

I find her mouth again and kiss her until she groans in the back of her throat.

'Does talking about cooking always turn you on?' she asks wryly.

'Only when you're doing it,' I reply.

We manage to sort out the food, in-between some rather heated interludes, but then Jen surprises me again by putting the kettle on.

'We never really finished our conversation about my exes,' she says. 'Now might be a good time.'

'Okay,' I gulp. It seems ironic that, while I'm struggling not to break my vow and take Jen upstairs, we have to talk about the guys who have already had that privilege.

'It's not as bad as you think,' she continues, setting out mugs and twisting open the tin of teabags. 'My first boyfriend was Jamie.

We were together in Year 11. I didn't sleep with him. Then there was George. I met him at uni, and went back to his room a couple of times. But it didn't last long. I used a dating app and met Ryan, but we just went on a few dates. He lived with his parents, and I didn't want to bring him back to my flat. That's it.'

'So… you only slept with George?' I ask. This is much better than my original estimates.

'Yes, technically.'

Jen pours hot water into the mugs.

'What do you mean, technically?'

'You know,' she says, 'like Americans say with 'first base' and all that.'

'What?' I'm totally clueless.

'There's a difference between going 'all the way' with someone and just… *doing stuff.*'

'Oh.'

I take my mug. I suppose this is to be expected. I can't help but feel nervous about my complete lack of experience. What if I'm rubbish?

'What was your first time like, with George?' I ask. I want to know, but I also don't want to know.

'It was all right,' she shrugs. 'I wouldn't say it was amazing. He was… nice.'

Nice? Ouch. I hope she doesn't say that about me if Katie or Deena asks her… I hope they don't ask her… Is it normal for women to talk about this?

'What I mean is,' she continues, 'you don't need to worry. You don't have to live up to anything. I may have done it before but it doesn't make me experienced.'

'I'm worried,' I confess, 'that I'm not going to be good enough for you.'

'I'm nervous too,' she smiles. 'But judging from what happens when we kiss, I don't think we're going to have any problems.'

58

Jen

Before Dan and Louise arrive, I send Katie a photo of my Jamaican style chicken dish.

Me: Not bad for a first try.

Katie: Memories!!!

Just the smell of it brings back Saturday afternoons at home, my mum singing in the kitchen… It's bittersweet because it's part of the past, but the sweetness is stronger than the bitterness.

'This is delicious,' Dan says.

'Thank you so much for cooking.' Louise smiles warmly.

It feels easier now, this new friendship, and Dan makes me laugh with stories of Michael's university escapades.

'We were at this country pub by a river, and some guys had hired a boat to get there. But then they drank too much and ordered a taxi. Michael insisted on rowing the boat all the way back.'

You can always trust Michael to do the right thing.

'I was wondering if you wanted to set a date for a stag do,' Dan asks Michael, while we're polishing off the treacle pudding. 'Also, if you put me in touch with your chief bridesmaid, we could even link up and have the hen do on the same day.'

'My sister Katie,' I grin. 'We have a wedding WhatsApp group—shall we add you?'

'Yes, great!' he says enthusiastically.

'Hopefully there'll be less memes now.' Michael rolls his eyes.

'How's the rest of the planning coming along?' Louise asks.

I show her the invites on my phone.

'We still need a photographer. Do you know anyone who won't charge a ridiculous amount?'

'My sister's at uni, and she's been doing a bit of photography,' Louise says. 'She took some great pictures at our cousin's wedding last summer, though she wasn't the official photographer. I could put you in touch if you like.'

'That'd be great.'

It actually feels like things are coming together. I thought it would be impossible.

'How's Grace?' I ask.

'She's good,' Louise grins. 'Although I have to say, it's nice to be out of the house and have a babysitter for a change! You feel like you're cut off from society when you're surrounded by nappies and psychedelic kids' TV programmes.'

'Is this dish Jamaican?' Dan asks.

'Yes,' I nod. 'My grandparents were from Jamaica.'

'Have you ever been there?' Louise chips in.

'Well, we're actually hoping to go this summer,' I reply, catching Michael's eye and smiling. 'Although we haven't been very organised about it yet.'

'Do you still have any family there?' Dan asks.

'Probably,' I answer vaguely. 'The trouble is, we lost touch with most of them. It's, er—' I pause to clear my throat. 'It's been ten years since my mum died.'

There's a moment of silence and I can't believe I actually managed to say it out loud.

'I'm so sorry,' Louise says, laying a hand on my arm.

'It's okay,' I say, feeling my eyes well up, and grabbing a sheet of kitchen roll. 'I've been thinking about it a lot, with the wedding…'

I start to sob. What a way to wreck a dinner party. There's a long pause as I try to pull myself together.

'I'm sorry,' I apologise, sniffing and giving my face carpet-burn from the roughness of the kitchen towel.

'You don't need to be sorry,' Louise says firmly, squeezing my arm. 'Let me get you some tissues.'

She finds a box and I gratefully dab my eyes.

'Weddings can be really hard like that,' Dan says sympathetically. 'You've got all these people around you who love you, and that's amazing. But you're always conscious if someone isn't there anymore. Or if there's tension between different relatives.'

'Our photos were a nightmare with all the different groups,' Louise says. 'You can't please everyone.'

'That's the problem,' Dan agrees. 'It's meant to be your day, but other people have expectations about what the day should be like.'

'Everyone has an opinion.' Louise smiles. 'But maybe this is a good opportunity for you to get back in touch with family you haven't seen for a long time. Weddings can really bring people together.'

I think I could get Katie on the case. She's great at tracking people down on social media.

'I'll help you with those.' Dan jumps up as Michael starts stacking plates.

'Thanks.' He smiles. 'How about we make some tea?'

59

Michael

'If there's anything I can do to help with the wedding stuff, just let me know,' Dan says, as we stand by the kettle.

'Thanks,' I answer hollowly. 'It's not the wedding I'm worried about so much. I'm supposed to be running a marathon in the morning.'

'What, as in the morning of the wedding?' Dan does a double take.

'Shhh!' I hush him. 'Jen doesn't know about the clash.'

'Well that's a recipe for disaster.'

I shrug helplessly.

'I don't know what to do. I'm raising money for a kid who's got cancer, and David's plastered my face on posters all over Whidlock.'

'Why can't he get someone else to do it? It is your wedding, after all.'

'I've been doing all the training for months now. I can't just ask someone to fill in,' I point out. 'Plus, it's my mistake. Marathons are usually on Sundays. I must have completely missed it in my diary.'

'I don't suppose running it the day after your wedding would be much better,' Dan says. 'Look, Michael, don't take offence at this, but... Sometimes you've got to let things go. I know you've trained and I know you might disappoint people, but at the end of the day, you're getting married and that's more important.'

'One of the parents is making a ten-grand donation. Ten grand!'

'That's a lot,' Dan concedes. 'But it's the principle. Even if someone came along with ten million, your wedding takes priority.'

'David thinks I can do both.' The fact that I'm using David's argument should alarm me. 'It starts at 9 a.m.; I'll be done by half twelve. Wedding starts at two o'clock.'

'What if you break your leg or something?'

'Unlikely,' I scoff.

'You need to tell Jen,' Dan says.

I sigh.

'You saw how much pressure she's under right now. I don't want to make things worse.'

'The whole point of you getting married is that you're going to share everything,' Dan says. 'You go through life together, sharing your burdens, and helping each other through. You can't fly solo anymore, Michael.'

'I'll try and talk to her,' I promise.

The next day, Dan and Katie ping messages back and forth on the WhatsApp group, and the hen/stag date is fixed for March. Dan promptly creates another group for the stags. My phone has gone into meltdown.

Setting it to one side, I look at our marriage prep assignment. I have to choose a compliment or positive quality to describe Jen for each letter of her name. I find a sheet of letter paper and write JENNIFER down the side, like an acrostic. I'm essentially doing a Year 7 poetry homework task.

As much as I try to forget it, Dan's reaction when I told him about the marathon troubles me. After all, he's a happily married man. I'm choosing not to listen to his advice, but to the laissez-faire attitude of bachelor David Clark, who doesn't tend to hold down a long-term relationship. Plus, Jen would argue that I shouldn't listen to David full stop, about anything. But the thought of pulling out revolts me. It goes against the core of my being: I've said I'll do something, so I should do it. It was, technically, a prior commitment before I got engaged. I'm furious at my own mistake, and I just can't accept that I will have to relinquish one of these two things. My training plan is all in place; I'm confident that my predicted race time is accurate. Why should I pull out and waste all that training? What would Bradley's parents think?

I think I should broach the subject of potentially changing the date with Jen. I chickened out last time, because of the invites, but I need to speak up. I open up my phone and the WhatsApp groups are full of unread posts. Katie's posted a 'wedding countdown' which gives us an exact breakdown of the days and hours before April 12th (88 days, 14 hours).

Maybe it's better to talk in person. I'll wait until tomorrow.

60

Jen

Following a number of concerns raised, the governors have decided to discontinue the new policy regarding relationships between staff members. We have sufficient trust that any staff with romantic connections will act in a professional manner on site, and we apologise for any negative impression this policy may have created.

Yours etc
Lavender Collins
Chair of Governors

I smile to myself as I read the email on Monday morning. Judy's conversation obviously went well. It's satisfying to think that David can't just get his own way all the time.

'Jen.' Michael walks into my room, and as I glance up at him from my laptop, I can see he's agitated. I close the lid.

'What's the matter?'

'I've been thinking.' He takes a deep breath. 'Don't take this the wrong way, but I've been wondering if we should change the wedding date.'

My eyes widen. Sure, it was a shock when he sprung it on me that he'd booked the church and signed us up for marriage prep. But now that I've got my dress, and the venue sorted, and Katie's made the invites, it would feel very annoying to change it now. Why on earth would he even want to?

The thought drops like a stone in my stomach. *He's read the email about the HR policy. He doesn't want to marry me anymore.*

'So now David says it's okay for us to date, you don't fancy the hassle of a wedding, do you?' I snap.

'I still want to get married!' he exclaims. 'But maybe we could shift it by a few days…'

'Why?'

'I made a mistake…'

'Oh really?' I say acidly.

'I don't know how it happened, but—'

Then the fire alarm sounds. I've had enough of listening to this anyway. I grab my coat and march out to the yard.

Students are pouring out of every door, and the noise of the rabble resembles a crowd of football fans. The day is barely beginning, and students are still coming in through the school gates, and facing the confusion of a fire procedure. Staff usher them into rows, looking harried. I don't have a form group now that I've taken on my new role, but I stand with the TAs and support staff. I can see Michael talking with Joseph Vermont, a stone's throw from David. Janet Patchell turns on a megaphone.

'All students should wait in a line with their tutor,' she says, her crisp tones muffled and distorted slightly. 'We need to wait until the alarm stops before we can go into the building.'

The noise level rises as more students arrive, and tutors walk around trying to register them. The problem is, no one knows who's absent anyway because no registers have been taken yet today.

Holly and Liam, two teaching assistants, are discussing the two Portakabins that were delivered over the weekend, which are now taking up a significant proportion of the yard. I zone out as I feel the familiar surge of anger mixed with anxiety. Why does Michael want to change the date? How much did the HR policy affect his motivation to propose? And then there's the issue of him turning thirty. Was I just a convenient choice, in the right place at the right time?

Though she thinks I'm a bit mad to be getting married so soon into the relationship, Steph didn't ever seem surprised that Michael proposed. But Joseph Vermont looks down his nose at me, similar to David Clark. They think I'm a bit of a joke compared to their slick professionalism. Well, no one's suing *me* at least! That's one thing I have.

Michael looks over at me and catches my eye, despite the distance of the yard and fifty rows of disgruntled students between us. I hitch in my breath. I still feel that funny flip of desire when I look at him, and the intensity of his stare suggests that he really wants us to be alone so we can talk, although that's not likely to happen. I *know* he isn't faking this. It's just that I can't shake the worry of him beginning to listen to David or his dad, the people who don't think I'm good enough for him. Just his comment the other day that he has more to lose, due to his house and assets, bugged me. He's got that self-righteous *I-worked-for-this* attitude, even though he was given a considerable leg-up by his parents. We're all working, but some of us get more privileges than others.

'We have been given the all-clear.' Janet's magnified voice interrupts my thoughts. 'Year 7, you may enter the building.'

'Are we doing a briefing?' Holly asks me.

'Yes, come straight to my room,' I instruct the group of support staff. I'm going to share with them which pupils they are working with this week, and what's coming up.

As we head towards the main entrance, I pointedly ignore Michael, but then David Clark calls to me.

'Jen, have you got a minute?'

Reluctantly I step back, allowing the group to overtake me.

'Did you check your emails this morning?' David asks.

I frown, wondering if he's making some reference to the HR policy.

'I read one or two.'

'So all good with the Portakabin then?'

I look straight at Michael, feeling my heart sink. He gives me a hopeful smile.

'I thought you'd appreciate a bigger classroom,' he says. 'And that you could make it into a support hub for students.'

When exactly did he decide all this? Why didn't he say anything for the entire weekend about it? The rage is back.

'I would *appreciate* being consulted next time,' I snap. 'Thanks for the advanced warning.'

'Not a very satisfied customer,' David remarks dryly. 'At this rate, we won't need a HR policy anyway, because you will have split up.'

'You didn't need a HR policy in the first place, as I believe Lavender Collins admits in her email to staff this morning,' I retort. 'Good to see the governors were willing to listen to reason.'

'I'm repurposing your old room to become a meeting room,' David informs me, with a satisfied expression. 'I hear it's decorated to a high standard.'

Unexpected tears start into my eyes.

'I don't expect you would understand what it's like to put your heart and soul into something,' I say. 'Excuse me.'

I push past to slot into the scrum of students swarming into the school, memories of being one myself suddenly resurfacing with the immersion. I walk, slightly unsteadily, thinking of how long it took me to transform what used to be a corridor with lockers into my cosy classroom. Years. Part of me knows that I can do it again, and it won't take that long, and that the Portakabin is a useful step up in terms of space, and setting up a designated area for support. But that's not the point.

I stumble into my bright orange room, my cat posters forming a colourful display, and the team are waiting for me. I grab a notebook and, shaking off my dazed stupor, read through the announcements I need to make. The bell rings and the team disperse.

Then Michael comes in. He's clearly waited till the end of the briefing.

'You didn't tell me,' I accuse.

'I honestly forgot,' he says. 'I thought you'd be happy you'd been upgraded.'

'You didn't ask.' I shake my head.

'Well,' Michael says, gesturing at the layered walls. 'I didn't think I had to. This used to be a corridor!'

'But it was mine,' I argue. 'I made it my own. Now I'm going to have to shift all this stuff into a freezing cold Portakabin and start everything from scratch all over again.'

Michael looks taken aback.

'Is this what it's going to be like being married to you?' I ask, feeling my anger build. 'I find out what decision you've made when it happens to me, like suddenly we're moving house or there's a new car in the driveway?'

'That's not how I wanted you to feel—'

'How would you like it if I did that to you?' I demand. 'If I said, "good morning Michael, I've moved you to a Portakabin. Collect all your stuff and get set up. Congratulations on your upgrade".'

'I'm sorry,' he says. 'I didn't think you'd react like this. But I really wanted us to talk more about the wedding date. I didn't have time to explain—'

'I've been spending the past few months, ever since we got together, saying we need to talk more,' I interrupt, holding my hand up like a stop sign in front of him. 'Now I've got to the point where I don't want to talk anymore. I have a ton of work to do and I don't have time for your confessions or apologies when you had the whole weekend to do that, and you didn't.'

Furiously, I grab a box which is half full of copies of 'A Christmas Carol', and start throwing items from my desk into it.

'I can help you—' he says, attempting to take the box, but I snatch it back.

'No!' I raise my voice. David Clark can come in and I don't care. 'Just… give me some space, Michael.'

'Space?' he repeats, dully.

'I'll let you know when I'm ready to talk,' I say.

It's not going to be any time soon.

61

Michael

I'm in serious trouble.

Jen's room upgrade has backfired, and now she's seething. I blunder through the day, trying to think up strategies for both (a) being honest with her about the marathon and (b) convincing her that I still want to marry her more than anything else in the world.

By break time, I've decided that (a) should be de-prioritised.

By lunch time, (b) is flashing red and marked 'URGENT'. Jen is talking to Steph in the staff room and then stops when I walk in. They both stare at me coldly. Mayday! Mayday!

'Do you want to grab a tea after work?' I ask Jen, nervously feeling like a teenager again.

'What, in the Portakabin?' she says disdainfully.

'No, out somewhere.' I try to pick something Jen will find irresistible. 'The snack van?'

The temperature in the room drops considerably. I thought she loved that place! I regroup and try again.

'Or we could go to my place?'

Memories of kissing Jen in the kitchen, while the kettle steamed, flash through my brain, before I remember that she hates me, so this is unlikely to reoccur. I reframe my expectations.

'Just, you know—' I clear my throat. 'To talk things through.'

It's not a euphemism but they're still giving me the Glare.

'Fine,' Jen says finally. 'But I'm bringing my dad's car so I can leave when I want to.'

I'm not planning on keeping her hostage, but I bite my tongue and leave her to continue scorching me over a spitfire, because I had the audacity to try and do something to help her without her prior knowledge or permission.

And she thinks *I'm* a control freak.

I have a limited time now to plan out what I'm going to say. What about the acrostic I wrote? It seems hackneyed and insincere in the light of what she's said today, even though it isn't.

My phone buzzes.

Rachel: My friend's dad has a vintage car. Could use it for the wedding?

She's sent over a picture of a navy blue VW Beetle. It looks awesome, and gives me a pang to consider how it's not a good time to forward it to Jen, as she might call the whole thing off.

Me: Thanks. It looks great. May not get a chance to chat to Jen about it today tho.

Rachel isn't fooled.

Rachel: Are you being a psycho again?

Me: I had an issue with the wedding date, but Jen took it personally.

Rachel: What's up with the date? You picked it.

Me: Yes. I forgot something.

Rachel: What is it, the dentist? Cancel it!

Me: It's complicated.

I find the nearest poster about the marathon, snap it and send it over. I watch the dots appear as Rachel types a message.

Rachel: WHAT?

Rachel: How did you do this?

Rachel: I thought you were the one who never screwed up.

Me: Thanks for the moral support.

Rachel: Does Jen know?

Me: No, and I'd ask you to allow me to find an appropriate time to tell her.

Rachel: Michael.

Rachel: You are supposed to be running a MARATHON on the day of your WEDDING. You have to tell her. Like, NOW!

Me: I tried, but the fire alarm went off.

Rachel: Lame excuse.

Me: If it were you, what would you say?

Rachel: I'm sorry I'm an over-achieving psycho.

I wait for the rest. Nothing comes.

Me: Is that it?

Rachel: Is changing the wedding date an option? You could ask the question, but also say, would you like me to pull out of the marathon? Give her the choice.

I know what she's going to choose, though. It isn't her who will have to tell Bradley's parents.

This weird thing happens with weddings; everyone gets really het up about the smallest little detail. Yes, it's a special day. But does it really matter what colour the waistcoats and neckties are? Will anyone remember if the favours were almonds or mints? What's the harm in shifting the wedding by a day or two? Why is Jen acting like I'm the unreasonable one?

To top it all off, I had a bunch of things I wanted to get done after school, so now I'm going to have to take them all home. At the end of the day, I carry my bag to the car, feeling more resentful than penitent.

'See you there,' I say curtly, climbing in and shutting the car door.

Jen says nothing, but slams her door with unnecessary force.

The acrostic feels a long way off now.

62

Jen

It's the worst time of year when it's dark at about four o'clock, and you barely see any blue in the sky. It's the taper end of the daylight when I pull up outside Michael's house, and with none of the usual emotions I usually feel.

He doesn't really mean it. He maybe just realised how close April was, and that we might need more time than he anticipated to plan the wedding. That's all.

I haven't mentioned this to Katie, as she designed the invites, which we're meant to be sending out imminently. I haven't messaged Deena and Clare either, because they were already suspicious of the HR policy being a questionable motive for a proposal. Please, Michael, just put this right, and then we can go ahead with everything just like we planned. Don't screw this up now.

Taking a deep breath, I leave the car and walk up to the front door. I hesitate for a moment; should I knock? It doesn't matter because Michael opens the door.

His eyes soften when he sees me. I want to put my arms around his neck and just forget the conversation ever happened. He's finally broken his 'no school night socialising' rule and he smells so good...

No. I need to be firm and strong. I step inside the hallway and unwrap my scarf, my back to him. I'm avoiding looking at him. His hands touch my shoulders and lightly shrug the coat off, and just his proximity is making my heartbeat quicken. Like a reflex, I twist around, and I didn't plan to but my mouth meets his. It only takes a moment for him to respond, pulling me closer, and I'm savouring his musky scent and the dark, delicious privacy of being alone in his house.

'I've missed you,' he murmurs.

'Mmm,' I say, and then my brain starts to refocus. 'You like me being here when you get in from school, hey?'

'It makes coming home a lot more exciting,' he says, kissing a trail from my ear to my mouth.

I move slightly to keep my mouth free.

'So why do you want to change the date of the wedding?'

He freezes, then pulls back, looking at me.

'I didn't think you liked the date,' he hedges.

'Well, given that it's on all the invitations, it was more a question of not making my sister's work a waste of time,' I say pointedly.

'We could put stickers on them,' Michael says. 'The new date, over the top of the old one. Just like I did with the—'

He breaks off suddenly. I frown at him.

'Like you did with what?'

'Never mind,' he says. 'I don't mind doing it.'

'What do you want to change the date to?'

'Just move it a few days, that's all.'

'Just a few days?' I repeat in confusion. I feel a spark of relief that he isn't wanting to postpone it by several months. 'So, it isn't that you think we need more time?'

'No,' he says, loosening his collar. It seems like a shameless tactic to distract me. I need to focus on being mad at him.

'Then what's the point?' I ask in frustration.

'I'd like to explain,' he says, 'but can we at least go and sit down? Shall I make some tea?'

It's a question that doesn't require a response. He heads off to the kitchen, leaving me to take off my shoes and arrange my bag neatly against the wall. He has a small table for mail. I pick up a large manila envelope that is blank, with no address. Maybe he's sending it to someone. As I turn it over to see if it's sealed, a sheet of paper falls part-way out of the envelope. I see the words 'Pre Nuptial Agreement' like they are branded onto my eyes.

'Michael,' I say.

Is this why he wants to change the date? So he's got time to safeguard his material possessions from me?

'Yes?' He appears in the kitchen doorway, and then sees what I'm holding. He gulps. 'My dad gave me that.'

'Do you want me to list all my worldly goods for you?' I can't keep the snarl from my voice. 'Worried I'm going to turf you out of your house?'

'He's a lawyer,' Michael begins.

'Do you trust me?' I interrupt.

'Yes, you know I do,' he answers.

'Did you not think I would find this insulting?' I brandish the envelope.

'I wasn't planning on saying anything…'

'What, you were going to do it behind my back?' I don't care if what I'm saying is irrational now. 'Surely you can't do that without me signing anyway.'

'I mean, I wasn't going to bother with it,' he says, impatiently.

'I don't want you to be reminding me of all the things that are yours,' I continue. 'Aren't we meant to be looking over our vows? *"All that I have I give to you, and all that I have I share with you."*'

'I'm not saying I disagree with that,' Michael says. 'Look, can you just, for once, think the best of me? Why do you think I'm trying to make you suffer?'

'I just need to know that you're one hundred per cent committed to me,' I say. 'You saying "let's change the date", and having a pre-nup in your hallway, isn't filling me with confidence.'

'I am not changing my mind about marrying you,' Michael says, fiercely.

'Then why do you want to change the date?'

I stare at him and watch as his face struggles for a moment.

'I made a mistake,' he says finally.

My stomach plunges.

'What, you didn't mean to get down on one knee and propose with strings playing in the background?'

'No, I mean about the date.'

'What do you mean?'

'You were right. I shouldn't have booked it without asking you first.'

He looks genuinely miserable. I let out the breath I've subconsciously been holding.

'I know I was angry with you,' I say, stepping towards him again, 'but it's all worked out for the best. We sorted a venue, I got a dress, and I don't know about you, but I'm looking forward to April 12th.'

I place my arms around his neck, hoping to recapture the romance of five minutes ago. I tilt my face upwards. His mouth is fixed in a grimace, and he looks lost for words.

'Really?' he says at last. 'I just… wanted to give you the choice to change it.'

'I'm happy,' I say, then press my lips to his.

It takes a few seconds, but soon he responds, and his arms move around my waist. 87 days and counting.

63

Michael

'Why didn't you tell her?' Rachel says in exasperation.

She rang me within a minute of me sending a confession text.

'I was going to!' I protest. 'Then she found the pre-nup that Dad gave me, and I thought she was going to break up with me.'

'The longer you leave it, the worse it's going to be when she finds out.'

'Mmm,' I murmur, distracted by my thoughts.

'Michael.' Rachel's tone becomes more serious. 'You do realise she is going to find out.'

'I can run it and be in my wedding suit by half one.'

'You don't know that,' she counters. 'Plus, that's not the point. It's about honesty.'

But I'd rather face Jen's wrath after the wedding, than risk her calling it off completely.

She's also stressed because not only has she been relocated to the cabin (my fault), but her aunt, who she hasn't seen for years, has contacted her.

'She wants to come over to mark the anniversary of Mum's death,' Jen says, sounding outraged.

'Do you not want her to do that?' I ask, confused.

'Where was she ten years ago?' Jen dumps a box of dictionaries on the cabin floor. 'I need a bookcase, by the way.'

'Okay.' I make a note in my planner. I promised I would sort out the furniture for her, to try to sweeten the pill. 'So she didn't come to the funeral?'

'No.' Jen arranges six different pen pots on her desk. 'All I knew was that Mum stayed with her in Jamaica.'

'Maybe she can tell you things about your mum you didn't know,' I suggest.

'I don't *want* to know.' Jen knocks a pen pot over, and a mish mash of pencils, rulers, and biros scatter. 'Argh!'

She crossly sets the pot down again and stuffs the pens back into it.

'Have you replied? Did she contact you on social media? Are you sure it's her?'

'I recognised her picture.' Jen rolls her eyes. 'I only have one Aunt Chevy.'

'Chevy?' I repeat. 'Like the car?'

'As in Chevelle,' Jen explains.

I'm reminded of this invisible wider network of Jen's Jamaican family. I still think it would be good to reach out to them about the wedding.

'I haven't replied yet,' Jen sighs, before I can voice my thoughts. 'Let's get through marriage prep, and I'll think about it after that.'

It's our final session this week. As we pour cups of tea and coffee, Jen chats away with Mattie and Violet like old friends. James is all right, though Benedict seems a bit of a bore. It's funny to think about where we'll all be in five years' time. Statistically, one couple will be divorced. I'm determined it's not going to be us.

'As our warm up activity, please read what you wrote about your partner to them,' Steve says.

We turn our chairs to face each other. I unfold my acrostic poem.

'*Joyful*

Energetic
Never a dull moment,' I begin, stopping to smile.
'*Nice doesn't do her kindness justice.*
If I could meet a million girls,
From all over the world,
Even then, the only one for me is Jen.
Really.'

She bursts out laughing and throws her arms around me.

'That's so sweet.' She kisses my cheek. 'Thank you. You want to hear mine?'

She pulls out her phone and opens a note.

'*Many have tried and failed, but Michael always wins.*
In every situation, he's prepared with a list.
Challenges are no hurdle; he continues like a pro,
He makes the impossible look easy and never accepts a 'no'.
At first he seems so focused that you wonder what's inside,
Exceptional and endearing, I
LOVE that I'm his bride.'

'Thank you,' I say hollowly. The words jar with my awareness of my enormous Marathon Mistake. *He makes the impossible look easy...* I think I'm going to be putting that to the test.

'Anyone want to share?' Steve asks hopefully.

'*Very Inspiring,*
One of a kind,
Loving and caring,
Excellent,
Tall,' James reads out.

Not sure about the last word but I politely clap.

'*Bombastic,*' Mattie starts, then bursts into giggles.

'*Elaborate,*
Nimble.
Effervescent.

*Dashing,
Intrepid,
Chivalrous and
Tenacious.*'

I continue to clap, bemused as I look at the Boring Egg-headed None-of-these-qualities Benedict, wondering if Mattie has cataracts, while Jen and Violet join her in laughing.

'*Mother*,' Benedict begins solemnly, and I fight a sudden urge to laugh.

'*A rose.
Tender in the breeze.*'

I swallow hard.

'*Ivy.
Love that never lets go.
Dancing freely.
A star.*'

'It's so beautiful.' Mattie dabs her eyes and throws her arms around Benedict as a reward for writing the worst poem I've ever heard.

Everyone says 'Ah' and claps, which helps me to disguise a bark of laughter as a cough.

'I'll go next.' Jen smiles and prepares to read hers out.

'You don't need to,' I say, my laughter effectively extinguished at the prospect of having her words heaping burning coals on my head again.

Too late. Jen reads it out and everyone claps enthusiastically, while I want the ground to swallow me up.

'You made it RHYME!' Mattie says, unnecessarily.

'Teachers, right?' Violet says, holding her own sheet nervously. 'Well, don't judge me on this.

*Jolly and jammy,
And*

Messy and manic,
Extraordinary, excellent,
Super and special.'

James catches my eye and gives an embarrassed grin. I join in the applause. There's a pause and I realise everyone is looking at me.

'Did you want to read yours, Michael?' Steve prompts.

'Er…' I hesitate. 'Not really.'

Violet giggles, but stops when she realises I'm serious. Steve moves on hurriedly, but not before I've seen the disappointment snuff out the spark in Jen's eyes.

'Now in many ways it's a silly task,' Steve says, 'but I want to make this point: when you're excited about getting married, it's easy to come up with all the things you love about them. In any long-term relationship, there will be times when you don't find it so easy. In fact, there will be times when you may not believe these words you've written anymore. Over time, you may hurt one another. But I want to encourage you to keep these name poems, and to consider this: it is your choice to see your partner in this way.'

I try to take Jen's hand, but she doesn't notice. Either that or she's ignoring me.

'Every relationship needs one essential ingredient to continue: forgiveness.' Steve pauses and looks around the room at each of us. 'Some of you have no doubt already had to forgive each other. I want to tell you a story from the Bible about forgiveness.

'A man had two sons. The younger one got tired and fed up, and asked for his share of the inheritance early. He then ran off, spending it all on parties, until he ended up with nothing. He took a miserable job, feeding pigs, and even envied the pigs' food, because he was starving.

'He thought to himself, "This is stupid. Even my father's servants have enough food to eat." He made a plan to go back home, apologise, and ask to be treated as one of the servants. He didn't think he was worthy to be called a son anymore.

'But on his way home, his father saw him from a long way off. He ran to meet him, and brushed aside his apologies. He dressed the son in a fine robe and announced a feast to celebrate his return.

'But the older brother wasn't happy. He heard that his brother had come back, and refused to join the celebration. His father went outside to ask him to come in.

'"I've worked so hard for you!" he complained. "You never gave me anything. He wasted all your money and now you're throwing him a party!"

'The father told the elder son that he loved him, and that all he had was his, but that they had to celebrate, because the younger son was lost, and now he was found.

'You may wonder what this has to do with marriage,' Steve continues. 'Well, I think all of us can either identify with the younger son, or the elder. Some of us are really aware of our mistakes. We often feel unworthy. We have to go back and ask for forgiveness, so that our relationship can be restored. That can be very hard to do. But until we do it, we can't enjoy the party. We'll still be stuck feeding the pigs.

'But others of us are like the elder brother.' Steve takes a few steps to the other side to emphasise the point. 'We don't feel we've done anything wrong. We don't feel that others deserve forgiveness. And we can't enjoy the party either.

'This story is often referred to as the parable of the lost son,' Steve says, 'but it's actually about two lost sons. Here's the thing: no one wants to 'lose' their marriage, or the love they have for the other person. But without a willingness to ask for forgiveness, and a willingness to give it, you will lose both your marriage and your love. It's a sobering thought, I know. But I need to be honest with you. Marriage is hard, a tough choice to keep going sometimes. But with forgiveness, even the worst problem can be overcome.'

'That's really why we're doing this,' Mattie says, after a pause. 'To have a fresh start.'

'That's a really good picture,' Steve smiles. 'Every day needs to be a fresh start; wipe the slate clean.'

Part of me longs for the simplicity of transparency. I turn to Jen, opening my mouth to confess the truth about the marathon, but then I realise she's crying.

64

Jen

I can't stop the tears; it's like the floodgate has opened.

'Sorry,' I mutter, getting up clumsily and heading for the toilets.

All I can think, over and over, is this: it's me.

I've been the elder brother, refusing to forgive my mum. But I've been the younger son too, trying to do everything my own way, and ignoring the feeling that I need to forgive her if I'm going to move on with my life.

I fumble in a cubicle for some toilet roll, and bury my face in it. Ugly crying isn't like in the movies, where you might possibly have a leaked line of mascara. I'm soaked with snot and tears and I don't know where it all comes from, and sobbing is like trying to inhale and exhale at the same time. It leaves you breathless.

'Jen?' Mattie's voice sounds tentative. 'Do you mind if I come in here?'

I can't stop crying to answer. She follows the noise and pushes at the cubicle door, which creaks towards me.

'Oh dear,' she says sympathetically, putting an arm around my shoulders and shuffling me out of the cubicle. 'There, there.'

She hugs me and envelopes me in her silk scarf and strong perfume. I try to regain control of my shuddering body.

'You cry if you need to,' she says, patting my back.

It takes some minutes before I can speak.

'I'm sorry,' I apologise, in the inexplicable way that we all do, like there's a global conspiracy to hide all emotions from view. 'My mum died ten years ago. It's very... hard... to for— to forgive her.'

I cover my face with my toilet tissue towel, which by now is pretty soggy and shredded.

'I'm so sorry to hear that,' Mattie says. She watches me blow my nose, and grabs another toilet roll.

'Why is it so... hard?' I ask, not really expecting an answer.

The question dies into the silence.

'A few years ago, Ben and I were on the brink of divorce,' Mattie says. 'He had an affair and I just felt like I hated him. Steve's dad is an experienced marriage counsellor so we agreed to see him before we made a final decision. Ben was distraught. He was so sorry and wanted to put things right but I just didn't know how we could move forwards.'

'What changed?' I ask, meeting her eyes.

'This.' Mattie holds out her necklace, a gold chain with a cross pendant. 'My mother left me this when she died. I was sat at my dressing table, going through my jewellery box, and I found it. I just held it in my hand, and I found myself crying.'

Her eyes are glistening now, and I feel fresh tears in my own.

'I remembered a verse I learned as a child: *"While we were still sinners, Christ died for us."* It made me see Ben differently. I'm a sinner too, not just him. My heart started to change.'

'And you forgave him?'

She smiles.

'Yes. Though it took a long time to trust him again.'

'And here you are, getting married again.' I smile back.

'Steve's right, though,' Mattie says. 'You have to forgive each other all the time. It's not a one-off. There will always be ways that you hurt each other. I wear this necklace to remind myself that His love never runs out for me. That gives me strength to forgive.'

'I want to,' I say. 'But I can't talk to her.'

'Your situation is different.' Mattie nods. 'It feels very different when the person you're trying to forgive is no longer with us. You're not doing it to repair the relationship, because they've gone, but I think you still need to go through that process. Have you considered getting some grief counselling?'

I think of Sylvia, the bereavement counsellor we met when we stayed with her in October half term. She gave me her number in case I ever wanted to talk.

'Maybe.'

I've always resisted the idea, but it's starting to sound like this is something I need to deal with. I don't want to start my marriage still dragging around the worst of the baggage from my past.

Then it strikes me: there's someone else I can contact to start dealing with the pain of my mum's death.

'Are you ready to go back in?' Mattie asks, assessing me in concern.

'Nearly,' I say. 'I just need to send a message.'

It's time to reply to Aunt Chevy.

Interlude

Alice was running, but the further she went, the more she forgot what she was running from. The path stretched out endlessly, and it felt as though the horizon would never draw nearer. She was stuck, with the sun always out of reach. Since leaving the prince behind, she felt like she had lost her direction. Her purpose.

Panting and clutching her side, Alice ground to a halt. She took several, heaving breaths, and wiped sweat from her brow. If only she had some water...

Her eyes were blurry and she closed them impatiently, willing them to refocus upon opening them again. When she did, she blinked. There was a well in front of her, made of stone, with a wooden roof. Sitting there, suddenly before her in perfect clarity, was her mother.

"You're... you're here?" Alice asked in disbelief.

"Yes," she answered simply. "Take a drink."

Wondering if this was a trap, Alice adjusted her belt (weapons all present and correct) and then took a tentative step forward.

"Here."

Her mother, no longer ghostly, was scooping up water into a cup and holding it out to her. Alice could see the droplets glistening on the side of the cup. It looked real. She looked real.

"It's not a shrinking potion," her mother said, smiling.

Alice unconsciously moistened her dry lips with her tongue, but forced herself to focus.

"Where did you go?" she asked, sharply. "I've been looking for you all this time. I was ready to give up."

"And yet, you're here."

She still held out the cup. Alice took it and sniffed it. It looked like cool, clear water. She took a sip and waited for a second. Nothing happened.

"You would have found me sooner if you had stopped running away," her mother said.

Alice gulped down more water, unable to resist the temptation.

"I wasn't running away; I was chasing you!"

"That's where you're not being honest with yourself," her mother said.

"What do you mean?"

"This isn't just about me."

Her mother took the empty cup, and for a moment, their eyes met.

"I don't understand," Alice said, defeated.

"You left Edward behind," her mother said. "Why?"

Alice turned her head, as though he would suddenly appear. How did her mother know about the prince?

"I didn't, I—"

"Alice." Her mother's tone was more commanding now. "No one is making choices for you. That door is the perfect example."

Following the direction of her gesture, Alice turned to see a door standing, impossibly, without walls, in the middle of the scenery. It looked like a door to nowhere.

"That wasn't there before," Alice commented, unnecessarily.

"You think it wasn't there before," her mother corrected. "Because you didn't see it there before."

"I'm tired of riddles," Alice snapped. "Where does it lead?"

"Into a maze," her mother replied. "He's waiting for you, you know."

"Edward?" Alice spoke before thinking, before she could stop herself.

Her mother nodded mildly, as if this was all very simple.

"You can run off again," her mother said, "but you'll never find the end of the road."

"What if I never find the end of the maze?" Alice countered.
Her mother sighed in exasperation.
"You'll find it, if you're together."

Document comments:

Michael Chase: This is so much better than the first version.

Jen Baker: I know.

Michael Chase: I feel I should have at least some credit for giving you the idea.

Jen Baker: Your head's big enough already. But I love you.

65

Michael

I should feel relieved that the marriage preparation course is over, but instead, the weight of the marathon pulls me deeper underwater. I'm hearing everything as though it's far away, echoing and distorted. Jen thinks I'm under too much stress at work and she's delegated most of the wedding planning to Katie, whose latest accomplishment is creating a gift list of hundreds of items, a bit like a kid with a catalogue at Christmas.

'Since when do we need a robot vacuum?' Jen says, scrolling through the list on her laptop while video calling her sister.

'They are so cool!' Katie gushes. 'You just turn them on, and off they go!'

'Take it off. I don't want to put high-ticket items on here like that. People will think we're being cheeky.'

'Isn't the whole concept of a gift list quite cheeky?' Katie returns.

'Plus, I think Michael's got enough kitchenware already,' Jen says. 'Have you got a blender?'

It's a moment before I realise she's talking to me.

'Uh, no,' I say. 'Should I?'

'They're great for soups,' Katie chirps. 'And for pureeing food when you have a baby.'

'Whoa!' Jen says. 'Can we just get married, please? Without you mapping out our future family life?'

'Just thinking long-term,' Katie says.

'*Very* long term,' Jen replies.

That's another thing we need to talk about, really. I sigh in emotional exhaustion at the thought of it.

'Okay, I'm happy with that,' Jen says, leaning back in her chair. 'You know what I'm going to ask you to do next, don't you?'

'Buy myself some designer shoes?' Katie asks hopefully.

'You wish,' Jen laughs. 'The seating plan.'

'Seriously?' Katie looks less than impressed. 'You will owe me big time.'

'I know.'

'All right. I'll give it a go.'

'I love you.'

The list of things to arrange, book, and plan is getting shorter. We met Louise's sister, Karen, and booked her as our photographer. Her work was stunning; she just seemed to capture lots of ordinary moments that made people look at their best. I remembered to show Jen the picture of the VW Beetle from Rachel, and she was happy with that, so Rachel asked her friend Sally's dad if he would mind chauffeuring us. Then when we got to my parents' house after the marriage prep session, and I still hadn't had a chance to ask Jen what was wrong, my mum had made six different varieties of cake and asked us to taste-test them, then asked if we wanted her to make the 'winner' as our wedding cake.

'I can do a traditional fruit cake too,' she said eagerly. 'But I thought you might like something more modern.'

'This is great,' I said. 'Jen, are you happy with this?'

'Sure.' Jen smiled, yawned, and went off to bed soon after.

The time is slipping away, and each day passing makes it harder to try to tell Jen the truth.

'Everything going well?' David asks me, meaningfully.

I give an annoyed shrug.

'It would be great if you could hire a stunt double for me.'

'Look, mate,' David says. 'We've worked together for years now. I want you to know I've got your back.'

So you're the first in line to stab it, I think, but don't say out loud.

'I've got it all figured out,' he continues. 'I'll take you to the starting point, and then I'll go and get changed and pick up Adele. Then we'll be there to meet you at the finish line, with your suit in the car, and we'll all go to the church.'

It dawns on me that David thinks he's invited to the wedding. I vaguely remember suggesting him when Jen first drew up the guest list. She shot that down in flames.

But now, I can't get to my own wedding without him.

I idly scroll through travel websites at lunch, rather than try to seek Jen out for an honest conversation. A one-way ticket to the Bahamas has never looked so appealing. I still haven't booked the summer trip I promised Jen, but I've lost motivation. The website's main image shows a couple who look like us: an average white bloke with a stunning mixed-race woman. I always knew Jen deserved better, and now it's only a matter of time before she realises.

'You've got the details for the cemetery?' Jen checks before we part on Friday.

My brain is still fogged up, and I look at her blankly.

'You know, for the memorial?' she says.

There's the proof: I forgot all about her mum's anniversary. Her aunt is arriving tonight and we're meeting at the grave tomorrow.

'Sorry, of course,' I stutter.

'You seem distracted.' Jen searches my face.

'Lot going on.' The words stick in my throat. 'Jen…'

'Yes?' She raises an eyebrow suspiciously.

Of the two earth-shattering things I need to tell her, I pick the lesser one, out of sheer cowardice.

'I invited David and Adele to the wedding.'

'What?' She shrieks loud enough that I check the corridor, in case he hears us. 'I told you I did not want him there.'

'I can't snub him like that,' I argue, hating myself for my own hypocrisy. 'He knows about it, and he's expecting to come. We need to send him an invite.'

'Well, maybe I'll add a few extra guests of my own, then,' she retorts. 'Like Sean.'

'Invite him if you like,' I say, with a careless gesture, even though the ploy worked: I'm annoyed. 'If you're fed up with me, maybe you can marry him instead.'

'It's ten years since my mum died tomorrow.' Jen hits me with that like a gut punch. 'I haven't got time for your petty attitude.'

And so another day concludes, where running the marathon on the same day as my wedding looks easier than telling Jen the truth.

66
Jen

Hugging Aunt Chevy is like clasping a lost piece of my mother. It brings tears to my eyes.

'It's been too long,' she says, surveying me, Katie and Dad and shaking her head.

She looks impossibly youthful, given that she's into her sixties. Her skin is smooth over her cheeks, unwrinkled; she wears long silver pendant earrings, and a mustard coloured scarf. Her eyes dance just like my mother's.

In the car on the way back from the airport, she has us laughing within ten minutes with anecdotes of the flight. If she had a Jamaican lilt she learnt from my grandparents, it's blossomed now that she's lived out there for twenty years.

'Nothing changes,' she says, looking at the rain, illuminated under the bright motorway lights. It's dark and the wipers are squeaking back and forth. 'It's weird, the things you miss.'

Katie smiles across at me. We're sat in the back like when we were kids. She's sleeping in my room tonight so Aunt Chevy can have her bed. It feels good to see her in person, not just on video call.

'Does Jamaica feel like home now?' Dad asks.

Aunt Chevy laughs dryly.

'In some ways,' she replies. 'But I was born here. I grew up here, with British friends, though people always asked me where I was from. They were surprised when I said "Bedford!"'

'Do you still have friends there?' Dad asks. 'We can visit.'

'That would be a trip down memory lane.' Aunt Chevy turns round to smile at us. 'Do you remember Sundays at Zion Hill?'

'I remember the food,' Katie says.

'Oh yes,' Aunt Chevy agrees. 'Sometimes I think old David used to shout 'Hallelujah' so loud just to make Dad finish his sermon a bit quicker.'

'And the fact that he was too hard of hearing to know what he was saying anyway,' Katie giggles.

'He's probably with the Lord now,' Aunt Chevy says, with a sigh. 'I'm an oldie now.'

I feel a stab of jealousy that Aunt Chevy gets to grow old and my mother's life was cut off so abruptly. It's odd how she is immortalised forever now in her 'prime'.

'Thanks for having me to stay,' Aunt Chevy says, mainly to Dad.

'It's no trouble,' he says, clearing his throat.

'Look at you two, all grown up.' She turns round again. 'Your mum would be so proud of you.'

I stare out of the window at the streaming rain.

Later, in my bedroom, Katie takes over my bed, wearing oversized pink pyjamas.

'Are you glad she's here?' she asks me.

'Yes,' I reply, then pause. 'It doesn't change how I feel towards Mum, but it feels like a missing thread that wasn't there last time.'

'You mean at the funeral?'

I nod. We don't ever talk about it.

'It's good to have more family,' she says. 'Why don't you ask her to help you plan your summer trip? You still want to go out to Jamaica, right?'

'Yes, but it's hard to think about it right now.'

I just want to get through the next twenty-four hours.

I wake up and I already feel like I'm crying, because I dreamed about her. That kind where you feel a tangible presence of someone being there, and you feel comforted. She didn't say anything, only smiled. But then when I wake up, the cruel contrast of loss burns me with the bitterness of the wind blowing a bonfire's smoke into your eyes. I want to sob but Katie's there, so I haul myself out of bed and head downstairs.

Aunt Chevy is already sat at the table with a cup of tea.

'Ah.' She clucks with her tongue as I hover in the doorway. 'You sit down and I'll make you one.'

She clicks the kettle on and shuffles round, already seeming at home as she finds me a mug and a teabag. She comes over and places a hand on my shoulder. I crumple and then she's holding me against her, tighter and tighter as I let myself cry. It's been ten years of being the strong one, ten years of looking after Dad and Katie, and finally it feels like there's someone to look after me.

'You shouldn't have had to go through this on your own,' Aunt Chevy says. 'I'm sorry I couldn't be here when you needed me.'

She makes my cup of tea, then sits next to me at the table.

'When Pearl turned up, I asked her what she was playing at. "Go home," I said. "You got to think of the girls." But she was in a bad place. She didn't know who she was or what to do. She kept going off with people, parties on the beach… I got a call from her one day. She was stranded and confused and needed me to go to find her. I had to miss work. I lost my job. I told her she had to pull herself together. Go to the doctor. I thought they would give her some anti-depressants. But they found a tumour.'

I hold the mug, out of habit more than anything else, and feel the familiar churn of emotions when I think about this.

'"Now you really have to go home," I said,' Aunt Chevy continues. 'She had no money. I had some savings but there was only enough for one ticket. I bought it for her, and she came back. You know the rest. I was searching and searching for a new job, and I finally got one. It was just before she died. I didn't have any money left to fly over here myself for her funeral, and even if I did, I couldn't ask for time off when I'd only just started the job. As time went on, it was hard to stay in touch. But this anniversary, I thought "enough is enough". I had built up my savings again, and I knew it was time to come back.'

'I'm so glad you did.'

I take her hand. I was so wrong about everything, so wrong to judge her.

'That's a pretty ring,' she says, noticing my engagement ring.

'I'm getting married in April,' I tell her.

My heart twinges. Maybe this is my chance to start clawing back some Baker territory in the Chase-dominated guest list.

'Why don't you extend your stay so you can come?' I ask.

'I'll look into it,' she promises. 'I need to get in touch with the church and see who's still around.'

'It would mean a lot to me,' I add.

Initially I'm saying this without really thinking about what I mean, but as I consider it through the day, the idea becomes more and more significant. If Aunt Chevy comes, someone from my mother's side of the family is there. Someone who is not white, who represents the Jamaican part of my identity (admittedly not something I've massively explored yet). Why should my wedding look like an upper-middle class networking event? And, to add to this, one of the first things Aunt Chevy does is to offer to braid my hair properly in cornrows. It's perfect timing, because it will protect my hair for the next few weeks before the hen do and then the wedding. Katie's keen to join in, so we spend the morning in the lounge together, using oils and laughing at rubbish TV shows, while Aunt Chevy braids our hair with amazing rapidity.

'You've let this go for far too long,' she scolds, tutting at my knotted mass of hair, looking frayed and brittle. 'I hope you're wearing a silk cap every night and oiling it.'

I wince, thinking of all the times I've slept over Michael's parents' house and forgotten to pack one.

'If you're here for the wedding, can you do our hair?' Katie asks.

'I got no credentials,' Aunt Chevy laughs. 'I can't do anything fancy.'

'I don't want fancy,' I say. 'But I need someone who understands how to style my hair.'

'No use getting a white hairdresser then,' Aunt Chevy says, definitively. 'If I'm here, I'll do it.'

In the afternoon, Dad drives us over to the cemetery. It has a bleak outlook over the railway line, and the tightly packed graveyard stones look like an optical illusion. It's raining again, and my life feels like it's in sepia. The greyness and gloom penetrate everything.

As we trudge across the car park, Michael's waiting, dressed in his long winter coat and holding a black umbrella. He could be an actor in a Dickensian period drama. I take his arm and lead the way to my mother's memorial. It's a modest stone with her name on it, the year of her death a sharply etched reminder of the worst time of my life.

Katie lays down some flowers and we stand there, getting wet in the rain: me, Michael, Dad, Katie and Aunt Chevy. I can't speak for the others, but if I'm honest with myself, I'm grieving more of what I wanted my mother to be, than the reality of who she was.

Mourning the loss of the mother I wanted. We're all crying, except Michael, who pulls a plastic wallet out of his coat.

'I brought a poem by Robert Frost, if you'd like me to read it,' he says to me.

Incapable of speech, I nod.

He reads:

'Nature's first green is gold,
Her hardest hue to hold.
Her early leaf's a flower;
But only so an hour.
Then leaf subsides to leaf.
So Eden sank to grief,
So dawn goes down to day.
Nothing gold can stay.'

In that moment, I love him more than ever.

67

Michael

When you're desperate to find the right moment to say something, it never arrives.

I've imagined a hundred different conversations with Jen, where she asks me about the marathon and I manage to effortlessly explain that I was wrong about the date, and where she accepts this without much of an argument. Not very plausible, I realise, but I'm never going to do it if I always imagine the worst-case scenario: Jen decides she hates me (it's a blurry line between love and hate sometimes), the wedding is off, and she breaks up with me. The thing is, Jen is quite an emotional person. She doesn't necessarily think about the pragmatic side. I've seen her eyes burning with anger at David and there's a list of offences she has never forgiven him for: using her essay when she was in Sixth Form, pretending he'd forgotten her name at the start of the year, and pressuring her to withdraw her application for promotion. Oh, and failing to take it seriously when a student threatened to turn up at her flat. Her laptop was stolen. Yes, I know he's annoying with his smooth-talking yet underhand ways, and listing his faults reminds me how out of line he's been, but still: the point is, Jen isn't very forgiving. She's already had to forgive me for pulling back when we first started dating. I was (misguidedly) trying to protect her from David's redundancy package. It took a while for her to trust me again. I don't want to wreck it all now.

WEDDING BELL TIME

The other problem is that, understandably, with the ten-year anniversary of her mother's death, she is super emotional right now. I brought tissues and an umbrella to the cemetery, and it's like *Wuthering Heights* out here with the rain lashing against our faces (Jen's favourite novel. I think she wishes I was more like Heathcliff. Although I would argue that the sociopathic elements to my character are not to be encouraged).

Chevy seems a refreshing tonic to this depressing situation. Jen's been stuck in the grey, littered streets of Whidlock all her life. I think part of the reason she struggles so much with her mum's decision to leave is that in some way she envies her, though she would never admit that. But Chevy brings sympathy; she's mourning the loss of her sister too. She also brings the sense of a wider world beyond this place, with her Jamaican lilt and her different way of seeing the world.

'That was beautiful,' she says approvingly, after I read out a poem. 'Now let's get out of this rain.'

We drive back to Jen's dad's house, and she makes this amazing fried chicken, all the time relaying anecdotes about Jamaica and Pearl, Jen's mum. I can see Jen's struggling to shake off the heaviness of the cemetery. Katie seems more at ease, laughing at Chevy. Their dad is quiet, but surprisingly relaxed as Chevy finds her own way around his kitchen. He isn't bothered by the mess; he's glad that she's there, happy to share in her memories.

'Now I want to hear about this wedding,' Chevy says, opening cupboard doors until she finds the seasoning she wants. 'I may be able to change my flight so that I can come.'

I smile, my guilt at filling most of the guest list allayed somewhat.

'That's fantastic,' I say.

'Where is it?' Chevy asks.

'In the town where I grew up,' I explain. 'On the coast.'

I fill her in with more details, while Jen sips her tea and looks out of the window. Katie starts chipping in with the things she's been organising.

'We don't have a florist yet,' she finishes.

'Hang on, let me check the date,' Chevy says, tapping on her phone screen. 'You know that April 12th is Easter Saturday?'

'Yes,' I reply. This fateful date is the only thing I can think about most of the time.

'A lot of churches don't allow flowers on that day,' Chevy says.

I frown.

'Really? Why not?'

Chevy rolls her eyes.

'Didn't you pay attention in church? Jesus died on Good Friday. He rose on Easter Sunday. The Saturday was a day of mourning and it's still part of Lent.'

'Can you check that?' Katie asks me.

'I can message Steve.' I pull out my phone.

'I mean, what are we supposed to do if we're not allowed flowers?' Katie muses.

'Well, you can use greenery,' Chevy suggests. 'It would look really natural.'

I send Steve a text and touch Jen's elbow. She gives a slight start.

'Sorry?' she says.

'Wake up, Jen!' Katie says. 'We have a new wedding crisis for you to worry about.'

'Great.' She sighs and pushes her chair back from the table. 'I'm just going upstairs to look for something.'

Katie raises her eyebrows at me and I shrug. Better to give her some space if she's thinking about her mum. Her absence gives me a unique opportunity.

'Chevy,' I begin, 'can you help me plan a trip to Jamaica?'

68

Jen

I find my mum's old jewellery box on the floor of my wardrobe, buried in silk scarves and crumpled up jumpers. I put her things away where Katie wouldn't find them and mess about trying them on. It's a wooden box, with a mother-of-pearl flower in the centre of the lid. Sitting on the carpet, I open it up, catching the smell of her perfume. It gives me a lump in my throat.

I find what I'm looking for: her wedding ring. I slip my engagement ring off, then try it on. It fits. Tears blurring my eyes, I slot my engagement ring on my finger, next to it. Then I cover my face with my hands and sob.

She won't be there. All I have left of her are little pieces, like this ring. I'm glad Chevy wants to come to the wedding, but she will be a visual reminder that my mum is gone. Part of me wanted to erase her from my life, because perhaps that would be easier. I could marry Michael, take a new surname, and start a different life. Now Chevy's here, I'm forced to face the reality that I can't delete her like an unwanted text message. When you lose someone, you can't just clear your history like a web browser. The familiar anger returns, as I think of all the things I want to say to her. As each of these ten years has gone by, I thought they might go away. But they haven't.

I look down at my two rings, nestled together on my left hand. Do I even want to wear this ring? After all, my parents' marriage was not exactly exemplary. She had an affair with a yoga instructor, then disappeared off to Jamaica. Yes, Dad forgave her when she came back. When I asked him how he could do that, he shrugged and said,

'I don't want to waste the time we have left together.'

Is that what I did? Wasted time being angry at her? But I don't understand how I could have felt anything different. You grow up trusting your parents to make the right decisions. When they don't, nothing is more bitterly disappointing.

I take both rings off, then put the engagement ring back on, holding the wedding band between my thumb and forefinger. I can see the markings etched on the underside of the gold.

'*Nothing gold can stay.*'

I repeat the last line of the Robert Frost poem, remembering Michael's voice reading it out at the cemetery. Nothing is permanent; it's the paradox of being human. Yet here I am, holding this ring. It has survived where my mother has not. I can take a piece of her into my future, if I want to.

Do I want to be like the elder brother in the story, refusing to forgive?

'I know you weren't perfect, but I'm not perfect either.' I speak these words to the ring, feeling the need to say them out loud. I bring the ring to my lips and kiss it. 'I want to forgive you. God, help me to forgive her.'

It's like a fist unclenching in my stomach. The stifling grip of anger begins to soften.

Mattie was right. He's the one who gives us strength to forgive.

'Thank you,' I breathe.

WEDDING BELL TIME

The ice starts to thaw as the snowdrops appear in the garden, and it's Valentine's Day. I reflect with irony that this time last year I was still single. Michael leaves flowers on my desk and a *Wuthering Heights*-themed journal, while I hide five creepy cat ornaments in his room and then put some succulents and a paperweight on his desk. We're seeing each other at the weekend, but between going through RSVPs to the invites, video calling his mum about the cake and the catering, and looking at Katie's latest draft of the seating plan, there's not going to be much time for romance. We still need to go through the wedding vows and pick hymns and readings for the ceremony, so that Katie can make us some booklets with an order of service.

I've managed to cling on to my writing time, and I feel like bringing Alice's mother back to guide her towards Edward has really unlocked the final part of the story. There's no longer a thread that trails off. I should be on track to finish redrafting before the Big Day, and then I can take a break. Michael's keen for me to self-publish it on Amazon, but I told him I just want to focus on one life goal at a time. That shut him up.

Life has also been a bit more fun with Aunt Chevy around. She and Dad have been looking at old photos and reminiscing about Mum, and she's cooked some amazing dishes too. My cornrows have stayed in and I feel much happier about the prospect of someone in charge of my hair for the wedding who actually knows what they're doing. Aunt Chevy has also promised to help decorate the church, since it turns out we aren't allowed flowers. Michael also suggested that we should add Deena's parents to the guest list, and Deena's mum has offered to help too. She's an expert in large parties and events, so I feel relieved that it's not just down to Katie (who'll be busy enough with her bridesmaid duties).

I got back in touch with Sylvia, and she's booked me in for some phone counselling sessions. It's a relief to know that I'll be talking about Mum and creating some time and space to think through everything that happened and how I should respond to it. Well, how I've already been responding. As much as I've tried to bury it, it's still seeped into my head, heart and thoughts and affected my life irrevocably. Admitting that is a massive step forward—although it feels like Alice wandering into the maze and not knowing whether she'll ever come out again.

Work is busy as usual. After getting over the shock of relocating to the cabin, I'm starting to appreciate having the extra space, and also a bit more seclusion (although Michael manages to appear regularly, despite not having the excuse that he's using my room as a corridor to get to his classroom anymore). I've had a few meetings with the support staff team and I'm more confident now in what we're doing, and what we need to prioritise. David hasn't been on my back about anything—probably because he's still fighting fires with the local authority.

From what Michael tells me, the plan to merge Whidlock with Prestfield is going to be open to public consultation soon. I don't think much of the consultation process because it seems to be a done deal, but the implications for all of our staff make me feel dizzy. They will need to 'redeploy' us, but there will probably be redundancies too. I haven't said anything to Judy and Liz, because I'm not supposed to know anything, and Liz is only just back to full time hours. We've been eating lunch together in the staff room, and she's been an absolute mine of information about additional learning needs provision. She's been through so many hoops as a parent with the local authority, so she can give me that perspective, and then I can put that together with the feedback from support staff to build up a much better sense of what we need to improve.

'We should set up a meeting,' she says, 'with my friend who works at Whidlock's special school. They could run some training for our support staff.'

'That's a great idea!' I say. 'We have some training days coming up and we need to organise something bespoke for our team.'

'When's my friend coming in for that creative writing festival?' Judy asks. She had put me in touch with her friend, who was a writer, back in October.

'Well, I had to change the dates a few times because of the school calendar.' I roll my eyes. It's notoriously difficult to arrange anything these days. 'We settled on the week before Easter.'

'So you're running a creative writing festival the week before your wedding?' Liz's eyes widen. 'How is the wedding planning going, anyway?'

'It's all right.' I shrug. 'Now that my aunt can come, at least someone will be there from my mum's side of the family.'

'I love the way she did your hair,' Liz says admiringly.

'It's a relief to have her around,' I say.

'How's Michael?' Judy asks. 'Isn't he training for a marathon?'

'Yeah.' I put down my sandwich. 'He's got to do some long runs over the next few weeks.'

'Is he stressed about it?' Judy asks, in a way that suggests that she thinks he is.

'I don't know,' I answer. 'He doesn't seem bothered about running the amount of miles.'

But when I think about it, Michael does seem preoccupied and distracted when we're together. He's got the usual pressures of his job, mediation between David and the rest of the Senior Team, and he's finding the constant pinging of messages on the WEDDING!!! WhatsApp group hard to handle. His mum has been on there posting pictures of cake stuff, which I think is really sweet and also makes me feel constantly hungry, but Michael backs off whenever I try to show him, and just says I can decide. The other WhatsApp group going crazy is the Hen Do. It's coming up in a few weeks' time, and Katie, Deena, Clare and Steph are proving a lethal combination.

Katie: Not gonna reveal anything but I can't wait!!!

Deena: Have we checked where the guys are going for the stag so we don't bump into them?

Clare: Before we rule that out, does Michael have any cute, single friends?

Steph: I highly doubt it, if David Clark is anything to go by.

Me: David isn't single.

Steph: That's not gonna stop him.

Deena: I thought Michael's guys would be more on the nerdy side.

Me: They are.

Clare: And your problem with nerds is???

Deena: Well, they're probably not even going to be out, are they? More like playing chess.

Steph: Chess can be sexy. All those pawns.

Me: Stop it! And they don't play chess.

Clare: Any singles??

Me: I think Kyle is. He's a lawyer too.

Katie: I think it says a lot about you and Michael that your best friends are lawyers.

Deena: You'll be calling us first when you get sued by some farmer.

Katie: Anyway, I have messaged Dan our plans so there will be no overlap.

Clare: Shame.

Deena: This is a HEN party! It's about us girls, no blokes allowed. You can meet the nerds at the wedding.

Katie: 53 days people!!

69

Michael

When it's finally half term, the last thing I want to do is stay at my parents' house and face a massive wedding to-do list, but Jen points out that it's our last opportunity to have an extended stay before the big day. I almost wish there was some way I could escape the house with Dad, but she's asked for his input on choosing hymns, which is an offer he can't refuse.

'This is a classic wedding choice,' he says, riffling through hymn music and playing the first verse on the piano. 'In fact, we sang this at our wedding.'

'Be Thou My Vision,' Jen reads from the title, then starts googling the words. 'What does this line mean: *"Thou mine inheritance, now and always"*?'

I look at her sideways. Is she trying to make a jibe about the pre-nup?

'It goes back to the tribe of priests in the Old Testament,' my dad says. I feel myself beginning to switch off. 'They had no land, because the Lord was their inheritance.'

'How could they inherit God?' Jen asks. She seems to be serious about this line of questioning. I pull out my phone to check my emails.

'It's more of a metaphor,' my dad explains. 'Instead of passing on land to their children, they would pass on faith. And instead of making their property on earth the most important thing, they were meant to make God the most important thing instead.'

'Which ties into God being our "vision", like in the title,' Jen says. 'It's quite archaic language, but I like it.'

'Billy Graham, a famous preacher, once said that the greatest legacy one can pass on to one's children is not money or other material things, but a legacy of character and faith,' Dad says. He loves to quote people.

'Wow,' Jen says. 'Michael, do you agree with that?'

'Hmm?' I look up from my inbox.

'Do you think that passing on a legacy of faith is more important than money?' Jen asks me.

'Sure,' I say.

'Maybe you should start making more time for church then,' she says.

I blink. Since when were we talking about church? A few months ago she'd never stepped inside one before. Now she and my dad are staring expectantly at me, waiting for me to have a religious epiphany. She sighs and turns back to the hymn book.

'I'll need to send the words to Katie to put in the order of service,' she says.

We're going to be here a long time at this rate. I start daydreaming about going out for a walk, to Bestward perhaps…

'Now, the seating plan…'

Oh help.

'I think I should go for a run.' I clear my throat.

'Sure.' Jen waves her hand, focussed on her laptop screen as she pulls up what Katie's sent over.

'Oh yes, when is the marathon again?' Mum asks, calling from the kitchen, but I've already headed out of the door, and it's easy to pretend not to have heard her.

I put my headphones in and start to jog, tracking the familiar territory of my childhood. The sun is pale but there's no frost on the ground today. I turn the corner and run down the street full of cherry blossoms, the pink forming bright clouds above my head. I love the freedom of running. I don't have to talk to anyone, answer any questions. My swarming thoughts start to calm, and I take in deep gulps of cool air.

Soon I've reached the stile, and I'm on the dirt track running alongside the clifftop, the sea foaming down below. The air feels clearer here. A seagull swoops and calls.

Running is easy and simple. I know the pattern of my movement, of my breathing. How it feels to reach different distances. When it comes to Jen, and the horrible secret of the marathon, everything is sickeningly unfamiliar and unpredictable. The burden of telling her turns my insides with guilt and fear. I know, theoretically, that lying is wrong, and that the longer I leave it, the worse it's going to be. But I'm still holding out for some kind of divine intervention that means I won't have to tell her.

After all, there's bound to be things she hasn't told me. What about her relationship history? She wasn't very quick to elaborate on that. Maybe there was more to it than she told me, things she withheld because she thought I'd react badly.

I picture the wedding day, Jen in a dazzling white dress, and then what happens when we are alone. What if I do everything wrong? I'm usually overly confident in my own abilities, but not in this area. I just want it to be perfect.

I switch my focus to the rippling water, and try to stop thinking about it. These things usually work out, don't they? There's no point worrying.

When I get back, I shower and then find a sheet of paper Jen's left on my desk.

'I, (name), take you, (name)

to be my wife/husband,
to have and to hold
from this day forward;
for better, for worse,
for richer, for poorer,
in sickness and in health,
to love and to cherish,
till death us do part,
according to God's holy law.
In the presence of God I make this vow.'

My eyes scan over the familiar words, but I find myself sinking down to sit on the bed, my hand shaking as I hold the page. This is the promise I am making. Jen might get cancer like her mum. We might go through hard times financially. Will I love and cherish her? Am I loving and cherishing her now?

Not if I don't tell her the truth.

I fold the page in half and stand up, fuelled by resolution. I stride downstairs with determination. I am going to tell her.

Just as I reach the bottom of the stairs, Mum comes out of the kitchen and smiles when she sees me. She takes my hand and presses it, nodding towards the lounge.

'They've been getting on so well.'

I can see Jen and my dad, looking at the laptop screen together and talking.

'I knew he would come round.'

I turn back to Mum and she has tears in her eyes. I pull her into a hug, smelling her familiar perfume and feeling her brittle shoulders.

'I'm so happy for you,' she whispers.

'Thanks, Mum,' I say.

I pull back and step forwards into the lounge. Dad and Jen look up.

'Come and see.' Jen beckons to me.

'Here, why don't you sit here?' Dad stands and gestures for me to take his place. 'I thought I'd make some coffee.'

'I was just putting some on,' Mum smiles.

'Great minds,' Dad says, and they leave us alone.

'We've got "Be Thou My Vision".' Jen scrolls down the document. '"Love Divine", and "Amazing Grace". What do you think?'

'They look perfect,' I say, covering her hand with my own.

She turns to smile at me, and I touch her jaw with my finger.

'I just read the vows. I need to tell you something.' I hesitate for a microsecond. 'It's about the marathon.'

'It's okay,' Jen replies, kissing my finger. 'David already spoke to me.'

What?

'He… he did?'

'Yes. You know, he was surprisingly decent. He does care about you more than I gave him credit for.'

I'm in a parallel universe. If I look out of the window, the sky will be purple with three moons.

'I agreed that I didn't want to stress you out any more than you already are,' she continues, 'so it's all fine and you don't need to worry.'

I exhale and feel relief immediately easing the tight knot in my stomach.

'I love you,' I say, cupping her face in my hands.

'I love you, too,' she replies.

70

Jen

Half term is over too quickly, and now the countdown to the wedding is really on. Aunt Chevy approved of all the hymn choices and then suggested that some of the choir from Zion Hill could sing. The trouble was, they all wanted to come.

'How about we hire a coach?' she suggests, speaking mainly to Katie as the chief wedding planner.

'I'm on it,' Katie says.

She's been home most weekends to help with wedding stuff, and also to see Aunt Chevy. She's turning into my PA, opening invitation RSVPs and logging everything on spreadsheets. She's got a Michael streak too.

'Your department has all accepted,' she informs me, which means that Judy, Liz and Geoff are coming. The Whidlock contingent is growing. 'Now you just need to confirm the hen do guest list.'

This has been tricky; I looked at all the women coming to the wedding, and then narrowed it down—mainly by age. But I wasn't sure what to do about Rachel, Michael's sister.

'Why don't you invite her, along with a friend?' Katie suggests.

'Okay.' I consider this. 'Her friend Sally is the one who's helping with the car. I'll see if they want to come.'

'Is there anyone we've missed?' Katie asks.

'What about Christina?' I ask. 'She was very involved with the proposal. I don't know her that well, but I'd like to make the effort, you know?'

'Sure,' Katie agrees.

'Do you need me to do anything?' I ask.

'Not at all,' Katie says firmly. 'You just need to be there. Everything is taken care of.'

That's what I'm afraid of.

The day arrives, grey and blustery. I had hoped for a lie-in, but Katie's too excited and bursts into my room with breakfast and Buck's Fizz on a tray.

'Happy Hen Day!'

'You are way too hyper already,' I groan, heaving myself into a sitting position. 'Isn't a bit early for alcohol?'

'Pssh!' Katie scoffs, sitting by my feet and shoving the tray onto my lap. 'Look, I even made you scrambled eggs.'

'That's because you always wreck it when you try to fry them.'

I pick up a slightly charred piece of toast and take a bite. This must be how our mum felt every Mother's Day when we presented her with breakfast in bed and she had to pretend to like it.

'Steph will be here soon to pick us up,' she tells me. 'I will lay your clothes out for you to make sure you are properly attired.'

I scoop up some egg with my fork and watch as Katie pulls out a pair of joggers from my drawer.

'Are we doing some kind of sport?' I ask suspiciously.

'Trust me, you'll love it,' Katie says.

When Steph beeps her car horn outside, Katie rushes around trying to find our wellies.

'Where is the other one gone?' she stresses.

'It's just underneath,' I say, retrieving it. 'You only had to lift a few things up.'

We're wearing hoodies and raincoats, and we dash out to Steph's car with a mild drizzle against our faces.

'I hope we're not wading through a river or something,' I say.

When I open the car door, Deena and Clare shriek at me.

'It's your big day!' Deena says.

'I thought that was my wedding.'

'Well, your big day before your wedding, then.'

'It's your big day with *us* before your wedding,' Clare corrects.

'How come you ended up as chauffeur?' I ask Steph.

'Everyone else had conveniently booked train tickets.' She looks in the rear-view mirror with a meaningful smile at Deena and Clare.

'Traffic's terrible, you know,' Deena says, with a wave of her hand.

'Where are we headed?' I ask.

'Somewhere you know,' Katie says.

Steph heads down the motorway; so far we could be going anywhere. But when she takes the exit, I look around at Katie in the back seat with Deena and Clare.

'Is this near Michael's parents?' I ask.

'It may be.'

I'm beginning to know the pattern of these roads much better, now that we've come here for marriage prep and at half term. The trees are looking greener, and the fields stretch out, with more livestock than before and groups of lambs. Steph takes a narrow farm track off the main road and the car judders along, thick hedging on either side. Finally, she turns into a gate with a sign saying 'Cherry Orchard'. Christina, Rachel and Sally are standing in a yard, and Christina is wearing jodhpurs and a riding hat.

'Are we going horse riding?' I ask Katie, hoping that Christina's not just using a horse as a mode of transport. I always wanted to do it when we were kids, but it was too expensive.

'We are going pony trekking!' Katie announces. 'And you can thank Christina; she knows the stable owners and she sorted it for us.'

I step out of the car and wave, slightly awkwardly, at the three girls I didn't know six months ago. Christina looks as dazzlingly perfect as ever, but I notice a slight blush as she says hello, and it makes me wonder if she's actually quite nervous. Rachel looks at home in these surroundings, with her athletic figure and clothes from leading outdoor pursuits brands. I haven't met Sally before, but she has the laid-back look of someone who gets along with everyone. She has a rounder figure, a mischievous grin, and a broad Bristol accent.

Katie takes it on herself to make all the introductions (despite not knowing half the group), but soon we're all going to be kitted out with riding hats and the awkwardness dissolves into excited chatter.

'Not long to go now,' Christina says, falling in step next to me. 'Are you counting the days?'

'I don't know what day of the week it is half the time,' I joke. 'I don't know… School is such a blur of busyness, and I am really looking forward to the wedding, but somehow it feels like a lot to get through before we get there.'

'Hard to see the wood for the trees.' She nods.

'How's your work going?' I ask, aware that being a doctor must be much more demanding than teaching.

Christina blows a strand of blond hair out of her face.

'It's pretty full on,' she says, pausing for a moment. 'You see so many people, so many desperate situations. It's hard to know what to do with it.'

'I don't know how you manage to do the Barn stuff as well.' I shake my head. 'You must literally not have a spare minute.'

'Oh, I like it.' She smiles. 'Honestly. I wouldn't do it if I didn't. If I get time off, I just feel restless. The shift patterns are so irregular; no one is in sync with you, you know?'

That's one good thing about me and Michael both being teachers: we get the same holidays.

'Thanks so much for all you've done to help us,' I say, finding more warmth than I expected towards this super-woman. 'And for today. I've never done this before!'

'Riding has always been part of my life,' she says. 'Rach and I used to come here every Saturday.'

'I thought she looked the part.' I glance across at Rachel and smile.

We form a motley crew: Christina and Rachel are clearly experienced riders, Katie is confident around horses but isn't a rider, Deena and Clare have done it once or twice before, Steph is good at all sports, and Sally is clearly not at all sporty. Rachel has to help her up onto the pony, and Sally gives a loud shriek and grabs the saddle, half slumped over it.

'Nice view,' Rachel jokes, as Sally's backside looms by her face.

She pushes her so that Sally can sit upright on the pony, and her hand lingers on Sally's thigh in a familiar way. It's just a moment, and then it's gone, but it's suddenly clear to me: they are more than just friends.

I remember Rachel crying, speaking on the phone, saying she couldn't tell them. I'm willing to bet that Michael has no idea. I don't want to predict what Ezra will do or say when he finds out.

It will be Armageddon.

71

Michael

David Clark on a stag do is a bit too much.

He's like a kid who's eaten too much sugar, buzzing in my ear like a fly, and I really wish that I had found some way not to invite him.

Dan's made a huge effort, setting up some orienteering-style treasure hunt around the city. We split into two teams, and Dan put David with me because he doesn't know anyone else. I bite my tongue as I watch him eagerly seize the third clue, butcher its meaning with the most unlikely interpretations, all in the superior tones of someone who is never wrong.

'The Bell; it must be The Bell,' he asserts. 'It's the oldest pub in Whidlock.'

'No, I think it's Otter's Tavern,' Kyle argues, in true lawyer style.

They bicker for a minute while I google the answer.

'Otter's Tavern,' I reply, enjoying David's momentary crushed spirit.

'I heard the girls are going there tonight,' Kyle says.

'Really?' I ask. This surprises me: I expected Katie to drag Jen to some lurid karaoke bar.

As we work out the right direction, David seems tense. Surely he's not mad about getting the clue wrong?

'You all right?' I ask, eying him.

'I think there may be a problem,' he says, enigmatically.

'What?' I press, my eyes narrowing with suspicion.

'I might be wrong…' David says this in the nonchalant way of someone who never admits they made a mistake.

We turn the corner, and Otter's Tavern is straight ahead. Then I see it.

A giant billboard advertising the marathon, the date in letters as tall as I am, is right next to the pub where Jen is eating tonight.

'I thought you already talked to Jen about it,' I say suspiciously.

'I told her that I was going to support you on the day so she could focus on the wedding.'

My knot of anxiety reappears, then sinks like a stone in my stomach, as if it never left.

'But you didn't tell her it was on the same day.'

I'm guessing the answer to that judging by his expression.

'Maybe we could buy some spray paint and deface it,' David suggests.

'What's he talking about?' Kyle asks me, looking confused.

'No,' I say firmly to David, then turn to Kyle. 'Jen doesn't know that I'm running the marathon on our wedding day.'

Kyle blinks.

'I know,' I say. 'David, I have to tell her.'

David shrugs. I pull out my phone.

'What, you're just going to phone her?' Kyle says.

'Why not?'

'Uh, because she's on her hen day,' Kyle says.

'I've put it off for too long,' I say, pressing the call button.

The phone rings. Kyle and David are watching me in silence. Finally, it diverts to the voicemail. Kyle stretches out his arm.

'You cannot say this in a voice message,' he says.

I hang up and sigh in frustration.

'What are you going to do?' David asks.
I stare at the billboard. Challenge accepted.

72

Jen

The pony trek is awesome from start to finish. The midway point is Bestward, and the girls all coo as Christina and I basically re-enact Michael's proposal. She does a great impression of Michael running around tweaking everything to be just right, and all my suspicion towards her melts away. She's genuinely funny and doesn't come across as interested in Michael romantically at all. To top it all off, she invites us back to her house for bacon sandwiches, and it's the first time that the girls get to see the barn.

'This is amazing!' Katie grins from ear to ear, and the joy is infectious.

I finally feel like I made the right decision, when I see everyone's reactions.

'This is going to be incredible,' Deena says, and Clare nods enthusiastically.

Rachel already knows the set up, but Sally is also keen to look at the details of where the wedding car will be parked and how the day will run. Steph is looking up local B&Bs, and then Christina's mum brings us a plate of fresh chocolate muffins.

'It will be great to go to a wedding where the food is actually decent,' Deena says, taking a huge bite of her cake.

'What are you talking about?' Clare says. 'Your sister's wedding had incredible food in abundant quantities too!'

'Well, yes, but other weddings are lame.'

'How many other weddings have you been to?'

'That's not the point.'

'Where are you going to get ready in the morning of the wedding?' Rachel asks me.

'I was just planning to be at home, really,' I say. 'It's not that far to drive here, as long as Sally's dad is okay with that.'

'Sure,' she says. 'We just need to check the road closures because of the marathon.'

I freeze. A funny, sick feeling turns my stomach.

'The marathon?' I repeat.

Sally, with no idea of the magnitude of what she's revealed, is scrolling on her phone, while Rachel's look of horror shows me that she knows what's going on.

'Yeah, the Whidlock marathon.' Sally holds out her phone to show me the poster.

It suddenly makes sense: Michael's cagey attitude, the sense I got that there was something he wasn't telling me… Well, I wasn't expecting this.

'Did you know?' I turn to Rachel.

'Yes,' she admits, blushing. 'I told him to tell you. He nearly did, but he was worried you would break up with him.'

'What's going on?' Deena says, finishing her cake.

'Michael's running a marathon… on our wedding day.'

I give a slightly hysterical laugh. When, exactly, was he going to tell me? Was he going to tell me at all?

Deena gapes at me for a moment.

'He's mental,' she says. 'What are you going to do?'

I look round at Katie, who doesn't look as though she has processed this information yet.

'I'm going to find him,' I say, fired up with indignation. 'And he's going to wish he'd told me the truth.'

73

Michael

'This isn't quite the way I wanted your stag do to turn out,' Dan says.

We're sat, like teenagers, on a bench by the pub, eating a McDonalds. It's starting to rain.

'Can you try and phone her again?' Kyle suggests.

'What's the point?' I sigh. 'I'll only look like a stalker if she has forty missed calls from me.'

My mood has dampened the atmosphere, but David is humming and tapping his foot on the pavement.

'What time is she coming?' he asks.

'Five,' I tell him for what feels like the twentieth time. 'It's St Patrick's Day and there's a special event happening in the evening.'

'That's what the shamrock hats were for,' Alex says. 'I saw a bunch of them in McDonalds.'

'What are you going to say?' Dan asks, quietly.

I run my hand through my (now damp) hair.

'That I regret not telling her. That I'm sorry. That I hope she'll still marry me.'

'What about that you're pulling out of the marathon?' he says.

'I don't think I can do that.'

'Why not?'

'The money,' I hiss, so David doesn't hear. 'You know I can't do that to the kid who has cancer.'

'It's not your job to fix everyone's problems,' Dan says.

'Hey, it's Mr Chase!'

I look up and see a group of Year 11 boys from my class, wearing green Irish rugby shirts.

'All right, Sir?'

'Mr Clark's here too!'

'Did you get a Big Mac, Sir?'

'Yes,' David replies. 'Now, I hope you boys are not involved in any underage drinking.'

'Just meeting some friends, Sir.' Toby, one of the tallest, grins at me. He could easily pass for eighteen.

The rain intensifies. The boys scarper off to find shelter, and Kyle finds a shop with an awning, a bit lopsided and faded, which we can stand under. A stream of water is flowing from the bottom corner.

'There they are!' Alex says, giving me a sudden nudge.

From the other side street leading towards the pub, there's a group of girls with bright pink umbrellas. I can just about work out which one is Jen, from her raincoat, and I dart forward, in front of the billboard.

'Jen!'

She looks at me, but she doesn't smile. Her pace quickens, and as I see the expression on the other girls' faces, I realise that there's a reason she hasn't been answering my calls and messages.

'When were you going to tell me?' she shouts, the rain spattering the pavement, her shoes creating a splash in each puddle as she stalks towards me.

'Now,' I say weakly, feeling my hair dripping onto my face.

It's not a good time to say it, but she looks absolutely stunning. People are stopping in the street to look at her, and it's not just because the umbrella catches their eye.

'Is this some kind of sick joke, some sort of weird achievement-driven thing, that you wanted to run a marathon and get married *on the same day*, the day before you turned thirty?'

The whole street is definitely staring now.

'I made a mistake,' I say, trying to just concentrate on keeping eye contact with her, but her eyes are pure fire and it makes me lose my train of thought and all the eloquent speeches I had thought up. 'I didn't realise. And then there was a lot of money involved…'

'Why didn't you just tell me?'

'I—I kept trying, but then there just wasn't a good moment, and I wanted to ask to change the date but then Katie made the invitations…'

'Katie made the invitations with the date that YOU booked! The date you booked before you even PROPOSED to me!'

I gulp. Her incandescent rage is beautiful but terrifying.

'I got it wrong. I made a mistake,' I repeat.

'Everyone makes mistakes, Michael,' Jen says, and her voice chokes up. 'But it's just you who insists on trying to fix everything yourself, and that it'll all be fine, it's all under control, and guess what? This time, it's not fine.'

'I'm sorry.' I reach out to touch her arm, and she pulls it back violently.

'I thought we agreed: no secrets,' she says, both tears and rain streaming down her cheeks.

'I know,' I say. 'When I saw the billboard, I wanted to be here to meet you. I wanted to be honest…'

'It's a bit late now, Michael.'

She steps backwards, looking up at the billboard, and shaking her head. Katie steps forward and puts an arm around her.

'Let's go inside,' she says.

The group make their way into the pub, Deena shooting daggers at me, and my sister comes forward.

'Give her some space,' she says. 'I'll call you later.'

My stomach is left churning as she follows the others indoors. I'm vaguely aware that I'm soaked through, but I can't bring myself to move. Dan and the other guys join me.

'I think that went well,' David says.

There's a moment of silence.

'Let's head back to yours,' Dan says.

74

Jen

I sit at the head of the table and cry, to a soundtrack of Irish music. My hen do meal has turned into a boardroom meeting of How to Handle this Crisis. A waiter approaches hopefully and Katie waves him away.

'You said what you wanted to say,' she says, putting her arm around me.

'What did he have to say for himself?' Deena asks.

'That he made a mistake,' I say, wiping tears from my cheeks.

'I'll say,' Deena mutters.

'He wanted to tell you,' Rachel says, not for the first time today. 'When he saw the billboard, he decided he wanted to be here to face you himself.'

'He probably thinks it's too late to call off the wedding,' I say bitterly.

'*Do* you want to call off the wedding?' Clare asks.

'I don't know,' I sob. 'I'm so mad at him!'

'We're *all* mad at him,' Deena says. 'No offence, Rachel.'

'None taken.'

'Can I get you some drinks?'

The waiter has reappeared, choosing the other end of the table this time so as to avoid Katie's death stare.

'We have a St Patrick's Day happy hour menu.' He hands a sheet of paper to Sally, decorated with green shamrocks.

'A pitcher of Guinness and a tray of Shamrock shots, please,' Sally says decisively. 'Jen, I think tonight you need to concentrate on having fun with your friends.'

'I ordered a hen party pack,' Katie says, grabbing a bag from Steph and putting a box on the table.

She grabs a butter knife and hacks away at the tape, nearly gouging part of her hand off in the process. She wrestles the box open and pulls out a tiara.

'Ta da!' she says, putting it on me.

'I don't really feel like—' I start, but then I notice what's in the box. 'Wait, is that...'

Deena grabs a packet of pink penis straws.

'Oh no!' Katie shrieks. 'It's the wrong pack.'

'I think it looks like exactly the right one,' Steph says, snickering.

'What's this?' Clare pulls out a magic wand, and then a giant pink badge saying 'Bride to Be' with L plates on it.

'There was a *classy* pack and then there was a *tacky* pack,' Katie moans. 'I clicked classy!'

'Clearly,' Deena says, fishing out a packet of pink bubble tubes.

'I'm so sorry,' Katie says, looking at me in mortification.

Clare silently retrieves a box with WILLY GLOW STICK in bold type.

I cover my mouth, then start to giggle. Rachel and Christina are looking uneasily at each other in a 'I didn't think it was that kind of party' sort of way. More laughter erupts from my end of the table. Steph pulls out a willy whistle and blows it, just as the waiter arrives with a tray of drinks.

'Right, let's do this,' I say.

75

Michael

'What if she rings me and tells me that the wedding is off?' I ask Dan, pacing my kitchen. 'Or worse, she doesn't speak to me at all, and I'm just waiting at the altar because I have no idea if she's going to show up?'

'If she loves you, I'm sure you will find a way to work through this,' he says, taking the cap off a beer and passing it to me.

There are cheers from the lounge: the guys are playing a FIFA tournament.

I shake my head and take a gulp of beer.

'I don't know,' I say. 'I thought David told her, but maybe I just wanted to believe it and I didn't exactly check. We're supposed to be saying these vows about loving and cherishing each other and I've double booked our wedding day.'

'Michael, I don't know why you see every mistake as being final,' Dan says. 'There's always a way. Perhaps you have to cancel; perhaps you have to let people down. But just because you've signed up to something, doesn't mean it's set in stone and you're going to be eternally cursed if you don't do it.'

'She said I always try to fix everything.' I run my hand through my hair. 'But I thought that was a good thing!'

'You have a lot to learn about women,' Dan says with a wry smile.

'What should I do now?' I ask, hopelessly.

'Let her enjoy her hen party,' Dan says. 'Go and see her tomorrow and then ask her what she wants you to do.'

'And what then?'

'And then do it!' He claps a hand on my back. 'No ifs, no buts, no get-out clauses. You have to show her that she's more important than anything else.'

'Right.' I sip my beer nervously.

'Hey guys.' David comes into the kitchen.

'I'm going to check on the game,' Dan says, giving David a smile before heading into the lounge.

David picks up a beer.

'Your friends are really cool,' he says. 'It must be nice to have friends like this.'

It's a rare chink in David's armour, but I'm not feeling very charitable at this moment.

'Well it looks like I'm going to need all the friends I can get, given that my fiancée and her crew hate my guts right now.'

'I'm sorry,' David says, and for once I don't doubt his sincerity. 'I know I've landed you in all this. I didn't mean to mess up your wedding.'

'It's my fault,' I say. 'I chose the wrong date. I should have just been honest with Jen from the beginning.'

'Are you going to pull out of the marathon?' he asks.

'I think I'll have to.'

We both look down at our beers, glumly. David's phone beeps.

'Oh no,' he says.

I look at him questioningly. He holds up his phone screen: WEDDING AND MARATHON ON THE SAME DAY? It's a video clip of me, standing in front of the billboard, and Jen saying 'Why didn't you just tell me?' Somehow, instead of being a shaky, blurry video that no one can see properly, whoever filmed it managed to frame it perfectly, with the bright pink umbrellas against the grey paint of the pub, and my face in profile against the giant billboard. It looks almost cinematic.

'Adele just sent it to me. You're going viral.'

It's my worst nightmare. What if Jen finds out? She had enough rage at being part of Adele's live stream.

'Does it say our names or anything?'

'No.' David scrolls down to check. 'But it won't be long before they find out.'

'The Year 11s,' I say, face palming. 'It might have been them who filmed it.'

'I think it's a bit good for one of them to have done it,' David frowns. 'But they were there, so they may tell the press who you are if anyone asks them for more information. Isn't it illegal to post a video of someone without their permission? Maybe we could get them to take it down.'

'Taking a video in a public place and posting it online isn't illegal,' I say mechanically, hearkening back to my days of studying Law alongside English. 'It's only if it's filmed secretly or in a private location like someone's home.'

'I guess it wasn't exactly a private setting,' David grimaces.

'What are people saying about it?' I try to peer over David's shoulder, but he holds the phone out of my reach.

'You don't want to read the comments,' he says. 'Rule number one of social media.'

'What are we going to say to Bradley's parents?' I feel sick at the thought of going to see them again, to confess that I can't do the marathon.

'We'll think of something,' David mutters, tapping away on his phone.

It's not exactly reassuring.

76

Jen

When I stumble downstairs in the morning, wearing a ragged pair of pyjamas, the first thing I see is the biggest bouquet of flowers on the kitchen table, and Michael.

'What are you doing here?'

He jumps to his feet.

'Jen—I love you—I'm sorry—please forgive me,' he blurts out in one breath.

'Nice flowers.' My eyes flick to the elaborate bouquet again.

'I should have told you,' he says. 'It was so wrong of me.'

'You're actually admitting you did something wrong?' I say skeptically.

'Yes.'

He looks at me, pleading.

'I can't stand being lied to,' I say.

Aunt Chevy walks in, looks at the two of us, and then turns to walk back out again.

'Sorry for interrupting!' she calls over her shoulder.

'What do you want me to do?' he asks, clear desperation in his voice.

'Be honest with me,' I say.

'Yes.' He nods. 'And what about the marathon?'

'Just… tell them you can't do it. Sign up for a different one.'

'Okay.' He swallows, but nods.

I wait for him to argue, but he doesn't.

'Do you want some juice?' I ask, walking to the fridge.

'No thanks,' he says, and something in his tone makes me look over at him again.

'What?' I ask.

'Someone videoed what happened outside the pub yesterday.'

'Sorry, what?' I shut the fridge door, making it shudder.

'It's online. Just so you know.'

'Where?'

'It's been shared on different platforms.' He shrugs. 'I just… didn't want you to be surprised by it.'

'Show me.'

He pulls it up on his phone. I watch the clip with a sense of horror. That's me, the Girl with the Pink Umbrella. I look MAD. I can see the view count is sky high and it's still being shared.

'Are the kids at school going to see this?' I ask immediately.

'There were some Year 11 boys outside the pub last night.'

I groan. It would be them.

'David thinks that some journalists might turn up at school tomorrow,' Michael continues. 'He suggests that we make a statement.'

'I can't think about this right now,' I snap, grabbing the kettle.

Juice is not enough; I need caffeine.

'I can write it if you want,' he says. 'I just need to apologise to Bradley and his family, and tell people that their money will be refunded.'

Just the thought of that poor kid makes my insides turn over.

'Slow down,' I say, and take a deep breath. 'Look, I need some time to process all this. I'll see you in school tomorrow and we can work something out then. Don't say anything to the press. Please.'

'Okay.' He nods. 'Jen, you know I love you more than anything, don't you?'

'I know,' I say.

But I'm still too angry to say it back.

I'd love to say I wake up on Monday feeling madly in love with Michael and ready to forgive him and move forward to the wedding, but I don't. After talking through every possible angle on the situation with Katie, she had to go back to Uni, and I had to think about what I was actually going to teach this week. I kept checking my phone for updates on the video, and Deena and Clare were posting on our group with advice too.

Clare: That's gonna be a PR firestorm if he pulls out of the marathon.

Deena: Shoulda thought about that before he signed up then!

Me: He signed up for the marathon in October, before we even got together.

Deena: So why did he book the wedding on the same day???

Clare: Human error, Deena. He said he made a mistake.

Deena: That's true.

Me: I don't like it, but I don't like landing him in it, either.

Clare: Why can't you suggest that people's donations support someone else running?

Deena: Because they wouldn't go to the kid with cancer then.

Me: I don't want to have to cancel my wedding.

Deena: You should not have to do that.

Clare: Look, hear me out, but can't you push the ceremony back a little later, to give him more of a buffer zone?

Deena: Are you actually suggesting that he should do it?

Clare: I think he's in a difficult position. He's trying to honour a prior commitment. Aren't you always criticising guys for not doing that?

Deena: His commitment should be to Jen first.

Me: I'm going to bed now.

As I arrive at school, wearing a slightly crumpled white shirt with a navy pinafore dress, my head isn't feeling any clearer. I shut my car door, grab my tote bag, and see Michael and David standing outside the main entrance, surrounded by a small group of people. Journalists. I can see David gesturing, and Michael looking... unusually helpless. I pull my bag strap over my shoulder, and tighten my jaw. I head straight towards them.

God, I don't know what to do. I don't know what to say. Help me.

'Is it true that you booked the wedding on the same day as the marathon to achieve two life goals in one day?' one journalist asks, holding a notepad.

There's a camera too.

'Is it true that the video captures the moment your fiancée found out the truth?'

'No,' I answer coldly, pushing my way through the small group to reach Michael.

I take his hand. He squeezes it.

'Have you spoken to the family of the boy you are fundraising for?' another voice asks. 'How will they respond to this news?'

'Are you still going to run the marathon?'

'Are you still going to marry Michael?'

The questions are fired at us simultaneously. I feel Michael's eyes on my face.

'Yes, I'm still going to marry him,' I say, as if any other response would be ludicrous. 'And yes, he's still going to run the marathon.

Michael is a person who honours his commitments. And I respect that. It's one of the many reasons I love him.'

I pass my tote bag to David, who dumbly takes it, then throw my arms around Michael's neck and kiss him. He hesitates for a nanosecond before wrapping his arms around me and squeezing me so tightly I can barely breathe.

'We will release a statement later,' I tell the press. 'David, what's Adele's YouTube channel called?'

'Dressed to Perfection by Adele,' he says mechanically.

'We will make a statement on Adele's channel,' I say, 'as long as she agrees to it. Now we need to go and teach.'

I pull Michael inside the heavy double doors with me, leaving David to stutter a marching order to the group.

'Did you mean it?' Michael asks me immediately.

'Which part?' I ask.

'All of it.'

'Of course I did!' I start to laugh.

'I thought you would never forgive me.'

'So did I.'

'I love you,' he says, his hands clasped over mine.

'I love you, too,' I reply. 'Now ask David to free us up so we can sort this out together.'

'Ahem.'

I look up and see David, lingering sheepishly by the door, having just left the press.

'Would you like me to ring Adele?'

Michael looks nervously at me. His jaw drops when I smile.

'Yes please David. That would be very helpful.'

I'm going back on camera, but this time, I'll be ready for it.

77

Michael

'Okay we're live in three, two…' David holds up one finger and then nods.

'Welcome, I'm Adele, and this is my channel, Dressed to Perfection. You may have heard about a teacher who's planning on running a marathon and getting married on the same day. On Saturday, a certain video went viral showing Michael Chase, under a billboard for the marathon, being confronted by his fiancée, Jen Baker. Well, I personally know Michael and Jen and I am delighted to be here with them now, to get first-hand the full story.'

Adele flicks her hair over her shoulder and turns to face me and Jen, sitting on bar stools in her makeshift studio in David's house. I try not to squint from the bright lights she set up in the corner.

'Michael, let's start with you. How did all of this come about?'

Just tell the whole truth, and nothing but the truth.

'I wanted to run a marathon. It's always been something I wanted to do. I started training and I signed up in October for the Whidlock marathon. The headteacher of my school suggested that I could raise money for one of our students, who has been battling cancer, and also for our school. I thought that was a great idea.'

'Were you engaged at that time?'

'No.' I give a dry laugh. 'I only met Jen in September. In October we were waging war on one another because we went for the same promotion.'

'Jen, what was your first impression of Michael?'

Jen smiles and leans forward elegantly.

'I thought he was driven and impossible to work with.'

She pauses here while Adele gives a high-pitched laugh.

'But then I got to know him. I realised that I had misjudged him.'

'When did you get together?' Adele asks, clearly loving these details.

'It was round about half term,' Jen answers. 'Then Michael proposed at Christmas, and I said yes.'

'A true whirlwind romance!' Adele says, looking at the camera, which is set up on a tripod. 'So what happened with the wedding date?'

'I made a huge error,' I say, looking nervously at Jen, who smiles encouragingly. 'I was really keen to book the church, and I forgot that the marathon was on a Saturday. Usually they are on Sundays. I didn't realise what I'd done until I came back in January and the Head had some promotional materials printed in order to raise more money.'

'And did you tell Jen?' Adele asks the key, burning question.

'No,' I answer honestly, feeling the sting of shame all over again. 'I know that I should have done. I have no excuse for my behaviour. I tried to hide it from her.'

'Jen, did you have any idea about this clash?'

'No.' Jen gives a wry smile. 'I was so focused on the wedding plans, I didn't really pay much attention to Michael's marathon.'

'So tell me what happened on Saturday.'

'It was my hen party,' Jen says. 'Michael was having his stag the same day. At the party, someone mentioned the marathon, and I suddenly realised that it was the same day.'

'What did you do?' Adele's eyes widen.

'I was really shocked,' Jen admits. 'Michael tried to call me a few times, but I didn't pick up. I wanted to see him face to face. I got my sister to find out where he was from his best man.'

'What were you doing at that point, Michael?'

'I was outside the pub, and I knew Jen was going there in the evening,' I say, remembering being sat on that bench in the rain. 'There was this massive billboard advertising the marathon. I knew she would find out and I wanted to be there to tell her myself.'

'So in the video that someone posted online, that was Jen confronting you because she had found out that day about the marathon?'

'That's correct,' I reply.

'What did you say to him?' Adele asks Jen.

'I think everyone who's watched the video will know my speech off by heart,' Jen remarks. 'But I basically told him that he should have told me.'

'And what's going to happen now?'

'We've decided that Michael is going to run the marathon,' Jen says, calmly. 'He's trained for it, he expects to finish it in good time, and we will run our wedding as planned.'

'Are you nervous?' Adele asks me.

'I'm more nervous about the wedding than I am about the marathon,' I say truthfully. 'Jen has been amazing. She is the best thing in my life, and I don't deserve her.'

'Jen, how do you feel?' Adele asks her.

'No one except Michael could have got into this crazy situation,' she says. 'But we're a team, and we're going to do this together.'

'Well I wish you the very best of luck with both the marathon and your big day, and I will be posting updates!' Adele faces the camera again. 'Don't forget to subscribe to Dressed to Perfection by Adele. Thank you so much for watching. Bye!'

David puts his thumb up and the red light flashing on the camera vanishes.

'Okay, how was that?' Adele looks at him.

'That was amazing,' he says. 'You all did really, really well. It came across as natural, and honest.'

'Let's take a look at the comments,' she says. 'How many views have we got?'

'A few thousand,' David replies. 'And in the comments, they are saying they are going to sponsor Michael.'

'I put the sponsorship link on there earlier,' Adele says.

'Thank you,' I say, taken aback.

'Thank you for asking me to do this,' Adele replies. 'I'm sorry about… what happened before.'

'I'm sorry too.' Jen surprises me by apologising. 'I was rude to you, and I just left. Thank you for doing us this massive favour.'

'How about we have some food?' David suggests. 'We never did eat last time.'

The weeks leading up to the wedding are absolutely insane. Adele's livestream gets more and more views as the story gets publicity from the local news team, and the video continues to be shared. The sponsorship goes through the roof. David and I meet with Bradley's family, who are unbelievably gracious to me, considering I made such a mess up of everything. They are overjoyed that I'm still going to run, and for the amount of money that's going towards Bradley's treatment and supporting their family.

There's a lot of public backlash as well, though. People say that it's just a publicity stunt and I'm not actually going to run the marathon. Jen comes up with the idea of Adele filming me and live streaming it at certain checkpoints on the day, which Adele agrees to enthusiastically.

'You don't have to be there,' I say to Jen. 'You'll be wanting to get ready.'

'I want to support you,' she says. 'I just don't know about the logistics of getting there and then over to the wedding, and all that.'

'Just stick to your plan,' I tell her. 'You get ready at your house with Katie and your bridesmaids, and I'll meet you at the church.'

'I can't believe it's happening,' she says, shaking her head. 'We're getting married!'

78

Jen

When Katie finishes for Easter, she comes home and sets up a 'wedding' office in the lounge. It's basically a pile of RSVPs, paperwork and her laptop, but she seems in her element. She's used this as an opportunity to micro-manage my whole life.

'Now, looking at your calendar, are you still running the writing festival this week?' she asks, peering at me around her laptop screen.

'No, David suggested that we should postpone it to the summer term.'

'You know, that's actually a good idea,' Katie says.

'Yes,' I agree. 'He called me into his office and said he was worried it was too much for me before the wedding. Not in a patronising way, but in a nice way. Even caring.'

'That's a transformation.' Katie raises her eyebrows. 'Are you sure he's not buttering you up before landing another HR policy on your desk?'

I roll my eyes and sip my tea.

'He apologised to me about that,' I remind her. 'I think he felt so bad about the marathon clash that he's turned into a cheerleader for us.'

'Well, he must be loving the press attention Whidlock's getting,' Katie points out. 'Half of Michael's sponsorship is going to the school. At this rate it'll be six figures!'

'I don't think so.' I smile. 'It's good to see some positive coverage. Maybe it will give us some leverage when the Council try to merge us with Prestfield.'

'But you still have asbestos.'

'The site has issues.' I nod. 'Is merging with another school the solution? Prestfield looks pretty crummy to me.'

'The reality is, they don't care.' Katie turns back to her laptop and taps on the keyboard. 'Now, shall we do a final check of the seating plan?'

'You can make sure I'm next to someone interesting.' Aunt Chevy comes in to snoop at Katie's screen.

'This is classified information.' She covers the screen with her hand.

'Okay, okay!' Aunt Chevy laughs. 'A parcel came for you.'

She hands me a tiny box.

'Have you got any scissors?' I ask Katie, who promptly hands over a pair.

I know what it is, but it still makes my heartbeat quicken. It's a red jewellery box with Michael's wedding ring.

'I'm going to get mine.'

I hurry upstairs and find Mum's wedding ring, and add it to the box. Two gold rings, side by side.

'*Nothing gold can stay*,' I repeat the Robert Frost line.

I know my dress, my shoes, the food and the favours will be things that perish and fade. I pray our love will be something that endures.

The day before the wedding, Michael kisses me under the relative shadow of the front porch.

'I am really looking forward to when this is all over, and it's just you and me,' he murmurs.

'I know,' I say, a twinge of excitement in my stomach. 'Good luck with the marathon. You'll be awesome.'

'I love you.'

With one lingering kiss, he tears himself away to drive home, and I return to the chaos indoors.

Deena, Clare, Katie and Aunt Chevy are all rolling up their sleeves to enthusiastically partake in the 'Beautify Jen' project. Dad has retreated upstairs, while the lounge is taken over with nail polish, make-up, oils for my hair, and a lot of fizzy drinks cans and junk food. It feels like I barely get a few hours' sleep before they're waking me up again, feeding me French toast and flapping about how we haven't got enough time.

'It's fine,' I protest. 'We've got plenty of time.'

'For you maybe,' Katie says. 'Don't forget about us too!'

It takes two hours for everyone to use the shower, by which point I'm propping my phone up, with Adele's live stream beginning. I can see Michael at the starting point, gathering with all the other runners, wearing a vest with a number pinned on the front. Please God, let him be okay.

It feels surreal, seeing clips of Michael running at various checkpoints: five miles, ten miles, fifteen… While I am zipped into my bodice and skirt, and Aunt Chevy fixes the veil so it just touches my shoulders. I test out putting it down over my face and back up again. I was nervous that my hair would just get caught in it and it would look wrong, but it actually looks really elegant.

'You look amazing,' Katie says, standing behind me and putting her arms around my neck.

I twist round to hug her. She's wearing her dress, but her hair isn't ready yet.

'I found something in Mum's jewellery box for you,' I say, finding it on my dressing table.

It's a tiny silver locket on a dainty chain.

'If you wear it, then we'll both be wearing something of hers,' I explain.

Katie's eyes fill with tears, and she hugs me again.

'The car's arrived!' Deena calls, looking out of the window.

'He's here early,' I comment, looking at the time.

'I said it would be good if they were here for the photographer,' Katie says. 'She's coming soon.'

'Looks like your Dad is finding solace outside with some male company,' Clare grins.

'He's well and truly outnumbered in here,' I comment.

'What's wrong with Michael?' Deena asks, pointing to my phone.

I turn and snatch it up. He's standing and shaking his head to the camera.

'My muscle just seized up,' he's saying. 'I'm going to have to walk.'

'You're at mile 22,' Adele says. 'You're so close now. You can do this.'

'I don't want to let anyone down,' he says, looking miserable. 'And I don't want to be late for the wedding.'

'We're all behind you, Michael,' Adele says.

The livestream ends, and I look up at the others.

'He's struggling,' I say.

'What happened?' Katie asks.

'Something about his muscle seizing up,' I say.

'The photographer's here,' Clare says.

'We need to go,' I say.

'What?' Deena asks.

'We need to go, right now,' I say. 'I need to be there for him.'

'You want to go to the marathon?' Katie's voice pitches into the stratosphere.

'I'll take Katie and the photographer,' I say, 'My dad can drive you and follow. Let's go!'

'I don't want to be taken!' Katie wails. 'I need my stuff!'

'Grab it, then!' I say, picking up my skirt with one hand and heading for the stairs.

'This was not part of the plan!' she shouts after me.

79

Michael

Everything was fine until I hit the twenty-second mile.

I was completely on track to achieve my goal of three and a half hours. It felt so easy. Now, it's like my body has just shut down. I'm hobbling along and people are passing me, including a group with a pacer for a four-hour time. Plus, this is all being captured by Adele at her checkpoints. The next time I'll see her now will be the finish line, but that's going to take a lot longer than I'd planned.

I think about Jen, standing at the altar waiting for me, a complete inversion of what's supposed to happen. The look of disappointment on her face. There's a lump in my throat I can't swallow away.

I know this is all my fault. Dan was right. I should have just quit while I had the chance, before this media circus took off, and I had to prove that I was actually running so that Bradley's family would get their money.

It's funny, I don't know why it pops into my head, but I feel like the prodigal son in the story that Steve told at marriage prep. I had all these grand ideas about who I was and what I'd do, and now I'm limping back, and I feel like I've failed.

God, please help me.

I keep putting one foot in front of the other, each mile feeling endless, and every minute going by makes my face burn with the humiliation of being so far off where I wanted to be at this point.

Finally, I approach the city centre. The central road has been closed, and the finish line is next to the billboard and Otter's Tavern. There's a huge crowd, and as I stumble forwards, there's a roar of noise. Odd.

Dazed, I fix upon the inflated banner that marks the finish line. Nearly there. Don't give up.

There's an even louder cheer, and then sounds of applause, whooping and screaming. Ahead at the finish line, Jen stands, in her wedding dress.

I think I'm seeing things. I heard about runners losing sight in one eye, their bodies shutting down due to the strain of running a marathon. Maybe I'm delusional.

She looks so beautiful. She's waving at me, but I can't do it. I feel my knees give way, and I'm on the ground.

'Michael!'

She's suddenly with me, lifting my sweaty, lifeless arm and supporting me to my feet.

'We're going to do this together.'

Her arms holding me up, we stagger to the finish line. I'm blinded now, by my own tears. There's a deafening wall of noise around me, but all I can do is sob into Jen's shoulder.

'I'm sorry,' I repeat, over and over.

'It's okay,' she says, her hand smoothing my back. 'You did it.'

Some stewards come over and usher us to the medical tent, and David and Adele follow behind us, Adele talking to her camera. Someone passes me a bottle of Lucozade.

'Is he all right?' I can hear Katie's voice just outside the tent.

'He crossed the finish line,' Jen says.

'Great,' Katie says, sounding as if she couldn't care less. 'Can we go now? It's your bloody wedding day!'

'You go,' I hear David say. 'I'll get him cleaned up and ready. Don't worry.'

'See you at the church,' Jen says, and kisses my cheek.

Then she's gone, and I'm left feeling as if it was all a dream.

'Come on,' David says, clapping a hand on my shoulder. 'We need to sneak out of the back here.'

He leads me out and ushers me straight inside the Otter's Tavern. A man is standing in the entrance.

'This is Michael,' David says, as if that explains everything.

Clearly, it does, as the man hands him a key and points us towards the stairs.

Grabbing hold of the bannister, I haul myself up the stairs and David opens a room with the key.

'Get yourself showered,' he says. 'We'll be getting ready in the next room.'

Feeling even more out of it, I stumble into the bathroom and turn on the shower. By the time I emerge, the room is clouded up with steam, and I can just about string a coherent thought together.

My wedding is in half an hour.

David has hung up my suit for me, and I mechanically dress, my stomach churning from hunger and nervous sickness. David knocks on the door.

'Are you ready?' he calls.

Slinging my sweaty running gear into a bag, I follow him back down the stairs. He's wearing a suit, and Adele is wearing a hot pink dress that's tighter than a vice, with a large fascinator in her hair. She totters behind David in six-inch heels.

'Car's just round the back,' he says, handing the keys over to the waiter and thanking him.

'How did you park it here?' I ask, as we pile inside.

WEDDING BELL TIME

'The landlord was pleased with the publicity from the video,' David says. 'He was happy to do us a favour.'

As I fasten my seatbelt, Adele passes me a sandwich.

'Don't get it on your suit!' she instructs.

I turn around to thank her, but she's holding her phone out to livestream again.

'We're now in the car, on our way to the wedding!'

Interlude

For some reason, it was night inside the maze. Alice wasn't surprised. After all, walking through a door in the middle of nowhere, with no walls, didn't make any sense. A low fog hung over the tall, thick hedging. The air smelled of conifers. The sky was cloudy so there were no stars or moon. Alice held her staff at the ready as she rounded each corner. Nothing.

For a horrible moment, Alice wondered if this was like the endless road. Was she destined to forever turn another corner in the maze, never reaching the centre or a way out?

The snap of a twig drew her attention. What was it, about twenty feet away? She started to run towards the sound, as best as she could with the twists and turns of the maze.

It was as if time slowed down and ground to a halt.

As she turned the final corner, she knew. She knew he would be there.

She stood, her chest heaving, and her breath curling like smoke into the mist. Edward was standing about fifteen feet away. He was holding his sword, but it was down at his side.

'Hello, Alice.'

'Edward.' She breathed out his name.

'Are you here to kill me?'

It looked like he was trying not to smile.

She shook her head. He already knew the answer to that question.

'What are you here for, then?' he asked.

He didn't try to close the distance between them. She lowered her staff.

'I don't know,' she answered honestly. 'I just knew that I had to find you.'

'You were the one who left,' he reminded her.

'I know,' she said. 'I'm sorry.'

And then he did smile. A cloud shifted and a silver moon glided into view, pearlescent in the dark sky.

The distance between them vanished as they met in the middle of the maze, in front of a fountain with a carved statue of a woman. It could have been her mother. But maybe it was a trick of the light (or lack thereof).

'It would have been easier for you to kill me,' he murmured, tracing a finger down her face.

'There's still time,' she whispered, her heart thumping.

When their lips met, it felt as though everything was fixed and made right again. All of the chaos made sense.

Under the moonlight, the statue smiled.

Document comments:

Michael Chase: Why does he ask her if she's here to kill him? Surely he must know how she feels by now?

Jen Baker: Love and hate are on the same spectrum.

Michael Chase: Do you often feel this type of raging violence towards me?

Jen Baker: Yes. It doesn't mean I love you any less.

Michael Chase: Maybe I should keep a shield next to the bed, just in case you wake up in the night after a particularly murderous dream.

Jen Baker: LOL.

80

Jen

It's a good job that Karen, the photographer, is as nice as her sister Louise. After snapping shots of me running down the finish line towards Michael, she jumps back in the wedding car and then suggests that we stop off by the coast for some pictures with the bridesmaids. Katie's stressing about her scheduling, but when we stand on the cliff top with the sea stretching out behind us, she concedes that the photos will be worth the detour.

'Anyway, we've got to give Michael a chance to get ready,' I reason. 'I don't want to arrive at the church before him.'

'There's no chance of that now,' Katie retorts. 'I've been following Adele's updates. They've arrived.'

'Don't we need to set things up in the church?' Deena asks.

'Dan's sorted all that,' Katie says.

'Okay.' I take a deep breath. 'Let's go, then!'

Driving through the streets in a wedding car, you get a lot of waves and attention. I feel like royalty as I put my veil over my face and grab Katie's hand to steady my nerves.

This is it. After all the planning and dreaming, we're finally pulling up outside the church, and this is my wedding day. The sun is warming me through the car window, and there are white, gold and green ribbons tied to the gates. Dad parks his car alongside us, and Deena and Clare step out and check each other's dresses. Karen hops out and starts snapping away.

'I'm going to go in with them,' Katie tells me. 'I'll come out to signal when it's time.'

I nod, and we look at each other for a moment, then she flings her arms around me.

'I love you,' she says. 'I'm so proud of you.'

I wipe the tears from the corner of my eyes, hoping that I don't have a complete emotional meltdown before I've even stepped inside the church. I watch as she leads the girls inside the church doors. Dad stands by the car door, and in truth, I've barely seen him all day. He's not a talker, but he's always been there for me. Even when I haven't been there for him.

He turns to me and smiles, opening the car door, and holding out his hand. I take it and step out onto the pavement, then I throw my arms around his neck and kiss his cheek.

'I love you, Dad.'

'I love you too,' he says, gently squeezing me back. 'You look as beautiful as your mum.'

'I wish she was here,' I say, and I can't stop the tears this time.

'She is,' he says, clasping my hand tightly.

Clinging to his arm, I walk down the path, the gold satin of my skirt shimmering in the spring sunlight. Inside the church door, the girls fuss over me, straightening my veil and smoothing imaginary creases.

'Ready?' Katie whispers.

I hear the piano and the beautiful, rich sound of the cello. Christina and her mum are playing 'Can't Help Falling in Love'. Deena and Clare walk down the aisle first, followed by Katie. I look at Dad and smile. We step forwards together.

Michael is standing by the altar, next to Dan, and I watch the wave of relief pass over his face. All the frustrations, the maddening overly ambitious life choices of the past few months, melt away as we smile. Our eyes are locked and everything else fades into the background.

'I love you,' he breathes.

It's one of those transcendent moments where everything is better than you imagined it could be. Aunt Chevy's church choir sing 'Be Thou my Vision' in perfect harmony, the sound echoing around the stone walls and arched ceiling. Steve leads us through the vows.

'I, Michael, take you, Jen… to be my wife.'

The way he says it makes my heart skip a beat. I'm holding my breath in light-headed rapture. I don't know how I manage to repeat my lines.

'To have and to hold… from this day forward… for better, for worse.'

We've certainly had a rollercoaster of ups and downs to get to this point. In the end, though, I know that Michael means every word of these vows. His inability to break a promise is definitely a good thing when it comes to this, as he told me all those months ago (not that I appreciated it then).

'In the presence of God I make this vow.'

If I'd never met Michael, I would never have come into this church. I wouldn't have had any idea what 'the presence of God' meant. There's still so much I don't understand, but I'm making this promise with absolute clarity on this: if our marriage is going to succeed, we have to keep on loving and forgiving each other. Today, it might be me forgiving Michael for running a marathon on our wedding day. Tonight, he'll have to forgive me for the choices I made in the past, because he waited, and I didn't.

But here we both are, wearing white and gold, and the dirt of the past has been replaced, and redeemed.

Dan brings the rings forward, and Steve gestures to Michael to take my mother's ring.

'I give you this ring…' He slips the band of gold onto my finger. '…As a sign of our marriage.'

His eyes shine with love for me, and there's no hint of censure as I say to him,

'With my body I honour you… all that I am I give to you, and all that I have I share with you.'

Our hands are clasped together, both gold rings on, and I am no longer Jennifer Baker.

'I now pronounce you man and wife,' Steve says, with a broad grin. 'You may kiss the bride.'

Michael lifts the veil over my head. Our lips meet, and it feels like coming home. When we turn to the congregation, I can see everyone I love clapping and cheering for us. I even smile at David and Adele, who stands out like a flamingo among penguins in her pink dress and fascinator ensemble.

'I think I might need to sit down now,' Michael says to me, smiling with clenched teeth.

Even that part.

There are so many precious and beautiful moments, but my favourite is when we go out to sign the register. Christina is playing again, and I sweep my dress into the side room, holding onto Michael's arm. He's limping slightly. Ezra and Heather follow us inside, and Heather flings her arms around Michael's neck, happy tears streaming down her cheeks. I step away slightly, to give them space, and Ezra meets my eyes. His own are glistening with emotion. He smiles at me, then wraps his arms around me in a warm, strong hug.

'You look beautiful,' he says.

My heart melts.

There's something about a wedding for sewing up a family more tightly with love and forgiveness, and as I finally have Aunt Chevy back in my life, it feels like this day has done more to restore wholeness than to just join me and Michael together.

After the service, Michael leads me out to the car, with Karen right behind us.

'How about a small detour to our favourite place?' he says.

Bestward. Maybe I'll get one of these pictures printed onto a huge canvas to hang in our living room, I reflect as I feel the wind lift my veil out behind me like an elegant version of a windsock. With the ruins of the castle around us, I could be a Shakespearean heroine or a pre-Raphaelite angel.

'Hello there!'

The Lady with a Dog is waving at us.

'You got married then?'

'Yes!' Michael shouts back in delight.

I love that man.

ACKNOWLEDGEMENTS

I had so much fun writing this book, and I'm so grateful to YOU now as you read this page! Thank you for joining me on Jen and Michael's journey. Since publishing 'Bell Time', I've been so thrilled to see other readers react to these characters, and I hope that 'Wedding Bell Time' has been the perfect next part of their story.

As always, Andy, I'm so thankful for your support, reading and awesome cover design. I hope you don't feel ruthlessly exploited! I love you. Megs and Josh, thank you for being so much fun. I love you too.

To my mum, for being my no. 1 fan. You're the best!

To Naomi, for reading this as quickly as you read 'Bell Time', and encouraging me with your feedback. I think together we've managed to diagnose a lot of neurodivergency!

To Roxy, for the most amazing BETA read! Wow. Your comments were so helpful and allayed my fears in giving Michael a POV.

To the Bookstagrammers, who have bowled me over with their passion for reading and supporting indie authors. Daria, Randi, Coco, Millie, Acrylic Reads, Introverts Booknook, and Tanya: thank you so much.

Finally, to my Lord and Saviour. I give this story to You and pray that You get all the glory. Amen.

Sophie Toovey is an English teacher and writer. She loves Jane Austen, and a good romcom by Mhairi McFarlane, Lindsey Kelk or Rachel Lynn Solomon.

Connect with Sophie
Sign up for news of future releases at sophietoovey.com
Listen to audio chapters for free on Youtube
Instagram @Sophie_Toovey
Twitter @SophieToovey
Tiktok @sophietoovey

WEDDING BELL TIME

The Day of the Dice

Coming Soon

It's the future, but it feels like the past. Elise farms the land with a community of ten families, the last people left on Earth. She dreads the Casting, where boys roll dice to choose which girl they are paired with for enforced child-bearing, a system established by her aggressive uncle, General Hunter. Elise discovers her mother's death in childbirth could have been prevented, but the General wanted her dead. Now she fears the same thing will happen to her.

But when Elise travels on the only boat to a forbidden island, she discovers there are other survivors. She returns determined to escape forever, but her plan depends on the privileged William. Their cover-story romance feels increasingly real, despite her cousin Alice's best attempts to keep them apart.

Elise begins to consider what it would mean to stay and challenge her uncle's harsh regime, despite the risk of history repeating itself. Torn between love and freedom, Elise will have to carve out her own path for the future she wants.

"*Pride and Prejudice* meets *The Hunger Games*, *The Day of the Dice* is a richly written, complex and compelling YA speculative fiction novel which asks us to consider what it means to be in love, what it means to be free and what sacrifices we make for the people we love." (Anna Mainwaring)

Printed in Great Britain
by Amazon